Praise for
Juan José Saer

"Brilliant. . . . With meticulous prose, rendered by Dolph's translation into propulsive English, Saer's *The Sixty-Five Years of Washington* captures the wildness of human experience in all its variety."
—*New York Times*

"What Saer presents marvelously is the experience of reality, and the characters' attempts to write their own narratives within its excess."
—*Bookforum*

"A cerebral explorer of the problems of narrative in the wake of Joyce and Woolf, of Borges, of Rulfo and Arlt, Saer is also a stunning poet of place."—*The Nation*

"To say that Juan José Saer is the best Argentinian writer of today is to undervalue his work. It would be better to say that Saer is one of the best writers of today in any language."—Ricardo Piglia

"Juan José Saer must be added to the list of the best South American writers."—*Le Monde*

"The author's preoccupations are reminiscent of his fellow Argentinians Borges and Cortázar, but his vision is fresh and unique."
—*The Independent* (London)

Juan José Saer

la grande

Translated from the Spanish
and with an Afterword
by Steve Dolph

OPEN LETTER
LITERARY TRANSLATIONS FROM THE UNIVERSITY OF ROCHESTER

First edition, 2014
All rights reserved

Library of Congress Cataloging-in-Publication Data: Available upon request.
ISBN-13: 978-1-934824-21-4 / ISBN-10: 1-934824-21-6

This project is supported in part by an award from
the National Endowment for the Arts.

ART WORKS.
arts.gov

Printed on acid-free paper in the United States of America.

Text set in Bodoni, a serif typeface first designed by Giambattista
Bodoni (1740–1813) in 1798.

Design by N. J. Furl
Wine glass illustration designed by Fabio Meroni / studio Slash

Open Letter is the University of Rochester's nonprofit, literary translation press:
Lattimore Hall 411, Box 270082, Rochester, NY 14627

www.openletterbooks.org

For Laurence

la grande

Was it I who was returning?
–Juan L. Ortiz

the solid things were gone, and only
what was transient remained.
–Quevedo

e vidi lume in forma di rivera
fulvido di fulgore, intra due rive
dipinte di mirabil primavera.
–Paradiso, *XXX 61–63*

Le cadavre exquis boira le vin nouveau.
–Abbreviated Dictionary of Surrealism

TUESDAY

WATER SOUNDS

HALF-PAST FIVE, GIVE OR TAKE, ON A RAINY AFTERNOON in early April. Nula and Gutiérrez are approaching, at a diagonal, the corner of an open, nearly rectangular field bordered at one end by a mountain sparsely covered in acacias, and behind which, still invisible to them, the river runs.

The sky, the earth, the air, and the vegetation are gray, not with the metallic shade that the cold in May or June brings them, but rather the greenish, warm porosity of the first autumn rains that, in this region, can't quite extinguish the insistent, overwhelming summer. Both men, walking neither fast nor slow, a short distance apart, one in front of the other, are still wearing lightweight clothes. Gutiérrez, walking ahead, has on a violently yellow waterproof jacket, and Nula, who hesitates at each step, unsure where to place his foot, a red camper made from a silky material with a slick and shiny texture, that in his family dialect (it was a gift from his mother), they jokingly call parachute cloth. The two bright spots moving through the gray-green space resemble satin paper cutouts collaged on a monochromatic wash, the air the most diluted, and the clouds, the earth, and the trees the most concentrated grays.

Nula, because he'd come on business—to deliver three cases of wine, a viognier, two cabernet sauvignon, and four local chorizos ordered the week before—and planned to visit a few other clients that afternoon, had dressed somewhat carefully, and besides the red camper has on a new shirt, a white, lightweight, short-sleeve sweater, freshly ironed pants, and shiny loafers that explain his cautious advance in contrast to the other's inattentive, sure step and constant chatter as he carelessly and noisily sets his muddy rubber boots on the saturated patches of grass bordering the narrow, sandy path or in the sporadic puddles that interrupt it.

The gray background lends the red and the yellow an almost extravagant, overwrought brilliance that intensifies their presence to the eye in the empty field while paradoxically, somehow, causing them to lose, to the mind, a good portion of their reality. In the desolate poverty of the landscape, the striking garments, possibly because of their price (the yellow one, although it's European and more expensive, nevertheless looks more worn-out) produce an obvious contrast, or constitute, rather, an anachronism. The excessive presence of singular objects, though they break up the monotonous succession of things, end up, as with their overabundance, impoverishing them.

Calmly, concentrating on each word, Gutiérrez holds forth with disinterested disdain, half-turning his head over his left shoulder every so often, apparently to remind his company that he's the one being spoken to, although because of the distance that separates them, the open air, the movements that disperse the sounds he utters and, especially, the forceful sound of the boots against the puddles and submerged weeds, in addition to the concentration demanded by the protection of his loafers and pants, Nula can only fish out loose words and scraps of phrases, but in any case getting the general point, even though it's only the third time he's met Gutiérrez and even though their first meeting only lasted two or three minutes. From what he gathered at a previous meeting, as he listened with surprise and curiosity at some length when he brought the first three cases of wine, when Gutiérrez talks, it's always about the same thing.

If Nula imagined himself summarizing those monologues in a few words to a third person, they would be more or less the following: *They—people from the rich countries he lived in for more than thirty years—have completely lost touch with reality and now slither around in a miserable sensualism and, as a moral consequence, content themselves with the sporadic exercise of beneficence and the contrite formulation of instructive aphorisms. He refers to the rich as the fifth column and the foreign party, and the rest, the masses, he argues, would be willing to trade in their twelve-year-old daughter to a Turkish brothel for a new car. Any government lie suits them fine as long as they don't have to give up their credit cards or do without superfluous possessions. The rich purchase their solutions to everything, as do the poor, but with debt. They are obsessed with convincing themselves that their way of life is the only rational one and, consequently, they are continuously indignant at the individual or collective crimes they commit or tolerate, looking to justify with pedantic shyster sophisms the acts of cowardice that obligate them to shamelessly defend the prison of excessive comfort they've built for themselves, and so on, and so on.*

The vitriol in the sentiment contrasts with the composure of his face each time he looks over his left shoulder, with the calm vigor of his movements, and with the monotone neutrality of a voice that seems to be reciting, not a violent diatribe, but rather, in a friendly, paternal way, a set of practical recommendations for a traveler preparing to confront an unfamiliar continent. His words aren't hastened or marred by anger, not cut off by interjections or indignant outbursts; instead, they pass easily and evenly across his lips, interspersed here and there with a Gallicism or Latinism, and if they sometimes stop or hesitate for a few seconds it's because in the three decades living abroad, one of them, relegated by disuse to some dark corner of the basement deep inside himself where he stores the incalculable repertory that constitutes his native tongue, is now slow to rise through the intricate branches of memory to the tip of the tongue that, like the elastic surface of a trampoline, will launch it into the light of day. His discourse is at once ironic and severe, spoken with a distracted intonation, difficult to peg as either authentic or simulated, or if the almost sixty-year-old man who uses it does so to communicate either a contained hatred or rather as a solipsistic and somewhat abstruse humorous exercise.

With regard to their ages, Nula is in fact twenty-nine and Gutiér-rez exactly twice that, which is to say that one is just entering maturity while the other, meanwhile, will soon leave it behind entirely, along with everything else. And although they speak as equals, and even with some ease, they refrain from the familiar *tú* form, the older man possibly because he left the country before its general use came into fashion in the seventies, and Nula because, as a commercial tactic, he prefers not to use the *tú* form with cli-ents he didn't know personally before trying to sell them wine. Their use of *usted* and the difference in their ages doesn't diminish their mutual curiosity, and even though it's only the third time they've met, and though they've yet to reach a real intimacy, their conversation takes place in a decidedly extra-commercial sphere. The curiosity that attracts them isn't spontaneous or inexplicable: to Gutiérrez, although he's as yet unaware of the exact reasons for Nula's interest, the vintner's responses the day they first met seemed unusual for a simple trader, and his parodic attitude when they met again, as he mimed the typical gestures and discourse of a merchant, interspersed with discreet allusions to Aristotle's Problem XXX.1 on poetry, wine, and melancholy, enabled him to glimpse the possibility of a truly neutral conversation, which would be confirmed immediately following the commercial transactions of that second visit.

The first meeting didn't last more than two or three minutes. Dripping wet, Gutiérrez emerged from his swimming pool and walked toward him across the neat lawn with the same indifference to where he placed his bare feet, Nula recalls, as he shows now, the rubber boots stepping through puddles that interrupt the path, or onto the wet weeds that border it. Nula had been recommended by Soldi and Tomatis, among others, and had spoken to him, Gutiérrez, on the phone the day before to set up the meeting for eleven thirty. Because this took place a few weeks before, in March, it was still summer. In the harsh, radiant morning sun, Nula watched Gutiérrez advance toward him from the white rectangle of the pool, itself framed by a wide rectangle of white slabs on which sat three wood and canvas lounge chairs—one green, one red-and-white striped, and one yellow—all inscribed on a smooth, green landscape bordered at the rear by a dense grove, and flanked, beyond a stretch of green earth, by the white house on the left and on the right by a pavilion with its obligatory grill and a shed that likely contained tools, bicycles, a wheelbarrow, a lawnmower, and so on. *I don't know if it was actually Gutiérrez, but whoever built it must've been inspired by those California houses that, from what I've learned on television, are made for people who've succeeded in life thanks to some righteous or dark arts,* suggested Tomatis the day he recommended Gutiérrez as a client. It actually wasn't such a luxurious house, but in any case it was definitely the most expensive in the area around Rincón, and even though Nula had never been to California he'd seen a lot of the same shows growing up, and so as he took in the assemblage as Gutiérrez, dripping wet, approached him, he realized that, as usual, and possibly for purely rhetorical purposes, Tomatis had exaggerated.

11

Instead, what surprised him was Gutiérrez's physical appearance. He'd expected someone elderly, but this was a vigorous man, with a flat stomach, with proportioned angles, tanned by the sun, and whose gray hair, as neatly cropped as the lawn surrounding the swimming pool, and abundant rusty gray body hair, which must have been black in his youth, sticking, because of the water, to his chest and shoulders, arms and legs, increased rather than diminished the impression of physical vigor, so much so that, considering the contradictory situation—less luxurious house than anticipated and younger owner than imagined—Nula thought for a few seconds that he'd come to the wrong address. The contracted and somewhat deformed shadow that, owing to the height of the sun, gathered at the feet of the approaching man could have indicated, in an indirect way, a somewhat more complex inner life than his appearance and the conventional tranquility of the setting it moved through suggested.

—I didn't know how to let you know that I couldn't meet you today, after all, Gutiérrez had said. And Nula:

—Clearly it's the time for taking the water and not the wine.

Gutiérrez had laughed, shaking his head toward the pool.

—Not at all, he said. What happened is I received an unexpected visit this morning.

Just then Nula realized that although Gutiérrez had left the pool the water sounds continued: someone, invisible from where he stood, was still splashing and swimming around. At that moment, in a fluorescent green one-piece, its shoulders bent, with that same abstracted, preoccupied manner, tanned and maybe slightly more solid than five or six years before, the body of Lucía Riera, which Nula had come to know so well, was emerging up the metal ladder from the side of the pool closest to the house. Without even looking at them, Lucía had thrown herself onto the green canvas chair next to the pool. Gutiérrez had followed Nula's surprised expression somewhat worriedly, and a shadow there seemed to suggest that an explanation of some kind was called for.

—Don't imagine anything irregular, he said. She's my daughter.

The customer is always right, I get it, Nula had said later that same night to Gabriela Barco and Soldi at the Amigos de Vino bar, where he'd run into them—they changed bars frequently for what they called their "work dates"—*it comes with the territory and, thanks to my stoic indifference, costs me nothing. But I actually know Lucía Riera, married to the doctor Oscar Riera and separated for some time I believe. It's true that I lost touch with her for several years up until this morning, but I know perfectly well who her parents are, though I never met them. A man named Calcagno, a lawyer, was her father—he died several years ago—but her mother, barring evidence to the contrary, is still alive. It took effort not to punch Gutiérrez in the teeth when he told me she was his daughter, and I wasn't just furious but stunned too, because I couldn't believe he'd lie so blatantly, and I was even a little embarrassed that he'd dare do that to me. He must have sensed something like that in my face because he got serious and polite and solemn and said he'd walk me out. We left it that I would call him to set up another visit, something that, obviously, I don't intend to do.* Nula stopped, satisfied he'd conveyed his indignation, but when he looked up he saw that Soldi was avoiding his gaze. After a few seconds, Soldi looked him straight in the eyes and, somewhat sheepishly, said, *And yet there are those who say that it might be or at least could be true. You should probably look for something else to get indignant over.*

And so, out of curiosity, Nula had called Gutiérrez again the following week, and they set a day and time for the second meeting. In a sense, the practically imperceptible incident, which didn't quite mean anything in particular for either, but drew them both for a few seconds from the neutral and conventional territory where mercantile transactions are understood to take place, had made them mutually interesting and enigmatic in their own way,

13

something that both took silent note of during the short telephone conversation when they set up the second meeting, and which they took pains to conceal when, several days later, they were once again face to face. The wine sale took place quickly—a case (six per) of viognier and two of cabernet sauvignon to start, plus four local chorizos—and once it was settled, the bill and the check signed and the receipt in Gutiérrez's hands, they took up a conversation that lasted more than two hours, on various topics that had little or nothing to do with wine, and during which, every so often, Gutiérrez elaborated his serene, disinterested soliloquies about *them*, the inhabitants, referred to with ironic disdain, of the rich countries he had lived in for over thirty years. They had sat down on a bench at the back of the courtyard, under the trees, after touring the property inside and out, though its details, if they sparked Nula's interest from time to time, seemed invisible to their owner. Their respective biographical details, which certainly interested them, did not form part of the conversation, at least in a chronological way, although every so often some personal element cropped up or was taken into consideration, like for example the medical and philosophical studies that Nula abandoned in succession, and his project, before selling wine, of writing his *Notes toward an ontology of becoming*, or the reasons (never clarified, and cited as a means of formulating an aphorism rather than an actual confidence) that had propelled Gutiérrez abroad: *I left in search of three chimeras: worldwide revolution, sexual liberation, and auteur cinema.*

Finally, at around four thirty today, without calling, Nula had brought the wine. He parked the dark green station wagon in front of the white gate at the main entrance, just as Gutiérrez, coming out of the house, was preparing to lock the front door.

—I have the order, Nula said as he stepped from the car. Were you heading out?

—On an expedition in the area, replied Gutiérrez. Looking for an old friend. Escalante. Do you know him?

He'd never heard of him. According to Marcos Rosemberg, he lives in Rincón, on the outskirts of the town, but on the city side, about three miles away, and Gutiérrez had decided to invite him to a party he was planning to throw on Sunday and to which he was thinking he, Nula, might come too. Nula looked at the greenish sky and the dark horizon and, without saying anything, had laughed sarcastically.

—I would also like to order some more wine, knowing the habits of some of my guests.

And so, after carrying the three cases from the station wagon to the kitchen, Nula filled out another order: more white wine, more red, and more local chorizos. When they came out to the front gate, Nula looked at the heavy sky and said:

—Actually, the walk is tempting, even though it's definitely going to rain and I have a couple of clients waiting for me.

In fact, he regretted it the moment he began speaking, but the quickness and frank satisfaction of Gutiérrez's response immediately erased the fear of having shown his feelings too openly: Gutiérrez's sincerity neutralized his own. They still didn't know each other well enough to be spontaneous, and their reciprocal attraction stemmed from what they hadn't figured out about each other: Gutiérrez's dubious paternity and, in addition to the sudden emotion he showed when Lucía emerged from the pool, Nula's singular conversation, blending, sometimes without a clear dividing line, commerce and philosophy.

When they reach the upper right corner of the rectangle they've been crossing at a diagonal, the bright yellow spot and the red one that follows it start up the mountain covered with acacias, at the same pace as before, neither slow nor fast, in a straight line toward the river. There is no path, but the ground is almost pure sand, so not much grass grows among the trees, and the rain, rather than softening the earth and forming puddles or wet layers of mud, had packed it down, and the two men walk on ground so hardened by the water that their footsteps hardly leave a trail. Clumps of pampas grass, gray like everything but the yellow earth, lay across the sandy ground, though when they reach the river, the vegetation of the island, on the opposite shore, some fifty meters away, seems more green, and the sand on the slope more red, a brick-like red that's almost orange from the sand mixing with the ferrous clay, in contrast to the pervasive grayness: the river, lead-colored and rippled, is darkening with the afternoon at the end of a rainy day that hasn't once seen the sun.

—Southeast, Nula says when they reach the shore, pointing at a downward angle toward the leaden water and the waves that crest its surface in the direction opposite the current. His voice, as though it issued from someone else, sounded strange to him, not during its fleeting sonorous existence, but in the soundless vibration it left in his memory as it faded, perhaps caused by the silence that had taken hold after the sound of the scrape of their steps on the sandy earth had disappeared. The soft breeze from the southeast is only perceptible on the water. Or maybe Nula and Gutiérrez can sense it on their faces, but, accustomed to the inclemency, they don't notice what they feel. Each of them surveys the landscape with the same withdrawn expression he might have assumed had he been alone in this deserted place, the details each observes not coinciding with the other's, each of them assembling it therefore in his own way, as though it were two distinct places, the island, the sky, the trees, the red slope, the aquatic plants at the riverbank, the water. For several seconds, Nula's thoughts are absorbed by the leaden, rippled surface, each of the identical, curling waves, continuously in motion, that swell and form an edge which could best be represented not by a curve but rather, more precisely, by an obtuse angle, seeming to attend the visible manifestation of the becoming that, by presenting itself through repetition or a counterfeit stillness, permits the coarse heart the illusion of stability. For Nula, who often catches himself observing the same phenomena that once occupied his *Notes*, the island ahead, the alluvial formation, is proof of the continuous change of things: the same constant movement that formed it now erodes it, causing it to change size, shape, and place, and the coming and going of the material and of the worlds that it makes and unmakes is nothing more, he thinks, than the flow, without direction or objective or cause, of the time that, invisibly and silently, runs through them.

—See that? They're all the same, he says.

Gutiérrez looks at him, surprised.

—The waves, Nula says. Each one repeats the same disturbance.

—Not the same one, no, says Gutiérrez, without even looking at the surface of the water. His gaze passes curiously over the island, the air, the sky, darkening from the fading light and from the mass of clouds, a denser gray, that have been moving in from the east.

Gutiérrez doesn't seem to notice that Nula is watching him openly, as though he were concentrating on what he sees less because what surrounds him is particularly interesting than because moving his gaze over the landscape allows him better access to what's happening inside himself. What little Nula knows about him makes him an enigma, certainly, but with a touch of irony Nula tells himself that ultimately even the things that are familiar to us are unfamiliar, if only because we've allowed ourselves to forget the mysterious things about them. *Quantitatively*, he tells himself, without a single word corresponding to his thoughts, *I know as little about him as I do about myself.*

Even what they know about him in the city is fragmentary. Everyone knows something that doesn't quite coincide with what

17

everyone else knows. The ones who knew him before he left—Pichón Garay, Tomatis, Marcos and Clara Rosemberg, for example—had lost touch with him for more than thirty years. One day he just disappeared, without a trace, and then, just as suddenly, reappeared. From that group, the first to make contact with him, and completely by accident, had been Pichón Garay. *I was on the afternoon flight back to Buenos Aires, and he asked the man sitting next to me to change seats,* he wrote to Tomatis a week after returning to Paris. (Pichón had spent a couple of months in the city, liquidating his family's last holdings, and in mid April Tomatis and Soldi had taken him to the airport, where he caught the afternoon flight to Buenos Aires, which at that time connected with a direct flight to Paris.) *Before sitting down, he introduced himself. Willi Gutiérrez, did I remember him? It took me a second to place him, but he remembered everything from thirty years ago—El Gato's stories more so than mine, actually—and I'm still not sure if he knew which of us he was talking to. He said he saw us with Soldi at the airport, but he couldn't come over because he was checking a suitcase. He said you looked the same as always. For the fifty minutes the flight lasted he did practically all the talking, spouting off about Europe, and I learned that he's living between Italy and Geneva, but that he travels all over. His trip to the city lasted a day, of three in the country altogether. The afternoon before, he'd landed in Buenos Aires from Rome, slept at the Plaza that night, and the next morning had skipped up to the city to visit a house in Rincón that he was looking to buy (I didn't offer mine because it was all but sold), saying that he planned to settle in the area. That night he was staying at the Plaza again, and then back to Italy the next day. Our destinies, as you can see, are contradictory: he'd come back to buy a house, and I was there to sell one.*

According to Tomatis, the first people Gutiérrez had contacted when he moved into the house in Rincón had been the Rosembergs. *The first that I know of,* he'd clarified, *because from what I can tell, he lives in several worlds simultaneously.* And Nula, who'd met up with Tomatis for coffee and to sell him some wine, had responded: *Just like everybody else.* And Tomatis, in a falsely severe tone, said, *Don't get cute, Turk, I'm serious. He lived a double life before he left, one that even his closest friends didn't know about, and now he's come back to it.* Tomatis's suggestive tone apparently implied that he might know more than he was saying, and when, about a month later, after his first trip to see Gutiérrez, Soldi, in the Amigos del Vino bar, reluctantly hinted that Gutiérrez might not be lying when he said that Lucía was his daughter, Nula remembered the suggestion, but for now nothing quite makes sense as he stands on the riverbank, watching the leaden, rippled surface of the water, and his hand reaches into the camper's inside pocket for his cigarettes and lighter.

The real estate agent (who in fact was representing an agency from Buenos Aires in the transaction), a guy named Moro, was also one of Nula's clients. His assignment consisted in picking Gutiérrez up at the airport and taking him to see the house in Rincón, or rather on the outskirts of Rincón, at the north end of town, on the floodplain opposite the highway, where some new money had moved early in the 80s because they hadn't been able to buy in the residential section of Guadalupe, which other, wealthier people had bought up first and transformed into a kind of fortress, with private security and everything, blocking so many roads that the buses were forced to change routes. Moro figures that Gutiérrez must be very rich. Leaning toward Nula over the desk in his office on San Martín, like he was sharing a secret, a large map of the city hanging on the wall behind him, riddled with different colored pins no doubt distinguishing the current states of the diverse property that his agency administered, Moro, rocking his comfortable swivel chair slightly, looking over his shoulder to check that no one was listening, though there wasn't anyone but them in the office, narrowing his eyes and lowering his voice, had hissed, admiringly, *I figure you'd have to measure it in palos verdes,* that is, by the millions.

The house had belonged to a cardiologist, a Doctor Russo, a public health secretary in the government that followed the military dictatorship. According to Moro, this Doctor Russo, who now lived in Miami, had been implicated in the disappearance of funds allocated to improving hospitals and the Public Assistance program, not to mention a shady story concerning bribes to pharmaceutical labs, and even as a businessman he'd been blemished in the eyes of the law, having served on the board of the Banco Provinicial, where, after his tenure, something like a hundred million dollars turned up missing, and not to mention the fact that the board members had passed around low-interest loans that were meant for poor people to buy a modest house somewhere, but which the board used to build mansions for themselves, some in Mar del Plata, and abroad even, in Punta del Este, in Florida, and in Brazil, north of Río de Janeiro, with the end result, according to Moro, that between the board and their rich friends all the funds for the preferential loans had been spent, and the hundred million dollar discrepancy caused the bank to go under, so none of them had to return the money they'd taken. A judge took an interest in the case, but the investigation went nowhere and anyway the responsible parties were already living in Marbella or Punta del Este or Florida. This had been the case with our Doctor Russo, who'd sold the house in Rincón and a bunch of others around the country, bought, according to Moro, with the money he'd made as a cardiologist and the dividends from his private clinic, and had left for Miami.

According to Moro, Gutiérrez's visit to the house didn't last more than ten or fifteen minutes. He walked through the interior rooms first—the six bedrooms plus the large living room, the bathrooms, the kitchen, practically bigger than the living room, all of it on a single floor—and then, at the same speed, went out to explore the grounds, the grove at the back, the pavilion, the tool shed, and the swimming pool with nothing at the bottom but a puddle of muddy water where several generations of dead leaves were putrefying and in which a copious family of toads had taken residence. Gutiérrez spent the whole trip back to the city interrogating him about painters, about people specializing in cracked swimming pools, about the chances of finding a woman to take care of the cleaning, and a gardener and caretaker, about someone who could fix the thatch roof over the pavilion, and so on, and so on, like the house was already his, and without uttering a single word for or against it—a place which he, Moro, knew hadn't been signed for in Buenos Aires—Gutiérrez spoke of it as though he owned it. To Moro he'd seemed like a nice enough guy, though slightly off: he was calm, quiet, polite even, and he always had this friendly and somewhat distant smile pasted on his face. Moro said that he ended up feeling slightly uneasy, in any case, because everything he said or did, the usual stuff you do when you're settling a deal, seemed to confirm something for Gutiérrez, something he'd come searching for, and that ultimately he, Moro, realized that Gutiérrez was looking at him like some kind of museum piece or some exotic fish in an aquarium that he'd traveled thousands of kilometers to see firsthand. Moro told Nula that he'd been told by the Buenos Aires office to take Gutiérrez out to a fancy lunch at a place on Guadalupe where all the celebrities in the city, starting with the mayor, took important visitors, but that Gutiérrez said he didn't want to take up any more of his time, that he wanted to spend some time alone before the flight and would prefer to be dropped off near the grill house on San Lorenzo, a place that had its fifteen minutes back in the fifties, but which had turned into just another dark neighborhood dive. Nula knew the place well; in his last year at the university he and a group of classmates would go there to learn to get plastered. The place wasn't actually that bad, just like the fancy

21

place on Guadalupe wasn't that good. But he stopped himself from saying this because Moro was already saying that he'd seen him again that afternoon. At around four, he'd passed the estate agency without coming in, walking slowly along the shady side of the street, like people from the area did, gazing at the storefronts, the houses, and the people with a discreet look of indulgent satisfaction. According to Moro, he'd seemed happy, and since just then he was walking south out of the agency to visit a property they wanted to put up for sale, and since this was the direction that Gutiérrez was also walking, totally by happenstance and without meaning to he ended up following him for several blocks. Moro said that finally he, Gutiérrez, after looking at his watch, had gone into the arcade—even though there are five or six others, everyone calls it that, *the* arcade, quintessentially, because it was the first in the city to open, in the late fifties, and all the others, which are more modern, more important, and more luxurious, have to be referred to by their full name—and took a table in the courtyard. Moro sat thinking for a moment. He was just over forty, already pretty bald and with a bit of a paunch, well-dressed and friendly, a spontaneous sort of friendliness that had nothing to do with his business, but which actually came from his private life, because in fact he'd inherited the estate agency, a flourishing family business started by his grandfather and established in the area for over seventy years, meaning that, not having any financial problems of his own, he could lend a personal turn to business matters, reflecting in a disinterested way about people and what they did. There wasn't a block in the city, or in the neighboring smaller cities and towns, or likewise in the surrounding countryside, where you wouldn't find the proverbial signboard: ANOTHER (in red letters printed at an angle in the upper left corner of the white rectangle), in the center in larger, black letters MORO PROPERTY, and below that, in red letters again, FOR RENT (or FOR SALE). And so whenever Nula would deliver his wine, the visits would last somewhat longer than with his other clients, although the sale of wine, because of the literary aura that surrounds the product, always overflows, to a greater or lesser extent depending on the person, into the private sphere. Nula was surprised to see him fall into such an introspective moment; from his expression, Nula could tell that he was trying to get his head around some unusual thought, something that he found difficult to put into words. Then he said, *While I was following him, I had this weird feeling I've never had before, and which, no lie, really bothered me. It was like we were walking down the same street, in the same place, but in different times. It occurred to me that if I walked up and said hello he wouldn't recognize me despite having spent the whole morning together, or worse yet he wouldn't even see me because we were moving through different dimensions, like in some sci-fi program.*

The day after his walk along the coast with Gutiérrez, Nula will see Tomatis at the southern end of the city, around six in the afternoon, behind the capitol building, and, stopping his car, will invite him in. *I accept,* Tomatis will say. *I'm waiting for the bus, but one that's full enough hasn't come along yet.* After exchanging some pleasantries, they'll end up talking about Gutiérrez, whose return to the city has, in fact, ended up causing something of a stir. Tomatis will tell him that, through his sister, he knows the couple—Amalia and Faustino—who work for Gutiérrez. The wife takes care of the house, the shopping, and the meals, and the husband the courtyard, the landscaping, the pavilion, the pool, and the garden. His sister relays the gossip from another woman, a sister-in-law of the first, who comes two or three times a week to help out around the house. Little things, purely circumstantial details (the couple is too earnest, according to Tomatis, to commit any sort of indiscretion) that Tomatis nevertheless interprets methodically and thus forms a general picture of the situation. *What I remember from thirty-some years back is that Gutiérrez left the city suddenly, that he stayed in*

Buenos Aires for a year, and that in the end the earth swallowed him whole. With other people who'd gone to Europe, to the States, to Cuba, to Israel, or even to India, we heard reports every so often, but with him nothing, not a single thing. It was like he'd died, gone missing, disintegrated, evaporated, or dissolved into the impenetrable, innumerable world. Although . . . now that I think about it . . . hold on, let's see . . . yeah, one night, many years later, in Paris, Pichón took me to a party where I met this Italian girl who, when she heard where we came from, Pichón and I, told me she knew a Gutiérrez who was from the same city and who lived between Italy and Switzerland and wrote screenplays under a pseudonym. His name was Guillermo Gutiérrez, but she didn't know what pseudonym he used for the screenplays. I'd forgotten that detail almost as soon as I heard it, and now, suddenly, it came back to me. Actually, the Italian girl was wrong, Gutiérrez wasn't from the city. He came from someplace north of Tostado called El Nochero. His grandmother, who was dirt poor, had saved up some money with the help of the church to send him to school in the city. He went to a Catholic high school, and, the moment he graduated, his grandmother died—it was like she'd been staying alive just to make sure her grandson was on the right track. He enrolled at the law school, where he met Escalante, Marcos Rosemberg, and César Rey, and they became inseparable. The four of them formed a sort of political-literary avant-garde that didn't last long—besides their youth and their friendship they didn't have anything in common, not even politics or literature. Since he didn't have a penny, unlike the other three, who despite being older still had school paid for by their families, Gutiérrez started working, a little bit of everything, until his Roman Law professor, who liked him, took him on as a clerk in his office, where he was partners with Doctor Mario Brando, a poet and head of the precisionist movement, as far as I know the most hateful fraud ever produced by the literary circles in this fucking city. But on that count I suggest you consult with Soldi and Gabriela Barco, who are researching a history of the avant-garde in the province. I'll get off at the corner. Thanks for the ride. And Nula will answer, *Not a problem. But what was it you were telling me about the couple that works for him?* And Tomatis, with a studied gesture of indifference, will downplay its importance, while letting slip—unintentionally, of course—two or three melodramatic and mysterious little details: *This and that. Nothing really important. But if push came to shove I believe we'd find that those two, although they haven't known him long, would sacrifice their lives for their new boss.* And then, before getting out, he'll discuss the weather and other mundane things.

But Tomatis will only tell him these things tomorrow, at around the same time, after another cloudy day that, as it ends, will nonetheless allow fragments of pale blue, faintly red from the last rays of an already disappeared sun, though still clean and luminous, to shine through the breaks in the gray clouds that high winds will begin to disperse. For now, though, as he takes a cigarette from the pack and brings it to his lips, the air and the rippled surface of the river, both an even, leaden gray from the double effect of the dusk and the increasingly low, dark clouds, remain in shadow. Two meters away, Gutiérrez, his silhouette sharply outlined against the darkness, over which his bright yellow waterproof jacket glows with an attenuated splendor, seems absorbed by an intense memory or thought, so much so that his arms, separated slightly from his body, have stopped in the middle of a forgotten movement. Less than a minute has passed since they stopped at the edge of the water, but because they've been silent, separated from each other by their thoughts, time appears to have stretched out, seeming to pass not only on the horizontal plane that their instincts recognize, but also on a vertical one, to an inconceivable depth, suggesting that even the present, despite its familiar brevity, and even along its unstable, gossamer border, might actually be infinite. Gutiérrez, apparently remembering that Nula is with him, returns to his open, slightly urbane manner, and smiles.

25

—I was time traveling, he says.

—And I was riding the present, trying not get bucked off that wild bronco, Nula says.

—Which luckily can sometimes be a gentle mare, says Gutiérrez.

—If we keep developing the metaphor, we're going to end up in the zoo.

—Screenwriters are contractually obligated to use the primary local material. In London, it's always got to be cloudy, and don't dare forget to fill the Sahara with camels, says Gutiérrez, a quick spark of retrospective disdain in his eyes. And, bringing his hand to his forehead, he rubs at something as he raises his head and looks up at the sky. A drop, he says.

—Two, Nula says, touching his nose while scrutinizing the dark clouds. Looking back down and around himself, he thinks of his red camper, his white pullover, his new shirt, his freshly ironed pants. He looks at his loafers, where a rim of yellow mud has formed along the entire perimeter of their soles and a few stains of the same yellowish substance have stuck to their insteps, and he makes two or three involuntary gestures, at once ambiguous and contradictory.

Gutiérrez watches him openly, laughing, as if his misfortune amused him, and then, deliberately reaching slowly into an interior pocket of his raincoat, the wide and open kind, like a marsupial pouch, that some of those coats have, he withdraws an umbrella with a short handle, where he presses a metal button, and the canopy of smooth and glowing fabric divided into seven different colored sections unfolds with a sharp sound, sudden and exact, and a perfection that approaches the theatrical. The sections of the canopy represent the color spectrum, red, orange, yellow, green, blue, indigo, and violet, with identical segments, and the composite of the two men and the umbrella form a multicolored blotch that is clear and mobile and that stands out sharply against the gray background darkened by the double effect of the clouds and the dusk.

Nula, slightly stupefied, takes in the umbrella's multicolored apparition, but he doesn't rush to shelter himself under the canopy's limited circumference, typical of the shelter offered by collapsible umbrellas, despite their price. Nula's reticence to seek the protection that placing himself shoulder to shoulder with Gutiérrez would offer has two motives: the first is that for now he's sensed only a few sparse and scattered drops that couldn't yet be called an actual rainfall or even a spitting one, and the second is that just as the multicolored canopy is unfolding, giving the impression that the two phenomena had been synchronized deliberately, in one of the pockets of his camper his cell phone has started ringing. Moving a few steps away mysteriously, he puts back the cigarettes and lighter that he'd just taken uselessly from his pocket. (He actually smokes very little, but he tends to carry cigarettes to share with clients, though today, he can't really tell why, he feels a stronger urge to smoke than usual.) Nula pulls the cell phone from his other pocket, and, with a subtle gesture of apology toward Gutiérrez, turns his back to him as he brings the phone to his left ear and answers the call. Gutiérrez observes him patiently but skeptically, isolated within the imaginary cylinder that the umbrella's circumference projects toward the sandy ground, forming an illusory refuge for surveillance, and when he moves his arm slightly and the multicolored circle shifts onto an inclined plane the ideal shape to contain him becomes a truncated cylinder.

Although for a man of almost sixty, however well he keeps himself up, youth tends to seem insolent, and although Nula's full and virile twenty-nine years, the fastidiousness of his clothes, and his apparent self regard seem overly manifest for his taste, Gutiérrez watches him indulgently, almost with pity, thinking that the energy the young radiate—so stimulating that, subjugated by it, they confuse it with the essence of their own singularity—they might not actually deserve. The indulgence is erased when Nula, turning around, raises his voice and makes two or three comical faces in his direction, shaking his free arm as he explains to the person on the other end (later he'll explain that it was his boss) that, because he's with an important client (and he extends his arm and wags his index finger at Gutiérrez with an exaggerated and complicit smile) he has to cancel the two appointments he has for later in the afternoon. Apparently, the person on the other end of the line lets himself be easily convinced, and from the things he says, Gutiérrez realizes that Nula, without having to insist much, but by the sheer effect of his communicative euphoria, has induced his boss to call the clients and reschedule their appointments for the same time tomorrow. Nula shuts off the apparatus and, stowing it in his pocket, takes two or three decisive steps toward Gutiérrez.

—Free as the wind until tomorrow morning at eleven, he says when he reaches Gutiérrez's side. And he turns his head sharply upward again because suddenly and silently a dense rain has started to fall. With two hops he reaches Gutiérrez, claiming for himself, in a tacit way, a portion of the meager protection offered by the umbrella.

Without really knowing why, Gutiérrez, who likes every kind of rain, prefers that silent kind, without storm or wind or thunder or lightning, and which forms gradually, almost surreptitiously, of low, dark clouds, so loaded with water that, from this excess, they split, suddenly, and empty themselves upon the world. In general, it will fall in the afternoon, and, often, after the warm spell of a wet day. Indifferent to Nula's somewhat ostentatious irritation (he's almost pasted to him, and, shuffling his feet impatiently, seems to want to incite him to keep walking), Gutiérrez watches it, not in the sky, which has brightened a bit and where the drops, despite their size, are invisible, but rather on the plants, on the yellowish ground, on the river, where, as they collide, after an incorporeal flight in which they seem to cross an extrasensory void, they rematerialize. Gutiérrez's senses perceive the rain across the deserted expanse that surrounds them, while his imagination projects it over the contiguous and distant spaces they have crossed and that, despite their imaginary provenance, are complemented by and confused with the empirical plane that surrounds them. What he perceives from the point in the verdant space where they find themselves, his imagination likewise assigns to the entire region, where, for the past year or so, after more than thirty years away, he has been living. And he thinks he can see, in the leaves that shudder silently as the drops fall, in their impacts with the yellow earth, and, especially, in the agitation that the drops cause as they cover the rippled surface of the river over an infinite number of simultaneous points, the intimate cipher of the empirical world, each fragment, as distant and distinct from the present as it might seem—the most distant star, for example—having the exact value as this, the one he occupies, and that if he could disentangle himself from the grasp of this apparently insignificant present, the rest of the universe—time, space, inert or living matter—would reveal all its secrets. Gutiérrez senses that Nula has guessed his thoughts, or has inferred them from his demeanor, and so has suppressed his annoyed gestures, opting instead for what appears to be sincere patience and calm. He allows himself a few seconds more, and then, giving Nula a gentle push on the elbow, urges him on.

They advance in silence, a bit faster than before, but, from their demeanor, they don't seem worried by the effects of the rain on the expensive clothes they're wearing, and Nula especially, thinks Gutiérrez, after having postponed the mercantile obligations for that afternoon, no longer seems interested in the state of his shoes or the pulchritude of his red camper. Actually, because the multicolored umbrella is too small to cover them both completely, the rain now soaks not only the lower parts of their bodies, depending on their position and according to the rhythm of their stride as they hike over the rough terrain (from which the path has disappeared), but also cascades over the edges of the canopy onto their shoulders. The bright and mobile blotch that travels along the riverbank is startling, because of this very brightness, against the uniform gray of the landscape.

This is the exact impression that comes across, fifteen minutes later, to the inhabitants of the first ranches that, on its outskirts, a dispossessed stretch of land they seem exiled to, nonetheless marks the edge of the town. Many surprised faces mark their arrival under the rain from the sleepy and utter misery of the settlement, the only variation from the tedious and inescapable exclusion where poverty relegates them. Ten or fifteen shacks of straw, branches, cans, bags, and cardboard—refuse from the nearby dump—half falling apart or possibly never completed or more likely repaired and reappointed every so often with the haphazard and heterogeneous material offered by that same trash heap, constantly at the edge of collapse and in any case inadequate for living or even dying in, crowded together in a barren field among four of five sparse trees so ragged that they seem infected by the poverty, and where a mess of knick-knacks, busted chairs, dismantled wardrobes, rusted grates, broken toilets crumbling among the weeds, paper and plastic bags twisted and half-buried in the mud, trunks, animal and human excrement, leather, bones, and dead branches litter the narrow space between the structures, and where three or four chickens and a dozen dogs, all of them rawboned and afflicted, wander around. At the back of a plot of untilled ground, two thin horses, indifferent to the rain, nibble at the yellowed grass. The filthiness of the ground stretches over the fifteen or twenty meters to the water. The smell of rotten fish, of sewage, and of carrion rises from the riverbank, and the earth is covered with dirty paper, cardboard disintegrating in the rain, broken bottles and rusted cans, ashes clumped together by the humidity, and even the carcass of a dog, hardened and dried despite the rain soaking it, a carcass whose owner, in the previous weeks, had managed to suffer, die, rot, and dry out again, so that, at its death, what it left behind will end up as dust, returned to the earth, or as bone forever.

Some of the shacks are shaded near their doorways by a kind of eave propped up on a pair of twisted poles and under which a rickety chair, old crates, or a stack of two or three trunks serve as seats. Outside one of the shacks, a double car seat, on the ground, leans against the partition that frames up the entrance. The poles of an abandoned garden, in the open ground where the settlement ends, point, in parallel lines, toward the gray sky. Both adults and children watch them as they pass. Some come out of their shacks and stare openly, but, apparently, without interest. The multicolored anachronism they comprise—contrasting with the immense gray-brown blotch of the settlement, which also stains the vegetation, the animals, and the people—seems to activate slow, rusted sensory mechanisms in the inhabitants, consigned to some remote corner of their mind by lack of use. Gutiérrez, raising his free hand, offers a generalized greeting as they pass that the others fail to acknowledge, or acknowledge only later, behind the curtain of rain, when they have already passed and can no longer register it, not from suspicion or timidity, and much less so from aggression, but rather from stupor, from indecision, from indifference.

—I feel like a sideshow freak, Gutiérrez murmurs. I wish I'd never been born.

—It's not so bad, Nula says, also in a low voice, prefaced by the same short, dry laugh that, as he emits it, he realizes he uses only with Gutiérrez, meant perhaps to display a self-control that, in fact, is far from authentic. But I know what you mean, he adds. My father was convinced that the real problem with the world isn't poverty, but wealth, and that's why he had to die.

Turning his head suddenly, Gutiérrez observes him carefully, but all he finds is Nula's profile, because Nula, as though he hadn't noticed anything, continues looking ahead, into the rainy space that separates them from a crop of saturated trees.

—Someone *over there* traded in his car, and so your father had to get murdered, mutters Gutiérrez, turning back toward the trees that obliterate the horizon at the end of the landscape. And, after a short pause, the litany, which Nula could see coming, starts up again: *who've ransacked the planet and now seem determined to do the same thing to the whole solar system, all so that they don't have to resole their shoes and instead buy themselves a new pair every month; who build luxury resorts in the poorest areas so they can water ski and scuba dive and get a tan in the middle of winter and stay in bungalows that simulate a primitive existence but where they serve all-you-can-eat breakfasts and lunches that Roman orgy-goers would be embarrassed by, and especially at night when they go clubbing and swap wives and then complain when the locals kidnap a handful of them that they never hear from again, they, who would ravage everything to see their privileges maintained or amplified and are inclined to do the same over the ruins of the whole universe simply from the voluptuousness their dominion arouses.* And Nula, with resigned irony, thinks, *Yeah, but he bought himself Doctor Russo's mansion, two kilometers from a shantytown, and, according to Moro, you'd have to calculate his fortune by the millions.*

Though they walk downstream, the direction the river runs is not indicated by anything on the surface but the tension created there by the many rough and parallel waves, riddled with the projectiles of rain that pierce them as, pushed by the southwest wind, they encounter the resistance of the current. This tension is so uniform and the fall of the drops so regular that the rippled surface of the water seems less like a medium whose impulse is renewed continuously by the opposing forces that push it in contradictory directions than like a fixed, gelatinous substance that, because of some hidden tremor, trembles and vibrates constantly, and the drops that strike it, despite being always new, seem always the same, captured for a gray but distinct instant.

When they reach the grove and start to cross it, the tall crowns of the eucalyptus planted in rows parallel to the river—they have to turn away from the riverbank slightly as they approach the center of the town—shelter them from the rain, but at the same time the rain seems more real among the trees than in the open; the bark of the trees seems lacquered by the damp, and the ochre trunks, dark and shining where they're not covered with bark, soaked in water, make it more distinct, as do the drops that cascade from the branches, and the odor of eucalyptus that the water amplifies, and the soft but numerous sound that the drops, continuous and polyphonic, produce against the branches and the trunks, against the leaf bed rotting on the ground, against the earth. At their arrival, two or three toads, motionless at the foot of a tree, stiffen and puff up from anxiety, from anger, or from fear, and then immediately flee with ineffective and clumsy jumps in various directions, while in the treetops a tumult of leaves and wings produced by invisible birds—of considerable size judging by the sound's intensity—indicates that the presence of Gutiérrez and Nula has not gone unnoticed. As they leave the grove they are able to make out, beyond a narrow ditch so choked with weeds that it's impossible to tell if there's water at the bottom, the first houses, on the first streets, which apparently follow the straight line that the municipality assigned them, but, lacking sidewalks or gutters or even trees to mark the boundaries between street and sidewalk, are not yet fully streets; there are only a few isolated houses, built of unplastered brick or adobe, two or three per block, constructed along the outer perimeter of the rectangular territories that delimit the blocks, as in so many other towns, whose outskirts, though included within the urban space by the geometric design that demarcated them before the town was chartered, before materializing into houses, streets, life—an abstract idea of the town, diagramed with a ruler, in the same imagination of those who projected it—are confused with the countryside. Where the sidewalks should be there are weeds that, in some cases, extend from the sandy street all the way to the edges of the houses; sometimes, because the inhabitants have pulled them up, but almost always because their simple coming and going has eliminated the weeds, a thin path of bare earth has been opened from the fence (when there is a fence) to the middle of the street.

The rain seems more mournful in the empty town than in the countryside or on the river, and though the houses are becoming more and more frequent as they approach the center, and, here and there, though it's not yet dark, some are lit up inside, these lights do not manage to give an impression of shelter or well-being. In the front gardens the plants drip water, and at the foot of each—hibiscus (which in the area they call *juveniles*), roses, dahlias, chrysanthemums, and many others—lies a multicolored jumble of fallen petals flattened by the rain. Through one window, an old woman holding a forgotten *mate* in her hand meets their gazes but does not respond to their subtle greeting. In the side yards and rear courtyards, visible through screen doors or open gates, hanging clothes, propane tanks, blackened furniture, broken dishes, and brightly colored plastic toys, abandoned on the ground, shine with water. Finally they reach the town proper, but the neat cabins with their trim lawns and swimming pools don't lessen the oppressive feel, and not only from being empty in the middle of the week, because the ones that are lit up, with a new car parked out front or in a garage

34

whose door was left open, and even those where they can see people coming and going through the windows, also secrete tedium, if not affliction. In many houses the flickering lights, caused by the discontinuity of televised images they project, make patterns that filter through the windows, despite the curtains or shutters being closed, and Gutiérrez and Nula, without making any comment, as they advance through the silence that accompanies the splashing of their footsteps, under the multicolored umbrella that, like the yellow rain jacket and the red camper, glows dimly in the blue dusk, both guess, from the fragmentary sounds that reach them every so often—voices and music that retain their shape despite the lack of context and the distance—that in every house they're watching the same show, some afternoon soap opera no doubt.

Closer to the center of town, the sidewalks are fully formed, some are even made of brick, and on the streets immediately surrounding the square these are ancient structures, high above the street, bulwarks against the floods that, when they're heavy, Nula explains, can overrun even the highest sidewalks and flood the inner courtyards beyond. An illuminated doorway opens onto the high brick sidewalk and a uniformed guard—the watchman at the entrance to the police station—watches them curiously, slightly intimidated, apparently, possibly because of their expensive clothing, since it goes without saying that the wealthy inspire deference in the keepers of the peace and that they serve at their pleasure. Gutiérrez stops suddenly, and Nula, realizing it only after a few seconds, takes two or three steps beyond the umbrella's protective canopy and stops in the middle of the sidewalk without turning around. From where he stands, he can hear the sound that the guard's shoes make as he comes to attention, the exchange of greetings, and the cordial and intricate directions that the guard's heavily accented voice gives Gutiérrez to Escalante's house.

—It's on the other side of the square, Gutiérrez says when he catches up with Nula and they resume their walk under the umbrella.

Nula doesn't answer, but as soon as they reach the next block, lowering his voice, fractured slightly by some violent emotion, he says:

—A few years ago, there were lots of people who crossed that doorway and never came out again.

—Your father? Gutiérrez asks in a low voice.

—No. He was killed in greater Buenos Aires.

They fall silent again. Now that the dusk has reached the edge of night, more lights are coming on around the square. And because the streetlights are still off, a last luminescence, somewhere between gray, blue, and green, causes porous and dark reflections to shine, here and there, off the wet objects. Inwardly, Nula senses Gutiérrez's confusion, but out of cruelty pretends not to notice it in order to prolong his discomfort, telling himself, almost reflexively, but immediately feeling guilty for thinking it, that Gutiérrez must have had it good in Europe while so many were tortured to death, defenseless and blind, in the town they're walking through under the rain. Nula realizes that his cruelty doesn't come from any sense of moral superiority, but rather from the brutal suspicions that have been plaguing him since the moment when Lucía, in that green swimsuit, had stepped from the pool dripping wet, and, without looking at him once had sat down in the yellow canvas lawn chair. He's only just now realized that if she hadn't even glanced at him as she came emerged from the water it was because Gutiérrez had already told her he was coming. *Soldi can think whatever he wants,* he says to himself, *but I've known who Lucía's parents were for years.* The momentary attack of rage passes immediately when he hears Gutiérrez's slightly contrite voice.

—Now I get why you kept walking and didn't turn around.

Nula is about to say something about the terrible years they lived through—he was just coming out of adolescence—but his reluctance makes him adopt a gentle and benevolent tone.

—No, no, he says. I didn't realize that you'd stopped, and then I was looking at the square.

But he knows that, though he pretends to accept the explanation, Gutiérrez doesn't believe it. They cross the street, and when their feet touch the corner of the square, aimed at a diagonal, the streetlights come on suddenly. A kind of iridescent halo, like a floating vapor, forms around the globes of white light distributed around the square. And the rain, as it crosses the illuminated space, becomes visible and audible as it cascades over the branches and trunks of the giant rosewoods and the floss silk trees, pouring over the cobbled paths and dripping over an infinite number of points, not only in the square, but in the town, in the region, in the province, in the world. They leave the square and enter a dark street behind a white church. Gutiérrez stops and looks around, trying to get oriented.

—He said it was behind a church, a block and a half away, he says doubtfully.

—It must be there, Nula says. After his vindictive overtures just now, he demonstrates an exaggerated desire to cooperate in the search for this Escalante. But, while exaggerated, this desire is actually sincere; despite the rescheduled appointments, the interminable walk under the rain, the mud, and the damp, not for one moment has he regretted following Gutiérrez on the expedition.

They pass the church and start to cross the street. Despite the streetlight, which hangs in the middle of the block from intersecting cables that support the lamp and the shade that protects it, Nula, who is studying the houses on the next block for some possible sign of what they're looking for, steps into a deep hole in the sandy street, the only one full of water, where, with a hard splash, his left foot submerges to the ankle, causing him to pull it out so violently that the brown loafer, lodged in the hole, comes off and stays where he stepped.

—You fucking bitch! Nula screams, speaking to the universe in general, to the infinitely complex and therefore impenetrable order of things that, indifferent to his designs and desires, put the puddle in the street, at the same instant and in the exact spot where his loafer came down. He rolls forward, standing only on his right foot, turns, and jumping on one leg, returns for the shoe, but Gutiérrez, already recovered from the sudden agitation the incident caused— agitation manifested especially in the umbrella, which trembled, whirling down and up again, producing a brief, colored tornado that, in the dusky half light, took on a muted splendor—has already bent over and is pulling the shoe from the hole, and, straightening up, he holds it out to Nula as he simultaneously offers a precise and sober analysis.

—When your foot went in, he says, the water in the puddle splashed into the street, and because the hole is so narrow, the shoe stayed on top, with the heel on the edge; don't worry, no water went in.

—Look at my sock and pant leg, Nula says reproachfully.

And Gutiérrez, who did not let Nula's somewhat cruel silence when they walked away from the police station go unnoticed, and just as he's feeling guilty for having talked to the guard, thinks, despite his impassive demeanor, that actually Nula's current situation isn't altogether undeserved. Nula shakes out the shoe and slips it on, stomping his heel two or three times—in a possibly overly ostentatious way that his shadow appears to mimic—against the sandy street tamped down by the rain. They reach the sidewalk in silence, and Gutiérrez is starting to get irritated by Nula's persistent moodiness, when Nula, who seems to have realized something analogous to this, relents.

—What just happened constitutes the broadest cause for laughter, he says. And you didn't laugh. Thank you for that.

—At my age, you learn to control your emotions, Gutiérrez says, laughing gently to signal that he considers Nula a good sport and that his self-control allows him to concede a certain level of irony toward the misfortunes of others.

—Right now I could be in some warm office in the capitol, selling wine to some aide to the governor, Nula says, exaggerating his plaintive tone. And then, laughing as well, adds, But I don't regret a thing. This outing takes me out of my routine.

—If Ulysses had made it straight home, the *Odyssey* wouldn't exist, Gutiérrez says.

—Possibly, Nula says. But these days the epic form is an anachronism.

—As a professional screenwriter, that notion takes the bread from my table.

—Not just the bread, Nula says. The wine and local salami, too. Which, by the transitive property, takes it from mine.

They laugh. Their recent troubles seem overcome. Now, farther from the corner, the sidewalk is darker, and their shadows disappear into the darkness. The houses are neither rich nor poor. Some are very old, and abut the brick sidewalk directly; others have a small front garden, separated from the earthen path by a chain-link fence. A woman carrying a plastic bag emblazoned with the W of the hypermarket and loaded with provisions, is about to enter one of the houses, stooping to slide the bolt to the screen door. Nula calls out. The woman looks around nervously.

—Good evening, Nula says. Excuse us. We're looking for the Escalante family.

—You mean Doctor Escalante? she says.

Nula hesitates.

—Yes, that's right, Gutiérrez says. He's a lawyer.

—He's retired, the woman says. That's them next door.

The woman points to the next house over. There's a flower bed out front, behind a fence; an expanse of neat lawn around the side courtyard, with an enormous orange tree at the center; and, at the back, a garden, judging by the cane and wire plant trellises, visible thanks to the light that shines through the windows on the far side of the ivy-covered house. *Delicia! Delicia!* the woman shouts. After a minute or so the door opens and a feminine silhouette, apparently very young, is cut from the rectangle of light.

—What is it? she shouts.

—Delicia, it's me, Celia. There's two men here looking for an attorney.

The silhouette in the doorway hesitates a few seconds.

—Who are you? she finally shouts.

Gutiérrez steps up to the fence and shouts back, I'm a friend from abroad, coming by to say hello.

Suddenly, and inexplicably, the silhouette in the doorway starts to laugh.

—I know who you are, she says. Sergio's at the club. Sorry not to come out but I'm washing my hair. Good to meet you. Celia, honey, can you show them where the club is?

—Look, says the first woman. Go past the church and turn right. It's three blocks, on the river side. The sign says *El Amarillo.*

—Thank you, Nula and Gutiérrez say in unison, acting much more polite than if they were speaking to a man, somewhere more crowded, and in the middle of the day. They turn back the way they came, then right on the second corner, pass the church, and walk a block parallel to the square. After crossing the street again—Nula sees the same iridescent vapor haloed over the light at the intersection that covered the white globes in the square—they enter another street, darkened by the trees that border the sidewalk, but also by the night that has now fallen completely. To the west, behind them,

Nula imagines, the curtain of darkness must have already lowered completely, erasing the last fringe of blue light that hung on the edge of the horizon. They don't speak now, and despite the constant rubbing of their shoulders, forced together by the meagerness of the shelter and the irregularity of the sidewalks, their steps splash with the same rhythm. And though both, for different or possibly even opposite reasons, are impatient to arrive, each seems to have forgotten the other. In fact, they're only strangers, and despite the ease with which they exchange the words that the other finds suitable, precise, smart, and so on, both are unsettled by what they might come to learn when the respective opacities that mutually attract them are finally illuminated. It's possible this discomfort is caused, as often happens, by not fully comprehending that the curious attraction they feel comes from unwittingly associating the other with something they both want to reclaim, and which they've long kept hidden in some remote corner inside themselves. They cross the street again, onto another dark sidewalk. Halfway down the block, a wide strip of light, which divides the darkness in half, suggests that they've reached the place they sought. And, in fact, a tin sign hangs from a bar that extends over the sidewalk from the brick wall:

EL AMARILLO
Fish and Game Club

A rough, childish drawing of an elongated fish, painted the same bright yellow as Gutiérrez's jacket, decorates the metal rectangle under the name.

—We're here, Gutiérrez says, and, apparently forgetting Nula, who is left outside the umbrella's protective cylinder, takes a few steps toward the open door and inspects the interior. Nula walks up and does the exact same thing, with very similar movements, not realizing that, because Gutiérrez has his back to him and can't see that Nula's movements so closely resemble his own, someone watching them from behind would think that Nula is deliberately aping him. Suddenly, Gutiérrez closes the umbrella, turns around, and shakes it over the sidewalk to release some of the water. Through the space he opens as he backs up, Nula can see inside the club. It looks like a newly built storehouse, made of unplastered brick, and while the thatch roof is in perfect shape (having been built pretty recently), the floor, by contrast, is simply tamped-down earth. Two small lamps hang from one of the roof beams, and a few lamps are attached to the walls, but only two or three are lit up. Three small tables and their respective folding chairs, arranged somewhat at random, a bit lost in a space that could contain many more, are scattered around the room. Two long planks, some collapsed trestles, and a stack of folding chairs is piled up against a wall. At the back there's a counter and a set of shelves loaded with glasses and bottles, and next to that a yellowed household fridge with a larger door below a smaller one to the freezer, which, Nula thinks, some member of the club probably donated after buying a new one. When they appear in the doorway, a man with a full, smooth beard, standing between the counter and the shelves, stops in the middle of drying a glass, watching them with an inquisitive and somewhat severe expression. At the only occupied table, four men are playing cards and three others are standing behind them, following the course of the game. None of them appears to have noticed their presence yet.

The severe look of the barman at the unexpectedness of their sudden intrusion doesn't seem to intimidate Gutiérrez, who, Nula thinks somewhat anxiously, walks in with the same ease and self-assurance with which one of its founding members or even its president could have. Nula, following him submissively, wavers between disapproval and confused admiration, and is so surprised by Gutiérrez's determination that he's not even conscious of what he's thinking, which, translated into words, would be more or less the following: *Or maybe this is all so familiar to him, it's such an intimate part of himself that despite the thirty-some years away the words and gestures come on their own, reflexively or instinctually, or rather—and it would be offensive if this were the case—he thinks that the millions that Moro attributes to him give him the right to walk in this club as though he were actually its president.*

Without even glancing at the barman, Gutiérrez, scrutinizing each of the players at the table and the three men following the game behind them, walks slowly toward the table. He stops suddenly, staring at one of the four players, who is receiving, his eyes down, the cards that the player to his left is dealing. The man's hair, a slicked-back shell pasted to his skull, is thick and smooth; it's patched in white, gray, and black, like the hair of an animal. A cartoonist would represent it by alternating curved black lines with corresponding white gaps of varying width between them, and a few black, white, and gray blotches interrupting the lines to mark the spots where the black and white separate. Two hollows amplify the forehead that, along with his nose, comprises the most protrusive part of his face, which narrows into a triangle toward his chin. His skin is a dark and lustrous brown, its similarity to leather accentuated by the wrinkles on his neck, on his hands, and around his eyes, whose half-shut eyelids obstruct the view to his eyes themselves, which closely study the two cards he's been dealt as he prepares to pick up a third, just thrown across the greasy table, itself a brown only slightly darker than his hands.

—Sergio, Gutiérrez says.

—Willi, says the other man, his tone neutral, not even looking up from his cards.

Patiently, Gutiérrez waits. Nula is unaware that recognition, approval, confidence, and mutual history have just been exchanged, tacitly, by the utterance of their names. Gutiérrez hasn't said a thing to anyone else, but the others, who've now understood that they're not being asked for, don't seem at all interested in their sudden appearance. Only the barman stands alert, paused in the middle of drying the glass, but when Nula, to indulge him—because Gutiérrez hasn't looked at him once—makes a friendly gesture with his head, the man, as though the nod triggered a remote control, looks down and keeps drying. Escalante picks up the third card, studies it, places it over the others, and deposits all three, so perfectly aligned that they seem like a single card, face down on the table. He looks up at Gutiérrez. Then he stands up slowly, inspects the three men following the game, chooses the one that seems most qualified, and gestures for him to take his place. He walks around the table, and when he reaches Gutiérrez he doesn't hug him or shake his hand, only looks him in the eyes and gives him a soft nudge on the chest with the back of his hand. Gutiérrez smiles, but with a look of protest.

—I live practically around the corner, and it took me a year to find you, he says.

—I saw you once, in a car, but before I could put two and two together, you were gone, Escalante says. And another time you walked down my street, but you were with someone. How'd you know I was at the club?

—Your daughter told us, Gutiérrez says.

—My daughter? Escalante says. I don't have children. That was my wife.

Opening his eyes wide and biting his upper lip and shaking his head hard, Gutiérrez's face takes on an exaggerated look of admiration.

—It was no great feat getting such a young wife, Escalante says. For her, it was between poverty and me, and she lost: she got me.

It's difficult for Nula to sense the irony in Escalante's words; his tone is so neutral and flat that it seems deliberate. It's like he's talking to himself, Nula thinks, speaking to something inside. And he realizes that he's been thinking about how Escalante's wife laughed when, referring to Gutiérrez, she said, *I know who you are.* That cheerful sentence implied that she and her husband had already talked about him, and that there might be a sense of irony between them when it came to the subject of Gutiérrez. Meanwhile, when Nula sees them face-to-face, it seems impossible—unless they'd been avoiding it on purpose—that they never once met in the past year. Who knows what reason they might have had to delay the meeting, since they must have known that it would happen sooner or later. When they exchanged their names across the table of truco players without looking at each other, Nula realized, without understanding exactly what it meant, that despite their efforts at pretending otherwise, both men had been aware of even the most intimate details regarding the other for all of the past year. And then he thinks that it's not impossible that when he saw Gutiérrez closing the door to his house he wasn't actually planning to come to Rincón, and that only at that moment did he decide to go, because without him, Nula, he wouldn't have dared come looking for Escalante at home. And Nula is so absorbed in these thoughts that Gutiérrez has to say his name twice in order to introduce him.

—Mr. Anoch, he says, wine merchant. Doctor Sergio Escalante, attorney.

The overly formal manner of the introduction, in particular the use of their surnames and professions, underscored by his sober tone, suggests to the two men that Gutiérrez's regard for their persons goes well beyond these superficial details—antithetically, in fact, to these social characteristics—in the quarter of authenticity and courage, of hard-fought individuality, of nerve, of introspection, and of a fierce marginality. Without much emotion, both Nula and Escalante nod their heads, accompanying the movement with a brief and rather conventional smile to show that they've discerned, approvingly, the irony of the introduction. When he smiles, Escalante reveals an incomplete set of teeth almost at brown as the skin on his face, and, realizing this, he raises a hand to his lips. The teeth must have been missing for a while, because the gesture seems automatic, and its slight delay could be due to his familiarity with the other players, in whose frequent company he thinks it superfluous—his teeth are no longer a secret to them—but now a reflexive modesty has induced him to conceal his mouth, too late in any case, though Gutiérrez doesn't seem to have given the matter even the slightest importance.

As the other players resume the game, Escalante starts walking toward the bar, and Gutiérrez follows, but Nula is delayed by a survey of the damages the walk has caused to what he rightly considers a kind of uniform: the loafers (the left one in particular), as well as the cuffs of his pants, are covered in yellow mud, and a few splatters of this watery substance, which have already begun to dry, managed to reach his fly and even the front of the white pullover, two circles with a tortured circumference and a dense center, like a pair of symbolic bellybuttons drawn on the white material for some cryptic, supernatural purpose. And on the red camper—like on his pant legs—some damp stains around the shoulders illustrate that the shelter offered by Gutiérrez's multicolored umbrella has been less than perfect. But Nula, after assessing the results of the walk, shakes his head with a smile that, for some reason, unknown even to himself, expresses less annoyance than satisfaction, and, with a few decisive steps, joins the others at the bar.

—What'll you have? Escalante says.

Gutiérrez, apparently uncertain, slowly inspects the shelves. The barman, who has left the towel and the glass he was drying on the table, waits, with a calm expression, neither impatient nor servile, for Gutiérrez to decide.

—A vermouth with bitters and soda, on ice, he says finally.

Escalante asks Nula with his eyes.

—The same, Nula tells the man at the bar.

—Orange for me, Escalante says.

As the barman starts to make their order, Nula watches the two men. They've fallen silent, and don't seem in a hurry to talk. Finally, without a hint of reproach, Escalante says:

—You left so suddenly. Swallowed up by the earth.

—I was in Buenos Aires for a while, and then I crossed the pond, Gutiérrez says.

Escalante shakes his head thoughtfully. He's taller than Gutiérrez, but his extreme thinness, and possibly his seniority, make him look foreshortened in comparison. With his hawk-like nose, his brown skin, his prominent Adam's apple, and his dark eyes that despite being evasive (due to some ocular handicap, perhaps) gleam when they settle on something, a person, animal, or object, the cruel epithet *vulture* that people assign to lawyers seems even more apt to him, not to mention the indifference he projects for things of this world, and the self-control—with the exception of the gesture to hide his teeth, a residual concession to aesthetic considerations—so internalized by now that it seems like his natural state, a false cloak against everything that erodes us, ceaselessly, day after day, from the moment we're born to the moment we die.

—You did the right thing, not saying goodbye to anyone, Escalante says. And Marcos, have you seen him?

—He was the one who told me you lived in Rincón, as far as anyone could tell, Gutiérrez says.

—I used to run into him at the courthouse. But then he got into politics and I retired. I haven't seen him for years.

—Well, I came to invite you over on Sunday, Gutiérrez says. You can see him there.

Escalante bursts out laughing, and raises his hand to cover his devastated teeth.

—At Doctor Russo's house? he says. It's haunted. They say the doctor's ghost comes back from hell just to rob the guests.

—He's not in hell, Nula says. Worse, actually—he's in Miami.

—Sorry, Gutiérrez says. But I'm out of touch with the local mythology.

—It doesn't matter, Escalante says. So you're inviting me over? Will many people be there?

—A mixed bag, Gutiérrez says. But you and the Rosembergs are my guests of honor. The rest—forgive me, Mr. Anoch—comprise the glamorous court I've assembled to receive my old friends. The only one missing will be Chiche, but as our young friend would say, El Chiche deserved something better than Miami, and we'd have to fetch him ourselves from the inferno to get him to come.

Escalante's eyes, gleaming ironically under his eyebrows, arched and gathered around his nose, lock on Gutiérrez's.

—Did you know, he says, that I've been sleeping with my maid since she was thirteen and I was forty?

Gutiérrez, slow to find the appropriate response, puckers his lips into an awkward smile.

—I wouldn't expect anything less from you, he says finally. Always the good pastor.

Nula watches them curiously. Since the first words they exchanged, and possibly to conceal their emotions, their demeanor has been remote and caustic, but to Nula it seems that rather than express the reticence of alert, disillusioned maturity, that style has something juvenile about it, adolescent even, as though something

48

had been suspended in each of them over the thirty years apart that was automatically put in motion again at their first meeting. Calculating the difference in their ages—when Gutiérrez, without telling anyone, and without a trace, left the city, he still hadn't been born—Nula experiences the vaguely disorienting feeling that he's unwittingly crossed an invisible border, and that he's now moving through the territory of the past, perceiving with his own senses a pre-empirical limbo that preceded his birth. He feels like he's crossed into a space where nothing is real, only represented, like some character in the movies who, during a scene that takes place in a false airport, pretends to have just disembarked from a plane that carried him from a distant country, and he speaks of that country as though he'd really just come from there, but his words are empty of experience, they're just simulacra authored by someone else, and when they're spoken, to describe things that never happened, as interesting as these things might be, they must sound bewildering and strange to the actor. With their lightly evoked juvenile irony, the two older men also seem to have been spirited away, and now float in that parallel universe in which, during their first meeting after a prolonged separation, their lives seem to have paused years and years earlier in the other's imagination. The empirical decades that have passed while they were apart are surely an impenetrable and reciprocal mystery that—while they might spend the rest of their lives elaborating them for each other—they'll only manage to recover as a series of vague, irregular fragments. It occurs to Nula that, for now at least, those decades don't interest them: all they seem to want is to renew the interrupted course of shared experience that time, distance, and the temporarily-overpowered inconstancy of their respective lives had steered into the limbo where for now, exchanging measured, ironic lines that carry with them authentic pieces of information, putting the external world between parentheses (*where they've put me along with it*), they try to reunite.

And Nula's conclusion could be summed up as follows: *That's why he came in here like he knew the place. It's got nothing to do with the millions that Moro attributes to him. He's trying to act like he never left.*

The barman deposits the bottles, ice, and glasses on the counter, along with a dish of peanuts and another of green olives. Nula takes out a cigarette but (because he's lost in thought) doesn't offer one around, and, after lighting it, returns the lighter and the red and white packet wrapped in cellophane to his jacket pocket. When they've finished preparing their drinks, Nula holds out his glass, as though he's about to give a toast, and he's just about to add his own ironic comment when he realizes that the other two men, poised at the threshold of old age, have lapsed into thought after taking their first sips (Escalante drinks his orange soda straight from the bottle), and so he keeps quiet. Suddenly, he understands what Moro had been trying to explain to him at the estate agency when he described his meeting with Gutiérrez on San Martín and said that at one point he got the feeling that if he spoke to Gutiérrez the other man wouldn't even have noticed his presence because he seemed to be in a different dimension, like in some science fiction show. *The past,* Nula thinks, *the most inaccessible and remote of all the extinguished galaxies, insists, endlessly, on transmitting its counterfeit, fossilized luminescence.*

And yet, Nula realizes, they don't allow themselves, in public at least, either nostalgia, distortion, or complaint. They exchange words that, from the outside, seem formulaic, but which Nula can sense are loaded with meaning. They start talking about Marcos Rosemberg and his political altruism, exchanging a brief smile that Escalante tries to hide with his hand and that signals their tacit recognition of a certain disposition, crystallized some forty years before, that they attribute to Rosemberg and which seems to provoke both sympathy and disbelief. And Nula, who knows Rosemberg well, since he, too, is a client—Rosemberg was the first to suggest selling wine to Gutiérrez, saying that if he told Gutiérrez he'd sent him, he would definitely buy some—thinks he can guess that the sympathy comes from their affection for him and the sincerity they attribute to his political activities, while the disbelief, modeled after a self-fashioned image of the cynic, reflects their doubt regarding the actual likelihood of the efficacy of those very activities.

—And you? Gutiérrez says.

Before answering, Escalante considers Nula's presence, apparently asking himself whether or not it's the right time to disclose his personal life, and Nula, as he thinks this, and as Escalante looks him over quickly, tries to muster, not altogether convincingly, a look of neutrality and indifference. But the one that appears on Escalante's face after the inspection, when he begins to speak, doesn't indicate a favorable appraisal of his person, but rather something more generalized, a sort of philosophical posture or moral reflection through which he recalls how trivial and revolting anyone's private life is.

—Everything Marcos must have told you about me is true, Escalante says, and Nula remembers thinking, a few minutes before, that despite his apparent curiosity and subtle exclamations of surprise, they've both known everything about each other ever since Gutiérrez came to the city the year before.

—I was married, I was locked up, I gave myself to the game, for years, and then I got together with my thirteen-year-old maid. After I lost everything, I took up the profession again, trying not to exhaust myself, until I was able to retire. But my wife works now. He falls silent, and then, in a murmur, adds, *The perfect crime.*

—Balzac said that behind every great fortune there is a great crime, Gutiérrez says.

—Is that true in your case? Escalante says, and, from under his arched and graying eyebrows, joined at the bridge of his nose, he locks his smoldering eyes on Gutiérrez's.

As his only response, Gutiérrez nods his head slowly, in a pantomime of suffering, and recites:

> *I am the knife and the wound it deals,*
> *I am the slap and the cheek,*
> *I am the wheel and the broken limbs,*
> *hangman and victim both!*

Escalante listens to the verses carefully, motionless, as though
they were a riddle, a code, or an oracle, and when Gutiérrez finishes
speaking, his expression turns severe and brooding, attempting to
interpret, for himself at least, its possible meanings. Then, gasping
softly, he concludes, worriedly, *It wouldn't surprise me*, which, for
some mysterious reason, or which, in any case, Nula interprets as
such, apparently produces an inexplicable sense of satisfaction for
Gutiérrez.

When they finish their vermouth, Escalante, who hasn't finished
even half of the orange soda, offers them another round, which
they decline. Nula, his back to the bar, throws three or four peanuts
into the air, one after the other, and, twisting his head and rolling
his eyes to follow their trajectory, catches them in his mouth. Then
he is still again, and, looking across the room at the front door,
watches the rain cross, obliquely, the light that projects onto the
sidewalk against the backdrop of the night.

—Are you coming on Sunday? Gutiérrez says, signaling, indi-
rectly, their imminent departure.

—I have to think about it, Escalante says.

—If it's because of your missing teeth, Gutiérrez says—bringing
his hand to his mouth and removing a set of dentures from the
bottom row and leaving a gap in the middle of his bottom lip—I too
can reveal my true face to the world.

Escalante's own face, impassive up until that moment, has become unstable, covered in folds, creases, and wrinkles, on his forehead, around his eyes and mouth, as though he were making a tremendous effort to hide an emotion, and he darkens slightly, possibly because his skin is so lustrous and dark that the blood that flows to his cheeks can't quite turn them red. Finally, the creases on his face disappear and Escalante is able to smile, and when his hand, his fingers curled, starts to move toward his mouth, he notices the gesture and stops it at his waist, hooking his thumb between his belt and the waistline of his pants. Nula, languidly chewing his peanuts, slows the movement of his jaws until they stop completely and his mouth is left half open as he stares at the other men, as the barman does, and who does so with an expression that combines surprise and uneasiness and even anger. Gutiérrez, with a gesture that vaguely resembles a magician or a variety show host, and which consists of holding the dentures aloft for the public, has also fallen still, displaying the false teeth mounted on a bridge of pink substance that resembles the color of his gums, and ends with two metal hooks that must attach to the actual teeth, and when he returns Escalante's smile, his lower lip, sunken into the hole that has opened in the middle of his face, folds and collapses into his mouth, disfiguring the countenance that Nula, over the course of their three meetings, had started to get used to. Slightly agitated, Nula thinks, *And I thought he walked in here that way out of arrogance.*

—Alright, fine, Escalante says. Maybe you convinced me. Maybe I'll come.

While Nula thinks, *What strange people*, Gutiérrez, narrowing his eyes and rolling his pupils backward, reinserts the teeth and stops a few seconds to install them, tapping his upper row against the lower one to make sure they're in place.

—Chacho, Escalante says to the barman. Do we have anything our friends could take back with them?

—Let me see if there's anything in the fridge, the man named Chacho says.

—No, Escalante says. I meant in the water.

Escalante's preference immediately generates a certain regard in Chacho for the visitors—somewhat diminished by the scene he's just witnessed—and a resigned smile decorates the ambivalent manner with which he gazes, through the doorway that leads to the sidewalk, at the slanting rainfall that crosses the light against the dark backdrop of the night.

—I have a couple of catfish, he says. They're the first of the year.

—So they don't leave empty-handed, Escalante says.

A childish, intensely joyful look appears on Gutiérrez's face, which the barman notes with a spark of satisfaction and possibly even malice, and Nula, without hesitating, attributes the look to some idealized image of the local color that, during his years away, Gutiérrez had hoped to recover, and which, at this moment, by some unexpected and benevolent concession granted by the external world, is now really real. Chacho disappears into the back of the building, through a doorway next to the fridge.

—Don't walk past the dump this late, Escalante says. You'll be slaughtered and eaten up.

—Where oppression reigns, its victims are always suspect, Gutiérrez says.

—They came forth for no good reason, and now they squirm around like a bunch of larvae, Escalante says, and, with a hoarse laugh, adds, Just like the rest of us.

—Yet we claim to embody something more elevated, Gutiérrez says. Power, knowledge, wealth, tradition, and, worst of all, virtue.

—Larvae that pontificate, buy cars, and drink fine wine, Nula says, rubbing his hands together. My golden goose.

Chacho reappears in the opening that leads to the other room: he's now wearing a burlap sack shaped into a sort of cloak over his shoulders; he carries an enormous flashlight in one hand and a knife in the other.

—Do you know where it is? Gutiérrez says.

—Doctor Russo's place? Escalante says. I once brought charges on behalf of two or three poor bastards who lost everything they had because of him.

—See you Sunday, Gutiérrez says.

They tap each other on the arm and Escalante nods at Nula, a kind of economical greeting that is also a gesture of approval, as though, despite having exchanged only two or three conventional words with him, he were granting him something resembling a certificate of approval. Chacho comes around the bar, and his corpulence, while surprisingly greater than it seemed at first, contrasts with the energy and even agility with which he moves. Gutiérrez and Nula follow him, but Gutiérrez takes a couple of hesitant steps and then stops, turning back toward Escalante.

—I'll have you know, he says, that when a European pauses thoughtfully, pencil in hand, it's because he's doing a crossword puzzle.

—I imagined as much, Escalante says, without stopping, and practically without looking at him, as he turns back toward the table of card players, and Nula thinks, again, but with a shade of irony this time, *What strange people.*

They step out into the rainy night, and, under the entrance sign, Gutiérrez once again unfolds the multicolored umbrella, but Chacho is moving so quickly that he has to stop and wait, realizing that the others have been delayed by a couple of seconds. As soon as they leave the swath of light that projects over the sidewalk, Chacho turns on the flashlight and an intense white beam shines over the sandy ground, the uneven brick sidewalks, and the saturated weeds that border the street. On the next corner, as they cross the illuminated intersection, Chacho turns off the flashlight, but after only a few meters he turns it on again. They pass the last of the street lights, and the tall silhouettes of darkened trees ahead appear to block their path, but it wouldn't make sense to say that the trees interrupt the road: just like when they came into town from the north, the sidewalks and the street are now level, separated only by a ragged strip of weeds that reflects fragments of the white flashlight beam, and, strictly speaking, it's already hard to tell them apart and there doesn't seem to be either a street or a sidewalk anymore. In reality they now walk down what, had there been one, could have been considered the middle of the street. Seeing Chacho covered in the sack, Nula feels a bit ridiculous under the small, multicolored umbrella, his left arm constantly rubbing against Gutiérrez's right elbow, elevated because he's holding the umbrella in his right hand, making their walk so difficult that Chacho, just ahead of them, has to stop every so often to wait, but the rain, fine and silent, is too heavy to face unprotected. When they reach the trees that darken the path, Chacho leads them to the right, onto an embankment that is somewhat more slippery and wet than the rain-tamped, sandy street.

—This is clay through here, Chacho warns them, and slows down a bit. Nula and Gutiérrez move cautiously, feeling the wet mud against the soles of their shoes, squeaking under Gutiérrez's now hesitant boots. The flashlight beam, projecting over the earth, reveals a brilliant, glistening circle of reddish mud. After walking some fifty meters over the embankment, noisily and with a few slips and hasty acrobatics, and crossing a scrub, they come out on another sandy road. To one side stands a large, whitewashed ranch, a light shining through a small window, and, to the other, they can sense the splashing and unmistakable smell of the river. A sudden watery upheaval betrays the rise and immediate submergence of a large fish. Chacho probably hasn't even heard it, and though Nula and Gutiérrez are both familiar with the sound, it produces, because they don't often hear it, a sense of pleasure.

Chacho, passing the flashlight beam quickly over the roof and white facade of the ranch, says, *That's my house*, and turns back toward the river.

A cluster of young acacias struggle near the riverbank.

—Watch your step, the water's up, Chacho says, and he stops so suddenly that Nula and Gutiérrez, pressed together under the umbrella and colliding as they brake, almost run him over. He passes the bright beam over the trees, the earth, the bank, the water, and eventually the light collides, somewhat weakly, against the vegetation on an island across the river. As the light beam retraces the same path, in reverse, Nula is able to make out, on the surface of the river, the parallel waves pocked with rainfall and formed by opposite forces, the downstream current and the wind from the southeast, apparently the same ones they saw upriver earlier that day, and whether they're the same waves or identical waves it's difficult to know, because the law of becoming, manifested here as false repetition, constructs its shabby platform of permanence right in the eye of the whirlwind.

A red canoe, shining in the rain, rocks gently among the reeds. Three damp ropes, tied to the trunk of a tree, extend from the water's edge. Chacho studies them a moment and then, crouching, grabs one of the three, lifts it slightly, and starts to haul it in, energetically but carefully. Then he turns around and extends the flashlight to Nula.

—Shine it here, please, he orders politely. Obligingly, Gutiérrez raises the umbrella slightly, not enough to cover the other two, and Nula, with a hint of treachery, thinks he must want to play a part in the scene—singular, at least to men from the city—that is developing in the rainy darkness. Pulling up on the rope, slowly, carefully,

Chacho takes out a wooden cage built from a wine case, its interior compartments disassembled and a few panels added to the outside to cover the openings without closing them off completely, allowing the cage to fill with water when it's submerged.

—Shine it here, Chacho repeats, brusquely, and, releasing a few hooks, opens the lid. Nula points the flashlight at the opening, and the white circle shines into the bottom of the cage. Two gleaming, silver fish with long whiskers and trembling dorsal fins twist desperately inside, and, lunging spastically, they collide and crash against the walls of the cage. With a single, deft movement, Chacho, who, in his burlap cloak, looks like a priest at some ancient ritual, grabs one of the fish by the middle, near the dorsal fin, and without straightening up, moves it slightly away from the cage into the flashlight beam, flips it belly-up, and splits it with a single incision, liberating it, Nula thinks, from the spasm of agony that still convulses the other, removing it forever from its strange fishy universe, as incomprehensible to the fish as to the three men standing overhead, a universe that, as cruel and adverse as it might seem, has yet to be seized from his associate struggling at the bottom of the cage. After splitting the fish, Chacho drops the knife on the ground, inserts his free hand into the open belly, and, in one tug, yanks out its guts and throws them into the river, causing, as they hit the water, a sudden upheaval, a noisy and violent tremor, as other, hungry fish struggle over the unexpected offering. Chacho places the dead fish on the ground, picks up the knife, and, with the same quickness, carries out the same operation on the second fish. Then he carries both fish to the water and washes them in the river, and then his hands, and finally, standing up and taking from his pocket a wrinkled plastic bag emblazoned with a green W from the hypermarket, drops the two fish inside and extends the bag to Gutiérrez.

—Here, he says.

Nula follows their movements with the white flashlight beam, but because of how close they are the circle is constrained and the only things that appear in the beam of light are their arms, a section of their bodies at waist level, and the plastic bag, whose logo Nula recognizes. Gutiérrez's free hand goes into his pocket and comes out with a few bills, moving toward the hand that's just given him the bag; this other hand shakes vigorously in the white light while Chacho's voice, from the darkness above, firmly protests.

—No, sir, I couldn't. Those fish belong to the club. When you need some more, I can sell you some of my own if you want.

—Thank you, Gutiérrez says in a grateful voice (maybe too grateful, Nula thinks, not feeling, because he's never left the area, the same fervency toward this altogether commonplace situation) from some vague space in the rainy darkness between the white circle that illuminates the lower parts of their bodies, on the sandy riverbank, and the multicolored umbrella above their heads.

—If you're going to Doctor Russo's house, don't go by the river side at this hour, Chacho says. Take the road instead. It's easy from here.

He holds out his hand for the flashlight. The quick movements, the change of hands and direction, make the beam of light land randomly, a fleeting disorder, on fragments of distant and near things, on trees, on the grayish, slanting rain, on the earth, the river, and their bodies, disparate moments of space and time floating in the blackness, which to Nula seem a more accurate representation of the empirical world than the double superstition of coherence and continuity that men have grown accustomed to under the constant somnolence that the tyranny of the rational enforces. They move away from the river again. Chacho walks at the head of the group, through the young acacias punished by the rain, by the season, and, most likely, by the rise and fall of the water. The coastline silence is undisturbed by the rain, and when they have moved far enough from the water that they can no longer hear its rhythmic splashing at the riverbank, all that is heard is the sound of their steps, snapping, scuffling, against sand, water, weeds, wet mud, a complex but sustained rhythm interspersed with the ephemeral dissonance of scrambling or involuntary interjections. When they are close to the ranch, Chacho veers off to the left, and the flashlight beam tracks from his sandals some ten or fifteen meters ahead, illuminating what appears to be a road. Above it, at a distance that's difficult to measure, possibly two or even three blocks ahead, appears a row of streetlights, shining tenuously.

—This here runs into the road. When you get there, turn right, to the north, and it's only a few minutes to the Russo place. Here, he says, and puts the flashlight back in Nula's hand. Give it to Doctor Escalante tomorrow or the day after, or bring it by the club.

—Thanks for everything, Nula says.

—Not a problem, Chacho says. Good luck.

—Right, Nula says. Now that it's over it's stopped.

—So it goes, Chacho says, laughing, and he disappears into the darkness. They listen to the fading sound of his sandals, which must be completely soaked, snapping as they hit the ground. Gutiérrez stands motionless, looking into the darkness where the other has disappeared.

—Sergio must have some good left in him, for his friends to treat us like this, he says in a low voice, but loud enough for Nula to hear. Then he turns and walks alongside Nula, who shines the light across the successive fragments of ground they venture over. When they reach the first streetlight, Nula turns off the flashlight, and though a few small, isolated ranches have begun to appear, they keep to the middle of the road. Three horses are pastured in the darkness, near an unplastered brick house. Out of curiosity, Nula turns on the flashlight and illuminates them, but the horses don't even look up: all three are in the same position, their necks angled toward the ground, their teeth pulling at the grass, their heads still, two of them parallel to the street, facing opposite each other, and a third, who's only visible at the hindquarters, its tail shaking slightly. Nula turns off the flashlight.

When they reach the paved road Nula slips climbing up the embankment and Gutiérrez grabs his arm with the hand that carries the plastic bag—the other holds up the multicolored umbrella—to keep him from falling over. They cross the road so as to walk against traffic, and their steps become noisier, but also more firm, against the asphalt paving. For a while, they walk without speaking. They pass a brightly lit, empty gas station on the left, and on their right the main road into town, the illuminated, perpendicular streets that extend from the road toward the town center, the square, the levees built up against the floods, the river. Every so often, the headlights of an oncoming car force them to step onto the shoulder, into the mud and saturated weeds, and when the car passes they step back onto the pavement, moving more easily again. For a good stretch they seem to have forgotten each other, but every time headlights appear against the black backdrop of the lamp-lit, asphalt road, gleaming in the rain, they step sideways in a way that appears practiced and synchronized, without advance notice, deftly and exact, onto the shoulder. In the quickly approaching headlights the invisible rain takes on a fleeting, grayish materiality that is vaguely spectral, dense, and slanting, pierced by the beams, shining, and then, as they pass, is suddenly swallowed again by the darkness. And after the car has passed, Nula turns on the flashlight and the circle of white light, at once steady and mobile, restores it.

Of all the witnesses from that time, Gabriela Barco said, *he's turned out to be the most useful—he remembers everything*. And Soldi: *He can recite from memory entire books that the authors themselves don't even remember writing*. After he first met Gutiérrez, by the swimming pool, when he happened to run into the two of them at the Amigos del Vino bar and Soldi hinted that Lucía might actually be his daughter, they started describing their interviews with Gutiérrez on the literary scene in the city during the fifties. *His Roman Law professor, Doctor Calcagno—that is, Lucía Riera's legal father—got him a job at his firm, where he was partners with Mario Brando, a firm that, by the way, was one of the most important in the city at the time,* Soldi said. And Gabriela: *Brando was the head of the precisionist movement; the precisionist specialty consisted of integrating traditional poetic forms with the language of the sciences. They made some waves at the time. Gutiérrez, though he had nothing to do with the movement, saw Brando constantly, because he worked for him, and while his bosses went about their political and literary lives, he did all the work for the firm. He worked there for a while until one day—it was Rosemberg who first told us this, but Gutiérrez later confirmed it, implicitly—suddenly, without saying goodbye to anyone, and without anyone knowing why, he disappeared. The other day, Gutiérrez explained why he left: besides his three friends—Rosemberg, Escalante, and César Rey—he didn't have anyone else in the world.* Because they were working, Soldi and Gabriela had a stack of papers on the table, and Soldi's briefcase, as usual, sat open on the chair next to him, within reach, containing papers, books, index cards, pencils, and so on, which he would arrange and rearrange. He grabbed a notepad, and, while he talked, consulted the notes that he'd been taking during the interview, which they'd also recorded: *He remembered the first and last names of almost every precisionist because Calcagno had taken him to quite a few meetings and because Brando, who never invited the group's members to the law firm, would sometimes send him on errands for the group. Brando was a true strategist, and Gutiérrez says that despite his apparent lack of empathy, his talent for publicity and organization was undeniable.* And Gabriela: *Not only does he remember everything, but the act itself, when our questions require it, seems to cause him incredible pleasure. All it takes is a name, a date, or the title of a book or a magazine, and he starts talking in that calm voice, which doesn't change even when he's recalling polemics, betrayals, or suicides. He seems to get the same pleasure from it that someone else might get from describing Paradise, but he doesn't try to gloss or hide anything, and in that same smooth, even tone, he can be ironic, disdainful, mocking, and cruel.* Turning the pages of his notebook, backward, rereading his notes to find what he's looking for, Soldi continued speaking without looking up: *Before leaving, he said, he burned all his papers, stories, poems, and essays, and he left for Buenos Aires intending to commit himself to writing, but he happened to meet a movie producer who offered him a job proofreading screenplays that were about to be filmed. And with what he made from that he left for Europe. As a joke, he recited a few poems that he'd written at the time, and that, in his own words, despite having been burned before he left the city, had been impossible to forget, which illustrated the Buddhist belief in reincarnation: not being able to forget his own poems proved that he was paying for his crimes in another life. I jotted down two verses: "The rigging will never see this port / there will be no other moment for your sadness."*

Nula's cell phone, from the bottom of his pocket, announces a call. Lost in thought, he only hears it after the third ring, and, passing the flashlight to his other hand—he only turns it on now when passing cars force them onto the shoulder—he takes it from his pocket and brings it to his ear. Addressing himself to the person on the phone, who calls from some unspecified place, but at the same time to Gutiérrez, who walks beside him silently in the darkness, Nula shouts:

—Where am I, you say? I'm on the river road, north of Rincón, soaked to the bone under a toy umbrella. It's raining buckets and for the last three hours I've been with a client who decided to tour the landmarks of his far-off youth. Because everyone knows that when it comes to the Amigos del Vino, as the sales manager taught us during the practicum seminar, the customer is always right. Is everything set for tomorrow, both at the same time as today? You're a genius, Américo. Thanks. I'll call you tomorrow.

Nula hangs up the phone and puts it back in his pocket. That was my boss again, he says. He's perfectly obedient, as you can see.

—This drenching has earned you a roasted catfish, Gutiérrez says.

—Are you inviting me over for dinner? Nula says. I accept, if I can bring the wine.

—Why not? An astonishing country, where everything is free, Gutiérrez says.

But it is written that tonight they won't eat together. A light is on in the house when they arrive, and a compact black car is parked next to Nula's green station wagon. Nula turns on the flashlight and casts the beam over the cars, the front of the house, the trees in the side courtyard, and finally shuts it off.

—A visitor, Gutiérrez says, and pushes open the gate, the same white gate that, Nula recalls, Gutiérrez locked before they started their hike along the river.

—Come in, I'll introduce you, Gutiérrez says.

—Is it family? Nula says, following obediently, feeling his heartbeat accelerate and trying, simultaneously, to keep his voice steady when he speaks, in such a high-pitched tone that he's forced to cough in the middle of the sentence in order to recover his usual gravity. But Gutiérrez, who moves toward the door, closing the umbrella, doesn't seem to hear him.

—Come in, he says again, even friendlier than before. He's about to put the key in the lock when the door opens from the inside, so suddenly that Nula jumps, an involuntary, barely audible exclamation escaping from his mouth. But Lucía, smiling, is already standing in the illuminated, rectangular doorway, and, receiving Gutiérrez, gives him a quick, noisy kiss on the cheek. Gutiérrez steps aside, and, with a slightly mysterious half-smile that Nula, stupefied by his emotions, tries unsuccessfully to interpret, assumes the need to offer them an utterly conventional introduction.

—Do you know each other? Mr. Anoch, enologist and philosopher—but which comes first? Lucía Calcagno.

Nula is about to stammer something, but Lucía preempts him.

—No, she says, still smiling, and offers her hand.

No, Nula thinks, as he holds out his own. *She said no.*

—Good to meet you, he says, his voice breaking. They shake hands two or three times and then let go.

—I had some stuff to do in the city and when I was on my way back to Paraná it occurred to me to come say hi.

—Great idea, Gutiérrez says, shaking the plastic bag. There's two catfish here begging for the oven. Come in, come in, he says to Nula again.

Nula stands frozen in the doorway.

—No, thank you, I'll leave you to your family, he says, thinking, constantly, and evermore intensely, as they say, *She said no.* Another time. Sunday.

After the door closes behind him and he starts to walk toward his car through the rainy darkness, Nula shakes his head in disbelief. *She said no*, he thinks, and a dry, sarcastic, inward laugh escapes his lips. The headlights, when he turns them on, illuminate the entire facade of the house, the white wooden gate, the white walls, the space that separates the gate from the front door, the trees growing alongside the house, but the image through the windshield, pearled across its surface by droplets of rain, is disintegrated and luminous. The white surfaces, even the white, lacquered wood bars of the gate, seem paradoxically more irregular, and the contours of things more uncertain, lines seemingly drawn by a seismograph, and the lights from the house, or from the headlights bouncing off the white gate, refract in each of the drops stuck to the windshield, a static flicker that the wiper blades, after he starts the engine, take several passes to erase, a pointless exercise, in any case, since after each pass, new drops fall, luminous, from the black heights of the countryside and cover the glass again. He puts the car in reverse, then goes forward, then reverses again, and finally starts down the sandy path toward the paved road. The glimmer disappears, only to reappear each time the headlights of an approaching car reflect off the drops that, despite the ceaseless arcs traced by the wiper blades, their trajectory accompanied by the same resonant sweep, accumulate repeatedly against the glass. Holding the wheel with one hand, Nula takes the cigarettes and lighter from the pocket of his camper, moves the pack to the hand resting on the upper portion of the steering wheel, takes out a cigarette, and, after putting it between his teeth and lighting it and releasing a thin cloud of smoke, returns the cigarettes and lighter to the camper pocket. (He wasn't wrong when he thought he'd be smoking a lot today.) He shifts slightly in his seat to find a comfortable position, grabs the wheel in both hands, and accelerates slightly by applying unconscious pressure to the gas pedal with his foot. With another short, sarcastic laugh, which makes the cigarette quiver, shaking his head back and forth, he mutters, *She said no! She said no!* He laughs again, and though he thinks he gets the complexity of the situation—he doesn't realize yet that the situation might be much more complicated than he imagines—there are, undoubtedly, traces of bitterness in the sarcasm.

The enormous hypermarket complex appears to his left, its eight theatres, its parking lot, its coffee shops, its cafeteria, and its restaurant all seemingly deserted despite the grandiose display of lights and colors hovering in the darkness of the countryside. The lights shine off the wet bodywork of the fifteen or twenty cars scattered around the parking lot, none of them near the main entrance. A year before, the land that is now occupied by the hypermarket was just a swamp in the middle of an empty floodplain—constantly under water, even when it was dry everywhere else—between La Guardia, where the road splits toward Paraná, and the branch of the river from which the city rises. Nula hesitates a few seconds, slowing down, deciding whether or not to turn into the complex; on Friday, Amigos del Vino starts a week-long promotion there, and he wants to finalize a couple of details with whomever's in charge, but immediately he changes his mind and accelerates again. The network of lights and colors passes, then reappears for a few seconds, fragmentary, in the rear-view mirror before it disappears completely. Now the road widens into four lanes, and is lit up by tall, downward-curving poles projecting onto the reflective asphalt. The city lights appear overhead, to the right the straight line of lamps on the waterfront, and, to the left, less regularly, the lights on the port, on the avenues converging toward the river, on the buildings of various heights that stand out from the rest, on the regatta club. The car reaches the bridge. It's so brightly lit that the city, despite its multiplicity of lights, appears dark on the other side. *She said no,* Nula says again, and, to underscore his disbelief, shakes his head in such a way that the cigarette, which he hasn't taken from his lips since lighting it, and which he's consumed a good potion of by now, vibrates in the air, disturbed by the words he says, by the movement of his lips as he shapes them, and by the negative sign, turning his head from left to right and right to left, several times, in the darkness, that expresses his at once ironic and confused bitterness. The combination of these movements causes the smoke that rises from the lit end of the cigarette and from his lungs, though his nose and mouth, to form a turbulent cloud between Nula's face and the windshield, where the rain drops, swept aside by the wiper blades, rematerialize, obstinately, and it's through this cloud that Nula, leaving the bridge, with another short, dry, and sarcastic laugh, sees the first rain-soaked streets as the car enters the city.

Gutiérrez also ended up alone early. Lucía didn't accept his invitation to dinner, and left for Paraná almost immediately after Nula's sudden departure. And so Gutiérrez has put the fish away in the fridge, and, to counteract any negative effects of the rain, has taken a hot shower, eaten some cheese and grapes he found in the fridge, and settled into what, with self-directed irony, he calls *the machine room* (satellite television, videocassette player, video camera, computer, printer, modem, radio, compact disc player, telephone, library, record collection, video collection, and so on), trying to work for a while. The *millions* that he's unaware of Moro assigning him are in fact imaginary. It's true he has some savings, and that the sale of a screenplay for *Wolf Man* two years before secured him his best fees ever for a movie, even though it was never filmed, but there's nothing in the world that could get him to stop working, and at this moment he's editing two other screenplays for which he's already been given an advance, so he couldn't abandon them even if he wanted to. Though it may be expensive for the area, the riverside house—the people in Buenos Aires who sold it to him never mentioned Doctor Russo, and he only heard the name after he'd moved in—cost him much less than an apartment in Rome or Geneva would have, and actually its location isn't inconvenient: if he had to make a Thursday afternoon meeting in Rome, for example, he'd simply have to take the Wednesday morning flight at nine fifteen from Sauce Viejo, connect in Ezeiza three hours later, and he'd be at the Piazza de Popolo for lunch by noon on Thursday. Luckily, the Swiss producer, his longtime employer, is also an old friend; he considers Gutiérrez reliable, his principal collaborator on screenplays, and though he never knew Gutiérrez's reasons for moving to Rincón, and never completely approved of the decision (for personal rather than professional reasons), Gutiérrez knows that he can depend on him, and while the producer's business continues to operate they'll continue to work together. Since he's been in Rincón, he's already made two trips to Europe, one to Rome and another to Madrid, but a week later he was already anxious to finish his work and return to *Doctor Russo's house*. (Everyone calls it that, and one night Marcos pointed out that, wherever he was, in this world or the next, the doctor had once again managed, nominally at least, to hijack another man's home.)

After working a while, almost till midnight, proofreading an Italian screenplay, Gutiérrez gets up and goes to the kitchen for a cold glass of water. Still on the table are the three cases of wine Nula brought for him and, in a plastic bag, the local chorizos. Gutiérrez stops in front of the wooden cases and scrutinizes them for a moment, as though he were trying to guess what they contain, then he opens the fridge, eats two or three grapes from a plate, and, after pouring a glass of water, takes it to his office and leaves it on his desk. He takes a few sips, and then, from a metal box in the second drawer, he pulls out a black and white photograph.

It's an enlargement of a photograph of Leonor Calcagno, from the late fifties, when she was twenty-three or twenty-four. It was taken by a street photographer in front of the suspension bridge, the major tourist attraction in the city—along with the Franciscan convent, built by the natives in the seventeenth century—since 1924, the year it was built, until 1983, when the flood knocked it down. In the desk drawer, in the same tin box from which he's just taken the enlargement, Gutiérrez has the original photo, in which he, in a light summer suit, is standing next to Leonor. The enlargement shows the blurry edge of his left shoulder, against Leonor's, covered by her flower-patterned dress. Gutiérrez knows every detail of the photo from memory, and every time he would look at it, during his first years in Europe, he would concentrate on Leonor's face, its features, its gaze, its expression. The idea for the enlargement came from thinking that, in the original photo, everything surrounding Leonor's face was superfluous, and the enlargement, ultimately, was a way of fixing, optically and chemically, on a specific point, not the image itself but rather the unstable attention of the viewer, the enlargement, at once benign and insistent, presenting the brilliance of a detail cleansed of the useless detritus of the surroundings. A photo of Lucía sits in a glass frame on the desk. Gutiérrez holds the photo of the mother up to the one of the daughter and compares them. Their similarity is apparent, but they're also very different. Lucía's features remind him of someone he knew or still knows, though altered, but despite how hard he tries he can't figure out who it is. He concentrates on the photo of Leonor again. It was the summer of 1958/59 and nothing had happened between them yet. They'd go for walks sometimes, pretty much out in the open. At the end of that summer, Calcagno, her husband, had gone on a trip.

Even though Calcagno was partners with Mario Brando, and was probably richer, and enjoyed a greater reputation as a lawyer, and was at least ten years older (and at least twenty years older than his wife), his admiration for Brando as a literary figure had practically enslaved him, something that happened with every other member of Brando's precisionist movement. Despite having been a cultural attaché in Rome during the first Peronist government, Brando had shifted to the opposition in 1953, and after the Revolución Libertadora he began occupying official posts in the provincial government. But it was his literary reputation, which overflowed the borders of the province—validated by his regular publications in *La Nación* and in various magazines in Córdoba, Chile, Lima, and Montevideo—that ultimately subjugated Calcagno, an expert in Roman law, an excellent litigator, and the one who did practically all the work for the firm. To his followers, the founder of precisionism was simply charismatic; to his enemies, he was an autocratic tyrant who demanded selfless devotion to the precisionist ideals, not to mention complete obedience to the leader of the movement. According to César Rey, who once threw a glass of wine in his face—this was sometime around 1957, when he was drunk at a dinner party—Brando was a talentless puppet who used his alleged literary gifts to charm the rich into giving him legal work or official posts regardless of who was in power. But there were many people who believed the opposite, and the precisionist movement and its leader enjoyed a considerable reputation. To Gutiérrez, Brando was a good writer of sonnets who tried to pass himself off as avant-garde. What bothered him was when Brando would give him work that had nothing to do with the firm, which fed a certain ambiguity that made people think that Gutiérrez, who was still very young and too financially dependent on him to protest, was one of his disciples. What at the time made him uncomfortable seemed useful in retrospect, since thanks to his work at the firm he made connections with the literary scene. Gutiérrez valued Calcagno, not only because he'd been a good professor or because he'd found work for him, but also because he was intelligent and sincere. But, along with other personal reasons, his strange devotion to Brando, who was inferior to him in every way, ultimately brought out Gutiérrez's contempt for him.

That summer, Calcagno and Brando had gone to a poetry festival in Necochea, and that trip had given them, him and Leonor, some space. They could see each other at any time of day without their time being limited, as it tended to be otherwise. They were at a point in their relationship when, no matter the subject, their opinions always coincided, something which they noticed every so often, euphorically, always with a renewed sense of astonishment. Gutiérrez still hadn't expressed his feelings in any straightforward way, but the increasing precautions they took not to be seen together revealed, though they didn't seem to realize it, the nature of their intentions.

They went out to a restaurant, a secluded place near the waterfront whose owner Gutiérrez knew. Since it was summer, there was hardly anyone there; if they weren't on vacation, most people still preferred to eat outdoors, at grill houses or beer gardens, to escape the suffocation of the hot nights. The owner sat them in an annex at the back that only fit a handful of tables, all empty but for theirs. When they were alone, their hands caressed on the table, unselfconscious, almost distractedly, and at one point Gutiérrez had stood and stepped around the table, leaning over to kiss her, just when the owner, who, because he knew him, was serving them himself, came in unexpectedly with something, and pretended not to have seen anything. Soon after that, when Gutiérrez got up to go the bathroom, the owner called him over and told him there was a room behind the restaurant that could be rented by the hour, but that he could have for the whole night and even the next day if he wanted, since it was Sunday and the restaurant would be closed, and that he could stay as long as he wanted since the room was actually separate from the restaurant and had its own entrance through the courtyard, and that he could return the key on Monday morning.

When he returned to the table, Gutiérrez already had the key in his pocket, but he waited a while before asking Leonor to the back room. He was afraid that she'd be angry and that the night would be cut short. He was sure she wouldn't accept, and he'd already decided that if she said no he wouldn't insist—he couldn't bear the idea that Leonor would be offended and stop seeing him—but when he finally suggested it, he was surprised by the open and straight-forward way she considered the idea, interrogating him at length about the owner's discretion and not about the intentions that a young law student might have regarding the wife of the professor who'd given him a job as a clerk in his firm. Actually, it was like Leonor hadn't understood that the point of going to the back room was to make love, and simply wanted to clarify the owner's ethics and his discretion, first of all, along with his sense of honor, his habits, and his family history. After discussing all of these points with Gutiérrez, Leonor seemed satisfied and accepted but said that they should wait until the patrons and two or three employees in the front of the restaurant had left. She would only go to the back room when, with exception of the owner, who would lead them through the dark courtyard and disappear, no one was left in the place but them. So they went on talking as before. About an hour passed, more or less, and the conversation was so animated that for a while Gutiérrez forgot that eventually they'd be going to the back room, and he was almost sorry when the owner interrupted them, around midnight, to lead them first through an old tiled courtyard with a large refrigerator, a covered balcony, and two or three half-open doors, then through a kind of storage room where, in the weak light, wine racks, sacks of flour, several folded chairs and tables, a soda machine, and two or three dozen bottles stacked around it were just visible, and then through another courtyard, with trees and brick path through flowerpots and vegetable beds. Finally, after opening the door to a small room attached to the back wall of the garden, whispering, *The switch is to the left when you go in*, and discreetly taking the money Gutiérrez had already prepared to give him when they reached the room, he disappeared silently into the dark courtyard that they'd just crossed, where the only thing that caught the weak light was the brick gravel path that had led them there.

They went in. At twenty-four, Gutiérrez was still a virgin. When he reached puberty, he'd masturbated just like everyone else, but in boarding school, where he'd been until he was eighteen, he hadn't had either the occasion or the stimuli for it, unlike his classmates, who, despite the vigilance of the faculty, never did without it, alone, in groups, in the bedrooms or the bathrooms. In college, he had to work to pay for his classes (in fact, two years passed before he could produce anything, since all the temporary jobs he found didn't leave him time to study) and after trying to go to bed with a prostitute a few times and failing, he'd stopped trying. The year before, César Rey, unaware of his virginity, had taken him to a brothel, and he was with one of the girls for a while, to no effect. The girl had gone about her work with complete earnestness for almost a full hour, every so often saying, *It's not getting up, honey, no matter how much I suck it and tug it, it won't get up*, and finally they'd given up and just talked until Rey came looking for him. But Gutiérrez knew he wasn't impotent—prostitutes just didn't turn him on. A few times he'd been with a friend, dancing or caressing her against a tree, in the shadows of a park, in a dark hallway, and his erection and orgasm had come, but that was at a time when women generally didn't sleep with their friends or boyfriends, and they all knew that by letting him rub up against her or put his hand up her shirt, and even helping to masturbate him, letting him finish against her thigh, or, what was less risky, in her hand, they would keep him calm and help him to wait for their wedding night. He was a virgin not because he wanted to stay pure or because he was impotent, but only because he'd never been inside a woman. After a few months had passed since he'd gone out with anyone, he started to think, with a sense of defeat, that he'd been denied the vitality that sex incarnated and that could allow him access to what at the time he called normality and real life.

The opposite was actually happening. That vitality, as he called it, that mythic force that the young seek out, was in fact contained inside him, and had been waiting, with exacting patience, for the chance to manifest itself. That night with Leonor he had five orgasms, *the first two without pulling out*, he thinks whenever he remembers it—not with a sense of pride or self-satisfaction for his virility, but rather with gratitude for something he hadn't realized was his, something that, unlike what happens to so many others, could only be manifested by a particular feeling (later, when the thing he'd felt during those months had vanished, he would realize that sympathy, admiration, friendship, and even respect, combined with a certain type of physical beauty, could allow him to periodically cash in his backlogged sexual quotas).

The availability of naked bodies produced at once a sense of euphoria and a sort of disbelief—it seemed inconceivable that the two wild animals who explored the most hidden parts of the other's body, not only shamelessly but in fact ecstatically, with ease and dexterity, with their lips, tongues, teeth, hands, fingers, and nails, gladly swallowing and sharing their fluids, who coaxed spasms and agonizing pleasure from each other, who communicated with breaths, murmurs, moans, screams, and insults were the same people who moments before, over a relaxed meal, had described their work, their artistic tastes, their small pleasures, their travels, their childhoods, and who, for months, had barely dared to look at each other, to let their hands touch, allowing themselves, even when they were alone, only polite conversation. Gutiérrez couldn't have imagined the double revelation that what was happening produced: a forgetting of the self and, paradoxically, the sudden awareness of being someone different from who he'd thought. Even now, as he examines the enlargement of her face, despite all her faults and failures, he has to acknowledge his debt to Leonor. For Gutiérrez, the person who could provoke that flood of ecstasy that at once transforms the person who feels it and the world he lives in, as imperfect as she may be, inevitably takes part in that splendor. Still, his continued devotion is directed less to the person than to the capacity, which, by some intricate design in the matrix of events, she, unaware of being a carrier, may have ignored or at least misinterpreted.

They copulated from midnight until the next morning, dozing off, half waking and starting up again, rubbing against each other with violence and tenderness. For the rest of his life, he thought about what happened that night. It taught him that love is filtered through desire, its own source, and that the parentheses of ferocity in which it traps its victims, who are also its chosen, are built of the illusion that in the wet embedment of their bodies the sense of solitude, which only increases in the act, is momentary extinguished. And it was this illusion that allowed the universe to seem transformed. When they turned on the light to the room, which was modest but clean and neat, they saw that in the bunk bed, the kind you find in certain family homes, there was a doll lying on the pillow, and, next to the bed, a bicycle against the wall. Before undressing, Leonor took the doll from the bed and placed it carefully on a chair. All night, every time his eyes found the doll, Gutiérrez got the feeling that she was looking back at him, and it seemed like in her frozen and at once vivid gaze there was a strange complicity with what was happening. The bicycle, meanwhile, provided him with what he called, mocking himself, as he often did, his *taste of the infinite*. In the subsequent decades he would sometimes get the sense, in the minutes that followed a satisfying sexual experience, that he was still in the room with the bicycle, and that a sort of continuity, or unity, rather, had synthesized his life, merging at once innumerable and fragmentary and disparate experiences that he'd for the most part forgotten. A sensory certainty of permanence, of rootedness on the edge of the ceaseless disintegration of things, of an indestructible, unique present, reconciled him, benevolently, with the world.

Their nakedness, their exhaustion, but also the summer night, the silence that settled in, and the desire that, though it only surfaces sporadically, is by definition infinite, and, like time, whose essence, in a sense, it shares, works unnoticed on those it transforms, brought them to the daybreak, to the morning, to the warm, empty Sunday. Before dawn, in the dark breathlessness of the twilight, a sparrow sang among the trees in the garden, and, with the first light, the goldfinches came, greeting the sunrise, the new day, with an excited racket that, Gutiérrez now thinks, is as splendid as it is absurd. And he sees himself again, naked in the bed, with Leonor sleeping naked beside him on the white sheet, twisted and soaked in sweat, and he can still hear, thirty-some years later, the clamor of the birds, who've once again forgotten that the same incomprehensible fire had come from the east the previous day, and the day before and the one before that, exhausting the sequence in an intangible past, previous even to memory, and who believe that the radiance that reveals the world and dissolves the darkness is meant for them alone and is happening for the first time, just like someone trapped in the magical halo of desire thinks that the feeling he gets from the rough touch of rough flesh is being manifested, finally, for the first time since the world began.

Of course, Leonor came to his house several times after that night; of course they happily made love again and again; of course they decided to run off to Buenos Aires or Europe or wherever; of course Gutiérrez arranged everything and of course Leonor changed her mind at the last second, choosing to stay with her husband, who heard the portion of the story, described as a strong mutual attraction, that, of course, did not include what they actually did. Of course, when he found out, Gutiérrez, who drank almost no alcohol at the time, got drunk and went looking for a whore to sleep with; of course, as usual, despite the girl's best efforts, she couldn't put him in the right condition. He woke up in an alley, lying in mud, his body aching and bruised. The next day he got on a bus to Buenos Aires, and, without saying goodbye to anyone, disappeared from the city for more than thirty years.

WEDNESDAY

THE
FOUR
CORNERS

FOR THEM TO MEET, SEVERAL THINGS HAD TO COINCIDE,
a few of which, for their importance, are worth mentioning: first,
that an inconceivable singularity led, because of the impossible
density of a single particle, to an explosion whose shock wave—
which, incidentally, continues expanding to this day—dispersed
time and igneous matter into the void, and that this matter, cooling
slowly and congealing in the process, according to the rotation and
displacement caused by the primitive explosion and owing to a
complex gravitational phenomenon, formed what for lack of a better word we call *the solar system*; that a phenomenon which owing
to an utter impossibility of definition we simply call *life* appeared
on one of the variously sized orbs that comprise it, that orb we now
call *the Earth*, cooling and hardening as it rotated around a giant
star, also a product of said explosion and which we call *the Sun*; and
finally, that one September afternoon Lucía walked past the corner of Mendoza and San Martín—where the Siete Colores bar now

81

occupies the spot that for years belonged to the Gran Doria—at the exact moment when Nula (who, after finishing his coffee, had been detained for a few seconds by a guy who shouted something from his table about a Public Law textbook) walked out onto San Martín and looked up, seeing her, dressed in red, through the crowd on the bright avenue.

Nula was almost twenty-four. Eighteen months before, the previous March, he'd decided to quit medical school and enroll in a philosophy program, where he studied the pre-Socratics and some classical languages and dabbled in German, intending to read Hegel, Marx, Nietzsche, and so on, but he felt too isolated in Rosario, where, because he didn't work, it was extremely difficult to get by, and so he came back to the city often, to his mother's house (his older brother, a dentist, was already married), where he could get room and board in exchange for occasional work and very little nagging. Medicine, he'd explained to his mother, could only be studied in Rosario, or in Córdoba or Buenos Aires, but with philosophy no particular establishment or diploma were necessary. For a philosopher, any place in the world, however insignificant it might seem, was, according to Nula (and many others before him, in fact), as good as any other.

La India—that was his mother's nickname, even though her family was from Calabria and her maiden name was actually Calabrese, because her straight black hair, her high prominent cheekbones, and her dark skin gave her the mysterious features of some exotic creature—narrowing her eyes and shaking her head in mock fury, had muttered, *And how much will that bit of insight cost me?* before cracking up laughing, signaling that she was already thinking of a compromise, which, in broad strokes, was as follows: lodging and meals while he was in the city and some cash for a few hours work in the bookstore until he finished his classes in Rosario, all on the condition that he came home with a diploma, even if it was just a doctor of philosophy. Nula—the Arabic version of Nicolás, which, because of how it's pronounced in Arabic should probably be written with two Ls to extend and roll the single L sound—accepted, more so to please his mother rather than to take advantage of her credulity, and kept commuting back and forth between the two cities for the next eighteen months. Chade, his brother, who had just started his practice, would also put some money in his pocket every so often. Chade, who was three years older, had been a brilliant, accelerated student, hoping, possibly, to find an equilibrium with his father's degenerative instability, blown around like a dry leaf by the winds of change and, after years of absence in the underground, murdered one winter night in 1975, whether by his enemies or by his friends it was unclear, in a pizzeria somewhere in Buenos Aires. Nula, meanwhile, who often wavered between enthusiasm and indecision, and who was prone to drifting (both inwardly and outwardly), routinely wondered whether he was having to occupy, in the unmanageable present, the same ambiguous place that his father had twenty years before.

With the legal bookstore across from the courthouse and a kiosk inside the law school itself, which Nula managed every so often and which suggested the comparison that his mother's business was as advantageously located as a brothel across from a barracks with an annex in the bunkhouse, La India had confronted their father's absence and had raised them and educated them both, him and his brother. But what kept them together, silencing their complaints and rebukes, was the fact that, though he was almost always gone, their father had never abandoned them. Every once in a while he would show up suddenly, loaded with presents, stay two or three days without once going out, and then disappear again for several months. After he died—Nula was twelve, more or less, when it happened—he was even more present than when he was alive. La India, pulling him once and for all from the clandestine shadow that politics had cast over him, filled the house with his photographs, his artifacts, traces of him, filling her conversation with her husband's stories, ideas, and sayings. Her refractory insistence on repeating them just as he'd said them would eventually turn them into genuine oral effigies. Nula knew that deep down his brother disapproved of this, but he was too attached to his mother to reproach her. Nula, meanwhile, who'd unwittingly developed an ironic, offhand manner with his mother—possibly so as to gain special treatment—objected every so often to the appropriateness of that cult with an ostensible indifference that to an expert's ear would have sounded pedantic and not the least disinterested. *But it's just that before the storm our life was a perfect picnic,* La India would sigh, often tending to speak in metaphor, her idiosyncratic way of employing the language ever since she'd begun to use it.

When they murdered him, Nula's father was thirty-eight, he had a deep receding hairline, and though misfortune had turned it prematurely gray, a thick beard, as was the fashion in the seventies, possibly to hint at the surplus virility implied by the political inclination of its bearer. And though the awful tempest of that decade had tossed him around like a dry leaf, the late fifties, while he was still young, was when his personality, or whatever you want to call it, had crystallized, and, at least at first, politics occupied a secondary place there. He left home to study architecture in Rosario, but like his youngest son years later (who, in turn, without realizing the symmetry, traded medicine for philosophy) he'd drifted toward economics, from which he declined into journalism. In 1960, he married La India, four months before Chade was born—La India was nineteen then—and they came back to the city. He studied business in high school, and so he ended up taking a job at a bank, but after a year and a half he stopped going. Handling money was nauseating, he said. No one, least of all him, realized that he was having a nervous breakdown. Nula had just been born, and since

84

there were now four mouths to feed, La India realized the time had come to get her hands dirty, so to speak. She started working at a legal bookstore belonging to a friend of her father's, across the street from the courthouse. Not long afterward, the owner stopped showing up, not even to settle the register at the end of the day. He preferred bocce over commerce, and he was the president of a club called The Golden Pallino in Santo Tomé, and so he ended up making La India a partner, and when he retired she hardly had to do a thing to become the sole owner. Even before his retirement she'd gotten permission from the university to install a kiosk, a sort of wood shack crammed with legal books, in the courtyard outside the law school. *A light bulb went off and I brought the horse straight into Troy* was her recurrent, self-satisfied metaphor. Yusef, her father-in-law, had helped her buy the bookstore. Though he never said anything to anyone, he believed the responsibilities that his son, in his point of view (which was nothing like La India's), did not appear capable of managing, should be for him to take on. His two daughters, who both lived in town (the youngest had already married, but the eldest, who never would, still lived at home), tried, solicitously, to console him. But it was pointless: the boy would be the scourge of his old age, and though he outlived him by several years, the ceaseless brooding over his son's incomprehensible life and death was what drove him to the grave. His grandchildren adored him.

He'd arrived from Damascus in the late 1920s, to work for one of his uncles in the fields outside Rosario, on the banks of the Carcarañá river. He hadn't yet turned sixteen. One day, a few months after he'd arrived, his uncle called him to the back of the courtyard, and, lowering his voice and looking around to make sure they were alone, took a knucklebone from his pocket and explained that there was going to be a game that night and that he was going to throw the knucklebone into the back of the courtyard, in the dark, and that he was going to tell him to go get it, and all he had to do was switch the knucklebones and instead of bringing back the one he'd thrown, bring back the one he was showing him, the one he'd just taken from his pocket. But Yusef, despite sincerely loving his uncle and owing him everything, had said no. It wasn't that he was scared, he said, and though he would have loved to please him, it just wasn't something he could do. His uncle seemed to understand his reasons and told him not to worry about it. Something must have happened with the knucklebones that night, Yusef realized, because his uncle was shot eleven times. He didn't die—he lived to be ninety-three with two bullets in his body that they were never able to remove, and died suddenly during a game of *tute*—but out of caution he left town and moved to Rosario, the mafia capital at the time. The impulsive *criollos* who drew their knives at whatever pretext or started shooting over a simple knucklebone switch-out did not correspond with what is commonly known as the proverbial discretion of the Sicilian brotherhood.

Look at any family, Nula would often think, *observing them specifically as a material phenomenon, and you'll see that they're just fodder for the Becoming—that everything is constantly moving and changing.* And, more or less, the thought would proceed like this: Any member of a family is first of all a shapeless substance, and his existence is only probable and random, and later, when he moves away from the virtual, purely statistical stage, he becomes an embryo, and a fetus, and then he's born. Once outside he becomes a baby, then an adolescent, an adult, an old man, a corpse, and then just matter again. The skeleton lasts the longest but after a certain period of time, as it fossilizes, it transforms. At this point, all that's left are a few petrified fragments, for which only the designs of the material world remain. In a family, meanwhile, the different ages are always represented; there are always embryos, fetuses, babies, adolescents, adults, and so on. And if it doesn't seem that way, if all that's left are adults and the elderly, it's because, in this case, only a fragment of the process is available for direct observation. Everything contained there appears and disappears, evolves and changes with time. Not for one second do the members of a family cease to enter and exit the world, transforming, changing in appearance, in size, in weight, the length of their hair or their nails, growing and contracting again, being born, and, each in his own decisive way, leaving the world and disintegrating once again. Everything, at every moment, is in motion, but it's impossible to know the speed at which things happen. Clocks only follow other clocks; what they measure has nothing to do with time. What is happening passes through a mental scheme they call *reality*, which is impossible to place either inside or outside of any person. One day, Nula said something to Riera that, in short, would be more or less the following: *All of existence is like the ship of Theseus, which, according to Plutarch, was conserved by the Athenians for many centuries as a kind of relic because it had transported the young hostages that the hero had saved from sacrifice in Crete. But over time, as it decayed, they would remove the planks that were too old and replace them with new ones, eventually in its entirety. These repairs were made many times. This is why, when the Athenian philosophers debated the concept of growth, the ship of Theseus was a contested example: some argued that it was still the same ship and others that it no longer was.* To which Riera, dismissively, as he often did when the topic didn't interest him, responded *Jerk-offs!* But Nula wasn't even paying attention: he was remembering how, during medical school, he would see the dissected bodies, their organs exposed, listening to his anatomy professor lecture, and wouldn't be thinking of organs or their function, but of more abstract things, like, for example, the fact that even if two bodies of the same sex had the same organs, each one was still unique, and that what really interested him wasn't the function or the specific pathology of those organs, but rather the relationship

87

between the general and the particular. So it made sense for him to abandon medicine for philosophy. Since then, in public, one of his provocative claims—like all young people, he had a considerable arsenal—was, *I'm only interested in the world in general.* And when he was in a good mood, or at a party, feeling playful with someone who could hold his own, as they say, blatantly feigning modesty, would announce: *Practicing the ontology of becoming is so simple: you just have to be aware of every part of everything and all the parts of the parts in all their synchronic and diachronic states.* And so on.

As kids, Nula and his brother would always spend their holidays in the village. They each had their own horse, just like their cousins, who their grandfather—maybe because they'd been born a bit later and didn't have his surname but rather the Italian one of his son-in-law, or maybe because Chade and Nula were a connection to the son he'd lost long before death, decisively, snatched him away—nonetheless seemed to love a little less. Or maybe because the two brothers who came from the city tended to imagine it this way, hoping, ever since they could remember, to make it true, from the time when that sense of shelter, consisting simultaneously of affection and severity, met the recollection of their first sensations of the plains. Tactile sensations, for example: the hot and quivering contact with the body of a sweaty horse; the sudden coolness on summer afternoons when they stepped into a shady corner of the immense courtyard; the slippery tension of a live frog struggling to jump from the hand that gripped it; the warm water in the pond and the contact with the obscure objects—animals or plants, it was unclear—that brushed up against them under the surface; their bare feet sinking into the dust on the street, when, on hot nights, they'd walk back from a dance with their shoes in their hands; the sudden burning on their calves at the moment when, crossing a field, they got tangled up in a cluster of nettles; the velvety skins of unripe peaches or the sticky feeling from the sap of the fig trees.

Or olfactory: the smell of the bitterwood, honeysuckle, and privet in bloom; of the outhouse at the back of the courtyard; of the alfalfa and the corrals; of the fires, woody at first and eventually combined with the meat cooking on the grill; of a kind of edible sawdust called *zatar* that arrived every so often from Damascus and was eaten little by little, making a small pile on a slice of bread and drizzling it with olive oil; of some chemical substance they couldn't pinpoint and of wet burlap in the village ice house; of the abandoned nests, a mixture of dry twigs, feathers, and excrement. Or taste: the flavor of a drink made with very acidic green grapes, mashed at the bottom of a jar and mixed with sugar, water, and ice; of the cigarettes made of dried corn husks and corn silk and later the real cigarettes and the first beers taken secretly from the store during the siesta and which they took to smoke and drink in a vacant lot behind the house; of the green, sweet stems they'd pull from the ground near the station and chew for a long time; of the rainwater that aunt Laila kept in a jar to *wash her hair*; of the mandarins and oranges that on winter nights they'd put to warm on the coals of the fire; of the Syrian food, mint, squash, lemon, eggplant, wheat germ with raw steak and onion, and, in the summer, stuffed with ice flakes; of the *mate* brewed with milk and sugar for breakfast. Aural: the black space of the night that would erupt into a multiplicity of planes when, for some reason, the dogs in the village started calling and responding in the darkness; the whistles of the trains that passed full speed through the village, or the clattering of the endless freight trains that, also without stopping, passed through slowly; in the fields, the sound of the livestock, the snapping of the grasses or the shivering of the corn when they pulled an ear off to eat it and put the silk to dry; the subterranean knocking of the tuco-tucos, the cries of the lapwings and the crested screamers at the water, and the cooing of the doves at midday in the summers; the hooves of the horses crossing town at a walk or a trot and so rarely at a gallop that when it happened people would come out to the street to see if something was wrong; a complicated, rhythmic sound, the creaking of leather, wood, and metal of the sulkies, wheelbarrows, and pick-ups; the conversations in Arabic between his grandfather and other Syrians or the family members who lived in town or who'd come to visit him from the surrounding villages or even from Rosario or Buenos Aires and once even from Colombia; the unsettling sound of the windmills at the bends in the Carcarañá when the wind picked up; the clatter of the bocce balls in the court behind the store; the Sunday mornings, the radio they'd take outside if the weather was nice to listen to *The Syrio-Lebanese Hour* on the Rosario station, the mournful voice of Oum Kalthoum filling the sunny courtyard, the house, the orchard, and garden, under the arcades covered with vines or enormous wisteria; the Arabic words: *bab* (door), *khubz* (bread), *haliib* (milk), *habibi* (darling), *badinjan* (eggplant), *watan* (homeland), and so on. And visual too: the empty horizon on the plain, always the same wherever you were; the swarms of yellow butterflies that would land on the damp parts of the street after the sprinkler passed and take off all at once and land in another puddle father off; the planters blooming with dahlias, snapdragons, daisies, and pansies; the outskirts of the village, which already were and also weren't the countryside; the horse-drawn carts that passed at a short trot and whose driver, without even turning his head to see if there was anyone there, would direct a greeting that consisted of slowly lifting the hand that held the reins toward the corner where the store was located; the signal that dropped suddenly when a train was approaching the village, and the people waiting for it running from their houses and crossing the tracks in order to reach the station before the train; the dirt roads, sloped and dusty on dry days and covered with black mud and mess the rainy days, and always, always, straight, endless, and deserted; the owls perched on the posts of the barbed wire fences, motionless and rigid, as though they were effigies of themselves painted on the wood; the guinea pigs with metallic blue tufts crossing the road slowly when a vehicle or a rider on horseback was passing; the rabbits running full speed from the undergrowth and the whistling ducks flying high, slowly, stretched out, forming an angle; or the motionless dust kicked up by cars and which on still days hung over the road for a long time; the dogs that copulated during the siesta, the male balancing precariously, trembling slightly, over the female; or the foal and the mare that once, at a distance, Nula had been watching, and saw that, as they caressed, stroking each other's necks and muzzles, the foal's penis was slowly engorging. (Each time he remembered one of these sensations, Nula put it down in his notebook.)

His grandfather was one of those assimilated "Turks" who, if he dressed like a farmer or a horseman and didn't open his mouth, with his straight black hair, his tightly clipped beard, and his skin toasted by life in the open air, could pass, among strangers, as a gaucho or a farm hand from the area, or one of those *santiagueños* who, in the thirties and forties, came en masse from the villages on the plain to harvest corn. And even when he spoke he didn't have much of a foreign accent: he'd learned Spanish well, with the exception of four or five hitches that his vocal organs probably couldn't adapt to, and which betrayed his origins. He was anticonservative, a yrigoyenista, and a *bitter* antiperonist (that was the epithet he used), and he liked to recall how, during the coup in 1930, a drunk gaucho had ridden horseback into the store, and he'd taken his revolver from the counter drawer and unhooked his riding crop from the wall, and hitting the horse with the crop, had backed him into the middle of the street. And yet he read *La Nación* and *La Capital*, and every month received *Selections from Reader's Digest*. He dressed in three different ways to fulfill his three main roles: for his work in the fields, where he had a few cows; for his general store, where he sold everything from *yerba mate* to freezers and at one point even cars, and of course clothes, fabric, paint, and what have you; and finally for his trips to Rosario, for business, family matters, or social occasions like weddings, baptisms, wakes, or parties at the Syrio-Lebanese club. In the sixties, he had a truck for the fields and around town, and a car for longer trips. Nula remembered hearing, without understanding completely because he was still too young and his parents only hinted at it, that after he was widowed he'd taken up with a mysterious lover in Rosario. Laila and Maria, his two daughters, wouldn't have tolerated that kind of behavior in the village. When Nula was older, La India told him that his father had spotted Yusef once in Rosario, and that his grandfather, who was with his lover, had pretended not to see him, but in any case the relationship between the father and the son had already fallen apart by then. In terms of religion, his grandfather considered himself a fervent *Apostolic Roman Catholic*, which might have been an implicit way of underscoring his superiority, not over the Jews, of whom he seemed unaware (although, when he played truco he always teamed up with Feldman, the pharmacist, who was one), nor over the Muslims, whom he loathed, but rather over the Maronites and the Orthodoxists, who seemed more skittish than true heretics to him, preferring those extravagant variants despite having recourse to the Roman Church. He attended mass every Sunday and took communion every so often, and if the priest came by for something for himself or for one of the poor people in the village, he didn't charge him, but he didn't like knowing he played cards on Saturday night and would keep from going to those games so he wouldn't have to see it.

They brought his son back to the village to bury, near his mother and an older brother who'd only lived a couple of weeks and who, as was the custom then, had the same name. At first, La

India had objected, because she'd planned to cremate him and scatter the ashes, but then she thought it would be better to leave him near his father, to see if the proximity, after the incommensurable separation, could reconcile them. She was left with, as she would often say to her sons in her colorful way, *the perfect picnic before the storm*. They had killed him in a pizzeria in Boulogne, near the Pan-American highway, and La India passed through the village to drop off the boys and pick up their grandfather on her way to Buenos Aires. The police interrogated them for a full day before releasing the corpse, and at the end of the interrogation a clerk read them the section of the report that referred to the event itself. He'd apparently set a meeting one night, for nine o'clock, but he'd arrived well before that and had changed tables twice. According to witnesses, at ten of nine a car parked outside the door. Three men were inside; the one who was sitting in the passenger seat got out and stood on the sidewalk, leaning against the open door to the car, which was still running. The waiter at the pizzeria said that when his father saw them he stood up too, reaching his hand into his jacket to get his gun ready, not looking away, but the man who took the shot had already been in the pizzeria for a while, drinking a beer at a table behind him and pretending to watch a sports program on the television, waiting for the car that would pick him up after the execution; he shot him four times in the back, shot him again where he'd fallen, and, according to the waiter, ran out and got in the back seat of the car, where someone had already opened the door from the inside, while the guy who'd gotten out of the car sat down again next to the driver, who'd pulled away at full speed, barely giving the others time to close their doors. After La India and her father-in-law were given permission to take the body from the hospital and had seen it to the funeral home's van to take back to the village, they decided to pass by the pizzeria. It was a winter dusk; an icy rose stained the sky opposite the west,

93

where the sun had almost disappeared behind a bank of clouds darkened by their own shadows, projected by the back light. In the empty pizzeria, the lights and the television were already on. They spoke with the waiter and the owner; when he realized who they were, the cook, who'd been kneading dough near the oven, put down his work, and without opening his mouth once, approached to listen. The owner didn't seem too happy that they'd come—he must have thought the visit could be compromising—but the waiter, who'd tried to help him, and who seemed truly affected by what had happened, showed them the spot where he'd fallen and tried to console them by saying that he'd died immediately, almost without realizing what was happening. He followed them to the door. Before they left, the grandfather put a few bills in his hand, which he ended up accepting after a brief but sincere resistance. They went back out to the street, onto that anonymous corner of the tortuous outskirts of Buenos Aires, with its little houses of unplastered brick, its cheapjack markets, its narrow, musty courtyards, its small shops and supermarkets, its loud furniture, its gardens, its shanty towns, its warehouses and its factories, its toothless girls, its old mestizos loaded with plastic bags, its vendors from Santa Fe, selling pills and candy, newspapers and soft drinks, at the bus terminals to Córdoba, to Rosario, to Resistencia, to Catamarca, to Paso de los Libres, or to Asunción. In the infinite solitude of the icy dusk the otherness of the world turned more oppressive and enigmatic among the masses that seemed to dissolve, lost, into the darkness.

They arrived in the village at dawn, almost at the same time as the van. They held the wake without even opening the casket, and buried him that same afternoon. Many people came to the cemetery, friends and acquaintances from the village or from neighboring towns: Italian or Spanish farmers who were clients at the store, old Arabs who owned or had owned stores in the surrounding towns, childhood friends of the deceased who'd gone with him to primary school and who'd stopped at that level, staying in the village, because the others, the ones who'd pursued higher studies, with the exception of the notary and the veterinarian maybe, were scattered around the world. The grandfather's priest friend had been dead for some time, so a young priest gave the mass. La India was about to object to a religious ceremony, but then thought that, having decided to return him to his father, she had to abide by the rules implicit in that choice, and that, in the end, death, which erased so many superfluous things, did so with disputes over religion too, but mostly because while for most of his life the dead man had thought he'd freed himself from it, at his burial, apart from her and his two sons, who were in a sense the only foreigners there, it was clear that the small world he'd escaped was now reclaiming him. His death had wiped away the inconstancy of the inextricable external world, and it was the unyielding procession of his childhood that now accompanied him to the tomb. The turmoil he'd submerged himself into, intending to give it a new order and sense, ended up forcing his return to that preconscious place where, in the shelter of history, in the territory of emotional and sensory immediacy, things were as they seemed despite this or that resistant opacity, which his adult years, with absolute certainty, would reveal. For the grandfather, however, the opposite occurred: his naïveté when he'd left his neighborhood in Damascus at fifteen to conquer the world had allowed him to face, lucidly, everything he'd found himself entangled in, making, at each opportunity, the decisions that seemed most just and which no doubt were, because their succession had brought him steadily closer to what he was seeking. He'd left his family—the mother and sisters with whom he still corresponded regularly at that time, exchanging gifts, like the edible sawdust *zatar*, and the brothers who'd moved to Colombia and Mexico—had left *the oldest city in the world*, as he liked to say, with childish pride, when referring to Damascus, and then had crossed the ocean and a good portion of the plains in order to settle in a little village on the banks of the Carcarañá, and, with the little his uncle left him when he left for Rosario after the shooting, had started a family and managed to make a small fortune, nothing exceptional, but enough for himself and for each of the millions of poor bastards who crossed the ocean from Genoa, from Galicia, from Marseille, and even from Dakar and from Tripoli; who came from Spain and from Italy, from Syria and from Lebanon, but also from Portugal, from Morocco, from central Europe, from Serbia or Belarus, from Ireland or from Japan, fleeing from oppression, from war, from pogroms, from the Ottoman Empire, from the secret police, from political or religious persecution, from hunger, from poverty, from their destiny. They scattered across the plains, where new ravages awaited them—violence, xenophobia, exploitation, mysterious illnesses, an early grave in a foreign land—and ended up gathering together on land parsed out by the government, eight square blocks that bordered the railroad, which they called a town and named after the first person to arrive, or whatever name he chose, often the name of a woman, thus marking the end of their epic wandering and the start of their sedentary, agrarian life. Yusef, his grandfather, was among these millions of men, and it hadn't gone too poorly for him, owing to a few personality traits that popular magazines call ambition, tenacity, rational self-interest, intuition, cunning, perseverance, and so on, and so on, and which they use to explain *a posteriori* the unfathomable crisscrossing of accidents that determine, from the forms that the fugitive—and by chance purely imaginary—evidence assumes in the dark matrix of any event, the thing they call destiny.

In any case, his grandfather had survived that adventure with total certitude of its objective necessity; if he'd had doubts, they were only the practical kind. And when it seemed he'd reached

the climax of his ambitions, reality, which often resists an obedience to desire, pulled him, through the conflict with his son, from
the legible and linear world he'd made, and submerged him in
murky contradictions of an unaccustomed type. What had been
clear became tortuous, incomprehensible. The value of sensations
and events began to escape him. With the death of his wife, who
was younger than him, he'd already intuited that the logic of the
world could be cut off or obstructed at times by unexpected clot-
ting; with that of his son, it was the natural order of the universe,
which he'd always believed in, that had been disarranged. Over
the few years he survived after his son's death, the world, corroded
by his unanswered questions, crumbled little by little into chaotic
fragments. Within weeks after the burial, his straight, stiff, black
hair and neat black beard, which to strangers marked him as an
old *criollo*, turned completely white. A year later they found several
tumors of a cancer that the doctors never managed to pinpoint.
They operated in Rosario, and when he recovered after his first
treatment his daughters convinced him to go to Damascus to see
his mother, who was over ninety years old, but a couple of weeks
before the trip he received news that she'd died. He bought a death
notice in *La Capital*, with a photo he'd gotten two or three years
before, compensating for his son's hasty and somewhat shameful
burial, and asked the young priest—whom he no longer charged when
his servant came by for something—for a mass, which many people
attended, of course the Arabs from Rosario and the surrounding
towns, many of whom, it goes without saying, were Orthodox or
Maronite, the Jewish pharmacist, the Italian and Spanish farmers,
clients, friends of his daughters and his son-in-law, Enzo's family,
and, of course, Nula, who was already shaving by then, with his
mother and his brother. After the mass, the family received their
guests in the courtyard, under the arbor—this was in October—and
once the formalized condolences had been carried out, the guests

tried to change the conversation and animate their host, but his grandfather, whose lips permanently wore a pained but courteous smile, would not open his mouth. He canceled the trip to Damascus, of course, though he still had his sisters, and his health kept up for a while longer, but eventually it declined again, imperceptibly for those who saw him daily, but alarmingly for those who saw him only once in a while. He no longer went out to the fields or attended the business, and though early in the day he paced the courtyard giving orders to the two boys in charge of the house and the garden, later on, after lunch, which he barely touched, his daughters would make him change clothes, and, washed and well-combed, would sit him in a straw chair in front of the store.

Across the broad dirt road stood the rail line and its sheds and station house. The villages on the plain liven up a little at the end of the afternoon, most of all on hot days when the sun, from which there isn't, in the fields, any defense, declines to the west. The sprinkler truck waters the roads and damps down the dust so that when cars pass, or sulkies, or even bicycles or men on horseback, they aren't forced to suffer a dust cloud. The grandfather, his eyes dim and absent, would watch the passage of the trains, cars, and people who sometimes stopped to greet him. Very infrequently, his eyes would light up, weakly, with a fleeting spark: he'd think he recognized an old friend in the driver's seat of a passing car, but it would take him so long to raise his arm in greeting that when he managed to wave his hand a little, at a certain height, the car was already two blocks away. A pretty horse at a trot was also pleasurable for him, because he'd always liked horses; and it was also pleasant sometimes to watch the children who, after being washed and scrubbed by their mothers, their older sisters, or their aunts, went out to play, still chewing on enormous chunks of homemade bread slathered with butter, dusted with powdered sugar, and smeared with *dulce de leche*. But that was it. At first, he'd get up every so often and take a few steps along the uneven brick sidewalk, but toward the end he never moved from the chair. By the next fall, he started refusing food, and since he barely weighed fifty-two kilos, they had to hospitalize him and feed him through a tube. One cold morning he stopped breathing.

When he saw him in the coffin, shrunken by death and by his suit and shirt, oversized because of the illness—his uncle Enzo had shaved him and tied on a blue necktie with colored stripes, its bulging knot resting on his Adam's apple, disproportionately large because of his thinness—Nula was able to observe, for several minutes, the discreet, blue tattoo on the back of his right hand, which covered his left hand, over his abdomen, consisting of three dots arranged in a horizontal line. It had always intrigued him, and though as a boy he'd asked his grandfather what they meant, he'd never gotten a satisfactory response, making it seem like one of those topics that, because of the evasive responses they get, children resignedly consider themselves unfit for. Many of the Arabs who visited his grandfather had similar discreet, blue tattoos on their hand, their wrist, or their forearm. Growing up, Nula had grown so used to seeing them that he ended up not noticing them. But seeing the tattoo on the back of his hand again, he had the confused sense that their location, and whatever reason he'd had for having them imprinted on his flesh, in death, those three blue dots, however enigmatically, betrayed an authentic need. He knew that those three dots were a sign, a message, but he couldn't tell to whom they were directed. And although two or three years later, when he thought of them, he still believed that they were a custom of another time and place, archaic and mysterious, where ritual and taste favored those marks on the body, by strange mandate or simple habit, it was only much later—he was already married and had abandoned his philosophy studies in Rosario to earn his living selling wine in the city—that he realized what the tattoos signified.

One night, he was watching a Monteverdi opera on television, *The Return of Ulysses*, and at the recognition scene, when Eurycleia, the old nurse, realizes that the beggar, from the scar on his thigh, is Ulysses, who has returned incognito to Ithaca, Nula, hitting the open palm of his left hand on the back of his right hand, shouted so unexpectedly that Diana, concentrating on the music, jumped. *Nostoi!* he practically screamed. And then, lowering his voice, as though in apology, *I've been trying to remember that word for so long.* They continued listening in silence, and, when the opera finished, Nula went to the library and returned with a copy of the *Odyssey* opened to the start of Book XIX. *"Nostoi" means "the returns" in Greek,* he said. *They were a series of epics that recounted the return home of the Greek heroes who'd fought in the Trojan war. But almost all of them were lost; only the return of Ulysses survived, and a few loose fragments of the others. I've been trying to remember the word for days, because I felt like it had some connection to my grandfather's life. And now I know why. First of all, because of Ulysses's scar from a tusk wound he got when he was a boy, when he went boar hunting once with Autolycus, his grandfather, like my brother and I used to hunt with our grandfather Yusef.* But it wasn't just about him, about his childhood memories of his grandfather taking them out to the fields to shoot partridges and wild ducks, but rather about his grandfather, about the recognition of Ulysses by the scar on his thigh, and if he shouted suddenly it was because he finally understood the purpose of those blue tattoos, on their hands, on their wrists, on their forearms, and possibly on other parts of their bodies that weren't publicly visible: those signs inscribed on their flesh anticipated the *nostos*, the return, which they assumed would be so far from the moment of departure that their bearer would return to his place of origin so disfigured by inclemency and disillusion, by the silence of distance and the contempt of time, by the frayed rags of experience and of being, their only conquest, that they thought it prudent to

mark themselves with an indelible sign so that they could be recognized by those who'd seen them off, and who still awaited their
return, patiently, in their homes or in Hades.

After his grandfather's death, Nula took fewer trips to the town,
though later, when he started medical school in Rosario, he would
sometimes go up for the weekend. He didn't need to catch the bus
at the terminal, because his apartment was close to school, and the
bus, before leaving the city, had to take several loops through the
one-way streets near the terminal, and one of those loops passed
right by his house. Sometimes he'd run into a family friend who
recognized him, and other times he'd travel with his eldest cousin,
who was studying to be a veterinarian—his youngest cousin was
still at the Jesuit school—and who always told Nula that when they
graduated they'd open a joint practice for gauchos: one of them
would treat the horse while the other one examined the horseman.
But, little by little, without knowing why, they grew apart, and
when Nula dropped out of medical school and took up philosophy,
they stopped seeing each other altogether.

What happened at the pizzeria caused a rift in the family that
only widened with time. On one side were his aunt Laila, La India,
Nula, and his brother, and on the other side his aunt Maria, his
uncle Enzo, and their three sons. The more distant family, their
friends, and acquaintances fell to one side or the other. Nula, who
couldn't stop thinking about what had happened, and though he
wasn't sure whether or not to approve of his father, possibly because he often felt their resemblance too closely, couldn't stand it
that anyone else, even his father's own sister, would judge him.

But there were other reasons for his detachment from the town
and his family. He'd drawn a low number in the draft, and because
of this escaped military service, which gave him a year advantage at
school, a stroke of luck that, from some dark, hidden, machinations
inside himself, he refused to take advantage of. It took him more

than two years to realize that what interested him wasn't so much the nomenclature of the individual organs, but rather, as he liked to proclaim every so often, *the viscera in general.* In fact, it had always depressed him to imagine one day running his own practice, his day filled with actual patients while his thoughts wandered always to their *causes*, though his perplexed indecision and his erratic imagination never bothered to find a way out of the problem. Around this time, he started seeing his life like an mechanics shop where the cars, the engines, the toolboxes were all in disarray and half-assembled, and though the incessant, fugitive process of becoming never for a single second stopped manipulating them, changing their shape and position, they would always be in that same state of incompletion. The world became contingent, uncertain, and the inextricable threads connecting things, which could be untangled only in certain dark places, began to interest him more than things themselves, simulacra sitting there in plain sight as though that's all there was to it. The way his uncles and cousins criticized his father bothered him less for its moral or political pretension than for its predictable submission to the world of appearances. After several months of hesitation, of conversations over drinks, of reading, he enrolled in the philosophy program. And, after accepting La India's conditions—*Around here, pal, let he who wants fish dig his own worms*—he started commuting between Rosario and the city. When he ran out of money, he'd go back to his mother's house, and two or three times a week he'd take over for the girl who worked the kiosk at the law school, who, because she was a student, had to close up when she had class or an exam to study for. But Nula didn't just go back to the city when he was broke. Despite the rude and offhand way that La India treated him, often to parody a threat, Nula knew that, whenever she was close by, though he didn't quite know the reason, he'd always be protected.

On one of these trips, by chance, he saw the girl in red on the street, just as he was coming out of the Siete Colores bar, on the corner of Mendoza and San Martín, occupied for years by the Gran Doria. As we were saying, it was not only necessary, for the meeting to happen, that an unknown combination of pressure and temperature caused an inconceivably dense point of space and time, which are ultimately the same thing, at a given moment, to explode and scatter, violently, in a stampede; that in certain regions it curdled and stabilized—it's impossible, we know, for Nula to calculate the velocity of the event with absolute certainty—into the thing we call our solar system, for example, and that on one of those cooling igneous orbs a set of chemical reactions made possible the appearance of something that for lack of a better word we call *life*, it's not really clear why, with all the incalculable consequences that brought with it. Not only, as we've said, did all that have to happen, in addition to the innumerable series of interconnected events that took place thereafter, these difficult to verify as well, but also, and in addition, as he turned toward the door, when he was just reaching the exit, a student sitting at one of the tables near the windows that faced Mendoza had to shout a question about a specific edition of a Public Law textbook, whether they had it at the main bookstore because they didn't at the law school kiosk, and by answering him Nula was delayed another thirty seconds, because otherwise, if the student hadn't called out to him, Lucía wouldn't have reached the sidewalk yet and he wouldn't have run into her as he walked out, and might have turned down Mendoza to the west to catch a bus at the Plaza del Soldado, or if, instead, he'd decided to walk back to La India's house for lunch, he might have turned up San Martín, and since he was more or less thirty seconds ahead of her, would've probably walked the twelve or thirteen blocks to his house without once noticing she was there.

Thanks to all of these coincidences, he'd bumped into Lucía as he walked out. It was just after noon, when the shops close and their employees dissolve into the crowd that comes and goes along the avenue and its cross streets. The buses fill up with people going home for lunch, with high school students, with bankers, with public servants. After one o'clock there's almost no one left on the street, but around noon, and later in the afternoon, in the city center, the crowds swarm anew, as they say. That bright September afternoon already anticipated that intimate and possibly organic, but also painful euphoria provoked in the species, most likely from its affinity with all other forms of life milling around the biosphere, and also from our consciousness of it, by the arrival of the spring. The fibers and tissues, flesh and organs, feeling the multiple effects of the weather appropriate for the needless, and, you might say, ad nauseam iterations of the same invariable, demented shapes, tense up in self-regard, in the fullness of the present, but memory, not necessarily in a conscious way, can't ignore that the fullness is temporary. The girl in red, tall like him, and clearly a few years older, with whom he almost collided as he walked out of the bar, surfacing from some preoccupation, looked hard at him, as though she was about to say something, but without opening her mouth she stepped aside and walked past. Without even taking the time to think about it, Nula started to follow her. They walked in the shade, which, despite the hour and thanks to the two-story houses, still covered a good portion of the sidewalk, and after a few meters, as she stepped into the street—they were on the San Martín promenade—Nula did the same, immediately feeling the warmth of the air and the light on his face and head. At first, less than four or five meters separated them, but Nula could see, in her posture and in a few uncertain movements of her head, that she already sensed that she was being followed by a stranger, and so he slowed down, to increase the distance between them, but even when he'd been following her more closely, despite the fact that her red dress hugged the full, firm shapes of her arms, her back, her buttocks, and her thighs, Nula didn't notice her body, ensnared rather by the memory of the quick, inquisitive look she gave him as she surfaced, momentarily—only to sink again immediately—from her thoughts. Later, a kind of sexual fury, more painful than pleasurable, actually, a transferred and rarely gratified salaciousness, would periodically entrap him, but in that first meeting and in others that followed it, the question of sex, though the immediate reaction of his senses indicated just the opposite, seemed secondary.

As they left the city center, there were fewer people in the street, which forced him to extend the distance between them by a few more meters, in case she happened to turn around, because if she recognized him as the man she'd thought she knew outside the bar, she'd realize that he'd been following her ever since. She walked at a steady pace, neither slow nor fast, apparently calm and sure, and her dark brown hair, with the same rhythm as the loud clicks that her heels made against the gray pavement—Nula had observed this when he'd been closer—bounced silently against her nape and the top of the back. After a few blocks, at the end of the promenade, she turned the corner, walked east one block, and, crossing the street, turned on 25 de Mayo, the first street parallel to San Martín. Now they walked on the sunny sidewalk, opposite the cars and the buses that moved south toward the city center. From a distance she seemed taller, and Nula guessed, without checking too closely, that when she made a quick pivot on the sidewalk, or when she stepped for a few seconds into the street, it was to avoid the broken patches of sidewalk he knew by memory, the missing paving stones or the potholes where, despite the week that had passed since it last rained, there still trembled a rectangular, stagnant puddle that had yet to evaporate. The red blur of the dress vibrated in the distance, mobile and vivid in the early afternoon sun that glimmered off the

105

windshields of buses, off the windows and the chrome bodywork of the cars, troubling the soft calm of the air.

Another thing that hadn't occurred to Nula was that their route was taking him straight to his own house. La India's apartment building was accessed in the middle of the block through an interior garden, faced on two sides by rows of apartments that divided the block without completely separating the two halves: despite the fact that the garden and the apartments took up the full depth of the block, the building stopped before the next cross street, and there was no other entrance but the main one, on 25 de Mayo. In the late forties, when they were built, the apartments were unusual and expensive—at that time they called them *luxury tenements*—and if they still conserved a sense of upper middle class dignity, time had mistreated them badly. Most of the residents were owners, and they'd formed a co-op, with La India as vice-president, to keep the complex in good condition and raise funds from the municipality for restoration. The main entrance, dominated by curves, granite staircases, and chrome banisters, evoked both the prosperous years of its construction and the avant-garde flirtations of its local architects.

On the next corner, Lucía changed sidewalks, crossed the street that intersects 25 de Mayo, and started down La India's block. Nula did the same, but when he saw that she had stopped at the entrance to his own building and was peering inside, curiously, he stopped at the corner to watch her. Lucía walked up the three staircases that separated the garden from the street and looked in, curiously, but also with a slow caution. Then, hesitantly, she disappeared inside. Nula was about to follow her in when she reappeared. She seemed dissatisfied, and also slightly disoriented. She stood thinking on the top step, quickly looked back inside, checked her watch, walked down to the street, took a few steps to the north, then turned around suddenly and started walking straight toward

106

the spot where Nula was standing. He was about to slip into the ice cream shop on the corner, owned by a friend of his mother, but he thought that if she wanted to interrogate him it would be better if it happened on the street, which was empty just then, and so he waited, looking right at her, watching her approach with that decisive step, neither slow nor fast, absorbed in her thoughts, as though she were measuring the words she planned to say when she reached him, but when she got to the corner she glanced up suddenly and gave him the same look she'd given him when they saw each other outside the bar, in which Nula thought he sensed a fraction of a second of recognition, but she sank back, almost immediately, just like before, into her thoughts, and she turned down the cross street. Playing it safe, Nula stayed where he was, and, as she moved down the tree-lined street, was easily able to study her. The pools of sunlight that filtered through the leaves and onto the sidewalk passed quickly over the body in red that advanced through the beams. Halfway down the block, Lucía stopped in front of a door, glanced cautiously inside, then kept walking. Nula started following her again. Just as she was turning the corner, Nula reached the door she'd stopped at and read the brass plate attached to the wall: *Doctor Oscar Riera, Clinical Medicine*. Afraid he'd lose sight of her, he hurried away, and reached the cross-street almost at a run, but he had to stop suddenly when he turned the corner, because she had stopped again and was staring, with the kind of concentrated attention that could have been called blatant indiscretion, into another house. Nula waited for her to keep walking and then started after her again. The girl's singular behavior worried him. Beyond its apparently strange, even comical or ridiculous aspect, there was also something slightly unsettling about it. He'd have preferred not to follow her, but at the same time he sensed that in the short half hour that had passed since he started following her, she had traveled deep into his own life. Lucía turned the next

107

corner and Nula sped up again. When he came around the corner he saw that she was stopped outside a house halfway down the block, leaning toward a door and pushing a key into the lock. Nula started walking faster and faster, hoping to exchange another quick look with her, but by the time he reached the door she had already passed through, and he just managed to hear the metallic sound of the lock as the key was turned from the inside.

He must have had a strange look on his face, because La India, who had been waiting with lunch, looked at him inquisitively once or twice, but, pretending not to notice, he only told her, in passing, that he felt like he might be getting sick. So La India prepared him an effervescent aspirin after lunch and he shut himself in his room till it was time to open the kiosk. Lying in bed, he lit a cigarette and gazed up at the ceiling. Lucía's strange behavior—he didn't yet know that was her name—must have had a rational explanation, and if what he came up with later had to be discarded, a kind of disquiet lingered. Only the last of the sudden stops in her strange circuit of the block seemed to have a rational explanation, since she'd obviously gone into her own house, or at least a house she had a key to. What intrigued him most was the symmetry of the four points: on the block (a perfect square) the four points where she'd stopped were, in fact, symmetric. The W point (for west), La India's apartment, was symmetrical to the E point (for east), also halfway down the block on the street parallel to 25 de Mayo; and the S point (for south), the office of Doctor Riera, was halfway down the cross street and symmetrical to the N point (for north), the house into which she finally disappeared. The facts were plain: she'd come to a stop exactly halfway along each side of the square that formed the block. That symmetry, if it followed some specific purpose, could be acceptably rational, but what troubled him was thinking that this specific purpose might be unknown or in fact (and has he began to suspect) nonexistent. He could also reverse the problem and think that it might not be the behavior itself that was troubling but rather the purpose that provoked it. And here Nula started looking for the most calming explanation possible, in which both the ends and the behavior itself were rational.

It occurred to him that the girl in red—oh how he wanted to see her again!—could've been an architect or an urban planner. On the one hand, she could have been inspecting the houses out of curiosity, and her strange demeanor was the result of her feeling somewhat guilty for her presumption and fearful of being witnessed. And the same could be said if she was an urban planner: after seeing the unique way the forties-era *luxury tenements* had been built, that is, with the entrance that, without quite dividing the block in half, nevertheless went the full depth, opening parallel to 25 de Mayo, she may have wanted to verify the effects of that strange construction on the buildings on the other three sides that, with 25 de Mayo, formed the block's perfect square. But those explanations, in fact, reminded him of Aristotle's distinction between arguments that are absolutely true and others, in contrast, that only appear to be, and, disheartened, he couldn't tell which argument belonged to which category. Not including the garden/ complex, the houses she'd stopped in front of were three typical middle-class homes from the fifties and sixties, just like so many others on the same block and on every other block in the neighborhood. Meanwhile, the girl's thoughtful expression and her somewhat extravagant curiosity suggested the opposite of rationality. No: after a detached shuffle through the most likely hypotheses, among which was the possibility that she was simply looking for a specific house, but without having much information to go on, Nula, hoping to maintain the self-respect of a *rational being*, a term he liked to borrow from popular philosophical jargon, he had to discard them all. The most likely answer, as far as Nula could see, of course, was that Lucía, in a manner of speaking, and, to continue with the architectural theme, *was missing a few bricks from her terrace.* Nula used the expression, he imagined, with detached, wry cynicism, not realizing that he was pinned to the bed by the unease that it provoked, by the profound conviction that even if it were true it wouldn't change in any way the decision that he'd made the moment that girl came into his life, and by his feverish summary of the events as he tried to make some decent sense of them: the look outside the bar, the compulsive way he'd followed her, the movement of the red blur as it moved along at an even pace, neither slow nor fast, down the bright sidewalk, the four symmetrical stops Lucía made on the perfect square that formed the block.

Now, driving back across the bridge, in the opposite direction as last night, coming back from Gutiérrez's, Nula, who has recovered his sense of calm after a night of sleep, once again remembers that early afternoon five years ago and the months that followed. The image of the girl in red walking ahead of him down the bright sidewalk is clear but impersonal, like any other distant memory, but the cloudy morning, threatening rain, that he moves through in the present—the station wagon's clock reads ten twenty-nine—his empirical surroundings, are somehow more elusive and vague than that tiny, red blur, vibrating and shuffling brightly in the center of his mind. Ever since he watched her step out of the swimming pool, and especially after running into her the night before at Gutiérrez's, when Lucía declared, as calmly as anything, that she didn't know him, that red blur has taken over his thoughts. The blur but not yet Lucía herself, just the stylized sensation of the red curves in the midday sun, without the tangled pattern of the months that followed.

Last night he stopped by the wine bar, but there wasn't anyone there he knew, so he went home. Diana, who according to Nula could spot an ink stain on a black wall in a dark room on a moonless night, when she saw the state of his shoes and his pants, and also the two muddy yellow rings on his white sweater, asked him, feigning more surprise than she felt, where he had been, but Nula, who is hardly blind to his wife's suspicions of the evasive nature of his personality, given to wandering, had offered his usual response—*Business*—knowing that, while unsatisfying, will disarm her temporarily. She'll counterattack, as they say, later, when they're in bed. Then he put the car in the garage and went to play with the kids, since Diana prefers to feed them before he gets home and then put them to bed early. The truth is no one, least of all him, knows when he might get home. At around nine thirty they ate, talked, cleaned up together, and then worked a while in the library, both absorbed in their own thoughts. They were the average middle-class couple of their time—the end of the twentieth century—and though they had some financial support from their families, they had to work for their living, at things that were different from what really interested them. Diana, though she was missing a hand, was a talented illustrator and painter, and designed posters for an ad agency. Nula, as we know, did not pretend the wine selling was anything but a means for financing his philosophical projects. While they were together they performed the ritual of domestic life with ease and even sincerity. At around eleven they brushed their teeth and went to bed, lying next to each other, flipping through the same magazine, and, after turning off the light, after Diana's hardly systematic and rather parodic interrogation, trying not to make too much noise so as not to wake the kids, who were sleeping in the next room, taking real pleasure from it, though, because of their youth, without yet realizing that when it comes to sex the other's reality and the thing that resists desire are the other's ghosts, as they did two or three times a week, tense and sweaty, they copulated.

Diana was born with the umbilical cord wrapped around her wrist. They had to operate, and she lost her hand. Because she was in fact very beautiful, and they were used to talking openly about it, sometimes, when they were alone together, having fun, Nula would sometimes whisper in her year, *you're just five fingers away from perfection.* Diana liked hearing him say that, but Nula knew that her jealous nature was a result of the stump. Reality, meanwhile, validated her suspicions: Nula cheated on her often, telling himself each time that he really loved her but was incapable of establishing a direct correlation between love and fidelity. Compassion, which can be a part of love, is alien to sex. Desire is neither compassionate nor cruel; it has its own laws, and Nula let himself be governed by them. His only concession was a compartmentalization of his sex life. Possibly to silence his own misgivings, he often said that it's absurd to find fault with an act of servitude. And every so often he resigned himself to his disloyalty with the thought that if, as a student of philosophy and wine merchant it was possible to supply his own ethics, when it came to sex the precepts of a moral sensibility ceased to make sense. *Sex is the common stock of the scorpion, the sardine, the rabbit, reduced to a solipsistic, repetitive, proliferating mania. It precedes morality infinitely and will infinitely outlast it,* he liked to announce, especially in the preliminary stages of a new relationship, though he in fact discussed these matters often with his wife, who watched him closely, at once wary and delighted.

Diana's stump inspired pathos, but it also excited him. Although she'd gotten used to it, and although a set of positive attributes, beauty, intelligence, talent, among other things compensated for the absence of the hand, Diana felt different, but when she tried to explain it to him, Nula would correct her: *Not different, unique.* In a sense, that stump, when contrasted with her other attributes, gave her an extraordinary singularity, and it was that singularity that seduced him. Nula, who was used to feeling two hands grasp his shoulders in a hug, felt a singular shudder when the warm, smooth edge of the stump rubbed, softly, against his back. And if he imagined that when he took the stump in his hands and stroked it and kissed it he was showing his love for her, most likely it was out of love for his own sensations that he did it, or rather out of love for the possession of that unique person who belonged only to him.

Nula crosses the bridge and turns onto the highway. The rain from the day before, which continued well into the night, has not yet dried, and the gray air blends into the horizon. The vegetation is still gray, but the low, dark clouds have been replaced by a high dome, a clear, even gray that releases sparks of water against the windshield, but these are so tiny and so scattered that they don't even manage to coat it. He passes the enormous, brightly colored hypermarket, an eye-catching anachronism at the edge of a swampy expanse, and then La Guardia, before turning onto the road to Paraná. When he crosses the bridge over the Colastiné river, gray like everything else, he sees that the multiplicity of rippled, geometrical waves driven against the current, which he saw with Gutiérrez the afternoon before on the Ubajay, north of Rincón, are gone, and concludes that the southeast wind is gone, and when he looks hard at the low-lying vegetation on the island surrounding the asphalt road, he sees that it, too, is motionless. Before reaching the tunnel he sees, three or four kilometers ahead, above him, in the hills, beyond the main channel of the Paraná, the small, quiet city that, paradoxically, took the name of the excessive, turbulent river. Inside the tunnel, he starts going over the list of things he has to cover with the regional manager of Amigos del Vino, Américo, and when he emerges in Paraná, at five of eleven, he realizes that this trip could have been made the next day, as he'd planned the week before, in order to prepare the promotion at the hypermarket, but it had been impossible to wait that long to try to find Lucía.

If I was as fat as he is, I would've gotten out of the habit of working standing up by now, Nula thinks, as he does every other time he walks into the building and sees Américo writing in a ledger open on the tall desk where he works standing up, and which he himself designed for the carpenter, down to the millimeter. Hearing his footsteps, Américo looks up and watches him a moment over the tiny, oval-shaped reading glasses propped on the edge of his nose, and when he recognizes him he looks back down at the ledger as he offers a silent greeting that doesn't appear to affect his concentration. Behind his desk, at the back of the room, which was first used as a workshop and later as a wine distillery, stacked carefully in piles according to brand and provenance, giving the impression more of a stage set than a commercial enterprise, sit the cases of wine. To the left of the entrance, that is, to the right of Américo (who works facing the entrance), behind a glass wall that heightens the scenic effect of the room, Américo's wife and his secretary work, in what could strictly speaking be called the office, surrounded by metal filing cabinets, computers, and stacks of documents.

Américo is writing on a sheet of white paper sitting on top of the open ledger, tight lines riddled with strikethroughs, marginalia, and loose words inserted between the lines, above or below the ones he's crossed out. Concentrating on his work, not looking away from the paper, he gestures with an apologetic smile for Nula to wait a second. Nula puts the briefcase on the floor, next to the desk, and waits. Although everyone calls him *El Gordo*, Américo isn't really that fat, especially considering his height (1.80 meters) and his wife's scrupulous control of his clothing and diet, allowing him a certain agility, nor does he seem old, because his closely trimmed gray beard is lighter than his thick, curly hair, which gives him a youthful look. Only his fingers are truly fat, but the grayish hair that covers them to the knuckles, tangled and solid across his hand, evokes virility more so than obesity. Nula leaves him to his work and walks into the office. Chela and the secretary are surprised to see him.

—We weren't expecting you till tomorrow, Chela says.

—I'm a workaholic, and also I wanted to buy my wife a gift. I've heard about a shop here in Paraná, run by someone named Lucía Riera, Nula says, amazed at his capacity for inventing pretexts and offering them without stopping even for a second to think about it.

—I don't know a Riera, but there's a Lucía Calcagno, *Mis pilchas*, the most posh boutique in Paraná, Chela says. They have every-thing, Cacharel, Yves Saint Laurent, all the international brands.

—That must be her. Where does one find such a marvel? Nula asks, trying to hide his anxiety.

—Downtown, half a block from the square. I have a card around here somewhere, Chela says, looking through a drawer.

—Now I see why poor Américo has to work day and night, you have a special account there. Thanks, Nula says, and, taking the card and putting it in his jacket pocket, goes back out to the ware-house, just as Américo finishes silently rereading what he's written, moving his head back and forth, correcting a final word, a line, a comma, and so on.

—Ready! he shouts, satisfied. Should I read it?

—What? Of course—Nula feigns offense—I drove all the way from the outer provinces just for this reading.

—Don't waste your breath on a mule like me, Américo says, and Nula cracks up laughing, but Américo remains serious, silently re-reading one last time, before doing so aloud, for an expert audi-ence, the brief text he's been composing. Of the five decades of his life, Américo has dedicated more than half to the sale of wine, first as an importer until the crash under the dictatorship, when hyper-inflation and the volatility of the market busted him. With Chela's inheritance they transformed their current space, an abandoned warehouse, into a table wine distillery, bottling their own brand— *Aconcagua*—a name that according to his detractors referred to the liquid additive that Américo introduced into a Mendoza wine, but that business, also because of hyperinflation, failed as well. Some time later, one of the owners of Amigos del Vino, whom he'd worked with in the seventies, offered him the distribution rights for the northeast part of the country. And with the collusion, on the national level, of publicists and cardiologists, and the fortuitous global fashion for wine, through conventions, indirect publicity, and the inevitable rhetorical advancements that from time immemorial have accompanied the embarrassing consumption of alcoholic beverages, and wine in particular, things managed to turn around. In the regions that border the banks of the Paraná, as far north as Paraguay and south to Brazil, the Amigos del Vino, which, it goes without saying, found favorable ground, and without major obstacles, quickly prospered. And though the two previous failures had forced him to keep his current success in perspective, Américo, who attributes his good nature to having had the privilege of his mother's breast till the age of seven, is happy enough with the present, but this doesn't stop him from developing survival tactics in case everything falls apart again, as has happened periodically.

—Everyone in Entre Ríos is either a poet or a gangster, he says, as a preface, and ignoring the vaguely ironic but nonetheless friendly smile of his only listener, he starts: *Wine, the measure of civilization, a precious nectar in every land, contributes to the good health of its faithful companion, the human being. Independent authorities have by now proven many times over that wine reduces stress, dissolves harmful fats in the blood which imperil the cardiovascular system, and contains vitamins, minerals, and enzymes that are beneficial to the body. But, above all, wine satisfies the palate, strengthens friendships, and multiplies and perfects moments of celebration.* When he finishes, Américo pushes the tiny glasses to the end of his nose and, over the oval lenses, interrogates Nula with a look.

—Not bad, not bad, Nula says. But you have to add something about the French paradox, something about the vines, and something about the *sawyils*, he says. purposefully exaggerating the rural pronunciation of the word. And, if at all possible, he adds, finish with a set of more or less potable quatrains from Omar Kayyám.

—Good idea! Américo shouts, dipping his head slightly into his shirt collar in such a way that his beard covers the knot on his tie, and pointing at Nula with a fat, hairy finger on his left hand. But, he adds, it has to be quick. This draft has to go out next week to Resistencia, Corrientes, and Posadas. We'll print up colored cards with different stanzas of the lofty poet. Turquito, one of these days I'm making you head of sales and locking you up in the office so you'll quit your dicking around.

—You mean like this? Nula says, and glancing quickly toward the office to make sure that Chela and the secretary aren't watching, he forms a circle with his index finger and thumb on his left hand and passes the rigid index finger on his right hand back and forth energetically a few times.

—No comment, Américo says, pushing his glasses back up and signaling that he's ready to talk business with his salesman. Nula opens the briefcase, takes out a ledger and some loose pages. As he talks, Américo takes notes on a legal pad. Suddenly, Nula interrupts himself and looks at his watch.

—What time do the stores in Paraná close? I have to buy a gift for my wife.

Américo's only answer is an incredulous snort. He doesn't look up from the notepad, and stands frozen in the writing position, as though he were posing for a portrait—*Américo Scriptori*—and

117

when Nula starts talking again, the portrait starts to move, taking quick notes with abbreviations and symbols that, like some private language, will only be legible to him in the future. Nula reads from a list in which he took down, that same morning, while he drank a few *mates* in the kitchen, the topics he had to cover. Some are straightforward comments that require no response, though Américo, in his private script, writes them down in the notepad, but others demand certain operations, the exchange of the deposit receipts and checks, for example. Their primary topics are the two afternoon appointments, which Nula postponed yesterday because of his walk in the rain with Gutiérrez, with the governor's aide and the dentist that his brother, Chade, recommended, and whose wine cellar, with a capacity of a hundred and fifty bottles, he has to fill; Gutiérrez's new order, which he'll deliver tomorrow; the commission check that Américo owes him from March, if it's ready (Chela has it in the office); the group sale to the law school for that Friday, if it's ready; he also wants to order (on his tab) four bottles of merlot and two sauvignon blancs that he's planning to take to the cookout at Gutiérrez's, because it doesn't seem appropriate to drink his own client's wine; he should also take two local chorizos, for the governor's aide, which he promised as a sample (it's a typical gift for new clients); and finally, there's the promotional sale at the Warden hypermarket, which starts Friday afternoon, culminates on Saturday, and lasts another full week; he, Nula, will be there at five o'clock sharp, making sure the stand is ready and every-thing is set up; that same afternoon, on his way back from the city, he's thinking of passing by to finalize the details with one of the managers. When they finish, they go to the office to pick up the March commissions check. Chela takes it from a drawer, has him sign a receipt, and hands it to him. Afterward, Nula loads up the four cases of wine—two cabernet sauvignons and one viognier for Gutiérrez, and one with four bottles of merlot and two sauvignon

118

blancs for himself, plus the chorizos for Gutiérrez and two for the political aide—and before getting in his car he turns back to the doorway and shouts:

—You haven't heard the last of me!

—I'm expecting some good stanzas from your *countryman*, for the cards, Américo says.

When he pulls out, it's ten of twelve. Because his trips to Paraná almost never take him downtown—the warehouse is on the outskirts—he ends up taking several wrong turns along one-way streets and promenades before finding the square. *Mis pilchas* is just half a block away, like Chela said, but because he doesn't find a spot, he double parks and leaves the car running. The boutique isn't very big, but it does seem very fancy for the city, and though it's already twenty after twelve it's still open. Lucía is talking with another woman, and when she sees him in the doorway, she starts laughing and comes to meet him.

—I'm so glad you came! she says, and kisses him on the cheek, pressing herself momentarily against him and laughing even harder when she pulls away.

The only thing that occurs to Nula to say is, *I'm double parked*, and, puzzled and excited at once by Lucía's unexpectedly cheerful and affectionate reception, and by the at once full and tight curves of the body that was just pressed against his.

—Go park. I'll finish up with her and wait for you, Lucía says.

Without thinking for a second about the purpose and possible consequences of his behavior, an exceptionally strange posture for a young philosopher—just imagine Descartes, Leibniz, or Kant in a similar situation—Nula obeys and goes out to the car. A pleasurable, hard tumescence tries to force its way through the barrier, over his left thigh, of his underwear and pants, ridiculous obstacles imposed by what we call civilization to the thing, difficult to name despite its many names, that insists on displaying, for all to see, and at all cost, its superabundant strength, the very source of the becoming, as Nula himself calls it, without which that very same civilization, assuming an ultimate end to time and matter, wouldn't even exist. It's only when he starts looking, slowly because of the thick midday traffic, for an open parking space, that, behind his forehead, a few thoughts begin to knock around. He wonders, first of all, if sending him out to park the car has been a pretext for disappearing, which would force him to guard the entrance to the boutique all afternoon and cancel, again, the two appointments that he already rescheduled yesterday, something which even Américo, who enjoyed the sedative effects of the maternal breast, shield against all future adversity, until the age of seven, may very well consider inexcusable. As soon as he started to think, the hard tension over his left thigh stopped pushing outward, but Nula is too absorbed in his thoughts to ask himself whether the thinking made it disappear, or if instead its disappearance allowed his thoughts to return to their normal function. He diagrams the complications that Lucía's reappearance brings with it, and, curiously, realizes that what he wants more than anything is for his emergent friendship with Gutiérrez to stay sheltered from them.

But Lucía hasn't disappeared. She's waiting for him, smiling even more broadly than before, which intrigues him to no end, because the Lucía that he knew several years before wasn't in the habit of smiling so much. When he's just a few meters away, her smile becomes a laugh and mixes with a conventional expression of irritation, to which she adds a negative shake of her head.

—I had no choice but to say I didn't know you last night. I was so surprised, she says with a pleading, happy tone of voice that displays no remorse at all.

—Three times before the cock crows, to see me crucified, Nula says when he reaches her. Not to mention the catfish I missed out on, the first of the year.

—I'm serious. Forgive me. It would've been too much to explain, Lucía says, taking his hand. And then, giving him a long, suggestive look, asks, Do you forgive me?

Nula doesn't say anything.

—Come on, let's go to my place, Lucía says.

Though it's still overcast, the day, possibly owing to the time, seems clearer and even a little brighter. The little black car that Nula saw parked the night before in front of Gutiérrez's white gate is around the corner, and by day and up close it looks newer and even more expensive than the first time he saw it, in the middle of the night, in the rain, and in the state that its presence put him in. They leave the city center and head toward the residential district, in Urquiza park, above the city, from which, at any window or balcony in its cottages or apartment buildings, the full breadth of the Paraná is easily visible, far upriver to the north and downriver to the south, where it splits many times into a delta and passes through many channels around tangled islands, forming the estuary at the mouth of the river.

—I did it for him, Lucía says. He's so kind.

—Your father, Nula says.

Lucía doesn't answer. In the silence that follows, Nula, though he regrets what he's just said, also senses a charge of immanence between them. Nula secretly observes Lucía in the rear-view, and in the fragments of face he can see—her eyes, which are on the street, are outside his visual field—part of her right cheek, her lips, her chin, and the portion of her dark hair that covers her ear and half her cheek, he thinks he sees a slightly theatrical expression of determination, something a grave mission, or a sacrifice, would demand. Finally, they arrive. Of the many homes in the highest sections of the park, all surrounded by gardens, Lucía's is among the largest and the most well cared for, with a good view of the river, and sheltered at the back by a grove of trees.

121

—It's my mother's house, Lucía says when they're outside the car and she sees Nula staring at the white facade, the balconies, the varnished doors, the tile roof, the white slab path that leads to the house and bisects the immaculate garden and lawn. I moved in with her when I came back from Bahía Blanca. Come in, there's no one here. She doesn't get back till Friday from Punta del Este, and the baby won't be dropped off till five.

Nula doesn't interpret those last words as a supplementary incentive to accept her invitation, not only because it would be superfluous, but also, and especially, because he's busy interpreting the second thing Lucía said when she got out of the car: *when I came back from Bahía Blanca*, which he takes to mean, *when I got fed up with everything you already know about and moved here with my son*. Despite the fact that, objectively speaking, the decision was a reasonable one, it's difficult, if not impossible, for Nula to imagine Lucía without Riera. In his memory, they're always together, they represent a kind of combined existence, a single entity with two bodies, a complex mechanism whose movements, though difficult to predict, could be mapped out, represented systematically, its behavior described, once its particularities have been observed, repeating continuously, without being necessarily, if the problem does in fact have a solution, unexplainable. When they're inside, Lucía locks the front door, and Nula recalls the first time he saw her and followed her to her house after she'd walked around the block. The last thing he knew about her that spring afternoon was that, after going inside, she'd locked the front door. For the rest of the day the tiny metallic sound of the lock had echoed insistently in his head. And now, after hearing a similar sound, he's inside with her.

—Do you want a drink? Lucía asks.

—No, Nula says, distracted.

Lucía laughs quickly, and Nula, avoiding her gaze, half smiles. He's just been overcome by a question that comes back to him over and over, less a problem than a riddle with no answer or insight or threat: How long does an event last, not as it's measured by a clock? How long is a day for an ant, or, in the material world, how long does the sound of a coin hitting the floor last? Does it last only briefly and disappear forever, or does it vibrate indefinitely, does it have the same inextinguishable persistence common to everything that happens? Or does the totality of existence recommence at every instance of every event, as negligible as it may be, from nothing, its essence composed of perpetual, flashing intervals, infinitesimal and innumerable by any calculus that we know or that can be known? And this thing, which years earlier he wanted so badly to happen, in vain, and which is happening now, does it live and die fleetingly, like a momentary spark, or, to the more refined observer, does it last, at the same cadence and velocity as the birth of a star that burns for an equally fleeting, incalculable moment before it's extinguished forever?

—Come on, let's go up, Lucía says, and turns toward the stairs. Nula follows her, hanging back a step so as to observe, in anticipation, the body already intending to abandon itself to his whims, but she slows down, waiting for him to come up next to her, and as they start up the stairs each knows that the other knows what's about to happen, so they don't speak, or even look at each other. Only when they reach the bedroom, next to the bed, does she say, in a low voice, *I owed you this*, and then starts to undress.

For the first time in his life, Nula enters her, exploring the dark jungle of her tissue as though with a sensitive, vibrating probe, piercing the heavy silence of the organs that with exact and constant discipline, through some inexplicable design, sustain the attractive shapes that, for a given period, before disintegrating into darkness, giving way for the next wave fighting its way out, shimmer, fugitively, in the light of day. Despite the frenzy, the violent contortions, the pleasure of the skin, the hard and prolonged embraces, the damp caresses and the moans, Nula understands, in the minutes after they finish, when they are lying on their backs next to each other, that Lucía's gift has come too late, and that she's also thinking something similar. But neither one says anything. As a courtesy, Nula represses his usual impulse to jump out of bed, get dressed, and disappear, which takes over whenever he finishes the sexual act, and which is stronger than usual, and though he needs to piss, he refuses to let himself move even for that. His disappointment has been physical too: when he penetrated her, Lucía's cavity offered no resistance, as though he'd entered a hole too large and formless, whose walls were too distended to hug his penis—a vast and empty cave. Ever since the day he saw her for the first time, the impossibility of possessing Lucía's body had mythologized it, and his disappointment, which he tries at all cost to hide, makes him incredibly sad, though he tries to find a rational explanation for it, which translated into words would be more or less the following: *We suffer the illusion of sameness, but five years ago it would have felt different because our bodies, and therefore our sensations, were too. It's possible that childbirth distended the tissue, or maybe I'm accustomed to another kind of feeling compared to what I felt today. But the most likely explanation is that despite the apparent constancy that we take for granted even the most private corners of our being, corporeal or not, have changed and will continue to change till we become unrecognizable, especially to ourselves.*

—Are you going to the cookout Sunday? Lucía asks.

—I think so. Either way, I already have the wine I'm planning on taking in the car, Nula says.

—We didn't see each other today, of course, Lucía says.

—Of course, Nula says. But we should call each other *tú*; it would be strange for me to use *usted* with you, Nula says.

Lucía laughs again, the same quick laugh as before, when they'd just come in, but this time Nula senses a hint of resignation, almost bitterness, in it. He presses himself closer to her, wraps his arm over her shoulders, and pulls her in, possibly to compensate for his disappointment but most likely to conceal it, caressing her earnestly, but excessively, because he feels a genuine affection for her. But Lucía seems indifferent to his embrace, already thinking of something else. Nula asks her what, and she answers simply, without any apparent emotion, that she came to Bahía Blanca with her son two years ago, more or less, and she has sporadic encounters with Riera, who comes every so often to see his son, but it's impossible to live with him all the time. *There's no denying it*, Lucía says, *he's a monster.* And, curiously, Nula realizes that when she says this, instead of anger, there's a spark of malicious sympathy in her eyes, which stop for a fraction of a second as they wander over the immaculate ceiling. Nula laughs: *I have no doubt about that whatsoever*, he says, and Lucía laughs too, in a way that makes Nula think that she's still in love with him and that, like the complications of their relationship, the separation must have had multiple interpretations and causes, and now Lucía is telling him that he, Riera, likes Nula so much, that he always talked about inviting him to spend a season with them in Benvenuto when they were still together, but she couldn't take it any longer and it came down to giving in or leaving. *Of course*, Nula thinks, and the images that provoke this rise in his memory, painful as a burn, *but I saw them outside that awful house in Rosario that morning from the taxi.*

—It was the right decision, not giving in, he says.

Lucía clears her throat but doesn't say anything. She thinks.

—I've never known anyone like him, Nula says.

Lucía shakes her head. I got what I deserved, she says, but with a trace of contradictory pride in her voice.

She was probably thinking about him when she decided to go to bed with me, and she thought about him the whole time we did it, and maybe—maybe—she thinks, with good cause, that I'm too simple for her, too colorless, odorless, and flavorless compared to Riera, Nula thinks, somewhat surprised, and the idea isn't altogether displeasing, though most likely because it absolves him from not loving her like before. Apparently, what until today was mythologized has suddenly become instinctual and perverted. But he's already moved on to a more interesting puzzle, Gutiérrez, *her father*, and though the question struggles to come out, his tongue and his lips can't manage to speak it, and it's Lucía herself who, without warning, begins the story about Doctor Calcagno (*my father*), about Leonor (*my old lady*), and about Gutiérrez (*Willi*), as though she too assumed that explanations were in order. When she was a girl, she loved Doctor Calcagno a lot, but as she grew up, her father's incomprehensible subservience to Mario Brando, his partner at the law firm and the head of a literary movement that her father was also part of— *precisionism*, Lucía clarifies, sarcastically—distanced her from him, and by the time she was a teenager she despised him. Calcagno was a Roman Law professor and a talented litigator, much more so than Brando, who hardly did a thing for the firm, dedicating himself instead to literature, to politics, and to his social position— but still, Lucía says, her father obeyed him unconditionally. The firm made a lot of money, and they were the only two partners, but despite having a fifty percent stake, Calcagno was the one who did all the work. Brando, with his literary fame and his political campaigns and his family and social connections—his father had been a big industrialist and he'd married a daughter of General Ponce—clearly inspired confidence in the clients of the firm, which specialized in business, trusts, estates, land acquisitions, and so on. Calcagno ran the firm, and at the same time became a sort of lieutenant to Brando, sometimes even typing up his poems, despite being older and having an international reputation as an expert in Roman Law. (Nula knows that Calcagno wrote a textbook that he often sold when he worked at the kiosk.) But at any hour, day or night, if Brando called, Calcagno dropped what he was doing and immediately did what he was told. Once, Lucía says, just after she'd turned fifteen, Calcagno planned a trip to Europe, but at the last minute Brando demanded that he stay to prepare a book that was supposed to come out in a few weeks. She and her mother were forced to travel alone. It seemed to suit Leonor fine, but she, Lucía, had begun, at that moment, to detest her father. Lucía tells Nula that she cried the entire flight and that her mother, to console her, had said: *You shouldn't hate him, Lucy, he's a good man. But remember this: A man who's good all the time is never enough for a real woman.*

It wasn't until four or five years later that Lucía started to suspect that Leonor cheated on her husband, and moreover that Calcagno couldn't not realize it, meaning, if it was true, that he tolerated it. *I really love her, but my old lady is the stupidest person I know. She has the maturity of a fourteen-year-old, more or less. All she seems to think about is clothes, jewelry, travel, and men. Old age has made her crazy: she spends a fortune trying to stay young, on creams, tanners, treatments, and surgeries. Since her family was already rich and my father left her a fortune, she never worked or had any responsibilities. When I left Benvenuto, I wanted to support myself, but she set up the shop so I wouldn't have to go out looking for work. They didn't teach me a thing. No one even made me study something useful. It was taken for granted that I'd marry a rich man and spend the rest of my life like she had. And I ended up selling clothes.*

Because she'd heard that the air in Paraná, on the hillside, was less polluted than in the city, a flat expanse twenty nine meters below sea level, and that pollution damaged *the dermis,* Leonor sold the house she had in Guadalupe, which Calcagno had built half a block from Brando—on the recommendation of the man himself, who according to Lucía always wanted his slave close by—and moved in to the cottage in Urquiza that she'd inherited from her family. And Lucía came to live with her. At any rate, if you subtracted from the weeks that she wasn't traveling the time she spent at rejuvenation clinics; her amorous liaisons supposedly always with men her age or slightly older (*up till now in any case*, Lucía adds), from good families like hers, though she may have more than one going at a time; her seasons at the *pied-à-terre* she had in Buzios, she barely spends more than two or three weeks at the house in Paraná. Her brother managed her finances from his office in Buenos Aires. If not for the married men who at the last second refused to get a divorce in order to marry her, the airports closed due to bad weather, the decline of Punta del Este, the wrinkles, the aging, the illnesses, and death, and if her daughter, whom she clearly loved, had married someone slightly less repulsive than Oscar Riera, Leonor, in an astonishing correspondence with Leibniz—whom neither she, nor Lucía for that matter, had ever heard of—would have believed that the human species had been given without a doubt the best possible world to live in.

One day, just back from a trip to Europe, she called Lucía in Benvenuto and told her that she had some good news but that she wanted to tell her in person. At that point, Lucía had almost decided to *separate* from Riera (that's the word she used) and figured that spending a few days with her mother would help her make the decision, and by the next day she was in Paraná. And, after lunch, while the baby napped—they'd left early that morning from Benvenuto, changed planes in Aeroparque, and by noon they were already in Sauce Viejo, where Leonor had sent a car to bring them to Paraná—Leonor told her that her real father wasn't Calcagno but another man, the only one she'd ever really loved, and whom she'd found again in Europe, where he'd been living for more than thirty years. He'd left the city seven months before Lucía was born and never returned. She'd asked him to leave without telling him that she was pregnant, and he'd made the sacrifice of leaving the city without telling anyone. She'd found him by accident, and they'd started to talk again: they spoke on the phone every week. He lived between Geneva and Rome and he was a screenwriter. Leonor had told him the truth and the man wanted to meet his daughter. His name was Guillermo Gutiérrez, *but back then everyone called him Willi.*

—She, who never sacrificed a thing, asked *him* for the sacrifice, Lucía practically screams, sarcastically. And Nula, to give some visible register of his agreement, and to be polite, shakes his head and offers her a scandalized grin. Lucía's directness surprises him; but because Calcagno, whom she didn't respect anymore, had been dead for years, and Lucía was aware of her mother's diverse and complex love life, it wasn't altogether difficult to hear the news with a sense of detached surprise and even of curiosity. The revelation, which she was nevertheless skeptical of, and which came at the same moment as she was deciding whether to leave her own husband, promised her a new perspective on her life. Lucía had met Gutiérrez because he was a law student that Calcagno had hired at the firm, most likely so he could pass off the jobs from his partner Mario Brando, whom he didn't dare confront directly. Gutiérrez was more or less the same age as Leonor, which meant that Calcagno was more than twenty years older than his wife. Putting two and two together, Lucía realized that they were about to run off but at the last minute she, Leonor, had changed her mind, and so at first she didn't really want to meet him because it occurred to her that he'd accepted leaving, making the sacrifice she'd asked for, possibly letting her mother convince him just as subserviently as Calcagno accepted everything that she and Brando forced on him.

129

But her curiosity was stronger than her suspicion and skepticism, and she agreed to meet him. *I'm lucky I did. He's a wonderful man. I'm not sure he's my real father, but it's like he's the father I never had.*

Nula sits up suddenly and emphatically on the pillow, and seeing that Lucía, stretched out naked next to him, doesn't move, letting her eyes drift calmly, thoughtful more than anything, over the immaculate ceiling, his face takes on an inquisitive and peremptory expression, comical in its exaggerated severity.

—So is Gutiérrez your father or isn't he? he asks.

With the same calm detachment, slightly unsettling to Nula, Lucía, after reflecting a moment, lists the possibilities: First of all—*it may sound cruel, so please don't repeat this*—it would be difficult to prove (and to confirm at present) that Willi was her mother's only lover, and even if you accepted that Willi was in fact her *first* lover, it seems absurd to Lucía that Calcagno, if they didn't have sex, would have accepted Leonor's pregnancy. So even assuming that at the time she'd only had sex with Willi and Calcagno, there still remained the problem of knowing which of the two was her father. According to Lucía, Leonor herself couldn't be sure—as with most other things, she had the habit of confusing her desires with reality—though she says that after Calcagno's death she'd started thinking about Gutiérrez again, and Lucía believes that her mother was actually in love with him, but she didn't dare run off because she wasn't prepared to accept the risks it implied. Nula knows that Lucía, for her part, against Leonor's wishes, didn't hesitate to marry Riera, who'd just gotten his medical license and didn't have a penny, so in a way it's like she's her own mother's mother, which is why she describes her as a girl from a rich family married to a rich man, who hadn't been brought up to run off with a poor law student, a clerk in her husband's law firm no less. She'd only developed the romantic mythology in retrospect, despite having already admitted to Lucía that she'd had many lovers over the years—Nula remembers Riera one day telling him: *Sometimes my mother-in-law goes swimming in the Salado, in Santo Tomé, and even though it's crowded and isn't even sandy, people go there because they say the mud rejuvenates the skin and is good for the joints. Anyway, when the water reaches her waist, the temperature in all the surrounding rivers (remember that the Salado empties into the Paraná) goes up by several degrees*—and she idealized Willi Gutiérrez, declared him the love of her life, and started to imagine, though it may in fact have been true, that he was the father of her child. It was impossible to know the truth because even Leonor herself didn't know what it was, and even if she'd been lying she didn't realize it, so when she said that Willi was her father, she was convinced that it was the truth.

—The truth, Nula says, is incredibly easy to come by.

—No, Lucía says forcefully. No one's interested in the truth. Mother, though she doesn't realize it, is terrified of it not being true. And Willi and I have an understanding. He came into my life just when I needed him. And besides, as absurd as it may seem, he really does love my mother, and doesn't ask anything in return.

Slowly, pensively, Nula slides back down until his body is once again stretched out next to Lucía. The two naked bodes, with their pale regions at similar heights, from their waistline to the tops of their thighs—although when Nula saw her for the first time, coming out of the swimming pool, she had on a fluorescent green one-piece, her large, soft breasts, which are tanned, indicate that the rest of the summer she must have taken the sun topless—are motionless, and their anatomical differences, rather than becoming more apparent through their nakedness, seem to have been blurred by their stillness and moreover the thoughtful expression on their faces, or rather in their eyes, which, like a luminous spring, flows from the two pairs of dark eyes that are more open than usual, and is propelled onto the white ceiling. Suddenly, Nula's hand, stretched out alongside his body, gropes along Lucía's forearm until it finds her hand and grasps it. Lucía lets him take her hand to his lips and kiss it softly, but her eyes stay fixed upward. Without letting go of her hand, Nula leans over Lucía's breast and starts sucking on her nipple. Lucía rubs his head, but then pushes him softly away.

—No, she says. That's enough for today.

Nula keeps sucking, as if he hadn't heard her, but he's relieved and glad that she's rejected him, although he insists a bit longer before sitting up. The suction sounds strange in the room, reminiscent of an animal, and Nula's actions, along with the position of their bodies, which have shifted, reestablishes the differences that, a few seconds before, the stillness seemed to erase despite their anatomical differences.

—Are you hungry? Lucía laughs, and Nula exaggerates the suction sound and intensifies his movements, but abruptly he sits up and grabs his watch from the nightstand. And, looking at the time, he lies:

—No. I'm late, he says, and sits up on the edge of the bed. Can I take a shower?

—Does your wife smell you when you come home? Lucía asks, standing up on the other side of the bed.

—Let's shower together, Nula says.

—If it's just a shower, Lucía says.

Lucía takes him in the black car to the dark green station wagon, parked a few blocks from the boutique, and stops a few meters away with the engine running.

—You're my only friend, she says when Nula is about to open the door.

—I hope so, Nula says, pretending not to understand what she means with the word, which has just put up a barrier between them, removing from their relationship, despite the intensity of the statement, any kind of exclusivity. Only when he's outside the car, watching it drive away, while he looks for his keys in his coat pocket, does he realize that his simulated love, his too sudden relief, his insistence on making her feel more loved than his true feelings would cause him to, are meant for himself, who feeds and expresses them. The months when he suffered most were also the most intense of his life, starting from that September afternoon when, coming out of the Siete Colores, after a student had called out to him, asking about a Public Law textbook, besides many other coincidences that would be tiresome to enumerate, he'd bumped into the girl in red as he stepped out onto the bright sidewalk, and, without knowing why, drawn by the magnet of fleeting shapes that undulate radiantly in the morning sun, before finally disappearing, he'd started following her, caught in her aura for years without ever managing to have her, until an hour ago more or less, when, at the very moment of possession, the aura, suddenly, disappeared.

The temperature has gone up a lot since noon, though the sky is still gray, a high and even, almost white gray, and it's stopped raining; what's more, the hot air has dried the last traces of damp left by the rain the night before, and which, before midday, were still visible on the streets and on the facades of several buildings. He doesn't yet feel very hot, possibly because of the recent shower— in the end, they showered separately—but the blue jacket, despite being lightweight, begins to weigh on him. Inside the car it's hot: the body of the car has been heated despite the fact that the rays of the sun have been sifted through a bank of motionless clouds that intercepts them in the atmosphere. Nula hesitates between taking off his coat and turning on the air conditioning, and opts for the latter for two different reasons: first, because when he gets to the hypermarket, where he'll have to speak to one of the managers after getting something to eat at the cafeteria, he'll need to put the coat back on; and second, which is naturally the most important, because the air conditioning will protect the cases of wine and the local chorizos that he picked up at the warehouse. But as he leans over to put the key in and turn on the engine, without knowing why, a memory overwhelms him, and he ends up sliding the key into the ignition without turning it over, leans back in the seat, his eyes in empty space, and for several seconds abandons himself to a sudden insight, a new way of remembering a childhood memory, one among many others of the vacations he spent with is grandfather, in the town.

On summer afternoons, after the sprinkler truck had passed, or when the sun reappeared the day after it had rained, swarms of yellow butterflies would appear, flying in groups of twenty or thirty, landing briefly in the puddles or the damp zones left over on the dirt roads, and then, all together, lifting off and landing a little farther away. He'd also seen flocks of birds that flew together and changed direction all at once; and, when he was older, watching some television show, he'd be astonished by the schools of colored fish, all identical, that slid through the water with the same movements, so synchronized and exact that they gave the impression of being a single body multiplied many times but controlled by a single mind, or whatever you'd call it, difficult to place either in the individual—fish, bird, or butterfly—or dispersed across the group, unifying it through an invisible current of shared energy. He'd been able to observe the butterflies himself many times, and if as a child the group's precision didn't catch his eye—what interested him then was hunting them, not with a net or anything like that, but rather with a branch from a bitterwood that he'd use to leave them battered, their wings broken, torn to pieces and dying in the dirt road—as an adolescent it began to intrigue him and after he stopped visiting the town the memory of those groups of butterflies with their uncanny synchronicity, without his knowing neither how nor why, began to represent the image, and the proof even, of a harmonious, rational universe, and which contradicted his conception of a constant and accidental becoming in which, owing to the perpetual collision of things, *in the space-time cocktail, shaken alone and ceaselessly, without the help of any barman,* as he often said, every event, in spectacular colors no less fleeting or provisional than the afternoon clouds, happens. To the question, sounding very much like a provocation, that Soldi asked him one morning a few months before, when they were drinking a cortado at the Siete Colores, phrased more or less as follows: *What if every event, like this one for example, stirring a cortado with a teaspoon, whether contingent or not, since it's impossible to know the difference in any case, hasn't been developing since the beginning of the world?* Nula responded that there wasn't a beginning to the world and that strictly speaking there wasn't a world, since it hadn't been created and was always in the making and wasn't any closer or farther from a beginning or an end and would continue to change shape forever, that's all there was to it, and the integrity of things was just a question of scale; the cortado that Soldi was stirring, for example, was no longer the same one they'd brought him a few seconds before, nor were the two of them, nor anything else that comprised the infinite present.

In truth, the collective precision of the flight of butterflies, the way he remembered it from childhood, which some attributed to a supra-individual instinct, didn't match up very well with his theories. And now, just as he leans forward to put the key in the ignition, it's unclear from where, and with such intensity that he's not turned the car on instead leaning back motionless against the seat, he's had a realization that he's now trying to form into words, and as which would be more or less the following: *It's the observer, from a deficiency of perspective, who creates the superstition of a total identity in the butterflies' behavior. In reality, every swarm struggles to move, and the movements only appear harmonious because we're incapable of seeing in detail each of the individuals that comprise the group. It's as absurd to believe that all their movements are synchronized as it is to say that all Asians are the same. Our bodies simply aren't sensitive enough to make out the differences. A flight of butterflies, if we observed it at the appropriate scale, would look like a clumsy, disorganized and frantic attempt at harmony. We'd see that what from a distance appears synchronized is only a set of individual movements, more or less fast or slow, more or less agile or clumsy, more or less exact or flawed relative to their objectives, we'd see that, for example, their position in the air or on the damp earth relative to the edge of the puddle or the direction of their flight when they take off again are not the same, not to mention the variable efforts of each butterfly, the accidents in flight or on the ground—a collision with some insect or a bird, or even with a car that scatters them or crushes them all, or a miscalculated landing in the water or in a patch of mud from which they can't manage to take off again, ending up there, in agony, their legs or their wings muddy or broken. If we followed the flight of a swarm along the four main blocks of the town, along the railway, it would be interesting to calculate how many escaped and how many reached the end of the street, no doubt what we call a harmonious dance, universally visible evidence of what certain imbeciles call the wonders of nature, is nothing but a sequence of cataclysms and catastrophes in miniature.* Nula shakes his head, as though he's coming out of a dream, and pulls a slim, black oilcloth notebook from his inside jacket pocket, in which every so often he takes notes, but which serves primarily as a place to jot down details on wine, stocks, brands, quantity, and their primary characteristics. After thinking a moment, he writes, *Sensory deficiency makes chaos seem like harmony. Flight of butterflies.* He puts the notebook and the pen away, and, after turning the engine over, while he steers the car out from between two others that leave him little room to maneuver, he thinks, satisfied: *An orgasm—thank you, Lucía darling—though the act may be disappointing—sorry, Lucía darling—always refreshes the mind,* forgetting that last night, after having made love in a satisfying way with his wife, he dropped off immediately, without thinking about anything, and slept the rest of the night.

At an open bend in the park, on the hillside, he parks the car a few minutes with the engine running and looks at the river. A long island, stretched along the same direction of the current that formed it, divides the broad channel, several kilometers wide, into two nearly identical branches. The water is a milky gray, a reflection of the sky, and owing to the invisible sun whose rays nonetheless pierce the motionless clouds, appears to be coated in a brilliant varnish. For anyone who knows its violent rhythms, its treacherous pools, its tides, the brutal countercurrents at its mouth, its unpredictable depths, its droughts, its aggressive fauna, in spite of its deceitful smoothness, as it flows to the south, is more indifferent than calm. Born of ancient, prehuman convulsions, it nevertheless has much in common with humanity, who think they've domesticated it, and like a sleeping beast it tolerates them on its back until one fine day, rearing up unexpectedly, swallows them up, and then, a week later, or often never, vomits up the unrecognizable rags that are left behind. The year before, Nula had the opportunity to see it from Diamante, some fifty kilometers to the south of Paraná. It was a bright October morning, around eleven—that hour on sunny mornings when, as he realized when a cold forced him to stay home from school, the silence of empty places increases to an uncanny level. Although Diamante wasn't in his sales region, Américo had asked him to go see a client who wanted to put in a big order, which had to be taken care of immediately, because the salesman who was in charge of it was in Corrientes. He'd left the city around eight, and by crossing to Entre Ríos on the bridge over the Colastiné and then through the underwater tunnel, not driving into Paraná but instead turning directly onto the highway by the outer streets, he'd arrived in Diamante before ten and by quarter of eleven the sale had been finalized. The day seemed so beautiful as he left the client that morning that he'd been overcome with the desire, without apparent cause in the species, *to check out the river* before returning to

137

the city. And following the crude signs that pointed the way to the coast, he left the city center and turned onto a dirt road that, after passing a few scattered ranches, ended at a kind of peninsula, at the top of the slope. He got out of the car and walked to the edge; he was surrounded by some sparse grass, and though the slope wasn't very high, the peninsula projected outward, and the shrubs and short trees that grew along the coast, some almost horizontally because their roots dipped into the vertical riverbank or the steep slope above, not quite reaching the end of the peninsula, allowed an unobstructed view to the north, upriver, where great quantities of water seemed to flow out of the horizon. The opposite shore, somewhere near Coronda, was not visible, of course, though in the flatlands that end suddenly at the river it would have been visible from that relative height if it had been any closer. Nula knew that the shore was several kilometers in that direction, to the west, but from where he was standing its presence was purely imaginary. The river dropped from the north, its vast breadth fractured here and there by green alluvial islands, by banks of sand, by floats of water hyacinths that came from the tropics, or possibly from Paraguay or from Brazil, and ran aground among the islands in the delta. Having carved through colored earth, the water was red, though in some patches the surface, mixing with the clear blue of the sky, it turned a bluish rose. The reddish opacity of the surface was rough in the distance, most likely owing to the current that turned the water and made waves across the heavy masses on the surface, on which, here and there, foamy edges formed. But what struck him were the contradictory impressions it provoked: it obviously advanced, but it appeared static, and though the morning was bright, the surface was not reflective, and though it flowed to the south in silence, the ear, possibly due to the heavy rocking of the surface, seemed to hear a distant roar.

Nula looks for his cell phone in the side pocket of his jacket as he steers the car through the park, toward the tunnel, but when he accelerates downhill, he decides to call Diana after he gets out of the tunnel, so he leaves the phone on the seat. He feels like a cigarette, though since he started selling wine he's been smoking somewhat less so as not to distort its taste and smell, as they recommended during the mandatory wine-tasting courses, but, because of the air conditioning, he doesn't light one. Ten minutes later he's crossing the tunnel behind an interurban bus, and after the toll on the opposite side he passes it. On the island highway he doesn't see a single other car, but on the bridge over the Colastiné he passes a truck and two cars that follow it toward the tunnel. While he's crossing the bridge—the river is smooth, the same pale gray as the Paraná, in fact the source of its waters—he calls home, but Diana's voice picks up on the answering machine. *It's me. How are you? I'm just about at the hypermarket. Kisses. Talk to you soon,* Nula says and hangs up, relieved not to have to speak to Diana, since it makes him uncomfortable to lie when the adventure is still recent, which some nights forces him to wander around in the car or sit in a bar for a while before going home, to make sure that Diana will already be asleep when he gets there. At the exit for La Guardia he turns toward the city, and as he reaches the hypermarket, before pulling in to the parking lot, where there are a few more cars than in the morning, he can just make out the old waterfront clustered across the opposite shore of the lagoon, with its chic cottages whose tile roofs emerge sporadically from between the foliage. He gets out of the car, noting that the afternoon is hotter but unsure whether to attribute it to the climactic differences between the cities, one at altitude, the other on the plain, or to the contrast with the air conditioning, but as he enters the hypermarket its own air conditioning returns the sense of coolness to him.

Although he almost never buys anything, except on the days when he and Diana are stocking up (but even then she's the one who actually does the shopping), he likes to wander through supermarkets, possibly because it once occurred to him that they represent a grotesque version of his grandfather's general store. The principles are the same, like the water vapor that on a small scale agitates the lid of a kettle when the water boils, and on a large scale moves a locomotive. As a child he believed that it was the abundance and variety that attracted him to his grandfather's store, but as an adult, wandering through supermarkets, he realized that what affected him was actually the repetition. The stacks of cigarette packs, all the same brand, the rows of vermouth or gin bottles, all the same shape, their contents the same color as the glass, with the same black label, filling an entire shelf, or the pyramids of cans in the center of the store, which his aunt or his grandfather had built, patiently and meticulously, the night before, after dinner, produced a visual effect that he confused with abundance, not realizing that what attracted him to the jars filled with orange jellies wrapped in transparent cellophane, all the approximate shape and color of an orange slice, was the cumulative effect, further enhanced by their loose disorder inside the glass jar, which in itself had both a decorative and philosophical aspect, though as a child he was still too young to realize this, because the repetition, even of manufactured objects, is the thing that's most familiar and at the same time the most enigmatic: *Abundance can be oppressive or sublime, but repetition is always aesthetic, and its effect always mysterious,* he sometimes thinks. In the hypermarket, even the background music that most reasonable people are sensible enough to loathe seems necessary to him because it underscores the environmental shift that's produced when one passes from the disarticulated and contingent external world to the internal one, a change as stark as the one we feel when, as we dive in the river, we cease to hear the sounds of the surface world and move, half-blind, through the underwater silence. Nula thinks of the excessive lighting inside the hypermarket—and all artificial light, for that matter—as a prosthesis of our visual organs, and that even the building's construction obeys the same principles that combine abundance, variety, and repetition, because the complex, manifested spontaneously from the primordial swamp, contains not one but eight movie theaters. At the self-serve cafeteria, meanwhile, the repetition is sustained: the carefully-arranged, small round plates filled with mixed salad, tongue in vinaigrette, hearts of palm with ham, chicken salad, are displayed in sets of three, and the white rim of the plate frames in each instance an approximate design whose individual elements are arranged more or less in the same way. Nula picks out a chicken salad, a mixed salad, and at the hot section asks for a milanesa with egg and fries, and after serving himself a piece of bread, a carbonated mineral water, and some packets of mustard, salt, and pepper from alongside the register, he pays and sits down at a table near the window that faces the stream, beside which the Warden hypermarket, which everyone calls *the supercenter*, in such contrast to the swampy, impoverished landscape that surrounds it, seems like a magical illusion, a colorful mirage in a desolate, gray desert.

The thing that hadn't happened five years before, now, only recently, because she thought it would repay a debt to him, suddenly, still perplexingly, and so different from what he'd always imagined, and so unexpected, had happened. If he'd pushed up his trip to Paraná in order to see her sooner it was merely out of curiosity, rooted in what had happened the night before at Gutiérrez's, and he hadn't even been sure, if he found her, that Lucía would speak to him. The coincidence of seeing her there had unexpected consequences, as it did five years before, when despite his best efforts, after the first time he met her, to see her again, he only saw her by accident one afternoon, at the corner of his block, not the one with the ice cream shop but the next one, where his street met the street with the house she'd gone into (her own house, in fact), locking the door from the inside while Nula, from the sidewalk, listened to the metallic sound of the key turning. Because he was still dazzled by the red dress vibrating intensely in the midday sun, he couldn't imagine her dressed any other way, and so he always searched the neighborhood, or in the crowd downtown, for the bright red blur, the vigorous cluster of organs, skin, and muscles, enclosed like an organic capsule by its meaty and velvety skin, splitting the balmy September air. Since they first met, he'd passed her house more than twenty times and had taken an unreasonable number of walks around the block, posting himself for hours on the four corners in order to see if the girl dressed in red who he still didn't know was named Lucía would reappear, not only at the one that he rightly assumed must've been her house, but also at the three other symmetrical points that he'd seen her examine, including La India's apartment, along the four streets that formed the block. Any red dress, seen from a distance, startled him and triggered his approach with the hope of seeing her again, but it was never her. And so when one afternoon, on his way back to his house after having watched the kiosk at the law school all day, he bumped into her again, he was so absorbed in thinking about her that at first he didn't recognize her because she was dressed in white. She had on an immaculate linen suit, stiff and recently pressed, and her hair was pulled up, stretched tight at her temples and the base of her neck and spilling out at the crown of her head above the dark ribbon that held it together. She looked calm, freshly bathed. From the opposite sidewalk, he watched her cross the street at a diagonal, enter the pastry shop, and sit down at one of the tables facing the window, at the corner farthest from the door. Just like the first time when he started following her without knowing why, not thinking about it even for a fraction of a second he crossed the street at a diagonal, veering off from the straight line that was taking him to his house, and went into the shop. There were several empty tables, but without hesitating even to discuss it with himself he took the few steps that brought him to a stop in front of her. She looked at him a moment, without surprise or curiosity, like an actress during the first reading of a play, waiting for the actor next to her to finish reading his lines before giving hers.

—Is this seat taken? Nula asked, using for the first time in his life an expression that he'd read many times in certain novels and had often heard when he went to take an exam at school or he was asked to wait at some public office.

She didn't respond right away, and only looked at him, but Nula realized that she was thinking because the look she gave him was abstracted for a few seconds, cut off from the external world, while her thoughts, hidden, unstable, inaccessible to him, possibly sought, behind the forehead on which passing wrinkles implied some effort, the response that she was about to give and her reasons for giving it. Before speaking, and after her gaze had reconnected with the external world, she took a moment to glance at her tiny, silver wrist watch, then looked up again, the movement perhaps a bit abrupt because the bubble of dark curly hair spilling from the crown of her head vibrated slightly.

—No, of course. Sit down, please, she said, her lightness seemingly calculated and her intonation contrasting with her serious, vaguely preoccupied demeanor. As he was sitting down, Nula saw La India turn the corner toward the house, and though he lifted his hand and shook it several times to get her attention, she didn't seem to recognize him, but that same night, when she saw him come in, she greeted him by saying, *You already have a mother, but you're spoiled and now you always want two for the price of one,*

143

and he, worked up, was about to say, *I'm not the one with a cult of personality in this house*, but he felt miserable thinking it and kept his mouth shut.

—That was my mother, he explained to Lucía.

—Such a beautiful woman, and so young, Lucía said, as though she was thinking of something else.

—Allow me to introduce myself, Nula said. Nicolás Anoch, but my friends call me Nula; it means Nicolás in Arabic. I'm studying philosophy in Rosario.

—My husband studied in Rosario, too, but medicine. My name is Lucía, Lucía said.

—I dropped medicine for philosophy, Nula said. I got tired of opening and closing cadavers. They're all the same inside.

—My husband is Doctor Riera. His office is just around the corner.

—Yes, that's right, Nula said. I think I've seen the sign. Across from the municipal building.

—Directly across, yes, Lucía said thoughtfully. And then, studying him openly, she said, Your face looks familiar. Are you from the neighborhood?

—Yes, Nula said. I've lived half a block from here my whole life. In the luxury tenements. Are you a city planner?

—City planner? Lucía said with a dry laugh. How could I be a city planner? I'm nothing.

Disconcerted momentarily by her sarcastic interjection, Nula hesitated a few seconds, until it occurred to him to say, Would it be alright if we used *tú* with each other?

—Sure, Lucía said, and looked at the time again.

—Are you waiting for someone? Nula asked.

She was about to say something, but the arrival of the waiter interrupted her. When he left, they kept talking. Nula felt incredibly impressed to be at a table using *tú* with her, and reconciling himself

144

to what he'd gained up until that moment, a thousand times more than what he'd dared to hope for fifteen minutes before, he felt content with the exchange of pleasantries that didn't even seem like pleasantries to him because in fact they satisfied him completely. Even though the arrival of the waiter had kept her from answering his question, it was obvious that she was waiting for something or someone; she drifted in and out of the conversation, checking the time every so often, and never lost her grave demeanor even when she said things that seemed cheerful. They discussed the neighborhood, the good weather, the city, and though every so often Nula would bring up personal details, more so out of his childishly inflated sense of himself than as an actual seduction tactic, she didn't seem to hear them, or in any case she didn't seem inclined to tell him more about herself than the two or three things she'd said at first and which had more to do with her husband than with herself. More and more frequently, Lucía would look out at the street, scrutinizing the people who passed, as though she were looking for someone in particular, drifting off for several seconds before returning to the conversation. Her laughter, when she laughed, was always abrupt and not exactly happy, and a few times, Nula, confused, had to admit to himself that no matter how much he thought about it, he wouldn't find, at that moment in the conversation at least, anything to laugh at. His worries from the week before returned, although she appeared calm and relaxed, with no trace of mental disarray in her focused and attractive expression. She was friendly and warm, and though she didn't seem inclined to offer him any special favor, she treated him in a friendly, intimate way, possibly because she didn't take him very seriously, but Nula, growing slightly bolder, so as to not lose heart, told himself that it wouldn't be the first time that he'd managed to sleep with someone who hadn't seemed to take him very seriously at first. Even though that bravado wasn't quite convincing, he already knew that what might happen there didn't matter much, that he couldn't decide anything, that whatever Lucía might do, he'd already gotten caught in her aura and he was trapped there.

Eventually, it started to get dark. Lucía asked if he wanted to go for a walk and Nula followed her out. They crossed to the opposite sidewalk, hurrying to avoid the quickly approaching headlights from the next block, but rather than heading for her house, Lucía, saying that she still had some time, suggested that they take a walk around the block. When they reached the entrance to Nula's building, Lucía went up the stairs and started looking curiously at the two rows of apartments and the central garden, where the white-globed nightlights had already been lit. Forgetting Nula, she studied the entrance for a few moments and then, to disguise her excessive interest, came down the stairs to the sidewalk and asked him, *So this is your building?*

—Yes. The third apartment on the right, Nula said, gesturing in its general direction with a vague nod and thinking, *She's starting the same circuit she took the other day, but this time, whatever her reasons, I'm taking it with her, and for a while still, I think.* And they turned at the corner of the ice cream shop: La India's ice cream friend (he'd opened after Nula moved to Rosario for medical school), who was filling a cone, looked up, surprised to see him with someone, but Nula, watching him covertly, acted as though he didn't see him so as to not have to say hello. They turned onto the cross street, shaded darkly under the trees, and walked in silence to Doctor Riera's office, the dark interior of which she stopped to inspect, and then they kept walking, turned north on the street parallel to 25 de Mayo, and Lucía stopped halfway down the block, outside the same house as the week before, gazing inside through the half-open door with the same blatant indiscretion, and though the lights were on and apparently there were people inside, after a few seconds Lucía started walking again, more quickly than before, a severe look on her face. While up until then Nula had wished that she had been less distracted from the conversation, he now knew that he'd been relegated by Lucía to a kind of nonexistence and completely forgotten. The warm aura he'd have liked to settle into indefinitely aspirated and expelled him at intervals, without warning, and he couldn't tell if she was doing it in a calculated or a careless way. Finally they turned the last corner and reached her house. Lucía opened the door. The house was dark, and it was obvious there wasn't anyone there. Nula thought she'd invite him in, but just the opposite happened.

—Well, Lucía said. Thanks for the tea and the conversation. It was nice to meet you. Now you know the house, so you can visit me whenever you want. No need to call ahead.

She leaned over and kissed him on the cheek. Nula, over-whelmed, started to babble something, but she turned around, flipped on the light in the entryway, and closed the door. A few seconds passed before he heard the small metallic sound of the lock which for the last week, and for many years afterward, had echoed in his memory, familiar, translated from the hollowness of pure circumstance to the metonymic ether where things, dissected and reordered, producing both anguish and consolation, restore and represent the flawed and ephemeral experience. He took a few steps down the sidewalk, toward 25 de Mayo and his house, but he stopped suddenly, stood motionless for a few seconds, and then turned and started walking in the opposite direction. He passed Lucía's house and, without stopping, noted that the entryway light was still on. He reached the corner, turned right, and when he was halfway down the block, in front of the house that Lucía seemed to have a problem with, stopped and briefly studied the door that was now closed but which, like the Persian blinds over the side win-dow, where a few parallel rays slipped through the bars, allowed the light from inside to filter out. Finally he decided to ring the

147

doorbell; he hadn't been hesitating, actually he'd been standing there for no reason, not really knowing what to do, when suddenly, without thinking about it, and without knowing what would happen if they answered, he rang the bell. Almost immediately, as though he'd been waiting behind the door for someone to ring, a five- or six-year-old boy opened it and looked up at him.

—I think I've made a mistake, Nula said. Does the Anoch family live here?

The boy looked at him and without saying a thing closed the door again, possibly because they'd taught him not to speak to strangers, or maybe he'd surprised him in the middle of a solitary game, and unable to distinguish the game from reality, he'd acted in a certain sense deliriously, his abrupt behavior belonging to the character he was playing in the game and not to the normal way he'd act outside of it, or following, on the contrary, an accelerated logic whose intermediate stages he short-circuited, he'd figured that since that family didn't live in that house there wasn't any more reason for the door to be open. Shuffling through these possibilities, laughing to himself, Nula continued his circuit. He was deliberately doing things that made no sense to him, he thought, and he remembered a conference he'd attended at school. The speaker had said that humanity, after the death of the gods, forsaken to the magma of the material, had begun to realize that its actions lacked significance, but that each individual could, if he wanted, give them meaning and assign his own value. And he told himself that, in their reproduction, Lucía's enigmatic intentions would ultimately reveal their meaning. But he didn't learn anything more about them when he stopped at the nameplate that read *Doctor Oscar Riera, Clinical Medicine*, which he was able to read thanks to a streetlight between him and the trees. As before, the office was dark and silent, so after trying to peer inside without seeing much, he continued walking, turned at the corner with the ice cream shop without looking inside, and soon reached the entrance to his building. He went up the stairs that led to the entrance and was already walking to the apartment when suddenly the place where he'd lived since he was born looked strange to him, the garden where he'd played as a kid, the two rows of apartments separated by the hibiscus and the rosebushes, the glassy planters and the blooming hedges, fragrant in the evenings. Lucía's curious gaze had displaced his own, and explained the apparently permanent alienation he felt, which translated into words would have been more or less the following: *The strangeness of the world isn't in its unthinkable or distorted sectors but rather in the immediate, the familiar. It just takes an outside gaze, which can sometimes come from ourselves, however fleetingly, to reveal this to us.*

That night, in bed, he came up with several plans, to be carried out the next day, but discarded them all after deciding that none satisfied him. One thing was for sure: he'd taken Lucía's invitation at face value. The next day, though, he worked from two till eight at the law school kiosk, and it didn't seem prudent to show up too late at Lucía's because of the danger that she might not be alone. But by the time he got up his caution had vanished: after showering and eating breakfast, he walked out, turned the corner, and went straight to Doctor Riera's office. He rang the doorbell, below which a sign read *Ring the bell and come in*, and pushed through the half-open door.

A woman of a certain age, who must've been the secretary, or the nurse, or both things at once, came through the side door that led to an empty waiting room, and with a severe expression asked him his name. When he told her, she must have realized that it wasn't the name she'd expected to hear, that is, of the patient who'd made an appointment for that time (it was ten exactly), and she was telling him that he'd have to make an appointment for another time when a second door, which also led to the waiting room, opened and Doctor Riera appeared. Seeing him, Nula thought, *He's as beautiful as she is, even more so, for a man: as virile as Lucía is feminine. He's tall, well-proportioned, with an athlete's body and an intelligent expression. And his dark, curly hair makes him look younger than her, though he may in fact be older, thirty-five, give or take. His eyes are sharp, his clothes are neat, but because he's tall and upright, muscular probably, without an ounce of excess fat, even the worst clothes in the world would look good on him. His gestures are precise and natural. He doesn't seem to have a single defect. Clearly they're made for each other. They're like gods and I'm the larva that squirms at their feet and which they wouldn't even bother to squash. There's no doubt whatsoever that I'm finished before I even start. And how virile and melodious his voice sounds as he tells the nurse to let me through, that the next patient won't be there till ten fifteen!*

And then he was inside, a clean and tidy office, and Riera gestured to a chair, just in front from the one he sat in, on the other side of his desk. He took a blue index card and a fountain pen from a drawer and transcribed Nula's answers to his questions, his name, birthday, marital status, residence, and a few details about his medical history. Then Riera stopped writing and examined him, first with his gaze, then with the ritual question he must have asked every new patient, but in which Nula thought he detected a slight hint of scorn.

—What seems to be the problem?

Nula invented some sort of allergy, an itch on different parts of his body that came and went over the past few months. Riera looked at him for a few seconds and then, as they stood up, he said:

—Alright, you can get undressed.

—All the way?

—Not yet, Riera said. You can leave your underwear on.

He had him sit down on the examination table and took his blood pressure, then listened with a stethoscope, or directly with his fingers, on his abdomen, on his chest, and around his back. Then he told him to stand up and take off his underwear.

—Where does it itch? he said.

Nula gestured vaguely around his hips, his belly, his thighs, his head. While he put on a pair of rubber gloves, Riera started examining the skin more closely, murmuring *I don't see anything*. Separating his hair with his fingers, he quickly studied his scalp; with the tip of his index finger he rubbed his eyebrows against the grain, straightening the hair in order to examine the skin more closely. Then he told him to lay down again on the table, face up. He sat on a black leather stool and sank his fingers into his pubic hair, slowly and carefully separating the hairs in order to see the skin beneath. After a moment he stopped and then said:

—It's not lice. You can get dressed.

Nula stood up.

—Hold on, one second, Riera said. With two fingers on his left hand he lifted his penis and with his right hand palpitated and weighed his testicles, then with the same two fingers folded back the foreskin and studied it closely, even going so far as to squeeze it, expanding the orifice in order to see into it. Then he told him to turn around, and separating his buttocks he examined his anus for several seconds. While he took off the gloves and threw them in a cylindrical, metal receptacle, whose lid opened by pressing a pedal that stuck out from the base, Riera announced that he couldn't find anything in particular.

—It must be psychosomatic. How've you been sleeping lately? he asked. I can prescribe a tranquilizer if you want.

—No, not at all. I sleep really well, Nula said.

Riera watched him closely while he dressed, and when he finished, and their eyes met, it seemed to Nula that despite the gravity of his expression and his professional tone when he spoke to him, there was, in Riera's eyes, a tenuous spark of mockery.

—How much do I owe you, doctor? Nula said.

—Nothing, Riera said. When you're really sick I'll charge you. For now I'd rather not think of you as a patient.

He followed him to the door but their eyes never met again. The ten fifteen patient was already in the waiting room, reading a magazine, and he stood up when he saw them come in, deferential to the medical authority, like a private who comes to attention when a superior officer enters the room. Nula said goodbye without turning around and went out to the street. He was so preoccupied that rather than walk down San Martín, as he'd imagined he would, he returned home. He grew more worried the more he thought things over. He threw himself on top of his bed but the very moment he collapsed onto it, as if he'd bounced, he stood back up. A kind of anxiety was taking over him without his even realizing it completely: the visit to Riera's office, like the profanation of a sanctuary, produced both pride and fear, and he replayed over and over, in a fever, the doctor's gestures and words. Everything felt saturated with meaning, but a kind of multiple meaning, impossible to specify, one which changed direction each time he tried to force an interpretation through it. The couple that had just come into his life was taking on a disproportionate prestige, representing, with their physical beauty, their tact, their enigmatic behavior, a side of the world that his dark and tragic family life hadn't allowed him to know existed. Those two attractive, singular people, endowed with a glow more intense than anyone else he knew, appeared sheltered from contingency, from the vulgar details that underscored the mutability of perfection, a kind of gift, at once immediate and inaccessible, offered up by the external world. Even though it had its darker side, like the vaguely mocking look he'd given him after the examination, Doctor Riera's behavior nevertheless seemed more rational than his wife's, but his last words, with their irregular feel, seemed to contain a coded message or a warning. Nula spent the rest of the morning going over his questions, waiting for La India, who closed the bookstore at noon and would be on her way back soon after, but at twenty after twelve, when he went to the kitchen to pick at something because he was starting to get hungry, he saw that La India had left him a list and some money to go to the store on the boulevard to buy three or four things they needed for lunch. And so he didn't open the fridge, and instead hurried out to the street.

When he was almost back at his building he had to stop suddenly: he'd seen Doctor Riera climb out of a double-parked gray car, step between two cars parked against the curb, cross the sidewalk, and easily mounting the three steps that led to the apartments, disappear inside. Nula started walking again. When he reached the entrance he saw that Riera was standing with his back to the street, a few steps away, looking carefully at the two rows of apartments and the narrow, tidy garden between them, and not wanting to run into him, decided to keep walking to the corner, and because he didn't quite know what to do he stepped into the ice cream shop, which was empty just then, not even the owner was there, just a girl who worked the counter every so often when the owner was out, and who greeted him inquisitively.

—I forgot my key and have to wait for my mother to come home, Nula explained, but at that very moment he saw Riera's gray car turn the corner slowly and he gave the girl a look that could mean several things at once, or rather none, and in two steps, two leaps practically, he was on the sidewalk, just in time to see Riera double-park the car again halfway down the block, climb out, quickly cross the sidewalk, and enter his office. Nula started walking under the trees, uncertain if he should walk fast or slow, or whether or not he wanted to run into Riera, if he should or shouldn't ask him for an explanation—though he wasn't actually sure that his visiting the apartment building had anything to do with him—but when he reached the office and saw that the door was open and the gray car was still running, he sped up, and when he reached the next corner, weaving through the traffic, which was heavy at that hour, he crossed the street and stopped at the next corner, in front of the hardware store window. Every so often he glanced furtively toward the office, until finally, though he hadn't seen Riera come out, he saw the gray car pull away slowly, practically rubbing against the ones parked against the curb, intending to turn, surely, which in fact it did, stopping again, this time in front of the mysterious house that apparently provoked in Lucía, every time she passed its door, a kind of theatrical disapproval. Riera got out of the car and rang the bell. He didn't have to wait, because the door half-opened immediately, and though he couldn't see who'd opened it, because the person wasn't visible from where he was standing, Nula presumed it must not have been the kid from the night before because Riera's gaze, though it was directed slightly downward, was nevertheless inclined at the height of an adult, or in any case someone much older than five or six. For about a minute, Riera talked energetically with the person who'd answered, and eventually, smiling, he passed his hand through the doorway and made a quick gesture, and turning around, crossed the sidewalk and got in the car, at the exact moment that the door behind him closed. Riera pulled out again, slowly, and turned left at the next corner. Nula crossed to the other sidewalk and walked to the end of the block, intending to turn as well, and saw that the gray car was now parked in front of the house—now all that was missing, when he passed by, was to hear the small metallic sound of the lock that Riera turned from inside, but no, this time his prediction was wrong, too much time had already passed since the car turned the corner and stopped halfway down the block, and no matter how much he focused, slowing down considerably but not daring to stop as he passed the door, unsure why he'd been struck by an intense desire to hear it, that small, familiar sound didn't reach his ears.

Crossing his utensils over the few fries scattered across his plate, over the traces of egg yolk and toasted, oil-soaked bread crumbs, Nula leans back against his chair and, taking a drink of mineral water, decides that his lunch is finished. He smiles at his memories: the explanation for their behavior was much more simple than he'd imagined, and, at the same time, Lucía and Riera never really floated in that inaccessible, mythological space. His relationship with them started, lasted a while, and now, for the last hour, give or take, is once again unfinished, has entered that murky zone where, their cynicism exceeding their optimism, contradictory and awkwardly, the incomplete, mortal shadows that live there struggle over each other. His smile disappears and he sits thoughtfully for a minute, at the end of which, in order to move on, he takes his cell phone from his pocket and dials the manager of the supermarket.

—Anoch, he says. How are you? I'm at the cafeteria. I'm on my way to your office. You're coming for a coffee? Even better.

He decides to move to a clean table, and he's just finished settling down when he sees the manager, accompanied by a woman who entices him immediately, a decisive and professional demeanor yet conscious of the effect she produces in men, and who exchanges a probing glance with Nula, a momentary search for recognition which he's unsure if the manager has noticed or even if it's actually happened at all. Suddenly it's like his sexual encounter with Lucía a little while earlier had never happened. It's been discarded in the trash heap of the past, the incomprehensible limbo where, rather than vanishing suddenly, disappearing forever from the strange world in which things take place, we believe the events recently shuffled from the present go to rest, their tenuous threads unraveling in our memory, like the ghostly, colored silhouettes that linger on our retinas when we close our eyes and which disintegrate slowly behind our closed eyelids until they dissolve completely into the darkness. With an infantile yet detached curiosity, Nula wonders (as he does somewhat too often) if the manager and the woman have just come from doing the same thing that he and Lucía did a little while ago, together or on their own, indulging a different hunger than the one usually satisfied at lunch. And Nula imagines the possibility that just as he called them they were in the middle of an embrace, though they seem too clean, well-combed, spotlessly dressed, and too calm and sure of themselves to have emerged, less than a minute ago, from the paroxysm comprised of spasms, moans, sweats, discharge, and even tears, which shortly afterward, after a brief pause, anticipating the promise of the unattainable, desires its infinite and, if possible, even more intense and emphatic repetition.

—How are you? the manager asks, giving him a brief, vigorous handshake, and adds, Mr. Anoch, from Amigos del Vino. Virginia is in charge of the whole beverage department, alcoholic and otherwise. You're required to get along with each other.

Nula and Virginia exchange a long handshake until her soft, warm hand slides effortlessly from Nula's.

—Should we have a coffee? Nula asks.

—I can't, the manager says. But Virginia has carte blanche to make decisions for the shop.

—Don't take this the wrong way, Nula says, but I think a conversation alone with Mrs. Virginia—or is it Miss Virginia, I hope?—would have its own advantages.

—She's our secret weapon, the manager says. Don't let your guard down.

—And here we see them practicing their beloved national sport, Virginia says.

—You mean chivalry? the manager says.

—No, machismo, Virginia says.

—I dare you to find someone more feminist than me, the manager says, and looking at his watch, getting serious and thinking of something else, an urgent matter somewhere else in the hypermarket, he announces, *With the way I love my women!*

He shakes Nula's hand and practically runs away. As they're sitting down, Virginia whispers:

—Every asshole thinks he's a comedian.

Nula laughs and Virginia, satisfied that her comment has been well-received, reclines against the back of her chair, and looks around, smiling languidly, making her breasts rise and stand out from beneath the tight, pale green suit jacket. In her heels she'd seemed taller than Nula, but she must be more or less his same height. Her face is round and full, her lips fleshy, and her hair, dark and thick, curls down to her shoulders. She doesn't seem inclined to show weakness, not at work or anywhere else.

—Would you like a coffee? Nula asks.

—Yes, she says. But don't get up. They'll bring it to us.

And she makes a pair of signs to the cashier, the first consisting of curling the index finger and thumb on her right hand slightly, the fingertips pointing at each other, three or four centimeters apart, and the second of extending her index and middle fingers on her left hand, curling the other three into her palm, and waving the extended fingers in the air, very conspicuously, to specify the quantity, signs that, translated into ordinary language, would signify *two coffees*. Nula follows her gestures admiringly, and though she doesn't appear to notice, it's clear that she's used to being looked at in that way, and the gaze that would have produced distinct pleasure in someone else apparently slides off her shell, or ricochets against it, falling to the floor without having had any effect, like bullets off Superwoman's chest, or prayers to an indifferent divinity, cloistered in her sanctuary, more self-absorbed than uncaring or contemptuous.

—Friday around five is a good time to open the display, Virginia says, looking him in the eyes, probing, despite her professional tone, whether, ultimately, given the moment, she might decide, if Nula is worthy, of accepting her admiration. That's when people start coming in, and it doesn't let up till Sunday, she adds. During the week it's slower. You're staying till the following Sunday, right?

—Yes, Nula says. Too bad we ended up with Holy Week.

—That won't change much, Virginia says. We're open Wednesday and Thursday that week and lots of people come in, and we only close on Friday afternoon. And Thursday is like the night before a holiday.

—So you're saying that in his final moments on the cross, Christ authorized that the Warden hypermarket could open half a day on Good Friday? Nula says, and halfway through the sentence he regrets having opened his mouth.

—I don't think so, Virginia says. But our chain does have special permission from the Pope, and in any case the Vatican is one of our biggest shareholders.

—Heaven awaits us, then, Nula says.

One of the waitresses from the cafeteria walks over with their coffees and leaves them on the table. Nula takes out some money to pay, but Virginia stops him with a quick gesture.

—It's on the house, she says.

—I'll have to pay you back somehow, Nula says.

—You'll get your chance, Virginia says.

They drink their coffee black, and Nula takes advantage, when she narrows her eyes as she brings the cup to her lips, taking short sips so as not to burn herself, to study her openly, almost hoping that she sees him do it, her attractive, regular features, her skin tanned by the recent summer, her thick, curly hair, her slightly compressed neck holding up her motionless head, her wide, almost masculine shoulders, her breasts bulging from the lapels of her pale green blazer made of a light and silky material. When they finish their coffee, Virginia looks at the time and nods vaguely toward the supermarket.

—Come on, I'll show you the place where the display will be set up, she says.

Nula follows her obediently. They walk side-by-side, unreserved, familiar, like a couple who've known each other a long time, and Nula, completely indifferent to the Amigos del Vino's commercial interests, wonders what the best way would be to advance his personal, and even intimate, relationship with Virginia, what means he might have to make that self-possessed, alert creature, attentive only to the interests of her own desire, fix him, if only for a passing moment, with a look that conveys abandon and submission. And suddenly, she takes the first step in that direction.

—Since you'll be calling me Virginia, I'll want to know your first name.

—Nicolás, but my friends call me Nula, which means Nicolás in Arabic, Nula says, scrambling to respond, hastily, almost servile.

She laughs.

—What a strange name. It sounds pretty feminine. But I like it, she says.

—And in your case, Virginia, is there a discrepancy between the name and the person?

—I have a two-year-old daughter, Virginia says, and though their conversation is light, she continues to look around, verifying, apparently, that everything in the Warden hypermarket, where she has a certain level of responsibility, is or at least seems to be in order, adding, however, *I think you're big enough by now to know what that means.*

—I'll have to think about it, Nula says, noticing that Virginia's smile widens.

Leaving the cafeteria, they cross a wide passage that leads from the restaurants and the multiplex to the hypermarket itself (the heads of the business, the radio and television commentators, and the daily press call the group of buildings *the supercenter*), where the lights are brighter than in the cafeteria and in the passageway. Despite the windows facing the parking lot, numerous lights illuminate the giant space stocked with merchandise, and the same music, which in the cafeteria and in the passageway was almost inaudible, sounds somewhat louder. Almost all of the registers are closed, and because of this, though the place isn't very crowded, at the few that are open the submissive customers gather in lines. The white plastic bags are emblazoned with a bold and conspicuous W of the Warden brand. From his trips here with Diana, Nula knows that the red ones come from the meat section, the green ones, not surprisingly, from the produce section, and the blue ones from the seafood section, but the yellow, orange, indigo, and violet ones are hard to match with a specific product, though in practice the bags end up combined together at the registers, and are only correctly organized at the sections operated by specialized workers, like the butcher shop and the fish section. According to Diana, who often works in advertising design, that set of colors, which evokes the refraction of light, must have been the designers' effort to suggest, from the publicity office of the Warden firm, which branches into many countries, that the W hypermarkets, with their incalculable diversity, predicting and satisfying the infinite spectrum of human desire, contain the sum of all existence. Nula seems to recall that the bag that Chacho gave them with the catfish had a green W, and though he remembers that the woman who pointed to Escalante's house through the rainy darkness was holding a couple of bags from the same supermarket, he can't picture what colors the letters were. As they pass behind the registers, the people waiting in line look at them discreetly, and Nula hopes that the men think that his relationship with Virginia is more intimate than it really is, but it's obvious and demoralizing that, at least to the youngest among them, each of which must be wishing deep down that he could possess such a promising body, he, Nula, is invisible next to her. The aisles between the shelves are like streets, and instead of houses with doors and windows there's a series of labels, cans, cellophane, packages, cardboard boxes, jars, that continuously yield to other merchandise with other uses, other shapes, made from cloth, plastic, wood, rubber, metal, and so on. The section of bottles, mineral water, soda, beer, wine, and liquor is deserted, and, at an intersection, Virginia stops suddenly.

—What do you think? she says, gesturing to the shelves around them. To one side are bottles of wine, and ahead of them the snacks and the liquor, but in the rows that start again after the intersection there are more bottles of wine, more snacks and more liquor, the same rainbow-colored profusion of labels that despite representing, in many cases, specific objects and shapes, seem abstract in repetition and lose their representative quality and seem more like a pattern or an ornamental design. Nula stares into the distance, but he can't quite make out the end of the room through the infinite convergence of overloaded shelves that, beyond the food sections, hold the kitchen supplies, the tools, the clothes, the stationary, and, far off, hanging from the ceiling, a mist of wheelbarrows, colored globes, signs, and bicycles.

—A tactical position, he says.

—Starting tomorrow, they'll be announcing the wine tasting over the loudspeakers, Virginia says. And you had some signs you were going to bring?

—Everything will be here tomorrow, Nula says.

—Tell me about the product you're promoting, Virginia says. I was on vacation when everything was set up.

—It's a high quality table wine, Nula says. White and red. Our company is trying to launch more mainstream products.

—That sounds good, Virginia says.

—If the launch on Friday is a success, how about if we have dinner together? Nula says.

—Why not? Even if it isn't, Virginia says. I finish at eight. My daughter always goes out on Friday nights, anyway.

—And her father? Nula says.

Virginia laughs.

—What father?

—Oh right, Nula says. I'd forgotten that in your case the name and the person corresponded.

—That's still to be determined, Virginia says. In any case, if we have dinner on Friday I'll tell you a secret.

—About you? Nula says.

—About you, actually, Virginia says, smiling mysteriously. And suddenly, glancing at her watch, her professional demeanor returns.

—Tell your *friends of wine*, she says, that when they come tomorrow, ask for Virginia. Until Friday, then . . .

She hesitates a second.

—Nula, Nula says, fascinated by Virginia's promise and her enigmatic smile.

—Nula, of course, Virginia says. She turns around and walks down another aisle loaded with bottles, and when she reaches the next intersection she turns right and disappears. Nula stands motionless for several seconds, thinking about the promise that has suddenly rubbed Friday night tantalizingly against his imagination, and skipping over the nominal hours that in reality happen in a single block of time, and have done so since the beginning of the

162

world and will continue to do so indefinitely, he leaps over the monotonous sequence of events, arriving at the possibilities invented by his desire, which, though still incorporeal and fantastical, are more intense and gratifying than the uneven and fragmentary pieces of existence. Suddenly, the vivid anticipation that, however immaterial, is capable of triggering more than a few organic regions of his body, is completely erased, and the present moment, the brutal actuality of everything, at once transparent and impenetrable, engulfs him like a thick and hardening liquid into which things around him sediment, and where the things that move, like the hand that Nula lifts without knowing why, seem to decompose into infinite layers that only through an immense effort overcome their medium, a kind of soft glass, for a millionth of a second, before they disappear. Nula's utterly estranged gaze passes over the illuminated space, and he tells himself, *It's like the bright space in the mind into which our thoughts flow.* Even the background music seems to have stopped: its pervasiveness melts into the assemblage, and though it needs movement, change, tempo, its formulaic shape built of predictable developments and melodies, so similar to so many others, seems to pause it, a sonorous binding that halts its advance. *It's like the static nucleus of an atom of the becoming.* And then, in accelerating and colliding images, which translated into words would be more or less the following: *Otherwise, the clear part of the mind resembles that fragment of the exterior. It's like a fish tank. At the top, the brightly colored fish move silently through the light, quickly, then disappear, and some, brilliant and insistent, return again and again. But farther down, among the plants and the moss-covered rocks, the water is less transparent, clouded by old sediment, crisscrossed by vague, unrecognizable shadows, sometimes thrashing so violently that the water loses clarity all the way up, muddled by suspended silts that have been furiously agitated. Between the clear zone and the dark zone, between the bright, familiar layer and the unstable, murky depths, there's no line of demarcation but rather an uncertain, mutable border where both layers blend together and overlap, transforming each other. The lower one forks out and is lost in the depths of the body, seeking in the remote corners of the tissues and the organs the liquid that, decanted, clarifies at the bright surface, populated by the colorful, silent fauna of our waking thoughts.*

Hearing steps approaching, though unsure from where, Nula's left hand, which had been hanging in the air, drops, and he starts walking slowly back to the front of the hypermarket, without seeing anyone till he's far from the beverage section. Since he left the warehouse at noon, he's been planning to buy two cheap salamis, and he knows that near the cheese and cold cut cases there's a basket full of old, dry sausages in which he'll find what he's looking for. Digging through the pile, he picks the driest and, more importantly, the cheapest ones, and after paying for them at one of the registers walks out into the parking lot, having ended up with a plastic bag with an orange W. He senses, most likely in contrast to the air conditioned *supercenter*, that outside the temperature has gone up considerably, and when he looks up at the sky, he sees that the uniform cloud cover, a bright whitish gray, has begun to dissolve at the highest altitudes, leaving sections of a pale blue sky visible. But the sun, on this indecisive and melancholy afternoon, is nowhere to be seen.

In the car, before pulling out, he changes the label on the salamis, or actually, he tears the labels off the salamis that he's just bought, and then, carefully removing the ones from the two local chorizos, originally intended for the political advisor, attaches them to the salamis from the hypermarket, happily noting that they work exceptionally well. He knows that what he's doing is infantile, possibly unjustified and even unfair, but he refuses to give anything to the governor's political advisor, who years before was active in the same clandestine group as his father, surviving him by more than fifteen years, and who now, rather than trying to change the world like before, writes policy and edits speeches for a governor whose only merit, according to most people, *is that he doesn't steal*, who played in major tennis tournaments, reaching Wimbledon and the Roland Garros once or twice, and who's friends with a Hollywood actor who shows up in the city every so often to take him fishing upriver, at the north end of the province, for golden dorado and tiger catfish. As long as he's unsure about how the political advisor is still alive while his father is dead, Nula doesn't want to give him anything, but less from a mean prejudice than a superstition: while there's no evidence that the advisor is in any way to blame (he did live for a while abroad), it would feel like an insult to his father, a kind of treason, until he had undeniable proof of his innocence, even if the gift is from the company. The advisor himself had stopped him one day on the street, two or three months before, and when he learned that he sold wine he gave him his card and told him to come by the public offices. He sent his regards, more than once, to his mother, but when Nula relayed them, La India's sarcasm sparked his mistrust. *That guy once wanted to make the revolution with your father, and now he writes limericks for the governor to wrap his caramels in.* Nula is aware that sometimes, unfairly, the ones who mourn the dead bear a venomous grudge against everyone with the miserable audacity to go on living when they might have died in their place, but nevertheless he would've preferred that the advisor not have taken the political turn he eventually took, in solidarity with the dead, who were also his own. La India didn't accuse him of anything, apart from being alive maybe, not thinking that her husband, if he'd come out of that nightmarish time unharmed, might have followed the same course. And Nula took his mother's side, but one day La India herself called him, saying that the political advisor had come to see her and had given her some letters that Nula's father had written a long time ago, while he was an economics reporter in Rosario, in which he spoke about her, and insisting that she convince Nula to visit him at the public offices. La India had been moved by the advisor's gesture, which for Nula had come too late. His mother, most likely without hoping to, had passed her suspicion on to him. A few days later, though, he called him and they arranged the meeting that he'd had to postpone yesterday, and which Américo had managed to reschedule for this afternoon, because he'd suddenly ended up in the middle of the countryside, somewhere near Rincón, half-sheltered by Gutiérrez's multicolored umbrella. Though he didn't think the words, Nula had the vague sensation that what La India considered a touching gesture was in fact a confession of guilt. In any case, the suspicion belongs to him now, and he's decided not to give him the two local chorizos. Of course, he could just not bring anything, but he feels a juvenile need to deceive him, from the suspicion that, if the other is trying to do the same to him, his attempt, through his symmetrical deceit, will be momentarily canceled out.

But first he has to go see his brother's dentist friend. As the car leaves the bridge and enters the city, a ripple of despair passes over him and immediately vanishes, not giving him time to think about it or even to realize that it's happened. But in any case his mood changes, and the euphoria provoked by his imagined Friday night dwindles and leaves him feeling neutral, subdued, governed by financial matters, a thin varnish that covers, provisionally and laughably, the thing itself. The city is withered, in ruins. Nula sees its defects before anything else, but what he thinks he sees in the city, though he doesn't realize it, is actually a projection from inside himself. He arrives at the dentist's exactly on time. A nurse opens when he rings the bell and takes him to the waiting room, where two women and a man are reading old magazines. Five or ten minutes later, the dentist says goodbye to a patient who was in the examining room and gives Nula a friendly gesture to come in. He's a little older than Chade, but more candid and friendly; he seems more at home in the world than his brother. *Maybe his father was also a dentist and died in bed of natural causes, not riddled with bullets in a pizzeria*, he thinks, but no matter how much he tries he can't dislike him. Just the opposite: at some point during the meeting, which doesn't last more than fifteen minutes, Nula starts to think that the man could have a positive influence on his brother, drawing him from his constant, intense standoff. He, Nula, couldn't be friends with him: he's too transparent; he'd be the ideal company for a casual chat in a bar or on the bus to Rosario—Buenos Aires or Córdoba would be too much—for a wine tasting at the Iguazú hotel, or something like that, but not much more. He's apparently a pre-metaphysical being, without fears or regrets, the lack of the first sheltering him from the second, or, ultimately, Nula thinks, it might be the opposite. That more or less unconsciously open disposition is what's lacking in his brother. The dentist tells him that he's bought a wine cellar for his apartment with capacity for a hundred and fifty bottles and that's he's giving Nula free rein to stock it, thirty percent with white and seventy percent with red. He tells him the amount he's willing to invest, a considerable sum, and gives him a ten percent deposit. And as he follows him to the door he tells him that his brother is an excellent dentist, that he's well-respected by his colleagues and that he'll go far in the field. *He's a scrupulous professional, and liked by everyone, despite his reserved nature*, are his exact words. It's clear he doesn't have much time to waste because, Nula realizes, there are now five patients flipping through old magazines in the waiting room.

The meeting with the advisor lasts much longer. The governor's aide doesn't seem in a hurry to buy wine, as though all he really wanted to do was talk about vague, fragmentary, disconnected things with him. Every so often he mentions *Beto*—that's the governor's nickname, which everyone uses—gesturing with a slight nod

167

toward somewhere on the first floor where his office must be, and once in a while smiles ironically when he refers to him, possibly to demonstrate his familiarity with *the supreme leader*, as they call him in *La Región*, or possibly for the opposite reason, to suggest to Nula that even though he holds an eminent post as political advisor to the government, he hasn't sacrificed his right to critique it. He's dressed with the conventional elegance of a politician, suit, striped shirt, tie, and has on his desk a stack of printed pages which he was in the middle of correcting, with an expensive pen, when Nula interrupted him. He's affectionate, candid, and doesn't appear to give much weight to his current position; he apparently doesn't even seem to realize the contradiction with his past, much less to be embarrassed by it, and though all his gestures, his words, his actions, and his allusions seem to indicate that his situation is the most natural thing in the world, a damp glow in his eyes, which alternate, in conflict, between steady and evasive, betrays a dishar-mony, a lack of resolution, a wound that refuses to heal. Wrapped up as he is—and as he always will be—in his family history, Nula is unable to translate everything written in his look. All he sees is an effort to conceal, and implied by this same effort, the shame of still being alive, from the son of his murdered friend. But his father's execution is only a detail in a larger picture: with neither cynicism nor indifference, he thinks that he'd be able to toler-ate the advisor if some ulterior interest had justified it. His look says more than one, two, or a thousand murders could. It says, *We thought we were out there to change our lives but it turned out we were seeking death. And the victims forget the taste of oppression when, little by little, and almost without realizing it, they become the executioners.* It's possible that even he himself doesn't know what he's think-ing. The province of happy mediums in which he now survives, languishes, and drifts aimlessly, is comfortable enough and doesn't demand the kind of moral bargain that he's convinced he'd never accept anyway, though he doesn't deny that his political reversals obey philosophical positions that could be considered relativist, eclectic, and above all realist. But if his interior life were compared to an electrical system, one might say that, although on the surface everything seems to be working fine, in the damp, weak spark in his eyes, the glow too steady or too unstable, to an attentive observer, the constant threat of a short circuit is obvious. But Nula's suspicions aren't political, they're personal, because if the opposite were the case (and Nula is unaware of this), they'd apply to his father too. What's clear is that, while the advisor continues to feel suspicious, and though he still doesn't want to give him anything, he no longer wants to deceive him, and probably didn't even want to before going up to see him, because he'd forgotten the false chorizos that he was planning to give him. At the end of the visit he sells him a small quantity of wine that he'll deliver to his house next week. Nula packs up his brochures and the deposit check and walks out into the street.

Before getting in the car, he takes off his coat, folds it carefully, and lays it on the back seat. The parking lot of the government offices is hotter than he'd expected. The afternoon has grown spongy and humid, colorless, vague. Despite his two showers, the first in the morning and the second at Lucía's house in Paraná, he feels greasy and exhausted; something, he's not sure what, wraps him up with a sense of indecision, of sadness possibly, of oppression. He'd like to go straight home and not come back till tomorrow. He shakes his head slowly, with a long exhale, and gets in the car and turns the key, but for half a minute, give or take, he doesn't make the decision to move. As the day has progressed, certain regions inside him have grown opaque and confused, spongy like the afternoon light, ambiguous like the day itself, neither overcast nor clear, fall or winter, and finally coming to an end. When night falls, erasing not only the light but also the ambiguity, when he sits within

169

the bright circle under the lamp, after dinner, reading or drafting a clean copy of the hours that have passed since he last woke, he might feel somewhat better, and the agitated sediment that clouds the fish tank will settle, sinking back to the bottom, and above, in the bright layer, the sharply colored, agile, silent fish will flash again. He pulls out slowly from the parking lot and drives around the Parque Sur, moving down a wide, tree-lined street that curves southwest, but two blocks later he turns again, to the north, once again on a straight, broad avenue that leads to the city center. The sidewalks lined with one- and two-story houses are nearly empty, the houses seeming deserted at that hour—the doors and windows are shut and no one is looking out to the sidewalk, maybe because of the indecisive weather, or the hour, or the fact that there's really nothing interesting to see. Every so often, the first bags of trash appear on the curb. Halfway down the block, three boys, one no more than two or three years old, scruffy and filthy, have opened a bag and are digging through it. Getting a jump on the waste pickers, who've made a way of life from the rational exploitation of garbage, the boys rummage through the bags like animals, trying to satisfy some immediate need, hunger or thirst, or in search of some interesting object, a cardboard figurine, a piece of thread, or a shard of mirror, a lost coin without monetary value but which could become something distinct or a fetish or simply a toy, transporting them for a moment, through its imaginary value, or its precarious and recreational use, from the animal immediacy in which they exhaust themselves, to the tenuous, human expectation that poverty, from birth till death, ceaselessly, confiscates from them.

Two blocks later, he sees a man on the corner, staring south, and when he's about half a block away, Nula recognizes Carlos Tomatis, with his perennial blue jacket and his light-colored summer pants, but this time he has on a white shirt and a dark tie that, cinched tight around his heck, slightly pinches the tanned skin that hangs below his jaw line. Nula slows down and finally stops next to Tomatis and, rolling down the window closest to the sidewalk, opposite the driver's side, he leans toward the opening just as Tomatis's dark face appears in it.

—I'm waiting for the bus, Tomatis says, but I had to let a few go by because they weren't full enough.

Nula laughs and opens the door.

—Get in, I'll give you a lift.

Tomatis gets in and sits down, giving him a pat on the shoulder.

—I accept, but your good deed has deprived me of one of life's most exquisite pleasures.

Nula laughs again and shakes his head, indicating, with that slow gesture, the legendary incorrigibility of his passenger.

—So you're waiting for the bus? Are you heading home? Tomatis says he is, but Nula keeps talking. What brings you to such a remote neighborhood at this hour, and looking so sharp in your white shirt?

—It may sound like a lie, Tomatis says, but I'm coming from a wake. The ex-publisher of *La Región*. He retired a long time ago. But he was the one who hired me at the paper and who somehow avoided firing me for years and wouldn't even let me go when I decided I was finished with all that.

—He was a good person, then, Nula says.

—Bearing in mind that he ran a newspaper, there were still a few ounces of decency left in him, so I guess so, yes, Tomatis says, and after thinking it over a few seconds adds, sorrowfully, But he thought that running a newspaper gave him the authority to have opinions about literature.

—Well, Nula says, I sell wine but I still act like know something about philosophy.

—It's different, Tomatis says, and though he seems to consider the reasons for that difference for a second, he apparently doesn't think it necessary to explain them.

—You caught me in a good mood, Nula says. I have a present for you.

With a curious smile, his head turned slightly toward Nula, Tomatis waits for more details about what he's getting. But Nula, acting mysteriously and moving deliberately slowly in order to prolong the wait and in this way postpone indefinitely the moment of revelation, gestures toward the back seat.

—Back there, the white plastic bag, he says eventually.

With some effort, twisting himself in the seat until his knee is propped up on it, Tomatis leans toward the back of the car, where, alongside Nula's carefully laid out coat, there are two plastic bags, one blank and another with the large orange W of the hypermarket emblazoned on it. He picks up the first one and holds it up to Nula.

—This one? he says, huffing slightly and checking its contents. There's two salamis inside.

—No! Nula shouts. Bad dog! And then, lowering his voice, says, The other one.

Without mentioning that, in his clumsiness, the unmarked bag has fallen on his jacket, though luckily without opening completely, Tomatis picks up the other bag and turns around in his seat, and, somewhere between confused and disappointment, asks, A gift from the hyper?

—Nooo! Nula says. Not on your fucking life. I put it in the wrong bag.

Tomatis peers inside.

—I regret to inform you that some goblin has transformed the gold watch you planned to give me into another couple of salamis, he says thoughtfully, with feigned resignation.

—Those are no mere salamis, Nula says, those are two hand-made artisanal chorizos manufactured especially for Amigos del Vino, but because the labels came off I can't sell them. And I can't keep them either, because that'd mean I was skimming off the top. And because I obviously can't give them to just anyone, I take the opportunity offered by this encounter, which transpired thanks to a chain of contingencies that in the end turned about favorably, the death of the former publisher, your noble, compassionate reflection before his remains, a series of insufficiently full buses, and my appearance, to carry out the offering. They're yours.

—*Habibi*, this is so touching, it gets me right in the trigeminal, Tomatis says, exaggerating his emotion and taking on an overly serious expression and even bringing his hand to his chest and resting his palm on his heart. For a couple of handmade chorizos I'd be liable to send my grandmother off to chart the rings of Saturn.

And he's silent for a moment. A few seconds later, without really knowing why, he starts talking about Gutiérrez, about his leaving the city, his complete, definitive, and strange disappearance, and about his sudden and inexplicable return. Tomatis tells him that once, in Paris, he and Pichón had met an Italian girl at a party who said she knew Gutiérrez, that he was working as a screenwriter between Switzerland and Italy, but that he wrote the screenplays under a pseudonym. Gutiérrez had first come to the city because his grandmother, who was penniless—his parents had died years before—sent him to parochial school, from some backwater north of Tostado, thanks to the help of the parish priest. After high school he enrolled at the law school, where he met Escalante, Rosemberg, and César Rey, who were younger than him, and had more money, and for years they were inseparable. His Roman Law professor, Calcagno, got him a job at the firm he ran with his partner, Mario

173

Brando, the precisionist poet. Tomatis's sister knows a woman who knows the couple who works for him—Amalia and Faustino—that they seem to have a high opinion of him and would take a bullet for him. Suddenly, Tomatis stops talking about Gutiérrez, possibly to create, deliberately, a feeling of suspense that leaves Nula with a slight feeling of frustration.

Seeing the approaching corner through the windshield, Tomatis realizes that he's reaching his house, and returning to common-place topics, says, The weather's supposed to be nice tomorrow. I'll get off at the corner.

The same pat on the shoulder that he gave him when getting in the car is repeated before he opens the door and steps out, with some effort, onto the sidewalk.

—I can't wait to try them, he says, shaking the hypermarket bag with the two local chorizos. Thanks. I'll see you.

—On Sunday, first of all, Nula says. Without having understood completely, or possibly without even having heard him, Tomatis closes the door softly and disappears behind the car. When he pulls a few meters from the curb, a blood red light suddenly fills the rearview mirror, surprising Nula, who takes a few seconds to realize that the afternoon sun, after having been invisible for a few days, has reappeared suddenly, in the west. At the end of the street a red blur covers the sky up to a certain altitude, above which, like a gathered canopy, a uniform ceiling of clouds begins, motionless all day and now starting to fold itself up. The grayish vault is stained red, a brilliant red that, as it washes over the houses, the streets, the trees, its magnetic waves and tones in constant and impercep-tible transformation, makes it seem uncanny and remote, as though he were seeing it not from a mobile point, crossing it from one end to the other if he wanted, but rather from the source itself, from the very same red incandescence that stains it. Nula feels at once inside and outside the world, and though, like every other day, he's on his way home to rejoin his wife and children, whose company is in fact pleasant, he'd like to prolong his trip indefinitely and put off the moment he sees them, fearing that what has suddenly separated and isolated him, outside the world, will invade them when they're finally together.

Nula thinks of Lucía's gift, its useless, belated ease, not having left them with anything apart from a kind of void, and, possibly, mutual compassion. That mythical pleasure, so long delayed in entering the laborious, wandering train of occurrence, was snuffed out suddenly that afternoon and disappeared forever from the deceitful and brilliant constellation that, without knowing whether it beats inside us or in some remote corner of the external, we call desire. For years, Nula believed that Lucía continued to incarnate the persistence of that myth, made possible because there's matter, because there's a world, because in the beginning there was energy, force, and then mass, expansion, proliferation, from all those inconceivable accidents, making ever more intricate combinations, patiently and ceaselessly, sparking, in a constant flux, within the existent, eventually producing that one spark—him, Nula—and placing it one morning at the bar on the corner of Mendoza and San Martín, where the Gran Doria stood for years, along with that student who, just at the moment when he was turning toward the door, called out to ask him a question about a Public Law textbook, delaying him a few seconds, just long enough that, as he walked out into the street, he bumped into the girl in red and without knowing why, started to follow her.

THURSDAY

THE
FLOODING

SOLDI SMILES THOUGHTFULLY, IS THAT WHAT HE TOLD YOU?

It must be forty years since Tomatis last took a bus, if he ever took one, but every time someone sees him on a corner waiting for a taxi, because he only ever takes taxis, or something else, or nothing, he always makes the same joke, which, if it makes the other person laugh, has given him the same intense pleasure for the last four decades, more or less: *I'm waiting for the bus, but I had to let the last few go by because they weren't full enough.*

Gabriela, sitting next to Soldi, in the passenger seat, smiles too, thinking that, because as unlikely as it might seem, when she emerged from her mother's womb into the world "Carlitos" was already waiting for her, it's the first time she's heard the joke. Soldi, his elbow resting on the steering wheel, half-conceals his interlocutor, the wine salesman who, through the open window of his own car, a dark green station wagon, or a long hatchback maybe, has just relayed his encounter with Tomatis, yesterday afternoon,

179

on that corner at the southern end of the city. The two cars are parked facing in opposite directions, very close to each other, on the slope that leads from the asphalt to the sandy road, because they'd passed just as she and Soldi were returning from Gutiérrez's and he, Nula, was on his way there to drop off a few cases of wine, and so the two drivers had expertly lined their windows up, and after rolling them down and turning off their engines, had started to talk between the cars, Soldi's pointing up, toward the asphalt, and the other toward the sandy road. To see Nula's face, Gabriela would have to lean forward in a way that would feel uncomfortable, not only because it would force her body to contort slightly, but also because her attitude could be mistaken for a sign of excessive interest in the conversation that, in what might be considered a falsely casual ironic tone, Soldi and Nula carry on. And when she hears Soldi say that he and Gabriela actually have a date with Tomatis for seven at the Amigos del Vino bar, Gabriela lets her mind wander, gazing at the sky and at the landscape through the windshield and her own window, thinking, with a sort of gentle disdain, that their gossip is not that interesting, and concentrates instead on the luminous afternoon.

Over the past few days the rain has cleaned the air, which is now clear and warm. The sky is a radiant blue, and far above them scattered plumes of bright white clouds drift across they sky, so slowly that they seem motionless, and the sun shines as if those same rains had cleaned it of all its impurities. The first hints of fall have been hushed, and the early afternoon light has a shade of spring. And Gabriela thinks—possibly because what she learned about herself that morning predisposes her to the thought—that April is preparing to offer them, for next few days, a postscript to the summer, before the fall conclusively arrives. Soldi, Nula, and she herself all have on lightweight and light-colored clothes, and the slight heat that can now be felt, in a few hours, and tomorrow at the latest, will no longer require the diminutive. Even just now, when they were having a drink next to the pool before moving to the table in the large, cool, and well-appointed kitchen, she wouldn't have disliked going in the water. They'd worked with Gabriela since ten, and at noon, when they were preparing to head back to the city (Gabriela was impatient to call Rosario and Caballito with the news), Gutiérrez insisted that they stay for lunch: he had two catfish ready in the fridge, the first of the year apparently, which he'd been given in Rincón, pulled live from the river in front of him, a little more than twenty-four hours before. Gabriela had decided to stay for a few reasons: first, because clearly the invitation had caused Pinocchio (Soldi) intense pleasure; because the chance to eat those mythic fish this close to Rincón itself sounded really appealing to her too, especially because of how hungry she was; and finally, if they stayed for lunch they could work an hour longer, which would help the project move along, because within the history of the provincial avant-garde that she'd been preparing with Soldi thanks to a shared grant they'd gotten in Buenos Aires, precisionism was already taking too much time, too much space, and too much energy, because its history had ended up blending into their own lives.

When they'd stopped to talk between the cars, the catfish had been their first topic of conversation. *You ate the catfish, my catfish?* Nula had said in a parody of indignant resentment, hyperbolically emphasizing the possessive and telling them that on Tuesday night, after having walked for hours in the rain with Gutiérrez, just when he was about to be compensated by the baked catfish—the same ones they'd just eaten—an unexpected family visit had spoiled his dinner plans (he, Nula, had already offered to contribute a bottle of white wine from the car). Gabriela thought she sensed, despite the farcical tone, a slight tension in Nula's reaction, though she was unsure what might have caused it, but decided, finally, that it could be the result of a slight embarrassment, possibly caused by the undeniably pretentious competition between him and Soldi for superiority with regard to their friendship with Gutiérrez, the foreigner who enjoys a manifold prestige thanks to his years in Europe, his apparent wealth, and, especially, his enigmatic life. But the tension in Nula disappears almost immediately, as do the fish from the conversation, when he starts describing his encounter with Tomatis.

The moment they are living in is peaceful, if not benevolent. They're young, all three are under thirty, they're all healthy, and they've all bracketed out the darker things in life, the way an orator holds back a forceful objection that he'll have to confront later on. Gabriela thinks that Pinocchio and Nula's jousting is meant to show the other how at home they are in the world. The autonomous, savage hum that occupies their thoughts when they're alone seems forgotten in favor of the conversation, where their concentration produces an exchange of words that are vivid and sharp and which, while apparently spontaneous, were carefully elaborated before resonating in the external world and fading away immediately, leaving an immaterial and approximate meaning in each other's memories. With the impartial disposition of someone who, for the moment, can be indifferent, but also cautiously, Gabriela studies them: Soldi's dark profile, severe despite the smile that appears through his beard, contrasts with his childhood nickname, Pinocchio, which his mother, no doubt thinking he was the most beautiful little doll in the world, or at least the most helpless, had given him in the first days of his life. The shape of his nose and ears don't match up at all to his namesake's, and with regard to his moral qualities, Soldi is incapable of lying, meaning his likeness to the puppet must correspond to feelings that Gabriela attributes to his mother, unless, spinning even more finely, she supposes that, in giving him the puppet's nickname (if in fact she was the one who gave it to him), the mother, recoiling from the pain of childbirth, from her worry, from the fear for the son who would be with her till she died, had been tempted, unconsciously, to deny her maternity, and had given her son the nickname of the motherless marionette: *Unless the opposite is the case, and she thinks of herself as the kind and beautiful fairy who, with a wave of her magic wand, had given life to the wooden doll,* Gutiérrez says perfectly clearly somewhere inside herself, and her lips form an involuntary smile that causes Nula to look at her, confused, from the other car, and for Soldi, because of Nula's expression, to turn his head toward her with an inquisitive smile, more apparent in his eyes than on his lips, barely visible beneath the dark black beard, which is tangled and metallic though he keeps it meticulously trimmed.

—It's nothing, Gabriela says, so they'll go back to their cheerful, contented exchange, allowing her to keep observing them. Even more cautiously, Gabriela studies the wine salesman now: his expression is friendly and open, possibly too much so. Should she remind him that he isn't with two potential clients and doesn't need to lay on the charm so much? With some reluctance, Gabriela tells herself that she might be judging him too harshly, that this might be his natural way of acting, and besides he's an old friend of Pinocchio's, who talks about him often. Clearly he likes to dress well, although that could be a result of the work rather than a personal inclination. His hair is light brown and clean cut, and his forearm, resting on the edge of the open window, is covered with a fleece somewhat darker than his hair, which the summer sun must have bleached slightly. And though he must have shaved carefully this morning, his cheeks and chin and neck are already darkened by specks of beard that sprout abundantly on his healthy, coarse, and masculine skin—that capillary abundance, though controlled, from his head to his beard, his forearm, and, Gabriela is sure, on his chest as well, is the product of his being *turco*, which is to say, of Arabic descent. When they met a few weeks ago at the Amigos del Vino bar (he may not run it, but he does come and go behind the counter, serving himself and his friends, though he knows to never touch the register and notes down everything he drinks), he seemed really angry with Gutiérrez for telling him that he was with his daughter, whom he, Nula, apparently knew before, and very well, but when Pinocchio told him that it may in fact have been true, he calmed down, though for the rest of the time he was with them he remained uneasy and pensive. But when they saw him again a few days later, he'd already seen Gutiérrez again to sell him the wine, and by then seemed to have recovered his composure and his good humor—if in fact the cheerfulness that he displays now is not a professional but rather an authentic quality. A tractor trailer that she hasn't seen coming because of the direction she's facing passes full speed toward the city and startles her, not only from the sound of the engine and the roar that the enormous, heavy mass produces as it moves, but also from the vibrations, so violent that the two cars parked on the slope that leads from the asphalt to the sandy road shake too. The red trailer is covered with a dark canvas, its loose edges flapping because of the speed, and as it passes them, Gabriela can just make out a suggestion printed in black letters on the rear: VISIT HELVECIA, FOR THE GOLDEN DORADO. All three watch it move away, though Nula, with his back to the road, finds it more difficult, because he has to turn almost all the way around to see it shrink and finally disappear toward the city. Nula checks his watch but doesn't seem ready to leave yet; after a few seconds of silence that follow the truck's interruption of their conversation, Nula leans back against his seat, searching for her eyes, and asks:

—What's new with our local avant-garde?

Gabriela hesitates a few seconds before she responds, because she wasn't expecting the question and because there's a hint of irony in it, but finally she explains:

—The testimonies coincide and actually overlap quite a bit, at least at some points. We've divided the project into three periods, and have gathered different informants for each of them: the forties, the fifties, and the sixties and seventies. Luckily, there's a lot on paper.

Nula nods, pressing his lips and widening his eyes to show that he's giving her his complete attention, at once respectful and reflective. The attitude pleases Gabriela, because it seems to show that Nula is able to behave with some deference and stop himself from acting so arrogantly. Soldi, for his part, also leans back against his seat, making room for the two of them to see each other.

—The main problem is with the head of the movement, Mario Brando. Some people say he was a real artist, others think he was a fraud.

—That's so often the case, isn't it, Nula says.

—That's true, Gabriela says. But there's some consensus from trustworthy sources toward the latter option.

When she says *consensus from trustworthy sources*, Gabriela is thinking of Tomatis in particular, who, each time he refers to Brando calls him, somewhat affectedly, *that miserable fraud*, or, more simply, *Brando the Swine*. And she continues her explanation for Nula, while Soldi, upright against the seat back so as to not interfere in their visual field, also listening extremely carefully, appears to verify, with his eyes, the things Gabriela is saying. For the second period, the second half of the fifties especially, they have the testimony of Gutiérrez himself, in certain respects invaluable, because he worked at Brando and Calcagno's firm, where Brando was always assigning him work for the magazine. For the first period, they have Cuello, who ran a *criollista* magazine in the fifties, *Copas y bastos*, and for the sixties and seventies, they have, among others, Tomatis, who edited the literary supplement to *La Región* for a long time, where, by the way, he never published a

185

single line of his own work, but which was a platform that Brando often utilized. There are other informants as well, protagonists or witnesses, or both things simultaneously, at one time or another. Then there're the magazines, *El Río,* edited by Higinio Gómez in the early thirties; the three eras of *Nexos,* the official organ of the precisionists; *Tabula rasa,* an avant-garde magazine that started to come out in the mid fifties; *Espiga,* published by the neoclassicists of the '40s generation, who were the most competitive with the precisionists: like them, they mostly wrote sonnets; and, especially in the sixties, *Catharsis,* published by the *Instituto de Letras* out of the philosophy department in Rosario. Of course there had been a thousand other magazines published in the region since the turn of the century, representing every national and international tendency in art and literature, and which she and Soldi used for their general study of avant-garde movements, but all the ones she just mentioned had more or less a direct relationship with the precisionists. And then there were the literary supplements and the other sections in local and national papers. And, finally, a singular document, which they'd given Tomatis a copy of, and which they were thinking of publishing as an appendix to their book, but anonymously, because its author, an older man who still lives in the city, and one of their principal informants, doesn't want to be named because of his connection to the families of several members of the movement. It's the fragment of a tentative history, more or less novelized, written at the end of the seventies, *the decade,* in the words of its author, *that condemned so many decent people of both sexes to silence, to hiding, to exile, to torture, and to death.*

A familiar sound interrupts Gabriela's explanatory gloss: a horse approaching at a slow trot, its hooves striking quietly against the sandy ground, which, before she has time to turn around, starts up the embankment, scratching softly against the slightly inclined surface where the loose gravel left behind by the paving mixes with the sand. The horse and rider appear suddenly, very close to the car, so much so that, to see the rider completely, Gabriela has to lean her head out the window. And she doesn't regret it, because she immediately recognizes, with that fondness particular to city dwellers, a figure typical of the coastal countryside, so magnified by her young imagination, a figure represented thousands of times in oil, in watercolor, or in pencil or ink, or even in wood or in marble, by every kind of plastic artist, painters, sculptors, weavers, and illustrators, or recalled in verse and in prose, in elevated or popular language, rhapsodized in *chamarritas* and *litoraleñas*, captured in movement by documentaries or films of touristic or critical stripe: A boy of ten or twelve, with dark skin and hair, barefoot and shabbily dressed, riding bareback on a compliant horse that he urges on by kicking its sides with his heels, or by whipping it briskly on its flanks with a green branch. At the edge of the asphalt the horse stops, uncertain, though it's crossed the road countless times in its life, and the whips with the branch and the kicks become more vigorous, forcing it to brave the provincial highway, changing the sound its hooves make, now on the hard and resonant pavement. And when he reaches the other side, the opposite edge, where the saddest and dustiest weeds in the world grow, the sound of the hooves disappears, creating a sharp contrast between the proximity of the animal, its movements, and the silence with which it executes them.

Gutiérrez, according to Gabriela, who's just put her head back inside the window, noticing, meanwhile, a considerable difference in temperature between the inside and the outside of the car—as unlikely as it may seem, the air is warmer outside—Gutiérrez shows an extreme tolerance for Brando, despite being fully aware, at the same time, of his character traits. He seems to confuse Brando with his own youth, assigning to the former the supposed values of the latter. But he's a meticulous and scrupulous informant, and when he has some doubt he doesn't hesitate to consult his library so as to not overlook anything. Between 1956 and 1960, more or less, the years he studied law and worked at the firm, correspond to the third and final era of *Nexos*, during which three issues were published. Each issue of the magazine had less to do with precisionism and more with Brando's own literary and political career: though he'd been a cultural attaché in Rome during the first Peronist regime, he eventually withdrew from the government, going so far as to take part in the coup that overthrew it in 1956. Gutiérrez is aware of Brando's opportunism, but it doesn't seem to bother him. At first, the precisionists would meet at a bar downtown that they could all get to easily, but when Brando started to have political aspirations he'd choose more discreet locations—according to Tomatis, his goals demanded a group of literary disciples and collaborators, but since most of them had social and economic positions less relevant than his, he compartmentalized his relationships, to one side the rich and powerful philistines, and to the other his disciples, poor but useful for his literary career—Gutiérrez, who doesn't hesitate to recognize the truth to that statement, doesn't appear too scandalized by it, as though the years, the actions, and the protagonists of that lost world had lived a kind of mythic existence, drawn with hard lines in immutable roles they were forced to represent, and were therefore resistant to change, to analysis, and, especially, to ethical critique. According to Gutiérrez, around 1959, Brando spent a year working out the problems presented by the translation of a classical sonnet to the language of precisionism, which is true, because there are some examples of this from the last issue, which appeared in 1960. Apart from his remarkable memory and the pleasure he seems to draw from her and Soldi's incitements to explore it, Gutiérrez offers a number of supplementary qualities as an informant: that he can tell on his own what might interest them, that he's a talented student of people, an ethnographer almost, at least with regard to that time period. After more than thirty years away he's able to describe the small world in which the precisionist poets emerged, and where he didn't belong, with countless unexpected and invaluable details and a curious mix of indulgence and irony. What they've heard him say could be summarized and transcribed more or less as follows: *The group was an assortment of famous lawyers and public servants, liberals and addicts of the eleven o'clock Mass, philistine patrons and high school teachers, Peronists, conservatives, and radicals, wealthy and poor, led by an ambitious and scrupulous man with a visceral duplicity, and who'd deserve our hatred had his ambitions not been so mean and transparent: to become a minister in the provincial government or land some subaltern post in an embassy and have his name appear every so often in the national press. His most unfortunate trait was his avarice: despite the fact that he'd inherited a fortune from his father, who'd gotten rich from a pasta factory he'd owned in the early part of the century, and had multiplied his assets at the law firm, he always contrived to have his coffee paid for by his disciples, these poor bastards who had meal stipends from the public assistance office or from the national university. But he was a good leader, and when he put aside his darling precisionism he could manage to write a decent sonnet.* According to Gutiérrez, his indecent attachment to money had cut short his political career, because in '56, after the Revolución Libertadora, they'd given him a post as undersecretary of something, Gutiérrez didn't quite remember what, but Gabriela and Soldi already knew that it was Undersecretary of Public Works, which he was forced to resign from a year and a half later because he'd taken some liberties with public funds.

—He resurfaced in the seventies, Soldi says. In '76, his brother-in-law, General Ponce, the son of the other General Ponce, his father-in-law, tried to get him a ministership, but Brando pulled out and instead wrote a few articles justifying the coup. When Elisa and El Gato disappeared, Tomatis had gone to see him.

An intense expression appears on Gabriela's face. Of course, she'd known that story long before she and Soldi started their history of precisionism and the other avant-garde movements in the province. It feels personal to her, and though she never knew either Elisa or Gato Garay, she is aware of how difficult it must've been for "Carlitos"—that's how she's called him since she learned to talk, sometime before her first birthday—to go see Brando and ask him to intervene for his disappeared friends. That story is part of her family history, she heard it often during those years, whispered by her parents, and much later, after she came back from the U.S., where she'd gone to finish her literature degree, from Tomatis himself, not as a tragedy but rather as a farce whose subject wasn't his friends' disappearance but the personality of Mario Brando.

From the other car, Nula carefully studies Gabriela's expression, while simultaneously considering her, in a sincerely disinterested way, at least consciously, as a sexual object. Earlier, it seemed that she was studying him in the same way, but he's learned, especially after his marriage, that when other women undertake a similar appraisal they tend to do it simply out of habit, often without feeling at all implicated by it, and it's therefore the impression of having been observed by her shortly before that sanctions his own sexual consideration of her. Her face is full and attractive, accentuated by wavy chestnut hair and a vivid and mobile gaze. A slight blush had appeared on her cheeks, darkened by the recent summer, in a sudden concentration that caused her lips to pinch slightly and her eyes to glow and then narrow and her head to freeze, as though she were bracing herself against an old injury. But she recovers herself immediately and, returning to the present, adopts a languid and earthly expression and prepares to continue. Nula compares her to his own wife and finds some points in common, though it's not really surprising since they are the same age and come from similar backgrounds; Diana, though, seems to control her emotions better. Last night, for example, when he'd gotten home after having been with Lucía in Paraná and visiting two clients in the city, it was obvious that Diana would've liked more details about the way that he, Nula, had spent is day, but he knew there was no way she'd ask him, and he couldn't have given them anyway because on his moral spectrum (an extremely subjective one, in fact), silence is permissible but lying isn't. After dinner, they'd made a game of repurposing lines from Omar Kayyám for the promotional cards, and what made them laugh the most was how hard it was, because in the *Rubaiyat* the glorification of wine was always followed by the violent critique of one thing or another, power, religion, conformism, death, themes automatically prohibited from advertising language, and though Américo is a self-proclaimed agnostic, he has enough common sense to know that publicity shouldn't offend anyone's sensibilities. And it wasn't hard for him and Diana to realize that the tone of ecumenical tolerance that dominates official discourse in every corner of the planet has the same characteristics as advertising language. For example, one stanza read, *This night, two cups of wine, / will make me rich twice over,* which works well as a tagline, but the third verse, *although before I must reject reason and religion,* were useless as ad copy because they'd offend both the religious pretensions and the religious sentiments of the consumer. Another verse, *Without wine it's impossible to live or to drag this body along,* were also useless because the marketing fiction about alcohol pretends that wine is a pure pleasure that produces instant joy without creating any sort of dependence. And they couldn't pick any stanzas (there were many) in which Kayyám refers to death, because its proximity to mentions of wine would give the product a negative image, so instead they amused themselves by cutting and pasting verses and rearranging them in such a way that none of the counterproductive elements would end up on the cards. They had enjoyed themselves after dinner, and when they went to bed they were about to make love, but at the last minute Diana decided she didn't want to. Nula went to sleep annoyed, not because he wanted her so badly that night, but rather because he believed, without realizing it, that the sexual act with her would erase the consequences of what had happened that afternoon with Lucía, sweeping it more quickly into the past, a superstition that he suffered from every time he had extramarital relations.

From his privileged position, having had erotic contact with two beautiful young women the day before, Nula congratulates himself on his impartial and disinterested assessment of Gabriela Barco as a sexual object. It doesn't occur to him to think that Gabriela experiences something similar, and that she might have even more compelling reasons to consider herself authorized to it: having achieved the principal object of all amorous practice, she's momentarily indifferent to its secondary benefits, and the countless number of men who could have provided them to her are clumped together in an asexual mass, not counting José Carlos, her partner, an economist in Rosario who at one point in the two or three thorough and affectionate embraces the month before had managed to plant the seed of what, this morning, once she had the results from the second test, has begun to enchant and fascinate her, enveloping her for the duration of the process that has been initiated, a transitory and autonomous system inaccessible to others from several different points of view. The recollection of this fact flushes her tea-colored irises with a glow so different from the introspective fury that just now inflamed them that Nula, disconcerted, turns his eyes from Soldi to look at her, while Soldi himself, having been watching Nula, tries to look at Gabriela from the corner of his eye without surrendering his perpendicular position, his back upright against the seat so as to not block their visual field, without being able to see anything in particular in her face. And when Nula finally meets her eyes, from which, by now, any trace of emotion has disappeared, Gabriela continues. According to Gutiérrez, she says, Calcagno had given him the job at the law firm to help him with his own work, but less than a month into the job, Brando was already giving him work that had to do with the precisionist movement generally, and with his own career in particular, and so often that he soon became a sort of private secretary. Not only did he edit the magazine and set up meetings and arrange the movement's activities, but he also typed out its leader's poems and articles and sometimes even wrote his personal correspondence. Gutiérrez claims that Brando wrote lots of poems that had nothing to do with the precisionist aesthetic and which were better, as far as he could tell, than the ones he published, but she and Soldi hadn't been able to confirm this because the family—his wife was still alive and his two daughters, who'd both married naval officers, had moved to the south—refused to collaborate with them or even to see them, and except for a few pre-precisionist poems written during his adolescence and published in *La Región*'s Sunday literary page and in some student magazines, there was no trace left of his traditional poetry. Every so often, Gutiérrez would quote the first line of an alexandrine sonnet that, according to him (and he seems to be the only one who read it), was called "To a pear," and which went, Gabriela says, concentrating a second to remember the exact phrasing of the line she's about to quote: *Juicy immanence, the universe incarnate.* When he hears the line, Soldi, relaxing and turning toward Nula, as though he'd just woken from a dream, filled with a light and emphatic euphoria, interrupting Gabriela Barco without taking the trouble to ask, in a voice raised a bit too much by his sudden excitement, interjects: *Gutiérrez also remembers the first hendecasyllable of a precisionist sonnet*—he practically shouts, in the tone of someone proffering a revelation—*that apparently he never published or even finished. The line, according to Gutiérrez,* Pinocchio says, *goes, The scalpel scratches the epithelium.* And shaking her head and laughing, not at all put off by Solid's sudden interruption, Gabriela repeats, *The scalpel scratches the epithelium.* With a short, almost inaudible sarcastic laugh, Soldi flattens himself against the seat again and falls silent.

For Carlitos—Nula, who knows him less intimately than his interlocutors, after an infinitesimal hesitation deep inside himself, translates his name to *Tomatis*—Gutiérrez's claim that Brando, despite his intransigent declarations and his authoritarian manifestos, wrote non-precisionist poems in secret is plausible enough, first of all because a duplicitous discourse was innate to him, and also because if the ship of precisionism capsized, overburdened by all the neophytes that the movement had attracted, he'd have his lifeboat of traditional poetry ready. As Tomatis sees it, Brando was the most dubious experimentalist anyway, because despite his professed renovation of poetics through scientific discourse (first theoretical postulate of precisionism), he spent all his time denigrating free verse and insisting that traditional meter and rhyme should be the principal instruments of precisionism because, like music, they comprised a synthesis of harmony and mathematics. Tomatis says that the precisionists were the only avant-garde poets in the whole world, *and probably in the whole solar system and even in the known universe,* he'd sometimes add with a vague and disoriented look around him, *who between 1949 and 1960 claimed that the renovation of the sonnet was the fundamental task of any literary revolution.* He'd often laugh at them, saying that their canonical texts were *Popular Science* and the rhyming dictionary. And even today he refuses to take Brando or his followers seriously, and even though he doesn't admit it, allowing himself a momentary concession that could be interpreted as a veiled critique of the intellectual champion of precisionism, "Carlitos" Tomatis *is incredibly annoyed that Pinocchio and I are giving the movement so much space in our book.*

—We can't just ignore it, Soldi says, relaxing in his seat, speaking to Nula but turning back and forth to Gabriela, as though to ask her approval for everything he says. In the forties, he says, the movement created a stir, even on the national level. Brando regularly published articles in *La Prensa* and *La Nación*. Cuello, who is our principal informant for the first period, and who, for political reasons especially, thinks more or less the same of Brando as Tomatis, admits that the cultural life in the province was genuinely shaken by the arrival of precisionism. Like every belligerent avant-garde, they had almost everyone against them, and in particular Cuello's group—what you might call pastoral realists—which practiced a kind of social *costumbrismo* and constantly published polemics against the precisionists in *Copas y bastos*. Curiously enough, after 1946, Cuello and Brando belonged to the same political party that had just taken power, but inasmuch as one was basically proletariat, the other was an elitist bourgeois who some people even called a fascist. Cuello's magazine took its name from two verses in the *Martín Fierro*: *En oros, copas y bastos / juega allí mi pensamiento*, and in the first issue the editorial collective announced (and Soldi laughs as he quotes the line): *Cups to share with friends and clubs for the ones who call us out to the crossroads.* What do you think?

—No more or less aggressive than Breton and his friends, our *criollos*, Nula says, pleased to see that the comparison provokes an involuntary smile not only in Soldi but also in Gabriela.

And Soldi continues: The best literary magazine in the city was *El río*, which Higinio Gómez published in the early thirties, before he left for Europe. Since he paid for it out of pocket, more or less, Soldi says, when he left the city the magazine disappeared, and when he returned a few years later he didn't have a penny, so he stayed in Buenos Aires and went to work at *Crítica*. But in the forties, according to Soldi, of the three important magazines that came out more or less regularly, *Nexos*, the official organ of the precisionists, was the best. *Espiga*, edited by the neoclassicists, unlike Cuello and his friends' magazine, was in direct competition with Brando. Some time later, in the mid-fifties, a highly experimental broadside called *Tabula rasa* started coming out: About this, Washington, who'd just finished a stay at the psychiatric hospital, had once (in so many words) said, *Drivel without punctuation is still drivel, but in this instance, despite being typed in all lower case, this is Drivel with a capital D.* The other two magazines, *Espiga* and *Copas y bastos*, had preceded *Nexos*, which was first published in 1945, and in a sense its release shook our small literary world from a slumber, an awakening as rude as it was abrupt: Brando and his followers, with their radical and exclusive aesthetic, were trying to show that the others didn't really exist at all. According to Soldi, the defensive rejoinders from the magazines that the precisionists attacked, and even Cuello's present memories, those of a calm and stable old man, all brim with outrage and resentment. The precisionist manifestos were graphic to the point of personal injury, and while the novelty of their theories made them feel disoriented and out of fashion, the absolute certainty with which they were formulated seemed to demonstrate beyond a doubt that up until that moment they'd been living in darkness. That clamorous novelty, widely celebrated and discussed on the radio, glossed approvingly in the press, discussed on conference panels, in university seminars, welcomed assiduously by the papers in Buenos Aires and even in Montevideo and Santiago de Chile, had something offensive about it because it apparently intended to substitute not one magazine for another, not one outdated aesthetic for an innovative one, but rather a provincial and harmonious universe in which each act and each object was indexed and classified, for another, up till then unknown, governed by laws that up till then they'd neglected, and that was there to rearrange their very essence, as if something brilliant, perfect, and rare had come to unmask them as the disordered, coarse, and antiquated beings they really were. They'd gone to bed thinking they were artists and intellectuals and had woken up ignorant and backward provincials. The precisionists' autocratic doctrines and attacks undermined not only what they wrote, but also what up till that moment they believed they'd been. And, according to Soldi, the overlapping testimonies that he and Gabi had gathered for their investigation were unequivocal: the conflicts and bitterness had lasted almost fifty years, continuing even after Brando's death—from colon cancer in 1981—made plain by Cuello and Tomatis's reactions, and especially the more or less novelized history written by their fourth informant, the old man who'd been caught up in all those conflicts for more than three decades and who now prefers to remain anonymous.

Soldi stops speaking and thinks, as though he were searching for something to add. His curly, closely trimmed black beard, which starts at his sideburns and covers his entire face and part of his neck, leaves a small opening for his mouth, which despite its owner's silence has remained half open, possibly remaining available for the use that he may want to put it to once his search through the shifting, unstable, and highly deceitful corners of his memory yields the appropriate conjunction to his previous subject and the command arrives from the organs that transform memories into words, into sonorous material, and it can propel them into the external world. But actually Soldi has been distracted from the story because an unusual thought, but which he's had before, has crossed the narrow but brightly lit stage of his mind, filling it completely. In the midst of the literary conversation that Nula apparently listens to carefully, Soldi thinks of the extra-literary consequences that they might have had for the people implicated, as they say, by all those conflicts, ruptures, betrayals, all the enmity, hatred, verbal and even physical aggression, the slander and denunciations, the

197

acts of cruelty, the suicides, and all caused by disputes over vocabulary, form, themes, and exposure in print and on the radio. Soldi knows that there was something between the son of a friend of Cuello's, a young engineer, and the daughter of a precisionist, and that their respective families had done everything they could to break up the relationship. One of the editors of *Espiga*, who people said was sexually attracted to children, had ended up committing suicide, though it was never clear if it was because of the guilt or the rumors that, because of indiscretion or malice, were circulated among other literary groups, and even within his own. Gutiérrez told them about a time he accompanied a precisionist to a radio show, and as they left the studio two neoclassicist poets who'd been waiting to come in after them started beating down the precisionist and had to be pulled off him by the radio staff, and because Brando had introduced him, in an ambiguous way, as a member of the group, when in fact he was just a clerk at the law firm, Gutiérrez himself had received several threats and insults over the telephone. Cuello claims that Brando anonymously denounced the social realists as communists, and Tomatis, who admits that he doesn't have any other proof apart from what Cuello said, confirms it, because if Cuello had been capable of that kind of slander he wouldn't have been friends with Washington Noriega for over forty years, and besides, to him, Tomatis, those denunciations (most likely indirect and no doubt anonymous) seem like something Brando would've done. If their informants hadn't been as trustworthy, Soldi wouldn't have believed all those stories. The author of the text, who by now is very old, and who's made them promise a thousand times not to mention his name, talks about Brando and his friends in a sarcastic way that reveals a contained resentment, and fifty years of mulling over the same insults and meanness doesn't seem to have been long enough for him to say everything he has to say. But neither he nor Gabi enjoy those stories, they depress them, actually. By temperament, Soldi's own life is solitary and private—Tomatis is the only person who knows that he's had a long-running sexual relationship with a much older married woman—his inclination toward literature doesn't include the contingencies of its personalities, and is made exclusively of texts, ideas, and forms, and there isn't room for anecdotes or gossip, not even for biographies. Within that almost abstract relationship, it's hard for him to see how a difference in aesthetics could produce hatred rather than dialogue, or how a truly accomplished work could produce anything but admiration. He's ashamed of all the slag they've been collecting over the course of their investigation, and though he sometimes relates those stories to another person, each time he does so he feels exposed, as though he too had committed a base act, betraying himself first of all, but especially those dazzling, steely objects, made so curiously of the deft association of words, and seeming more permanent than the accidental, mutable, and empty transience of the material world.

Nula and Gabriela Barco wait patiently through those seconds of hesitation, and Nula looks into the distance, to the north, toward the place where the blue sky meets the horizon, an irregular green line interrupted by trees and shrubs, where scattered and apparently static cloud masses emerge, suspended over many points in the vast, blue sky. The sandy road that begins just after the embankment is slightly oblique relative to the bluish horizontal of the asphalt, and some three hundred meters off, more or less, is lost in an organic background, swallowed abruptly by the darkening green foliage, the borders of the yellow strip converging, through the effect of perspective, until they almost meet. *The horizon*, Nula thinks, *paradigm of the external, is in fact the result of a human impossibility: the parallels do not meet at an infinitely distant point, but rather in our imaginations. A good portion of the world exists because I exist. I should note this down but I'll wait till later—I shouldn't forget it—because if I do it in front of them I'll have to give them some kind of an explanation and if I tell them the truth it might sound pedantic.* But, contrary to what he's just decided, he reaches into the inside pocket of his jacket, pulls out his notebook, and opens it. Beneath the last note, which he wrote yesterday in Paraná, at around the same time, after leaving Lucía's—*Sensory deficiency makes chaos seem like harmony. Flight of butterflies*—he draws a horizontal line in the middle of the next space to separate it from the next note, and, with Gabriela and Soldi watching him discreetly, after thinking for a few seconds, as though he's alone, he props the notebook on the transversal rail of the steering wheel and without rushing, writes, *Optical illusion and external reality (Horizon, parallels, etc.).* When he finishes, he closes the notebook and puts in back in his jacket pocket, and then, clicking the end of the pen so as to make the tip disappear into the metal tube that protects the ink cartridge, inserts it, vertically, into the same pocket, hanging it in place by its clip on the edge of the pocket. Then he looks up and meets the gazes of Gabriela and especially Soldi, whose look expresses a combination of curiosity, surprise, and a vague and inexplicable satisfaction.

—It's nothing, Nula says. I just remembered an order I took on the phone this morning and I had to jot it down so I wouldn't make a mistake later.

Gabriela seems satisfied with Nula's somewhat hasty explanation, but Soldi furrows his brow skeptically, the inside edges of his black eyebrows gathering at the bridge of his nose while the outside edges rise to his temples. Soldi turns to Gabriela.

—Don't believe him, he says. He's writing an ontology of becoming.

—Is that all? Gabriela says.

—The problem demanded a sacrifice, and I offered myself, Nula says softly, narrowing his eyes, theatrically underscoring the humility of the philosophical martyr and apparently delighting his

200

interlocutors. Though he's flattered by the response, he considers it an obligatory gesture of courtesy to ask Soldi about the fascinating point at which he interrupted his story, the old man who knows so much about those literary skirmishes. How did they find out about him? How'd they contact him? How'd they gain his confidence? How'd they manage to get a copy of the text and how did they convince him that they were really going to protect his anonymity?

—My aunt Ángela, my mother's sister, Gabriela says. They're close friends, and she introduced us. Actually the idea for the history of the avant-garde only came up after we met him, isn't that right Pinocchio?

In the quick look that Soldi and Gabriela exchange, Nula senses a spark of collusion, or complicity maybe, and he's not wrong. Gabriela has left out of her explanation that, decades before, her aunt Ángela was in love with the anonymous author of the precisionist history, but he'd had to explain to her that even though she was the person he loved most in the world, women weren't his strong suit. Her aunt had remained single, and has lived with her friend for years in a platonic relationship. Those facts are only known outside the family by Soldi, who'd never reveal them, which explains why the knowing look that they've just exchanged is followed by a slightly awkward silence. Actually the last few ironic words they've traded conceal the fact that their interest in the conversation is starting to fade. It's difficult to tell the reason why some conversations follow that course, becoming quickly animated, lasting for a while at a certain level of intensity, and then, gradually, and sometimes suddenly, fading away and extinguishing. Talking is, after all, a physical activity, and after a while it gets tiring; the translation of thoughts into words, when they're often fundamentally different, the exercise of the respiratory system, and the muscle movements required by the practice of language inevitably produce a certain fatigue, but most of the tension comes from the effort required to filter out the internal hum, subduing it and hiding it and adjusting oneself to the external world, those two contradictory and mutually opposed infinities that nonetheless supply each other, existing because their opposite also exists, and at the same time, sooner or later, reciprocally, they annihilate each other.

Soldi, changing the topic, says he has a date with Tomatis that night at the Amigos del Vino. Would he, Nula, like to join them? Why not, he'll call Diana right now and ask her to come along, if she's free. Nula pulls out his cell phone from the side pocket of his jacket, but Soldi nods and waves goodbye—Gabriela has leaned back against her seat—and, turning the ignition key, pulls away. Nula, surprised, is frozen with the phone in his hand, and smiles hesitantly and inquisitively at Gabriela, who, turning around, shrugs and makes a helpless gesture, and as the car turns onto the asphalt, gives him a friendly wave.

—What's the hurry? she says.

—Hurry? Soldi asks, unsettled, surprised.

—Your friend didn't think we were leaving so soon, Gabriela says.

—I was trying to be polite and didn't want to listen in on a conjugal conversation, Soldi says. And besides, we've been blocking the street for a long time.

Turning around all the way in her seat, she sees that the dark green colored station wagon, or long hatchback, has started its descent toward the sandy road. Straightening up, absent for several seconds from her surroundings, she holds in her imagination the dark green shape moving slowly up the street and, when it gets to the first corner—in reality, one side of the street is all countryside and the other is dotted with two or three wooden houses in the middle of a wooded plot—it turns right, drives about twenty meters, and stops next to the gate outside Gutiérrez's house. Like an image projected by an external source, extraneous to her will, the scene, materialized briefly, without apparent reason, from the darkness, is interrupted suddenly, almost accidentally, despite its clarity, from the same consciousness where it had been projected, and Gabriela once again observes, with a kind of muted euphoria, the landscape that rolls past or that rushes to meet them as the car gradually picks up speed. Beyond the dusty weeds that grow on the embankment along the edges of the road, modest unplastered brick houses alternate with a few ranches and, every so often, with more-finished houses, plastered and whitewashed, with carefully installed thatch or tile roofs, with small gardens alongside or out front, with fruit trees or other larger shade trees, eucalyptus or acacias, mulberries or bitterwoods that have made it through the summer with their dense foliage still intact. All the vegetation, even the willows, abundant near the river, and which fade before the rest, is still green, and in the gardens the red hibiscus flowers, and those of other species of the same color, shimmer in the afternoon light, which the enormous masses of scattered clouds do nothing to block, fleeing from the sun (which is still high) and dissolving into a sky that's been cleansed by the previous days of rain. Every so often she sees people sitting at a table under the trees, finishing their meal in the shade. Many, and not necessarily the most finished or comfortable ones, are weekend houses, and some of the cottages, whitewashed and carefully looked after, reveal a kind of rural elegance, produced by the intricate, diverse, and ancient vegetation that protects them, adorns them, and distinguishes them. Small, azure-colored swimming pools (the large ones only appear in Rincón itself, or in the residential neighborhood above the floodplain, where Gutiérrez lives), made of plastic, oval, or less traditional shapes, cloverleaf for example, show up every so often in the back yards, along with spherical mud ovens resting on a square brick base and grills in the open air or sheltered under a pavilion, clotheslines loaded with motionless, shining clothes, a motorcycle leaning against a tree, an old car or a light truck parked at the entrance, between the road and the front garden, chicken coops, corrals, vacant lots where a horse or a cow grazes, birds flying between the trees, or which appear from the foliage and land on the power lines or on the posts that spring up at regular intervals along the road, then taking off suddenly and flying off, shrinking in size and disappearing somewhere in the direction of the river. This section of the coast was less populated when her parents and her parents' friends, Tomatis, the Garay twins, Pancho Expósito, were young, and excluding Rincón, was considered inhospitable wilderness. The region, for years deserted and poor, had slowly been developed, first by small ranches scattered randomly over the countryside, then by industrial chicken farms, by brick factories, by otter hunters, shell miners, and fishing outfits, and later by union-owned recreational centers, by fish and game or bocce clubs, summer camps, and finally by people from the city who'd buy a small plot for pocket change and, as the story goes, would build a small cottage or a cinder block house or even a fancier, tree-shaded cabin with their own hands, or they'd hire someone else to do it. In New Jersey, where Gabriela had gone to finish her literary studies, opulence and poverty were only juxtaposed in large urban centers, in contrast to the coastline, at least around Rincón, which they're driving toward, where dilapidated cottages and ostentatious weekend houses coexist apparently without antagonism. After Rincón, the sandy roads that branch out from the asphalt into the countryside or toward the river, to the left or the right of the highway, are more and more populated, and every two or three kilometers, in La Toma, in La Bena, in Callejón Freyre (where the La Arboleda motel is located), there's a rash of businesses, butcher shops, bakeries, corner stores, tourist stands, nurseries, cigarette kiosks, phone banks, groceries, and drink stands. And all along the route, to La Guardia and even to the entrance to the bridge over the lagoon, crude tin or plywood signs advertise fruit, fresh fish, or meats. Through her euphoria, Gabriela sighs inwardly: that mythical place described in texts and in oral traditions, which her parents had often visited ever since her childhood, had become an overpopulated suburb of the city, so much so that they'd had to widen the asphalt road and put up traffic lights at the busiest intersections. According to Soldi, heavy bottlenecks formed on Sunday nights with people coming back to the city. To top it off they'd filled in and cleared the swamp around La Guardia and, virtually overnight, the loud anachronism everyone calls *the supercenter* had sprung up. But smiling and narrowing her eyes, feeling the sun through the windshield warming her face, she thinks that luckily they can't change the pleasant weather, at least not yet.

Soldi is completely oblivious both to Gabriela and to the supposed attractions of the road. He's recalling, analyzing rather, the morning that they've spent with Gutiérrez, first of all the interview, which started inside, continued at the back of the courtyard, under the trees, and was extended by the swimming pool while they drank a glass of white wine before going into the kitchen to eat. With a sort of juvenile haste, he, Soldi, had grabbed the yellow canvas lounge chair, which had caught his eye immediately, and sat down while the others continued standing, because he'd been momentarily stuck by the fear that Gabi or Gutiérrez might take it first, but he'd barely sat down before he felt guilty and stood back up, just as the others were arranging the other two lounge chairs, causing Gutiérrez to look at him quizzically and start back up to his feet, but Soldi, with a cryptic smile, gestured casually for him not to stand up while he pretended to arrange something in his pants pocket, as if he was afraid he'd lost or forgotten something, and sat back down. Of their three principal informants— besides the author of the anonymous text, there are many others, but as sources they're more fragmentary and weren't as close to the events—Cuello, Gutiérrez, and Tomatis, Gutiérrez is the most impartial and scrupulous. Cuello knew Brando's father, who was also a friend of Washington's, and according to him, and he's not the only one who's said this, the head of the precisionist movement was even hated by his own father, but Cuello, despite his efforts at objectivity, has an excessively negative perspective on the subject. And just hearing the name Brando makes Tomatis furious, and he treats the precisionist aesthetic with the same irritated disdain as he does its author. Only Gutiérrez strikes him as impartial, though Soldi can't suppress a slight doubt that always accompanies that assessment: *Maybe too much so.* Clearly it's pleasurable for him to recall that period of his life, for reasons that probably have nothing to do with precisionism. They'd already discussed that issue several times with Tomatis: first off, it concerns his youth, and the distance from which he remembered it over the years had caused him to end up confusing his own feelings with the place he'd come from and he'd idealized that time without realizing that it's himself and not everything else that he's remembering, blending space and time and the internal with the external. But neither he nor Tomatis feel completely satisfied with that explanation. There's a darker side to it, which Gutiérrez can't talk about openly with people he only knows slightly, and about which he let something slip during Nula's first visit, surely thinking that he was a simple wine salesman with no personal connection to his friends or acquaintances. It's hard to tell if Gutiérrez is aware that, besides the two or three friends he's told, many people he knows already suspect it, and some have even been discussing it, more or less openly, since he came back to the city. But there's something else about his surprising composure, something embedded inside him, disconnected from the external world, a complete seed that needed no cultivation and that sprouted alone, something he's probably not even conscious of, and now Soldi realizes that he'd driven off suddenly in the middle of

206

the conversation because, behind the urbane banter that the three of them had passed back and forth between their cars, and which he'd of course enjoyed, he, Soldi, had needed to be alone a while to reconsider the various impressions that Gutiérrez had left him with that morning. Two or three times during their interviews over the past few weeks he'd heard him say, *I chose screenwriting because I wanted to disappear better as an artist, because a screenwriter doesn't have his own existence, and to disappear as an individual, I use a pseudonym that apart from my producer no one knows.* That declaration, spoken in a lighthearted, cheerful tone, had intrigued him, and it seems to him to reveal something more than a straightforward professional or private discretion in Gutiérrez, but he can't tell what. Soldi suspects that Gutiérrez's generous but exact critiques are in fact the consequence of the sort of tolerance that doesn't exclude the person who offers them, and if he himself is their first object, he's also the last one he thinks deserves it. But it's a cold tolerance, unburdened of the emotions that inspired it, an ultimate calm that sees the whole universe and all its parts, as infinitesimal as they may be, as lost causes from the very moment when, appearing suddenly and incomprehensibly from out of nowhere, as colorful as they are illusory, they bloom.

That attitude seems to be confirmed by his sense that as soon as anything appears in the world, whatever the reason, a catastrophe immediately gets to work on it, dizzyingly slow but sure to destroy it, with himself as the clearest example of that process. Clearly he treats the things around him—the house, the furniture, the garden, the countryside, the city, the world—and especially those that belong to him, as though they were foreign, with a gentle indifference, without suspicion or pretension, seeing only their use value, and he, Soldi, when he's visiting the house, often gets the feeling of possessing them more than their owner, in any case of using them more carefully, as though it were he and not their owner who was aware of their true value. The only possession that he seems to claim is the precise memory of his years in the city, starting when his grandmother, who was his only family, had sent him from their insignificant, remote village, to parochial school, hoping that he'd finish high school so she could rest in peace, and what happened afterward, the law school, the three somewhat older and richer classmates—though anyone would've been—Rey, Escalante, and Marcos Rosemberg, the Roman Law professor who noticed his poverty and took him on as a clerk in his firm, the harsh conscription as occasional secretary to Brando and the precisionist movement, and the final days in the city, events so closely linked and so obscurely experienced that for a long time afterward they produced suspicions, inquiries, and conjectures among his friends until finally they forgot about him, and which caused him one fine day to disappear from the city without saying goodbye to anyone and then reappear and move in just as suddenly almost thirty-four years later. In his memory those years are inexhaustible, and if every memory, like every event, as insignificant as it might seem, is by definition infinite, then Soldi wonders if the interviews with him and Gabi allow Gutiérrez to relive them over and over, with meticulous tenacity, drawing to the clarity of his present consciousness a multiplicity of details that he might have considered disappeared forever, and which he finds still surprisingly fresh and vivid in some lost corner inside himself. His total lack of hope regarding the possibility of recovering the vividness of his past experience down to the minor details, among which one might have to include precisionism, is what produces that calm tolerance, that lucid indulgence of even the most malicious acts and the most sordid gossip. It's as though he were telling his interviewers, *They're the only years I was really alive, so I have to take them as a whole because they were so few that I don't have the luxury of rejecting any part of them.* And Soldi thinks that Gutiérrez has a point: With the stories we were told as children, before going to sleep, which we wanted to hear over and over, always exactly the same way, we wouldn't have let the narrator censor the sad or violent parts, or the ones that, because of the accumulation of details, delayed the advance of the plot or the arrival of the climax. All those elements of the story, happy or dramatic, moral or immoral, enjoyable or painful, had the same value, formed a part of it, were the whole story and not just its parts, and the most intense sections wouldn't have had any meaning or the capacity to touch us if the transitions that sometimes may have seemed superfluous hadn't held them together.

Soldi imagines that Gutiérrez is aware of the base acts, but simply observes them from a distance or glosses them unemotionally, not as though they made no difference to him, but rather as though he'd exhausted all his supplies of anger and outrage a long time ago. During lunch, for example, his customary monologue about *them*, the inhabitants of the European countries he's lived in for over thirty years, which he never names, never calls them *the Italians, the Swiss, the French, the British, etc.*, and not even *them* in fact, unless the construction of the sentence forces him to use the pronoun, that monologue which at times becomes a soliloquy, as though he were articulating thoughts that aren't even directed to the people present, isn't spoken either with gravity or violence but rather with a calm and ironic, almost delicate tone, as if he were referring to a hopeless case that doesn't deserve more than a distant and dispassionate description, possibly thinking that even the most atrocious crimes, repeated ad nauseam, become monotonous and comical: *Society there is as chaotic as a natural phenomenon, and just like someone with a roof over their head tolerates the rain, they get along by trading their workdays for extravagance, which, like the air they breathe, they can't do without, allowing themselves to be treated like slaves, not realizing that even if they could take a step in any direction it would make them an accomplice in the most atrocious crimes. And because the glut has temporarily dulled their instincts, they've traded ethics for a guilty conscience, and if because of that same excess the rest of the world declines, deprived of everything basic, they'll let twelve-year-olds in other parts of the world work fourteen-hour days when they're not getting raped by the perverts on vacation in those places or worse yet buy newborns and adopt them as their children when they can't have them any other way, all so that their own children are well-fed and well-dressed and get what they consider to be a decent education. The ruins of the places they've sacked, pyramids, temples, devastated jungles, empty savannahs, ravaged geological layers, fossils that they lay claim to by giving them ridiculous names, all serving as decoration, as a mirror to what they insist are their souls, which they insist are fabulous, rational, and profound. And they've transformed the few livable places left in those wasted lands into kitschy destinations for their so-called holidays, the so-called setting for their supposedly unforgettable so-called pleasures. Their bestial sensualism isn't a product of their own desires, which have become incomprehensible to them because of their philistinism and the constant, ubiquitous brainwashing, bombarded as they are by political and commercial propaganda, rather they're the byproduct of generic stereotypes and secondhand needs inculcated by that very same propaganda. They refer to themselves as individualists and yet whenever they open their mouths all that comes out are clichés so fashionable that they end up being interchangeable with anything that their worst enemies, who pretend to be different, might have on hand. The religions they practice don't commit them to anything, nothing more than following a soccer team, and their obedience is certainly less stringent than to their weekly magazine subscriptions or to the guidebooks that dictate their mindless travels. Even though they wiped them off the face of the earth a long time ago, they pretend they're still shaped by the precepts dictated by their gods, which according to them sanction their commerce and their genocides as long as every once in a while they donate their old clothes and unwanted food, their table scraps in a word, though it's well-known that the god they adored kept them on their knees or treated them like rabid dogs or forced them to wash their bodies before they asked it for anything—always the same irrational fantasies, of course—and the others, the ones they all feel proud to have descended from, pretended to live in a brotherhood of rational and benevolent deities when in fact, and for no other reason than their thoughtlessness, jealousy, resentment, and cruelty, they would descend from Olympus to betray them in battle, demand the sacrifice of what they held most dear, rape their mothers and wives and daughters and transform them into rocks or animals. Evil was already engraved by fire in the natural order before they multiplied it insanely with science, technology, commerce, and religion, their avarice causing them to speak of it euphemistically and, when they couldn't control it any more, infecting every corner of the world with it. But they're happy as long as they're well-educated and can condescend to foreigners, and even though everything they pretend to know they've read in newspapers or heard on the radio, they're ashamed when they have to put their pets on diets so they don't lose their figure.*

Soldi laughs, and Gabriela turns toward him and, intrigued when she sees his bearded profile, smiles too.

—Gutiérrez, Soldi says. The things he said at lunch about Europeans.

Gabriela's smile widens.

—He has a talent for description, she says. It must come in handy for his screenplays.

Soldi makes a vague movement with his head and shoulders, and once again serious, returns to his thoughts. Gabriela, staring abstractedly through the windshield at a random point on the pavement that shifts and changes as the car moves—only the distance between herself and the car remaining constant—"sees" the dark green station wagon again as it moves down the sandy road, turns to the right, and stops next to the white bars of the gate. Now she sees Nula getting out of the car, pushing the half-open gate, stopping at

211

the white front door, and hesitating a few seconds before deciding to ring the bell. His walk through the garden with Gutiérrez, as she sees it, is halting and fragmentary. Maybe, as with herself and Pinocchio before lunch, they sit down in the lounge chairs next to the pool, or maybe they sit down at the bank of trunks under the trees at the back (eucalyptus, acacias) where she and Pinocchio had once sat while they waited for Gutiérrez, who'd stepped out, to the city, leaving a message telling them to wait so they could resume their interviews. But now they're inside, standing next to the round kitchen table, inspecting some wine bottles they take from the cardboard cases. They might have a cup of coffee, or Nula might simply drop off the order, take his check, and return to the city. Gabriela looks back at the road they've been leaving behind, and which gets more and more narrow as the car advances, first through the side view mirror and then through the rear window: no short, dark green station wagon appears on the straight and empty pavement. No, he must still be there, trying to make another sale, or reporting, in his ironic, juvenile way, the conversation they'd just had, between their cars, on the embankment that descends from the highway to the sandy road. Maybe they've settled their business and have moved on to what Pinocchio referred to earlier as the *ontology of becoming*, Nula, with that provincial womanizer attitude, being of course, alongside Pinocchio, a real expert. *But he doesn't really have the fingernails of a guitarist*, Gabriela tells herself, using an expression so conclusive and circular, smoothed and polished by its infinite iterations in popular speech, that for a fraction of a second it displaces the images that had occupied her, the words that comprise the expression imprinted on the bright stage of her mind like a neon sign switching on and off periodically against the black background of a dark, obscure city. But she's not sure that he doesn't have those fingernails: simply put, he shouldn't act so sure of himself. Now she sees him again in the lounge chair by the pool,

212

drinking coffee and discussing philosophy, exhausting the declensions of the verb *to be*. And Gabriela recalls a story that her father told her once: he and Tomatis were leaning over the railings of the suspension bridge, watching the water, and it occurred to Barco to ask, *Carlitos, in your opinion, what is a novel?* And without hesitating even for a second or looking up from the water swirling around the pillars of the bridge several meters below, Carlitos had answered, *The decomposition of continuous movement.*

Now she's the one who laughs, and Soldi, intrigued, looks sidelong at her.

—Carlitos, Gabriela says. One day my old man asked him for a definition of the novel and he answered, *The decomposition of continuous movement.*

—The decomposition of continuous movement, Soldi repeats, nodding slowly. And after thinking it over a second, says, Of course, in the sense of representing, through an analytic and static form what in fact is synthetic and dynamic.

—That's more or less it, Gabriela says, except with fewer -ic adjectives.

—Cheeky! Soldi says. Let's stop by the Piedras Blancas beach before we head back to the city, even though there're no rocks, and much less white ones, for six hundred kilometers in any direction.

—Just for a minute, she says, because she's anxious to call Caballito and Rosario with the news, though she knows it's too early to call because her father must still be at the courthouse and José Carlos still teaching class at the university. She'll call later, after six, before their date at the Amigos del Vino. Her mother is home of course, probably in bed, where she's spent most of her time for the last two or three years, after she stopped wanting to get up, or shower, or go out, or do any work for the firm, or go back to the courthouse. She's not being eaten away by sadness or anguish, which would inspire sympathy, but rather something incomprehensible, which is confusing and at times revolting, a slow and apparently permanent flood of indifference. It's not worth giving her the news: within minutes of getting it, tangled as she is in her tremulous labyrinth of heavy thoughts, she'll forget it forever. Though she'd always been quiet, sometimes, in the middle of a party, she'd suddenly pull out some funny observation, some ironic or sarcastic comment whose unexpected elegance and precision always produced laughter in her surprised listeners. And she'd often sing, in an intimate, solemn voice, accompanying herself on the guitar, sometimes to songs she'd written herself by putting her favorite poems to music. During the black years she'd defended political prisoners with almost more courage and tenacity than Barco himself, to the point that on two or three occasions she'd been *detained* at a police station or at some army post, but because her family had come from Germany, in the southeast, their embassy protected her, and besides she was already too well-known by then to be disappeared. She'd survived so much, calmly and bravely, and one day the thing that had been slithering from the dark and remote corners inside her, probably since the moment she began to take shape in her mother's womb, burst to the surface and when it had her it dove to the bottom till she blacked out, it confused itself with her and made her hateful by force of its insistence, it, the indifference, overpowering her completely.

In La Guardia, where the river road splits toward Paraná, the traffic is heavier, despite the fact that the road widens all the way to the bridge between the cities, and Soldi is forced to slow down behind a double-decker green bus on its way to Buenos Aires. In the opposite lane, cars, buses, and trucks move along at a slower speed, resigned to the caravan. In the hypermarket parking lot, beyond the countless parked cars that fill the designated spaces, a red tractor trailer, the top opening covered with a dark canvas, is parked near the warehouse entrance, and as they pass Gabriela turns around to see if there's anything written on the back of the trailer, where to her satisfaction she's able to read, in large printed letters, VISIT HELVECIA, FOR THE GOLDEN DORADO.

They pass the hypermarket, and before they reach the bridge Soldi turns off to the right, though still in the direction of the city, down a narrow parallel road that ends suddenly at a white curb, forcing them to turn right again, this time parallel to the waterfront on the opposite shore. The paving ends after a few meters and the road turns to reddish dirt—they must've mixed the earth with gravel or ground brick to make it harder—at the end of which, some two hundred meters ahead, there are a few cars parked along a recently installed chain link fence. Soldi slows down and maneuvers the car, reversing slightly to straighten it out, and parks facing the same direction as the others, perpendicular to the fence, in the ample space between a white truck and a light green Citroën. The soles of their shoes scratch against the gravel as they walk toward the entrance, and their shadows, which at midday had been compressed and reduced at their feet, have begun to stretch to the east, recovering a more or less recognizable human shape. Hanging on the fence itself, to one side of the gate, a small white sign with blue lettering announces, PIEDRAS BLANCAS TOURIST CENTER. As he passes the sign, Soldi, without further commentary, nods toward it and emits a short and sarcastic laugh.

The sunny beachfront—a section of which, off-limits to swimmers and decorated in white rocks and used as a mooring area, proving that the specifications on the white sign at the entrance were not superfluous—is almost empty, a condition explained by the fact that the season officially ended a few weeks ago, a closure validated by the rain over the past few days. Gabriela and Soldi, though, felt the heat of the sun on their faces, on their naked arms, and on their heads the moment they got out of the car. A good portion of the blue sky is visible over the open beach, over the water, over the low-lying city crowded against the opposite shore, and it's

215

clear that most of the massive white clouds that had earlier given a deceitful impression of stillness have disappeared, though the ones that do remain, too scattered to block much of the sunlight, seem just as motionless and vast. Several pitched roof buildings sit between irregular-shaped planters covered with shining grass that the recent rains have reanimated; the most important of these houses the bar-restaurant and the others serve as changing huts. There's a play space for kids, with a curved bridge, painted blue, which ends at a platform with a sort of cabin and a horizontal yellow wheel, elevated on an axle, whose function is difficult to guess. Gabriela and Soldi walk past the bar, where a few tables, sheltered by umbrellas, are occupied, toward the shore fortified with white rocks that possibly serve to keep the water from eroding the sand too quickly. The planter closest to the water, the only one bordered by white-painted cement, is heart-shaped, and a flagless flagpole stands at the upper vertex, where the two halves of the heart meet, and which narrows as it deepens. Soldi emits another short, sarcastic laugh, but Gabriela barely hears him because she's looking at something in the distance, at the far end of what strictly speaking would be called the beach, two people, a young woman and a two- or three-year-old child who seems to be her daughter, playing, hand-in-hand, mirroring each other's movements, at the edge of the water: both have straight black hair that bounces over their shoulders, dark skin, not sun-tanned but naturally so, dressed alike in short-sleeve yellow T-shirts and faded jeans, and so identical from a distance, were it not for their size, that the daughter could be taken for a miniaturized reproduction of the mother. Gabriela realizes, meanwhile, that the mother and daughter represent not only a sequential order but also a continuum between the internal and the external. Of course what she's seeing isn't repetition, Gabriela thinks, because the girl, though she appears identical to her mother, as she takes shape in the external world, adds something new to it, something that never before existed, because no two splinters of time are the same, and therefore the simple accumulation changes everything, the present, the past, the future. In the external world, the girl interiorizes the mother from whom she's separated, and one day, because of that same appropriation, she'll bring her back into the world again. It suddenly seems to Gabriela that the whole universe is being played out in those two people of her same sex spinning hand-in-hand at the edge of the water. A vague happiness, not altogether disconnected from the warm April sun, the clear day, and the nearness of the water, comes over her, and her forgetting that she has personal reasons to feel happy might indicate that with her pleasurable shudder she now incarnates the Whole that is at once outside of her while, generously, containing her.

Beyond the bar, two or three sailboats—sails furled and decks empty—are anchored, several meters from shore, near the beach on the Piedras Blancas side of the river. Breaking up the sandy expanse are several trees, an acacia, two young eucalyptus, and two or three others whose species Soldi can't identify at that distance. A group of single-color umbrellas, reds and yellows, are scattered around the empty space, separated from the two-colored ones, divided into ten alternating segments, also red and yellow: the brightly colored canopies project black circles onto the sand without the two circles coinciding completely, the position of the sun causing the black circle to be displaced slightly with relation to the red or yellow circle that projects it. Their feet scratching lightly against the sand, Gabriela and Soldi move away from the "port" toward what strictly speaking would be called the beach. When she senses their presence, the woman in the yellow T-shirt stops playing with the child, watches them a moment, and then, taking her own reduced image by the hand, moves away from the water and starts walking slowly toward the exit down a path that opens between the trees. Gabriela, slightly mortified by their departure,

217

nevertheless acts as though she hadn't seen them. Where the white rocks end the ground elevates to a high lifeguard tower, a white wooden structure consisting of a fixed ladder topped with a seat, and which because of its height dominates the whole beach, whose perimeter is marked by a semicircular chain of red buoys, one end of which is attached to the shore at the edge of the white rocks and the other to some vague spot beyond the shore. Not only are there no bathers, there are no lifeguards; the few people there are sitting at tables around the bar, under the shade of the umbrellas. It's quiet enough that as they approach the damp edge of the shore they're able to perceive the almost inaudible murmur of the water.

In the windless afternoon the almost transparent surface is furrowed by long, delicate wrinkles, parallel to the beach, that appear motionless and whose circulation is only visible in the final curl coming and going along the surface, betraying, inconspicuously, its movement.

—It's not really noticeable right now, but there's a rising tide, Soldi says, and he and Gabriela, simultaneously though in opposite directions, observe the river around them. The wide channel, two hundred meters across, framed at one end by the seawall at the waterfront, and to the north, on the Guadalupe side, by a circular expanse a few kilometers in diameter that everyone, even the cartographers, refers to as *the lagoon* because of its shape, though everyone knows that actually a branch of another branch of another branch (called rivers, streams, tributaries), and a few others that form the Paraná on its way to the delta, spill together on a northward bend to form the lagoon, then turning south again form the city's port, eventually meeting another channel that, with many others, will return the dark current to the breast of the father that at some indefinite point, or everywhere at once starting at the first thread of source water upriver, engendered it. Soldi says that the beach seems so new because the floods, two in recent years, have submerged it. It had been rebuilt for the third time, Soldi says stoically, at the start of the season that had just finished. The '82 flood washed away the Guadalupe beach and several of the houses that had been fearfully built up around it, and the water level never went back down at that spot in the river. And with *him*, Soldi says, nodding to the south, the one in '82 *shook him up*, and the one the next year finished the job. Gabriela surveys the section of the suspension bridge that still stands a few blocks away, half of it more or less, the part closest to the city; halfway down, the structure drops off, suddenly, into the void. Several twisted black cables hang from the metal arch closest to the severed end, holding it in place. Behind the ruin, cars, buses, and trucks move slowly and indifferently down the parallel highway bridge, built twenty years before in anticipation of the immanent collapse. Soldi and Gabriela look at the remains of the bridge in silence, both slightly upset, although a slow, abstracted smile appears on both of their faces, wide enough that it's even visible through Soldi's curly, black beard. They both seem to have discovered, simultaneously, the two boys, much younger than them, leaning against the metal railing, no doubt enjoying the coolness of the river after a long walk before going home, taking a quick shower, and returning to the night's rituals and promises. Resting their forearms on the metal railing, they watch the water swirl around the cylindrical cement pillars, and for a while they stand silently at the edge of the beach, feeling the three o'clock sun warming their bodies and faces. Gabriela and Soldi, without having agreed to, both observe them. They're facing upriver, toward Guadalupe, and they recognize them easily, despite the distance. To the west, on the city side, the cloudless sky is a uniform, bright red stain, like melting lava, and on the other side, to the east, the night is rising. Suddenly the tallest one, the one who's most calm and most patient, without warning but neverthe-less gently, asks, *What is the novel?* And the other one, who's slightly

219

younger, without even looking up from the whirlpool, says, *The decomposition of continuous movement.*

When he leaves her at the door to her aunt Ángela's, Soldi offers to pick her up that night on his way to meet Tomatis at the Amigos del Vino bar, but Gabriela, before closing the passenger door, says she'll walk or take a bus, and crossing the gray pavement, heads toward the front door. Her aunt Ángela's house is like a thousand others in the city, with the difference that hers is much better cared for, and was chosen carefully and with a specific purpose, the intention of satisfying a particular aesthetic taste (on the opposite sidewalk, a very similar house from the same period, but practically in ruins, long ago began displaying the ubiquitous sign: ANOTHER MORO PROPERTY FOR SALE). And yet both houses have been in a good location—far from the city center but within the quadrangular perimeter of the main avenues—since the twenties, more or less. Her aunt's house has a front garden separated from the sidewalk by a metal door and a meter-and-a-half high yellow wall, and beyond the garden, behind a hibiscus heavy with flowers and two rose bushes, the yellow wall of the house itself, with a window and a door with frosted blue and yellow glass that leads to a covered gallery surrounded by four or five rooms. At the back are the bathroom and the kitchen, and behind these a larger courtyard with a medlar tree, a poinsettia, and an enormous magnolia, which has been there since the house was built and which provides good shade in the summer—only the magnolias lose their leaves, and the petals rain down on anyone who sits under its branches to talk on December or January nights. The red tiles in the gallery shine and the yellow walls all look recently painted, as do the gray doors, in front of each of which there's a multicolored doormat so new-looking that Gabriela feels guilty whenever she steps on them, even when she's barefoot. The parquet flooring in the dining room, the living room, and the bedrooms also shines, as does the furniture, some of which, like the dishes, antiques inherited after her parents' death, receive special treatment. Before she retired, her aunt Ángela had taught geography at the technical college, though she could've lived without working because both of her sisters, who were married, had renounced their inheritance, which wasn't enormous, but enough for one person. Because of the free time that being single allowed her, she'd been the one to care for their parents, who'd never wanted to leave the northern town where they'd been born and where they'd wanted to be buried. But her aunt didn't have the sad, compliant, and dark habits that so many nineteenth-century novels attribute to spinsters. She'd traveled ever since she was young, alone or with friends—she'd hitchhiked across Patagonia with just a backpack; she'd been to Mexico and Europe several times; to California and to Egypt; and, in recent years, when the weather was right, she'd take trips with her friends to the mountains, to the Iguazú falls, or to Brazil. The third sister, Helena, had married a Uruguayan doctor and lived in Montevideo, and Ángela regularly took the morning flight, which left at eight thirty, transferred at Aeroparque, and by noon was having lunch at the Mercado del Puerto. In fact, that afternoon she'd gone to the Córdoba mountains with a couple of friends. On the kitchen table, held down by a glass ashtray, there's a note:

Gabi dear, they're coming for me at one thirty, and we get back on Monday afternoon. I left a few things for you in the fridge, the two bottles of white wine and the chicken too, in case José Carlos comes for the weekend. Put it in the freezer if you go to Rosario, and don't worry, I'll make it for you Monday night when you get back.

You-know-who called this morning wanting to talk about your work on Brando & Co. He insisted again that his name shouldn't appear anywhere in the book. He doesn't mind that you've given a copy to Gutiérrez, but the fact that Tomatis has a copy too has him very worried. I tried to reassure him that Carlitos could keep the secret and told him that otherwise you and Pinocchio wouldn't have given him the manuscript. But he's afraid that Carlitos, if he thinks about it, will realize who the author is. I reminded him that Tomatis was still playing with blocks when the things he writes about were happening, which calmed him down a little, but, to be honest with you, I think our friend's fears are perfectly justified. The moment he takes one look at it, Carlitos won't have any doubt about who the author is. If he insinuates anything, you have to ask him to please be discreet.

Well, I should finish packing so I don't make the girls wait. Big kiss till Monday from your auntie.

Gabriela stands by the table with the note in her hand, thinking. With a preoccupied air, she takes a glass from the cabinet, pours herself some seltzer from the fridge, and picking up the sheet that she's just put down on the table, rereads it while she sips the seltzer. Though there's no one else in the kitchen or in the rest of the house to provoke her level of worry, Gabriela's expression, consisting of pinching her lips and slowly shaking her head in a vaguely circular way that isn't negative or affirmative, while she rereads the note and for several seconds afterward, is unmistakably doubtful. She and Pinocchio should have kept Carlitos from knowing who the author of the text was, which means it was without a doubt a mistake to give him a copy. But she doesn't think that he'd reveal it, and though it's true that he's been known to flirt with indiscretion for the sake of a joke, he only does so at the cost of people he considers undeserving of courtesy, Mario Brando for example. He does make cruel jokes about people he knows, but he's just as capable of making them about his best friends or about himself. Some of his jokes are legendary, like the one about the writer who'd been accepted to the Academy of Letters, and who they said had been a prostitute and who'd gone to sadomasochistic orgies when he'd first moved to Buenos Aires as a kid; Carlitos once said that he personified all three philosophical schools at once, the Academic, the Peripatetic, and the Stoic. But no, there's no way he would comment publicly on what he knew, given that she and Pinocchio had asked for his discretion. And besides, is there anyone left to listen? Gabriela's face brightens, her head stops its doubtful movement, and her lips, softening, recover their normal shape. She finishes the last sip of seltzer, leaves the empty glass in the sink, and, taking her aunt's note, walks to her room, opens a blue cardboard folder, and files the note inside along with several other papers. When she closes the folder, she freezes again and now it's her forehead that's pinched: And the wine salesman? Wasn't it irresponsible of her and Pinocchio to reveal so many details about the fourth informant? Although he doesn't have (nor will he have) access to the text before it's published, Nula knows more about its author's personal life after their conversation this afternoon than Tomatis and Gutiérrez combined, at least relative to what as she and Pinocchio have told them. His friendship with Pinocchio, though not very intimate, does validate the confidence, but his profession, which puts him in contact with many sorts of people over the course of the day, could offer many temptations, simply as a means for bragging—his overblown self-esteem is obvious a mile away—to prove his relationships in intellectual circles, or out of vanity, because those supposed relationships could help him close a sale or even engineer a sexual conquest. Gabriela sees the dark green station wagon again, moving slowly down the sandy road, turning at the intersection and parking some twenty meters ahead, alongside the white bars of the gate. Now she sees Gutiérrez and the wine salesman sitting in the lounge chairs next to the pool, drinking a coffee, and she thinks she hears Nula tactlessly telling Gutiérrez everything that he's just learned about the anonymous author of the novelized history of precisionism, which creates a double layer of complication, the first relative to the author of the fragment and the second relative to Gutiérrez himself, because

223

they've told Nula more about the fourth informant, not because they doubted his judgment but rather because they aren't close enough to Gutiérrez to discuss certain things. She's tempted to call Soldi and tell him all of this, but she realizes that he's probably still not home, and, feeling suddenly more tired than usual—she might be a little hungry, because the two catfish with salad actually turned out somewhat thin for three people—she lets herself fall softly, face up, on the bed, and stretching out contentedly, careful to keep her feet over the edge of the bed, she uses her feet to slide her shoes off at the heels, letting them fall with a loud thud against the lacquered parquet floor. Sliding to the center of the bed, she spreads her legs, stretches her arms alongside her body, and assuming a satisfied expression (like everyone else, Gabriela is in the habit, which by now is unconscious, of displaying her inner life with gestures and expressions, especially when she's alone), she smiles happily and half closes her eyes.

It's not actually worth getting upset over such improbable complications. Tomatis would never say anything, and as far as the wine salesman is concerned, apart from being overly self-confident, there's really nothing else to fault him for, at least for now—well, one thing, actually, maybe the shameless way he looks at women. Laughing, without opening her eyes, Gabriela shakes her head slowly, summing up, with this gesture, Nula's essential predictability, possibly some automatic program from his early years that's unconsciously set in motion every time he sees a chick. With gentle, condescending indolence, she puts Nula aside. She wants it to be after six already so she can call Rosario; Caballito can wait till tomorrow or even till the weekend, because she wants to be sure that she'll get her father on the phone rather than her mother, if she happens to answer, though she's usually incapable of even stretching her arm as far as the end table, where the phone is kept, and if her father is far from the house, in the garden for example, he has to run to answer it and usually comes too late. Besides, José Carlos should be the first to know—although he already has two teenage children from his first marriage, Gabriela knows he'll be happy. They've lived together for almost four years, but they've known each other since before she went to New Jersey to finish her degree. Actually, it's been several months since they stopped using protection, and they'd started feeling somewhat disappointed that nothing had happened yet, until finally her period hadn't come, and when it was almost three weeks late she decided to buy a test at the pharmacy; the result was positive, but to be sure she wanted a lab test, which settled all her doubts. Because Holy Week is coming up, she and Pinocchio decided they'd work till Wednesday with Gutiérrez and Cuello, and she'd go to Rosario to see her doctor—this morning, after getting the test results, she'd called for an appointment—and, if the doctor allowed it, she'd take advantage of the holiday and would spend the weekend in Caballito with José Carlos. When had it happened, Gabriela asks herself, when did she and José Carlos get what they were hoping for? After her last period, over a weekend in Rosario, they'd made love twice, the first time on Saturday morning—she'd arrived late Friday, after having spent the whole week working with Pinocchio, and José Carlos had taken part in a conference on economic planning at the university that had lasted two full days—and then on Saturday night, before going out to eat, and after a quiet day at home and then at a party that had lasted till late, they'd started up again. It must have been the second time, that night, Gabriela decides. They'd been talking and caressing each other for a while, mostly naked—it was still hot then—and she'd been getting turned on gradually as he played his fingers softly through her pubic hair, wrapping and unwrapping them and sliding them every so often along the damp edges of her opening. A reddish shadow covered the room, into which the last light of the afternoon filtered. They were happy, and though they seemed distant from the world, they were unwittingly working in its favor. When José Carlos's fingers dipped a bit more and pushed open the damp edges, she'd had the sensation, in which pleasure mixes with a slight and luckily passing anguish, of not belonging to herself, of losing herself in a remote, forgotten corner of her own body, where blood and tissue and fluids, the silent life of her organs, steered her toward divergent and external shores. She'd experienced that singular feeling from time to time, but never as intensely as that Saturday night. When she touched his penis, it felt silky and tense and quivering against the tips of her fingers and the palm of her hand, and when he entered her Gabriela thought it felt harder, thicker, longer, hotter, and wetter than usual—she'd thought this later, as she showered, because at that moment the sensations filling every corner of her body didn't leave much space for thinking—and the drawn out pleasure culminated during her orgasm in a kind of fury that made her muscles ache for days afterward and left José Carlos with his back covered in scratches. Gabriela had felt him finish with a thick burst of semen, and for a while after he'd pulled out she'd been sensitive there, and had liked the feeling of José Carlos's organ still being inside of her. Yes, Gabriela thinks, it must have been that time, it couldn't have happened in any other way but in the middle of that pleasure, and she happily abandons herself to that thought for several minutes, though of course she's aware that for its self-perpetuation that ancient, opportunistic, and single-minded substance could work under any conditions, *in vivo* or *in vitro*, and as long as contact happens between the two protagonists who must unite in order to guarantee its persistence it makes no difference whether there's pleasure or suffering, design or accident, love or indifference, consent or violation. Gabriela lies still, satisfied, smiling to herself, but suddenly, without warning, the smile is erased and a hard expression takes over her face, and when her mouth opens abruptly, as though her lower jaw had

226

unhinged, the hardness is transformed into confusion, irritation, anger: she's at Gutiérrez's house, sitting at the table with Pinocchio, and the owner of the house, who has his back to them, is preparing something at the stove, and when he turns around he's the wine salesman, and as a mean joke he's serving her a plate of live fish. Opening her eyes and crying out, Gabriela is suddenly awake and sitting up on the bed. The disorientation of the sudden dream gives way, in her recovered thoughts, to amazement: in the fraction of a second that she was asleep, the dream took disparate fragments of experience and constructed a new world as vivid as the empirical one, and whose meaning is as difficult to unravel. At an infinitesimal intersection of time, a tangential episode, endowed with its own time, unfolds into events that, were they put into the order in which they occur in reality, would take hours, days, weeks, months, years, the way a single sentence of a story can gather together centuries of empirical time.

Gabriela gets out of bed, yawning, waking up. She turns on the light, opens the doors to her dresser, quickly examines the clothes hanging there, and finally takes out a lightweight tan suit and an ivory silk blouse. Holding up the hangers in front of each other, she studies the combination of tones, and then, holding the two hangers away from her, the blouse on top of the tan coat, to see them better, she decides that the contrast works and that she's happy with the outfit. But when she lays the clothes on the bed, she realizes that the third, and most-visible, button on the silk blouse, which would fall in the middle of her chest, hangs by a thread, so she goes to the dining room and takes her aunt Ángela's sewing kit, an old red and black pastry tin, from the bottom drawer of the chest in the dining room. Her delicate yet agile fingers explore the contents of the box, scissors, thimbles, variously colored spools of thread, loose or packaged buttons of different material, shape, and color, a short piece of tailor's chalk wrapped in a rubber band, transparent boxes full of safety pins and tacks, two green pin cushions from which many different-sized heads emerge, and, at the bottom, several worn-out, greasy coins from past decades, worthless for years because of inflation, currency switches, or political instability. Gabriela sets the box on the table and takes out two or three spools of thread whose colors more or less correspond to the blouse, one white, another a flat yellow, and a third beige, but deciding that she'll have to choose among these for the one that most matches the blouse itself and especially the thread used to stitch the other buttons, she puts everything back in the red and black tin and takes it to her room. Sitting carefully on the edge of the bed so as not to wrinkle the clothes that she's laid out, she leans over the blouse and carefully examines the button, an iridescent mother-of-pearl circle with two holes in the center, and in particular the thread from which it hangs, a beige-like color, lighter than the one from the spool she's just chosen. Leaning closer, she concentrates on the thread, comparing it to the one that holds up the other buttons, which come stitched from the factory, and, in her memory, to the ones in the box. To resolve her doubt, she opens the tin and takes out the beige spool—too dark. The flat yellow, with a vaguely greenish-gray tint, seems better, and the white one clearly won't work. Yes, the yellow one will match the others best, and even though Gabriela knows that no one will be able to tell the difference, the detail doesn't seem at all superfluous, despite the fact that more than one person might laugh at her—she thinks of the wine salesman and his ridiculous joke, serving her a live fish, an idea that seemed plausible for him, even though it was from a dream—she could remind that person that distinguishing the differences in little things is good training for seeing them in bigger ones, like an ontology of becoming, for example. And Gabriela remembers the philosophy class in which they studied Plato, and the question from the *Timaeus* that she'd memorized, and which

228

had helped her get a really good grade on the final exam: *What is that which always is and has no becoming, and what is that which is always becoming and never is?* Gabriela imagines herself asking him this question, hoping to crush him—Gutiérrez, Pinocchio, Carlitos, and Violeta are there, and the scene takes place that Sunday, at the cookout, by the swimming pool—but Nula, smiling benevolently, though never losing his theatrical disdain, would respond, *Are we actually going to discuss becoming or are we just making riddles to humor an old fag who fled Syracuse disguised as a woman, like some vulgar tranny?* Laughing softly at his response without realizing that in fact it's her own and not Nula's, Gabriela loses interest in the becoming, and, putting the beige spool back in the tin, sifts though its contents until she finds the yellow one. Between the two, she chooses the green pin cushion that seems to have the thinnest needles, and leaving the needles and thread on the bed, passes her hand delicately under the silk cloth so as not to wrinkle or tear the blouse and then gently rips away the button, which comes off easily, though it leaves a piece of thread hanging from the end, which she's loosened but which she won't be able to remove herself despite the delicacy and dexterity of her *free finger samples*, as José Carlos likes to call them in jest, because of their tiny size, which means that she'll have to use the scissors to do it. There's one with a curved tip, and another one that's much larger, so she picks up the smaller one: she inserts the tip between the cloth and the thread and carefully pries the thread away so that in the end, when the thread is loose, she can pull it away with her fingers. When it's ready—the tip of the scissors enters farther as the thread loosens—she removes the scissors and finishes the job with her fingers. So as not to lose it, she's left the mother-of-pearl button on the lapel of the tan jacket, where it contrasts more against the dark background, rather than on the light bed spread, on which it would disappear and be difficult to find. Picking it up, she starts pulling out the thinnest needles from the pin cushion one at a time, trying them in the holes without managing to get any to fit, and then sticking them back on the pin cushion after the failure. Eventually, with the fifth needle—without realizing it, she's trying a needle that she'd already tried before, so for her it's the sixth, counting the needle she'd tried twice—it works, which is only partially gratifying for Gabriela because the needle that fits the iridescent button is so thin that she doubts whether the yellow thread would pass through the eye and then through the holes on the button, *easier for a rich man to enter the kingdom of heaven,* Gabriela thinks, laughing aloud, *where the ruling classes control the gates.*

Gabriela unrolls a piece of thread from the spool, some thirty centimeters more or less, brings the spool to her mouth, cuts the thread with her teeth, and, taking advantage of the movement, puts the end of the thread she's just cut into her mouth and moistens it on the tip of her tongue. Dropping the spool back into the tin, she prepares to thread the needle. The end she's just moistened is rigid and ends with an extremely thin filament that could easily pass through the eye, but the eye is so narrow that the filament bends as it touches the metal, without passing through the hole, and Gabriela has to bring it to her mouth and moisten it again. Like the first, the second attempt also fails, the filament colliding against the metal without sliding through, and Gabriela, remaining patient, once again moistens the end of the thread and attempts to pass it through a third time. Now, the filament passes through the eye, but it's so thin that even Gabriela's *free sample fingers* can't grasp it; her index finger and thumb, on several occasions, think they've gripped it, but when they pull at the rest of the thread the fingers come away empty, as if the filament, which is clearly visible on the other side of the eye, were an immaterial object, a mirage, or an illusion; the tips of her fingers appear to grasp it, though no sensation is transferred to them, and nevertheless the extremely delicate and in fact all but invisible tip of the thread has changed, twisted, coiled in on itself, as if the incursion of her fingers had produced a tiny catastrophe of a single miniscule point. Finally, on the fourth attempt, she grasps it, but when she pulls—now she can really feel the thread, dampened because she's put it back in her mouth in order to straighten and sharpen the point—the rest of the thread, rather than passing through, gathers at the entrance to the eye, because of an infinitesimal accident, but enough, in the present situation, to block its passage. The filament has undone the thread, unraveling it, and only this single filament of the thread's braid has passed through the eye, and the rest of the thread, come apart, furrowed and compressed at the eye, increasing its diameter, now wider than the eye of the needle and slightly undone, gathers at the entrance. Gabriela makes an irritated face, its exaggeration diverging profoundly from her calm interior (she's content, actually, and the difficulty of threading the needle, rather than annoying her, is in fact amusing), and she pulls out the thread, and deciding to change ends—the former has clearly suffered irreparable damage in the previous attempts—she moistens it carefully, rolling it several times over her tongue to infuse it thoroughly with saliva, and, concentrating, performs the same movement, slowly, carefully, but fails again. She has to try twice more, and on the third attempt, finally, she succeeds: the end that has crossed the eye is solid against her fingertips, and seeing and feeling how the thread passes cleanly through the eye of the needle produces a pleasure that is at once physical and mental. The yellowish thread ends up distributed across the needle in two unequal parts; Gabriela makes a knot in the longest end, the one that was undone by the failed attempts to pass it through the eye, picks up the mother-of-pearl button, puts it in place, and pierces the fabric from the back to the front, passing the needle through one of the holes of the button, which ends up hanging in the air, suspended along the thread that tenses as Gabriela expertly and gently pulls the needle outward until the knot at the back of the fabric hits it, and in doing so begins the first turn of the stitch; placing the button again, Gabriela passes the needle through, in the opposite direction, from the outside in, with the thread following and tightening the button against the fabric, and then passes the needle through the first hole again, inside out; after repeating this maneuver twice more in both directions she checks that the button is firmly stitched, and, removing the needle, vigorously wraps the end of the thread between the button and the cloth to ensure that there's enough space between the button and the fabric to allow it to pass through the buttonhole without wrinkling the fabric; finally, Gabriela ties off the end and, lifting the blouse, snips the thread with her teeth, and checking that she's done this almost at the edge of the knot, decides she's satisfied and carefully lays out the blouse on the tan suit again.

Although it's only ten after five, Gabriela decides it would be a good idea to start preparing now so she's ready by six; she can call Rosario and Caballito before she leaves for their date at the Amigos del Vino, and so, translating her decision into actions, she walks out to the tiled corridor and takes the short walk toward the back of the house, sidestepping the doormat that guards the entrance to her aunt's bedroom, opens the next door, where there is no doormat, and enters the bathroom. Maruca, the girl who's taken care of the house for the past seventeen years—she started when she was single, but by now her eldest son, who's Ángela's godson, is at least fourteen—responsible for the gleaming neatness that dominates even the most remote corner of the house, pays special attention to the kitchen and the bathroom, and when she turns on the light, Gabriela realizes that Maruca must've waited till her aunt left before she finished cleaning, because the mirrors, tiles, railings, shower, tub, toilet and bidet, plastic curtain, medicine cabinet, towels, shower caps and bathrobes, slippers, combs and toothbrushes, shampoo and soaps (rose-colored for the sink, green in the shower, white on the bidet), lotions, creams, powders, and perfumes are all clean and polished, each one in its place, so carefully scrubbed and arranged that as she enters, and as often happens in certain places, Gabriela perceives less the bathroom itself, which is displayed, overwhelmingly, before her senses, than the ideal that inspired its style, its arrangement, its cleanliness down to the millimeter, as though it were decoration, a hyperrealist illusion or some sample display at a trade show. It wouldn't be smart to take a bath under the circumstances, and so, after undressing and urinating, and before entering the shower, she turns on the tap and tests the temperature with the back of her hand as she adjusts the mix of cold and hot water, opening and closing the respective taps until she finds the appropriate level, and when she finds it she steps into she shower, closes the flower-patterned plastic curtain to keep the water from splashing out, and lets the warm rain soak her. Washing her hair carefully keeps her in the shower a long time, and when she finally comes out she dries herself off energetically, wraps her hair in a towel, puts on a bathrobe, slips on a pair of plastic and wood clogs, gathers her dirty clothes, and puts them directly into the washing machine in a small room behind the kitchen, in the rear courtyard. When she's back in her room, she opens the bathrobe and slowly examines her body in the dresser mirror. Are her breasts any larger? Apparently yes. And her belly? Gabriela looks at herself face on and then, turning sideways, gathers up the white bathrobe and studies the contours of her belly, unable to decide if it is or isn't slightly more prominent than usual. By the time she finishes drying her hair, dressing, putting on makeup, it's twenty after six. No one answers when she calls Caballito, which means her father hasn't come home yet, and José Carlos's cell phone goes straight to voicemail. Gabriela doesn't leave a message, and as she's hanging up an unexpected realization strikes her, a feeling that, paradoxically, combines defiance and pain: *In the end, this is happening inside my body, and whether anyone else knows it or nor, whether they like it or not, they'll always be outside of what's happening.*

She crosses, calmly, in the warm evening, the blocks that separate her from the bar, and when she arrives, she feels hot on her face and legs and damp on her temples—for several minutes, she's been walking down the street wrapped in a spring-like warmth, the seasons confused on her own skin, which, in contact with the air, has revived her flesh, her organs, and the spark that flickers behind her forehead, sensations related to other days of the year, to October and November. The door to the bar is closed because of the air conditioning, but through the window, sitting at the last table, she sees Tomatis, Violeta, and another young woman who she doesn't recognize. Soldi is standing at the bar, behind Tomatis, talking and laughing with Nula, who, from the other side of the bar, is uncorking a bottle of wine as though he were the bartender. Of the seven or eight tables in the tiny bar, the one at the back is the largest; besides theirs, only three others are occupied, and two young men are at the bar, near the entrance, drinking red wine and snacking on something. The real bartender—Gabriela's already seen him several times before—wearing a white jacket over a red and green check shirt, visible at the collar and at the wrists, who smiles when he sees her come in, is arranging some salmon slices on a plate. As she enters, a few somewhat loud exclamations erupt from the last table, causing Gabriela to check her watch to see how late she's arriving, because her friends' excessive happiness seems to suggest that they're already on their second or third glass of wine. But it's only seven fifteen, and there's nothing on the table yet, not a bottle, or glasses, or plates, nothing apart from an ashtray, a metal stand that, vertically, contains a stack of napkins, and a glass toothpick container. Gabriela leans in toward Violeta and Tomatis and kisses each of them on the cheek. Tomatis asks:

—Do you know Diana? The wife of our friend Nula, who as you can see is opening a bottle of Sauvignon Blanc, which honors us this night at the Amigos del Vino.

Gabriela steps aside and leans in to give Diana a kiss, and as their cheeks quickly and delicately graze, Gabriela's gaze lands on the stump on the end of her left arm; she controls her surprise in time, pretending not to have seen anything, but her face burns suddenly, and she hopes that her summer tan hides the blush. But from Diana's vaguely mocking expression—*How incredibly beautiful you are!*—she suspects that she must've noticed the look and is amused by her distress. Diana, possibly to calm her, raises her left arm and, with a slow and natural gesture, slides her hair behind her ear with the stump and then returns it to her lap, under the table. Hesitating, Gabriela continues standing next to the table, staring at the wall behind them, and after a few seconds the memory of the previous moments returns, as she crossed the threshold and closed the door, the tableau that has become fragmentary and confused by her intrusion, the bartender in the white jacket, smiling as she comes in, arranging, at the end of the bar near the door, oval salmon slices on a plate, the two people drinking red wine at the bar, the blurry patrons at the small tables near the entrance, and her friends at the last table, Tomatis at the head, his back to the bar, and to his left, their backs to the wall, Violeta and Nula's wife, and behind Tomatis, on either side of the bar, Nula and Pinocchio, talking and laughing as Nula uncorks a bottle, the noisy greeting from her friends, like actors sitting around a table on a stage, performing the arrival of an actress who plays the role of the friend, in a typical bar scene with some extras who play the parts of the bartender and of the patrons pretending to have a conversation, all forming a scene so external to her that Gabriela feels nostalgia for its loss in the bottomless abyss where it collected with the more remote past, the previous week, the years of her childhood, the centuries buried forever, the innumerable masses dispersed over the world and eventually erased, the first moment of the universe, despite the fact that it occurred only a few seconds before.

—My father was an architect, my ex-husband is an architect, my first son is in his first year studying architecture in Rosario, and of course I'm an architect, so I think there's still some hope of keeping these old ruins from collapsing; we might even modernize him, Violeta says to Diana, nodding toward Tomatis, who seems to draw extreme pleasure from the declaration, though he must've heard it several times by now.

Since they called him at *La Región* yesterday at noon to tell him about the publisher's death, Tomatis has been running around, from the paper to the wake, and this morning to the private cemetery, Oasis de Paz, in the north end of the city, more than half an hour by taxi. The publisher had retired years earlier, long before he decided to leave, but Tomatis would see him every so often and had even visited him the year before at the hospital where he was admitted a few days and from which no one thought he'd come out alive, but he lasted another year, until that Wednesday morning, the day after turning eighty-three. Although he'd edited the Sunday literary page for a long time, Tomatis didn't publish a single line in it after he started at the paper. In the first few weeks, he tried to include a few less-conventional authors than the usual group of contributors, all from the city and the surrounding region, and who were only read by each other, he even decided to invite some writers from Buenos Aires of differing political and literary tendencies to contribute, but about a month later, Tomatis and two other journalists with some literary sense were called in to discuss the upcoming issues of the supplement when suddenly the publisher appeared with a copy of the previous week's literary page and told them, in a way that, despite being friendly and cheerful didn't allow any room for objection, more or less the following: *Look boys, this is a mediocre city and La Región is a mediocre paper. Which means that the literary page has to be mediocre too.*

Thirty years later Tomatis still laughs, somewhere between incredulous and in awe, when he tells someone about it. And he'd admired the relationship they'd had too. The publisher, who'd been retired for a while, when he found out that Tomatis had decided to leave the paper, called him up to tell him it was a mistake, and when Tomatis told him that he'd already wasted too much time putting lipstick on a pig just to watch someone else butcher it, the publisher understood that his ex-employee, for some reason that he was unaware of, had lost the quality that had been so necessary to his work: his cynicism. And because his retirement had pushed him to the margins of power, because his children and the children of his partner, who'd died years before, had taken over the business, he said that it was good to leave, that it wasn't worth looking after such trivial things. He didn't say it out of cynicism: his was an average intelligence, his values were as relativistic as they come, and if old age and death hadn't existed he would have gone on defending those values and judging the world according to them. Tomatis was fascinated by that sincere, slightly myopic mediocrity that nevertheless forced him to be a shrewd deal maker. His father, who founded the paper, had been an anarchist, and he was a member of the Jockey Club. From that combination he'd retained a taste for the popular, which made him feel more comfortable at cookouts with the print shop staff or at parties thrown by the newspaper carriers union than at ceremonies with the Archbishop, with the governor, or with military officials (although, while he was running the paper, he never missed one). The ideals that turn out lucrative become loathsome or sinful according to the moral resources of those who, disinterestedly at first, insist they can live by them. He spent his free time laboriously translating Shakespeare in order to improve his English, and writing, even more laboriously, stories

237

about the peasants who lived along the river and the islands, and at the end he would shut himself up in his office to write them, ignoring everything at the paper, and eventually the heirs forced him to retire. He never doubted for a second that Tomatis's worldview was the exact opposite of his own, but he trusted his cynicism more than the sincerity of the other journalists, the ones who thought like he did but who were incapable of measuring exactly what had to be said and how to say it, as Tomatis could, thanks to his energy and his education. When he'd stop by Tomatis's desk, especially early on, he always, out of curiosity, tried to see what books he was reading, and if Tomatis, when he showed up at the paper, or before he left, passed by his office for some reason, most often to ask for an advance on his wages, he'd quickly swipe the book that he carried under his arm or in his pocket, looking carefully at the cover or thumbing through it slowly, knowing that their authors, of which he was totally ignorant, came from a world that he'd never be allowed into. In the obvious and natural indifference with which Tomatis treated the ostensible seriousness of the paper, and in the scrupulous and slightly humiliating (for the other journalists) facility that he had for doing his job, the publisher, who was aware of the strict limits to what he could demand, saw less an employee than a sort of counterpoint to himself.

Yesterday, Tomatis made the trip to the funeral home and stood a while before the publisher's impassive, sharp, and now pale face, unable to suppress, at first, the clichés that death occasions, like *What if he's faking it? What if he suddenly opened his eyes and sat up?* or maybe, *It won't be long before I'm in that box*, or, *Does cerebral activity continue briefly postmortem, in a confused, delirious way, at first neutral or increasingly painful, or less painful, until it becomes pleasant, which those who've come out of a deep coma or a long period of inertia have ended up calling limbo, inferno, purgatory, and paradise?* But then he remembered the call he'd gotten from the publisher when he found out that he was planning to leave the paper, and how he tried to make him understand, by his tone, that he, Tomatis, was the only one he still trusted to do things the way he understood them, because the new generation of publishers and administrators, under the pretext of "internal restructuring," as they say, had ceded control to the military dictatorship. Even for the publisher's visceral mediocrity, that control was dangerous—its hungry opportunism lacked the weapons of his kingdom, which were cunning and negotiation. And he, Tomatis, was the only one who knew how to use them, and though he didn't share those values, even disdained them, and actually worked constantly against them when he wasn't at the paper, while he was there he was the only one who could understand the need for them and integrate them to the work.

When he walked out to the street and stopped on the first corner to wait for a taxi, Nula offered to take him home, and on top of that gave him a couple of local chorizos that neither he nor his sister could really consider disposable after they'd cut a few slices before dinner. Violeta was having dinner with her mother and her grandmother, and afterward would stay over, so Tomatis went up to the terrace and worked a while in his room, with the window open and the door ajar, allowing a current of air to sneak in. But just now there was no breeze, in fact, and the atmosphere in the room, having been shut up the whole afternoon, in the increasing heat of the day, had become humid and stifling. He got up and went out back to the terrace and looked up at the sky, but neither the moon nor the clouds nor the stars were visible: there was only a hazy, gray dome, fading to black, and the sun that he'd seen, staining red the horizon and the low sky in the west, as he got out of Nula's car, had not dissolved the nebulous, smooth cap that had covered the sky the entire day. And so, when he went back to his room he didn't shut the door as he went in because in the open darkness of the terrace there hadn't been the slightest hint of a breeze. The night was warm and pleasant. Under the lamplight, Tomatis took out some white sheets of paper from a drawer, removed the cap from a black pen, and on the first page, where the date and location of the correspondence usually appear, he wrote, *Wednesday night.* And after thinking for a second, he began to write his letter. *Dear Pichón: Guilt always precedes the crime, and is even independent of it. Myths accept no refutation, they just are: thus, in the myth, Oedipus, though he doesn't know it, is guilty. The tragedy, meanwhile, translates the myth to the level of action. As I was saying on the phone Sunday, in this particular tragedy the development of the plot is more ambiguous, and the statements that trigger the disaster are merely verbal assertions and do not contain the slightest proof. Everyone says that Oedipus Rex is a detective story, which means that the rules of the genre force us to ask ourselves who benefitted from the crime and who had the opportunity, the means, and the motive to devise it and make it look like an inevitable misfortune. The plot, as I see it, is as follows: 1.) Oedipus arrives in Thebes, solves the Sphinx's riddle, and marries Jocasta. 2.) Oedipus's clairvoyance puts him in conflict with Tiresias, who'd been unable to solve the riddle and who sees in Oedipus a serious competitor, and also disrupts Creon's plans: after Laius's death he'd planned to overthrow and murder Jocasta and take the throne of Thebes. 3.) The shepherd, who did in fact abandon Jocasta and Laius's true offspring (who didn't survive) on Mount Cithaeron, and who foresaw the death of Laius and his attendants at the crossroads, fled not because he recognized Oedipus after so many years, but rather to save his own life because, as the only survivor and witness to the crime, he figured, rightly, that Oedipus would eventually kill him too. 4.) Creon sends him to Corinth to figure out why Oedipus exiled himself, and he learns that it's because the Oracle at Delphi predicted that he would kill his father and marry his mother, which meant that he had to put space between himself and his family to avoid incest and parricide. It's worth noting that, according to various*

240

traditions, the Oracle wasn't infallible—far from it—and not only was it often mistaken, forcing people to return for repeated consultations, but also its prophesies were generally formulated in such obscure ways that its visitors' interpretations were often mistaken. In this version of Oedipus, we can apply the domino theory to the successive Oracles: if a single one is false, the rest will be too; and if nothing in the tragedy, except the statements of the shepherd and the messenger, proves that Oedipus is actually the son of Laius, the only thing that's proven by the end is that superstition makes more innocent victims among children than among their parents. Oedipus consulted the Oracle because some drunk in a tavern in Corinth called him a bastard, which made him start to doubt his own identity. 5.) Creon plots, with Machiavellian cunning (avant la lettre), to eliminate Oedipus and Jocasta by making them believe that Oedipus was the child that Laius had sent to Mount Cithaeron because an Oracle had predicted that the child would kill him. 6.) Creon relies on the complicity of the shepherd and the messenger from Corinth, who have no choice but to follow his plans. Insidiously, Creon convinces Tiresias—who is old and all but senile and who detests Oedipus for humiliating him by solving so quickly the riddle of the Sphinx that he'd been unable to solve—that Oedipus is the son of Laius and Jocasta and the true source of the curse upon the city. 7.) The false testimonies from the shepherd and the messenger convince Oedipus that he's committed two horrible crimes, parricide and incest, and that the man in Corinth who called him a bastard had been telling the truth: Oedipus is unaware that, while he was certainly a bastard, he wasn't the same child that the shepherd had abandoned on Mount Cithaeron, but another. Creon had exploited the rumor, the false prophesy, the murder of Laius, and the wedding of Jocasta, weaving his own version of the story in order to achieve his goals. 8.) Jocasta hangs herself, Oedipus gouges out his own eyes and exiles himself to Mount Cithaeron, Creon takes power of the throne of Thebes, and the shepherd and the messenger, of course, were never heard from again.

241

*In the tragedy, it is suggested that Laius may not have been the
father of Oedipus, that some nymph on Mount Cithaeron, et cetera, et
cetera. Actually, what the myth suggests, constantly, is that returns, not
to mention "regressions" tend to be catastrophic. All returns contradict
the physical laws of the universe, which is always, or almost always,
expanding. Swimming against the current, and so on. Call me when you
get these notes, to talk them over. Carlitos.*

*PS. This Sunday I'm going to a monstrous cookout at Gutiérrez's.
Many ghosts of the past and a few tenuous silhouettes of the present will
be in attendance. I'm a hybrid of the two. Kisses to Babette and the kids.*

The next morning he woke up early and, because the weather
was nice, sat down to drink some *mates* while he read on the sunny
terrace. The mild, eight-thirty sun announced the return of the
summer. Enormous, dispersed white clouds, static, with vast blue
spaces between them, decorate the sky. Tomatis's gaze passes over
them gladly, thinking they foretell good weather for the days ahead.
The mass is at nine thirty, and the burial is scheduled for eleven,
but because it's for a local person of certain importance, Tomatis
knows that there's no point in rushing, and since he's decided to go
straight to the cemetery, avoiding the church, he still has an hour to
kill before he has to get ready. When he arrived at the cemetery, the
mourners had only recently set up around the family mausoleum,
transferred from the municipal cemetery, too exposed to the floods
of the Salado river, which every so often, before joining the Paraná,
overflows and inundates the whole western flank of the city. Oasis
de Paz, a private business, though it offers its own mausoleums,
also accepts transfers, *corps et biens,* from the families who can pay
for it. Concealing his skepticism, Tomatis listened to the eulogies:
from an advisor to the governor who'd once been a guerrilla and
who after living abroad for a few years had returned to the city, to
serve the democratic process, as they say, although since the return

of democracy the problems that had supposedly inspired him to take up arms not only persist but are in fact worse than ever; from one of the current publishers of the paper, an heir of the other family of owners; and from one of the editors, a sports writer, who recalled that the publisher had also been president of a soccer club, and that during his presidency the club had played in the first division. Tomatis, out of curiosity, has approached the wreaths and bouquets of flowers to read the violet cards: everyone's there, the government, the church, the banks, the industrialists, the two main soccer clubs, the television channels, the law school, the charitable organizations, the university. Seeing the crowd around him, analyzing the rhetoric of the eulogies, Tomatis realizes just how long—since his adolescence at least—he's been living with his back to the city that in turn regards him with considerable suspicion: Without a formal declaration of war, without explicit violence, his disdainful irony toward what the pages of *La Región* at one time had the habit of calling *the life blood of the city* had been reciprocated with suspicion and distrust. Nevertheless, when the ceremony finished and the guests began to disperse, a small group of employees and ex-employees of the paper, from editorial and the print shop, called him over as they made their way to the cemetery exit. At first they talked about the publisher, but soon they moved on to other things: dead or retired colleagues, the imminent move of the newsroom and print shop to a new location, modern and larger, in the north end of the city, and finally a discussion about the *Clásico* that the two local soccer teams would play that Sunday. The sports writer who had given the eulogy offered to drive him downtown, and they distributed themselves into two cars—there were nine of them in all—and Tomatis said goodbye at the cemetery gate to the five who were going in the other car. Tomatis was uneasy about making conversation with his ex-colleagues all the way downtown, but two blocks later the driver and the two in the back had already returned to the discussion of Sunday's match, analyzing the rosters, the fact that they were playing on such and such a field, and the recent history—trades, wins and losses, physical condition of certain players, and so on—of the two teams. Early on, when he'd just started at the paper, at twenty years old, the sports writers laughed at his affinity for literature, and so Tomatis took his vengeance on them by ridiculing sports and proclaiming, in all sincerity, that he'd never set foot on a soccer field, and now, listening to their heated discussion during the drive, he thinks that he could still make the same claim, but that his situation won't allow it—what from a twenty-year-old would have sounded like a provocation they'd take, today, as an insult, though it wouldn't stop them from letting the Sunday match take up the entire conversation, let alone ask themselves if the person they'd invited to travel with them was interested in the topic or not. *None of us have changed a bit in all these years, and we won't change any in the years that we have left to live*, Tomatis thought when he got out of the car on the corner of Mendoza and San Martín, at the Siete Colores, the bar where he had a one o'clock date with Violeta. She was working on an urgent project that was due that same afternoon, so they drank a coffee and made another date for seven at the Amigos del Vino, and when Tomatis showed up at seven on the dot, he saw that Violeta, refreshed and calm, was already there, and five minutes later, Soldi arrived. Tomatis had spent part of the afternoon correcting and expanding the letter to Pichón, and before coming to the bar he'd stepped over to the post office to mail it.

Gabriela, recovering from her indecision, instead of sitting down takes a few steps to the right and approaches the counter, just as Nula, turning his back to the room, has started to prepare something, his posture so similar to the way he looked in the dream that, elbowing Soldi, she whispers:

244

—Watch him serve us a live fish, realizing as she says it that Soldi is only laughing to be polite, because, as is to be expected, he hasn't understood where the joke is in what she's saying, and much less what she's alluding to. But Nula doesn't have a live fish in his hand when he turns around, but rather a dish of green and black olives.

—You got here in time for the first bottle, Nula says.

—I was thinking a while this afternoon about the question of becoming, Gabriela says point-blank. What does this sentence mean to you? *What is that which always is and has no becoming, and what is that which is always becoming and never is?*

—*Timaeus* 27, Nula says. An important but easily refutable moment of the dialogue on the topic.

—It suddenly smells like school in here, Tomatis says.

—Yeah, Diana jumps in. Finishing school.

—Key moment? Gabriela ventures. Obviously it's just a riddle to please an old fag whose corruptive political fancies forced him to flee Syracuse dressed as a woman, like some vulgar tranny.

Given the value of the joke, which has been told at Plato's expense a thousand times in similar or different ways since the third century before Christ, her listeners respond with a moderate smile, surprised at Gabriela's mysterious peals of laughter, unaware that what makes her laugh so much isn't the joke itself but rather the fact that she'd previously attributed it to Nula during an inexplicably hostile daydream, not realizing, when she did so, that it was not Nula but rather she herself that had made it.

—Pass those glasses to the table, Nula says to Gabriela and Soldi, who pick up three each, each glass destined to one of the six friends, and distribute them around the six seats that are either occupied or empty. Gabriela sits down to the left of Tomatis and Soldi, who also brings the dish of olives and places it in the middle of the table and then sits down next to Gabriela, across from Diana. Nula, who has been delayed a few seconds writing two or three quick symbols on a white receipt pad, arrives after them with the bottle and shows it to the group.

—In the arid lands at the base of the mountains, a chardonnay will become ponderous and will lose its fruit and lightness. A slightly more acidic grape holds up better. Ladies and gentlemen, he says, raising the bottle, Sauvignon Blanc from Mendoza! On the house.

And he starts to serve, expertly, carefully, a small amount of wine in each glass. Violeta reaches for the olives and Nula stops short and shouts:

—No! Wait till after you've tried the wine.

And when he finishes serving, before he sits down at the end of the table opposite to Tomatis, he raises a glass and gestures for a toast. The rest make a similar gesture, and Nula tries the wine, concentrating on the flavor so as to get the best description.

—White flowers, Diana says.

—And grapefruit, Violeta says.

—The summer sun wasn't able to over-sweeten it, Nula says. Clover. It's my favorite.

He sits down. Gabriela and Tomatis are taking a second sip, holding the wine on the tips of their tongues. Tomatis purses his lips and his mouth takes on a wrinkled and circular shape resembling a chicken's asshole. Satisfied, with his glass elevated, Nula looks around at the group, and then, leaning toward his wife, passes the back of his free hand over her cheek. Gabriela, for whom all that rhetoric (not without irony in the present case, of course) is slightly nauseating, notices Nula's gesture and is pleasantly surprised: she didn't expect that kind of spontaneous expression from the person whom, after the conversation they had between their cars this afternoon, and because of certain unmistakable looks that betrayed excessive confidence in his seductive powers, she considers the world champion of pretension. The (incredibly beautiful) Diana, meanwhile, having inspired immediate sympathy in Gabriela, seems to improve, transitively she supposes, her image of Nula, and even Nula himself. And in fact, all rhetoric aside, the wine is exquisite, and when she sees Violeta pick up an olive with a toothpick, she thinks that Nula's insistence that she not eat one before tasting the wine wasn't completely impertinent. Gabriela is hungry, and as she waits for something more substantial—this place serves, among other things, some delicious cheese empanadas and a very good prosciutto—she thinks a few olives wouldn't be a bad idea. But how to begin, with the green or the black ones? Violeta took a green one, left the pit in the ashtray, and now she's taking a black one. For Gabriela, the mixture of green and black olives in the dish constitutes a chaotic situation, and it befits a rational being to introduce order among the chaos: this is what Violeta appears to have done, unless she was choosing randomly with the toothpick. What's more likely is that she has some reason for choosing as she did. Before serving herself, Gabriela decides to wait for Violeta to pick a third olive—it's a green one—and decides to do likewise, rationalizing her selection in this way: the black ones tend to be stronger than the green ones, which means that it makes sense to eat a green one first, in order to taste it better, followed by a black one, whose stronger flavor will saturate the palate. The problem comes with alternating back for the second green olive, whose flavor would be neutralized by the persistence of the black one's much stronger flavor. Maybe, Gabriela thinks, plucking a green olive and bringing it to her mouth, the proper method consists of eating three or four green ones in a row and then switching to black. And when she bites into the smooth pulp of the green olive, she decides that this is the method she'll use from here on out.

Suddenly, raising a glass and holding it motionless in the air, in a parodically solemn voice, Tomatis recites:

If the drug called Day is the one you turn to
know that the people you'll buy from here
forget to mention the thing to fear
which, in the end, is that it's sure to kill you

The others laugh, nodding their heads, and Violeta, leaning toward him, congratulates him with a kiss on the cheek.

—*Juicy immanence, the universe incarnate,* Soldi quotes with a smile, as though they were in an improvised musical dialogue, looking sidelong at Tomatis to see what his reaction will be. And, bringing the glass of wine to his lips, he takes a long, meditative sip.

—The idea is copied, and ruined, by the way, from the thirteenth sonnet to Orpheus, Tomatis says, discarding, expeditiously, Mario Brando's verse, and with an air of having countered, many times, in the same way, Soldi's typical provocations. And after having simulated gratification (the former) and categorical triumph (the latter) the two look at each other conspiratorially, celebrating what technically speaking would be called an *inside joke.*

In fact, Soldi is trying, in a very direct way, to provoke Tomatis into talking about Mario Brando. Soldi knows that the subject is unpleasant for him, and Tomatis avoids it if possible or simply, with impatient skepticism or even ostentatious disdain, rejects it altogether. But in general even a minor incident, a phrase that might contradict his intransigent opinion of the person and craft of Brando, an aesthetic or moral judgment, a poorly told anecdote or an ambiguous estimation of the man, and so on, would be enough, notwithstanding his sworn silence and indifference, meant to ignore him into disappearance from the universe of opinion, to set Tomatis off on an interminable monologue from which Soldi, who's already heard it several times, draws fresh pleasure every time he hears it, not to mention the fact that new information which could be useful to the investigation always comes up. But Tomatis, with a satisfied smile, declares:

—The second bottle is on me, along with the appetizers that, I hope, will add to the experience. Speaking of which, Turk, the salamis—beautiful! My sister couldn't believe how good they were.

—Go ye into all the world, and preach the gospel to every creature, Nula says.

—Now your Phoenician soul is coming out. I was thinking your joke was designed to brighten our passage, but it turns out that it was just a publicity ruse meant to exploit me as a sandwich board, Tomatis says.

—What joke, *che*, what joke? Violeta says.

—I found him standing on a corner, so I offered to take him downtown, Nula tries to say, but Violeta interrupts him.

—Don't tell me he made that joke about the bus that was too full, she says. He told me that one day when I was still engaged to my first husband and started following me around everywhere expecting me to sleep with him.

—I had to wait years for it, Tomatis says.

—And the one about Propp, did he ever tell you that? Violeta says.

—Yes, Gabriela and Soldi say in unison, but Diana and Nula, with inquisitive expressions, wait for someone to tell them.

—Vladimir Propp invented the structural analysis of folk tales. Every plot element, shared among the stories, he argued, could be reduced to their function, starting from an initial situation (for instance, a king and his three daughters), which is represented with the Greek letter alpha, a sequence of variations follow, each of which represents a function: for instance, the daughters go out for a walk (function $\text{\ss}^3$) and they stay longer than they should in the garden (∂^1); a dragon kidnaps them (A^1); the king calls for help (B^1) and three heroes depart in search of them ($C\uparrow$, to indicate the departure); combat with and death of the dragon (M^1–Y^1); liberation of the girls (K^1); return ($\downarrow$); and compensation (W^3), Soldi recites, pretending to be exhausted when he finishes. The limited variable set, he continues, allows us to abbreviate every combination to an abstract scheme. Tomatis says that in Germany, where modern life is incredibly hectic and time is money, parents are too busy to read their children a story before putting them to bed, so they recite one of Propp's formulas instead. And the German children, who are very intelligent, like them a lot. Nula, don't forget this one tonight: alpha beta three capital A, A to the first B to the first up-arrow. H to the first dash Y one K four down-arrow W cubed. Your kids will love it.

—Fantastic, Diana says. Like a numbered joke.

—Propp may have been inspired by them, Tomatis says. And, standing up, he adds, Before the next bottle arrives, I beg your leave to relieve myself of the first.

He makes a gesture to the waiter, who is behind the register, that consists of pointing at the table and spinning his finger, and then, passing behind Nula, opens a door and turns on a light in the next room, illuminating the abandoned cinema whose bar Amigos del Vino rents out to use as their promotional location. The glass doors that lead to the street are shut, as are those that would lead him to the theater itself, and the staircase that once led to the mezzanine is blocked by several rows of stacked-up chairs. On the opposite wall stands the ticket window, intact, but the ceiling lights, which Tomatis has just turned on, don't allow him to see what's behind the glass. The bathrooms are to the right of the door, contiguous with the bar. Sometimes, during the intermission, when he was a teenager, Tomatis remembers, when he went to the bathroom to piss, if he was alone, he'd try to listen to the conversations and the sounds that came from the women's room, convinced that, because they came from an intimate place, they were sure to be exciting.

After pissing, and after looking around to make sure no one is coming in to catch him enjoying that humiliating pleasure, he farts, and then goes back out to the hall, but rather than returning to the bar he approaches the theater doors and, through the circular window, like the eye of an ox, in the center of the upholstered surface—in the fifties, when it opened, it was a luxury theater—he tries to see, through the dust that covers it, the dark interior of the large theater, hoping to hear or perhaps see, lingering in the darkness, the oversized, magnetic ghosts, black and white or in color, the simulacra of life that, night after night, were turned on and shuffled for a couple of hours across the bright screen, and then suddenly turned off, deposited in a circular metal container until someone decided to pull them out again to resume their repetitive, mechanical lives.

Rather than going straight to his seat when he enters the bar, Tomatis leans in toward Soldi and resting his hands on his shoulders informs him, in a weary and patient tone:

—By August of 1945, Brando was an avant-garde poet, but in April of that same year, as you can verify in the archives of *La Región*, he was still imitating Amado Nervo.

And because the waiter is standing with the bottle, waiting for him to taste it, he gestures for him to pour a drink, then lifts the glass and drinks it, holding it a while in his mouth and pursing his lips into a wrinkled circle again, and after a few seconds declares:

—Perfect.

Violeta and Soldi exchange a quick smile: they can already see that the bird will enter the cage. The waiter serves another round of wine and puts the bottle in a bucket of ice—the bucket, which sits on the counter and can hold two more bottles, was a promotional gift from a champagne brand—and then picks up a small plate of salami, one of prosciutto, and another of bread slices, all of which were waiting next to the bucket, and distributes them around the table. The place is so narrow that, standing next to Tomatis, he can pick things up from the bar and place them on the table without moving his legs, leaning to the left and to the right with professional elasticity in order to carry out the task. When his eyes meet the waiter's, Nula, tapping his index finger and thumb, indicating a certain size—which is to say, of the cheese empanadas—he asks the waiter, with a mundane look of course, to bring some, to which the waiter responds with a nod.

—Mario Brando, the biggest fraud ever produced by this fucking city, Tomatis announces with a sententious air, after which he grabs a piece of prosciutto with a toothpick and brings it to his mouth. And not only when it came to literature, he continues. Even his own father, who was a friend of Washington's, detested him. He was so cheap that when he organized the dinners for the precisionists he'd arrange beforehand with the owner of the restaurant not to charge him his share, arguing, rightly, that thanks to him every Thursday night there was a table with fifteen or twenty people there. And he was the one who profited, despite the fact that many of his disciples were dirt poor. And even though he was a millionaire, in '56, during the Revolución Libertadora, they forced him out of the government because he was a crook. Gutiérrez should know about that. One thing to note: there were no communists or open homosexuals or Jews among the precisionists. You, Turk, wouldn't have been accepted, he says to Nula.

—Me neither, Diana says, but for different reasons.

—I wouldn't join a literary movement that would have me as a member, Nula says, adapting the quote to the circumstances.

—And on top of that, Tomatis says, he was a dictator. He terrorized his disciples, humiliated them in public, and treated them like servants, and anyone who tried to leave the movement he'd prevent, by any means necessary, from publishing in the papers and magazines where he had influence, and on several occasions he

252

got someone fired from their job. His literary talent was mediocre, though, I admit, he had genius for machination, too much, possibly, relative to his pedestrian motives: money, though he'd already inherited plenty from his father, social status, and minor literary recognition. Despite his time as a cultural attaché in Rome and his travels through Europe, he was a bumpkin. Dante was his principal reference, and, because he came from Italians, he thought he had exclusive rights to him. He once wrote an article called "Dante and the little country"—it was published in the literary supplement—where he described Dante's relationship to Florence, and which in reality was just a comparison to himself, and as such lowered Dante to the level of a noteworthy provincial. According to Washington, when he retired from the pasta factory the elder Brando started writing literary essays about realism that were a thousand times more interesting than his son's articles.

—That's all true, but he does have some good sonnets, Soldi says.

Tomatis's eyes burn for a fraction of a second, but immediately an ironic smile forms on his lips, his eyelids narrow, and his head shakes slightly.

—You're trying to get me going, Pinocchio, he says, with a solemn and threatening voice.

—He already did, Violeta says.

And everyone sitting around the table, including Tomatis, starts laughing and takes advantage of the moment to take a drink of wine and grab a piece of meat or an olive (Gabriela now opts for two green ones followed by a black one). Putting his glass back on the table, Tomatis thinks for a moment before he continues. And, finally, he says:

—Yes, maybe he had two or three sonnets that weren't completely terrible. But none of those were precisionist. When he wrote more or less decently it was in the style of his worst enemies, the neoclassical poets gathered around the magazine *Espiga*. Brando insulted them publicly while he secretly imitated them, and meanwhile he imposed his ridiculous aesthetic, precisionism, on his disciples, who weren't allowed to publish a word without his say so.

Brando called himself an experimentalist, Tomatis continues, but was a plain-faced bourgeoisie. According to Tomatis, he lived and thought like a bourgeoisie. He married the daughter of an ultra-Catholic conservative general, as opportunistic as himself, who changed his political position with every changing government or circumstance. Brando claimed he had combined poetry and science, but his values and his lifestyle were as traditionally bourgeois as they get: he raised his daughters Catholic, and when they grew up he married them off to navy officers. According to Tomatis, he never went to church more than his social obligations demanded, but his wife and daughter attended the fashionable eleven o'clock mass every Sunday. His brother-in-law, according to Tomatis, was also in the military, and, like his father, gained the rank of general. Starting in the sixties, he'd often visit North American instructors in Panama, in Washington, at the School of the Americas. Because his entire career transpired in the shadow of General Negri, the celebrated torturer, he'd been given the nickname, even in certain military circles, of *secondary anticommunist*, in reference also to his subdued personality, a possible side-effect of his alcoholism. And, therefore, Tomatis says, because of all of this, he'd once been forced to ask Brando for a favor. Tomatis is quiet for a few seconds, remembering, reflecting maybe. Soldi's, Violeta's, and the others' expressions have also turned solemn. Gabriela lowers her head, possibly so as not to have to look anyone in the eyes, or possibly in order to listen better to what she's actually heard many times already, from Tomatis, from her parents, or old friends that Tomatis and her parents had in common: the disappearance of El Gato Garay, Tomatis's friend and the twin brother of Pichón, and Elisa, his lover for several years. She was more or less separated from her husband, who knew about the affair. And though she didn't live with Gato all the time, she would spend her weekends with him, and sometimes, when she wasn't busy with the children, whole weeks. El Gato spent practically all his time at the beach house in Rincón that had once been the Garay family's weekend retreat. El Gato lived on almost nothing, odd jobs from friends mostly, enough for food, for drinks, and for tobacco. He left the town less and less frequently; it was extremely strange to see him in the city. When Elisa visited him, her black car would be parked for days without moving, gathering sandy dust. Every so often they'd walk through the town on their way to the grocery or to the butcher shop, otherwise they were always in the white house, which was starting to fall apart, or in the rear courtyard, which could've been cleaned more regularly. They were an unusual couple, polite but not very demonstrative, and at that time being even slightly different from the people around you who put you in danger for your life. (Someone once joked that they were kidnapped because they didn't have a television.)

Simone, a friend of Gato's who ran an ad agency from which he gave him some work from home every so often, started to worry because Gato, who was usually punctual, was late handing in a small job he was doing, and he decided to go to Rincón (the house didn't have a phone) to see what was up. Simone says that when he arrived everything seemed normal. Elisa's black car, covered in sandy dust, was parked out front, the house was quiet, and the gate was shut. Simone opened the gate, clapped several times, crossed the rear courtyard, the hall, and, opening the screen door to the kitchen, knocked on the door itself. No one answered, and he was about to leave but he tried the handle and the door opened. When he was inside, a nauseating odor stopped him, and he was about to turn around when he saw a piece of raw meat rotting on a wooden cutting board on the stove. Next to the cutting board there was a large kitchen knife and an unopened packet of salt. The kitchen was clean and neat. Simone opened the fridge, in which he found a few bottles of white wine, some seltzer, and several tomatoes. Simone squeezed a tomato to see if it was rotten too, but though it felt a bit soft, he couldn't tell how long it had been there. Then Simone walked through the house, room by room, inspected the bathroom, and, closing the double kitchen door behind him, walked doubtfully through the rear courtyard until, suddenly, he realized what might have happened. He walked out to the street and after checking that it was empty got in his car and returned to the city. He shut himself in his house for several hours without knowing what to do, and when he returned to the agency he called Tomatis.

Ten minutes later, Tomatis was at the office. At the back, Simone had a small closet where he prepared coffee and stored various things, cardboard sheets, old panels, cleaning supplies. After closing the door, he told Tomatis what he'd seen, and Tomatis was about to bolt out to find Héctor, Elisa's husband, but Simone told him to stay a while because such a brief and agitated visit might awaken the suspicions of the guys that worked with him. So they drank a coffee and then walked out, still talking, to the main room, and after a few more minutes, Tomatis left. It was a difficult time for him: his marriage was falling apart, his mother was dying, Washington had died the year before, the whole world was collapsing around him, and he got drunk almost every night (soon enough, it would be every day, too).

Héctor and Tomatis drove to the house in Rincón and inspected everything: the kitchen, the bathroom, the bedroom, the courtyard, without finding a single sign of violence, of alarm, of sudden flight, nothing. All the clothes were in the closets and the bed was made. In the kitchen they found an uneaten loaf of homemade bread wrapped in a plastic bag. Except for the dust that had gathered over the past few days, the house was clean, in order. The paper basket next to the table where El Gato usually worked was empty, and they found the advertising copy that Simone had given him to correct in two short stacks on the table: a taller one, on the right, with the pages already corrected in red pen, and the other, shorter, on the left, which proved, according to Simone, that Gato had been working on them, but all the red pens he used were in the white ceramic jar where he usually kept them. Because El Gato was very organized, there was nothing mysterious about any of that. The rotten piece of meat—it must've been on the board, on the stove, for five or six days—suggested that if something out of the ordinary had happened, it must've been around dinner time: often, when they were together, Elisa and Gato skipped lunch and cooked for dinner, which was always around nine. Tomatis and Héctor guessed that as she was preparing to cook, sometime around eight, Elisa had taken the meat from the fridge, planning to use the knife to remove the fat, while El Gato kept working a while longer on the ad copy, and suddenly, at some point, something happened—probably just as Elisa was putting the cutting board on the stove—that caused him to put the pen back in the ceramic jar, and, leaving the two piles of paper on the table, he got up and went through the kitchen to the rear courtyard, where visitors and strangers usually entered, clapping their hands to announce themselves, as Simone had done when he went to check on him. In all likelihood, El Gato got up calmly because the chair was in its usual position against the table, though someone else might have put it back later. It was difficult to imagine what might have happened; no matter how much they tried, Héctor and Tomatis couldn't reach a single conclusion. They'd passed the time of spectacular kidnappings, meant to terrorize the neighborhood, when they'd arrive at dawn, seal off several blocks with sirens, police cars, military trucks, heavy weapons, and some-times even helicopters, and they'd take not only the whole family or a good part of it, sometimes leaving one person shot dead in the same bed he'd been sleeping in when they found him, but also taking the furniture, the television, the fridge, every object of value they could find, and destroying anything they didn't find useful. Now, the operatives, as they were called, were much more discreet. One morning, someone had watched from their balcony as they kidnapped a young man who was walking calmly down the sidewalk, not far from the center: a car had pulled up to the curb with the engine still running and three hooded men jumped out onto the sidewalk, pushing and hitting him, and shoved him into back seat, on the floor; two got in the back with him and the third got in the front, next to the driver. The car accelerated, pulled away quickly, and a few meters ahead turned at the first corner and disappeared forever. Because there was no one in the street, the witness thinks that if he hadn't been on his balcony, no one would have seen what had happened. Of course this witness wouldn't be crazy enough to report it to the police: just as the kidnapped boy (who was a more or less familiar face in the neighborhood) was never heard from again, no one would ever again see the witness were he to report the kidnapping.

Maybe she'd heard someone clapping in the rear courtyard, and Elisa, leaving the knife and the meat on the stove, had gone outside to see who it was. It was highly unusual for anyone, especially in winter, to show up at that time—or, in fact, at any time: they lived in their own world, self-sufficient and unaware, a shadowy, inexplicable place that almost no one, not even their best friends, approached. And El Gato would've heard the clapping, and, probably surprised, waited a moment for Elisa to come tell him who it was. Elisa would've turned on the outside light in the hall, and, opening the doors to the kitchen, the door itself and then the metal screen outside, would've gone outside to the courtyard, toward the gate. El Gato, worried that she was taking so long, would've placed the red pen back in the ceramic jar and walked out to the rear courtyard. All of this Héctor and Tomatis could easily imagine; the rest, ungraspable, escaped them. Something had happened in the darkness of the street, alongside the beach, that would deprive them of Elisa and Gato forever.

In town, nobody knew anything; nobody had seen or heard anything, no disturbance, no suspicious movement, no shouting, nothing. At the station they listened to them politely, even diligently; the new captain—the previous one had been killed a few years before, and the station was no longer such a dangerous place—took their report seriously and started making inquiries, but after forty-eight hours the investigation hadn't turned up a single lead or a single witness or achieved a single result. Héctor and Tomatis decided to go to police headquarters, to the courthouse, and to the federal police offices in the city. But they didn't learn anything definitive there either. In the best cases they received evasive responses, and in the worst, veiled threats. They knew that if Elisa and El Gato had in fact been kidnapped they had to act quickly; the longer they delayed the less chance there was that they'd ever be seen again. Ultimately, a kidnapping was the only plausible theory, because it was more than obvious that they hadn't fled, that there hadn't been an accident—the car was still parked out front when Simone discovered their disappearance, and Héctor, who had another key, drove it back to the city—not a car accident or any other kind: they never went canoeing or walking through town, where they were never seen except when they were out shopping. So Héctor and Tomatis decided to file a report at the federal police station knowing that the people who took the report were convinced from the beginning that it was a waste of time, that if Elisa and El Gato had really been kidnapped by the army or the police their simulacra of legal action wouldn't produce a single result. They did everything they could, and because Héctor had a verbal altercation with an army official, fearing that he'd get arrested or worse—at that time, anything was

259

possible—Tomatis calmed him down, took him home, and asked him not to get involved any more. Another possibility had occurred to him, a way to find out something or, if they had been kidnapped by the military, to obtain their release. Héctor accepted: in the end, there wasn't anything left to do.

The possibility that Tomatis was thinking of was to speak to Mario Brando, whom he knew was married to the daughter of a general and whose brother-in-law was General Ponce, the right arm of General Negri, captain of the military district, whom everyone knew was directly responsible for all clandestine activity in the area, every kidnapping, every assassination, every raid, and every seizure. It was said that Negri liked to participate, personally, in the bloodiest and most sordid activities, *in solidarity with the troops*, a rumor that he often bragged about. He'd said publicly several times that, *to strip the tree of subversion to its roots one has to dig broadly and deeply, and he was prepared to clear every inch of ground down to the last blade of grass in order to complete his task.*

Brando and Tomatis had detested each other for years, but their interactions maintained a veneer of civility. Brando hated Washington and all his friends, among whom Tomatis was one of the closest. Tomatis was a long-time editor of *La Región*'s literary supplement, where neither he nor his friends hardly ever published, and Brando, who was an assiduous contributor, couldn't afford to make an enemy of him. Tomatis was obligated to read his submissions before sending them to the print shop, and sometimes even when the proofs arrived, if there wasn't anyone else there to read them, and he felt a malevolent glee publishing them because they seemed to make plain their author's mediocrity, not realizing that the public to which they were directed may not have had the capacity to perceive it. Ever since he'd first heard of him, when he was seventeen or eighteen, Tomatis had considered Brando an impostor: to him, his bourgeois lifestyle and his avant-garde pretensions seemed irreconcilable, not to mention the happy accident, Tomatis thought, that his beloved precisionism attempted to combine poetry with science, the only intellectual activity that the comfortable bourgeoisie respected, because it was a way to make money, to increase their longevity, and to substitute a salaried worker for a cheaper machine. Tomatis and Brando lived in different worlds: they had different readers, different relationships with institutions, with enemies, and with allies, both literary and political. And while they moved in different circles and their ways of conceiving and practicing the literary profession were mutually opposed, there were a series of common spaces—the literary supplement of *La Región*, for instance—where inevitably, however much they ignored each other the rest of the time, like fragments of expanding material, their trajectories pushing them always farther apart, sometimes relatively, in the present moment, trying to avoid a collision, trying as much as possible, with icy deference, to disregard the other, their paths crossed.

And so Tomatis, playing, as they say, his last card, decided to go and see him. The possibility was dubious and, Tomatis thought, possibly dangerous. He was in the midst of the most miserable years of his life: the world was falling apart around him, his marriage was a shipwreck, and, every night, he tried to swim away from the wreckage, the misery, and the fury. He still had the strength to go to the paper, but soon he would stop that too, first for a short while, and eventually forever. And so he went to the publisher's office and, without explaining his reasons, asked him to arrange a meeting with Brando, and when the publisher didn't act surprised he figured he already knew what they were but chose to disregard them, less from politeness than from a sense of caution. Soon enough, the publisher called him over the internal system and told him that Brando would be waiting for him at his house in Guadalupe at eight. The speed of the response intrigued him. Had

261

Brando also guessed what would make Tomatis would put aside his reticence and decide to speak with him, or had the publisher, with his talent for finding a compromise even in the most irreconcilably contradictory situations, mistakenly let something slip about the reasons for Tomatis's visit, maybe suggesting, without specifying anything, that the paper was preparing a special supplement and that Tomatis wanted to ask him personally for a submission? For years, with the hatred and humiliation as poignant as ever (and even now, as he's telling the story in the Amigos del Vino bar), Tomatis wondered how he could have been crazy enough to speak to Brando, but would immediately reconcile himself to the certainty that, because it was the last chance they had to see Elisa and Gato again, not trying to see him would have been even worse. And so at eight on the dot he was ringing the doorbell at the house of Brando.

It was his father's house, built in the twenties from the wealth of the pasta factory, two or three blocks from the beach. The well-kept house was on a corner, but withdrawn behind a garden that occupied at least a quarter of a block. After his father's death, Brando had moved in. A light came on in the threshold and a uniformed servant opened the door, but rather than take him inside the house guided him through the trees to a sort of cubical pavilion topped with a semispherical cupola, constructed in an open space in the garden, and whose function Tomatis guessed immediately. It was Brando's office, in which he'd built his amateur observatory: every so often *La Región* published an article or an interview in which Brando described his astronomical observations with such insight that Tomatis once commented that Copernicus, Kepler, and Galileo—not a festive, happy bunch in the least—must have been doubled over with laughter in their graves.

The servant knocked, and immediately after hearing Brando's voice, which was delayed a few seconds before reaching them, opened the door and lead him through. Brando was dressed in a wool dressing gown, but with an immaculate shirt and tie underneath. Tomatis had the sensation that he'd walked into a theater to see a play that was being performed just for him. He was leaning toward the telescope and maneuvering it with a single hand to find an optimum view, or a more exact framing, or adjusting it with slight movements to follow, at every moment, the regular path of the bodies that he was pretending to observe, so that with his free hand he could hold the edge of the dressing gown closed at his thighs to prevent it from opening too much because of the angle of his body, despite the fact that he had on excellent quality, carefully ironed pants beneath. He lingered a while in that position, not finding the perfect angle, or in all likelihood pretending not to, thereby forcing Tomatis to wait for him, whatever his reason for visiting, paying off, in this way, the first portion of the debt that each thought the other owed him, the accumulation of interests that their antipathy, suspicion, aesthetic and political differences, behavior, or the circles in which they respectively moved, the tradition of accumulated gossip, slander, satire, and rancor, on top of what each had written, and so on, transformed into legend by the passage of time. Seeing him with his eye glued to the telescope sight, Tomatis felt a violent sense of obscenity, of a slithering, contented perversion, as if Brando were spying on a naked woman, although that understandable perversion would've inevitably produced less revulsion than seeing him intrude, with his indecent gaze, upon the intimacy of the stars. Finally, Brando straightened up, walked over to him, and invited him to sit down, while he himself sat down at a desk chair, behind a desk that, Tomatis observed, was built a few centimeters above the visitors' chairs, allowing him to look down on them and keep them in an imperceptible position of inferiority. For three or four minutes they exchanged pleasantries: it was obvious they didn't have anything to say to each other. And then, at a certain point, in an overly abrupt way, Brando stopped talking and, widening his eyes, looked at Tomatis inquisitively, but when Tomatis started to talk, tripping over his words at first, Brando leaned back in his chair and stared at some vague spot in the room above them, frozen in that position except for his hands, which, held in front of his mouth, met silently at the fingertips, with the fingers extended, as he must have done at the law firm when he met a new client for the first time. Overcoming the revulsion, the shame, the humiliation—after leaving he practically ran to the first bar he found and drank his first gin, and though it was barely eight thirty, he spent the rest of the night, till the morning, going from bar to bar, drinking—Tomatis started telling him what had happened to Elisa and El Gato, all their fruitless inquiries and the official reports they'd made, adding that Elisa and Gato were completely inoffensive and apolitical and lived in their own world, which could have seemed strange from the outside and might be interpreted mistakenly by someone with dogmatic and suspicious inclinations. After they'd exhausted all the possibilities, and though their family and friends' doubts were as strong as ever, Tomatis remembered that Brando had family in the military, and it occurred to him that they might obtain, though him, some help or information—Tomatis had thought, for instance, of General Ponce, his brother-in-law, which was why he'd called the publisher to ask for a meeting.

—You should have called me directly, Brando said with an icy friendliness that carried a vague hint of reproach. But he fell silent again and sat waiting. In reality, Tomatis had already said everything.

—A normal person, Tomatis says now, to the people listening to him at the table in the Amigos del Vino bar, though at least three of his five listeners, having heard the story many times and having thought about it often, know what he's saying by heart. A normal person would have reacted from the first words, asking for details, making some gesture or showing some emotion, but he just sat there with his impassive, conventional posture of polite attention and good breeding.

And when he finished speaking and the other's attitude remained friendly and attentive the silence became so oppressive that Tomatis started over and stumbled through the story again, but rearranged, fragmented and rushed, knowing already that Brando not only would do nothing, but also had introduced between himself and his visitor a kind of invisible wall against which his words were ricocheting. Tomatis's agitation was a mixture of incredulity and fury, but his story, although incongruent and superfluous, had to continue till the end because he also knew that the visit had to maintain a semblance of normalcy and that the slightest incident could be dangerous: if things went south, Brando wouldn't hesitate to call his brother-in-law to tell him what had happened. And so, when he finished, and the unbearable silence that met the first version of his story had returned and Brando continued to sit for long seconds, frozen in his conventional pose, staring at a vague point somewhere near the ceiling, Tomatis froze too, waiting, and though he was boiling inside, he affected a calm and patient demeanor. After an interminable interval, and after giving him a strange look, severe yet momentary, that betrayed what, below his formality and stuffy bourgeois appearance, he was really thinking, Brando stood up. Suddenly, in a mundane and conventional tone, as though he hadn't heard a single word that Tomatis had just said, he asked:

—Do you want to see the moon through the telescope? It's very beautiful tonight.

Trying to keep his voice from trembling, in the same tone, Tomatis responded:

—Some other time. It's getting late.

—I'll walk you out, then, Brando said.

—No, no, Tomatis said. I know the way. Good bye.

Brando didn't respond, but as he was walking toward the door Tomatis could feel his gaze burning a hole in neck. When he was in the courtyard, in the translucent, frozen, winter night, he realized that, despite the cold air, he was sweating. The round and brilliant moon that was rising from the river illuminated the shadows between the trees and reflected off the grass around Brando's observatory. In the street, he stood a moment on the corner, hesitating, and finally decided to walk toward the beach, hoping that one of the summer bars would still be open at this time of year. As he walked away, the interview with Brando seemed more and more incredible, more unreal, as though it had never happened, or as though he'd dreamed it, because in the normal world, where he'd been living up till that moment, it never could have; it had happened somewhere else, where the laws of the nightmare ruled. And so, because of the absurdity of the meeting, its reality, as he left Brando's house in search of a bar near the beach, faded away. The only thing that remained, troubling him, was the strange look, severe yet momentary, that Brando had given him before he stood up from his chair.

Brando died of cancer three years after that meeting, although tonight, as he's recalling it in the wine bar, more than fifteen years after the moment he saw, sparking darkly, across Brando's eyes, the flashing look continues, in his memory, to transmit its concealed, violent meaning, emerged suddenly from the most carefully protected corners of the external world, where, nevertheless, everyone's singularity is made and unmade, estranging everyone from everyone else. That look, intact in the memory of the one who received it, though the eyes it came from have been irrecoverable dust for years, still says, *You dare to come here trying to convince me that your disappeared friends are innocent, but I know you and I know every one of your associates, so I know in advance that they're subversives, and furthermore, that all of you, with all your false modesty, which can't hide*

266

the arrogance of your behavior and your opinions, are the very seeds of
subversion. I have work, I've run magazines, I've been a diplomat and
a minister, and on top of that I have one of the most powerful law firms
in the province, and all of you, I'm sure of it, ignore my poetry and
ridicule it when you're together, I know you do, getting drunk with your
divorcees and raising someone else's children. Free verse is your pretext
for hiding the fact that you're incapable of measuring a hendecasyllable
or using rhyme correctly. If your friends were taken, there was a reason
for it, so don't come here with some story about their innocence. If I were
you, I'd watch my step: I still haven't decided anything, but it wouldn't
take much for me to pick up the phone and describe this unspeakable visit
to certain people who wouldn't have any problem coming to find you at
home one of these nights to give you once and for all what you deserve.

FRIDAY

THE
WINE

THAT DAY AND THE DAYS THAT FOLLOWED, AND FOR
several years afterward, he asked himself whether adults realized
that sex existed. It happened the summer before his father's murder,
just after he'd turned twelve. He was in a cornfield, *inside* a cornfield rather, during a siesta at the end of January, himself, Benito
(his uncle Enzo's nephew, whom Nula thought of as a cousin), La
Cuca, and her little brother, El Bebe, a boy who was almost ten,
boarded with the Jesuits in San Lorenzo, and who followed Nula
everywhere when he spent his vacations in the town. His puppy-
dog admiration amused Nula: El Bebe imitated everything about
him, agreed with everything he said, and whenever they sat in a
field or on the sidewalk outside his grandfather's store or on the
benches at the train station or alongside the swimming pool at the
town club, and they fell silent, El Bebe stared at him, spellbound.
That canine devotion often suffocated him, and, to rid himself of
his slightly asphyxiating dependence and to rest, even though he

271

did like him, he would lie and tell him that he had to go out to the fields with his grandfather or stay home and study for March. Obediently, El Bebe, who believed everything Nula said, resigned himself to not seeing Nula for a couple of days, time he took advantage of to go hunting in the country with other boys his age or slightly older, who smoked in secret, told off-color stories, and claimed a sophistication that Nula was sure he didn't possess, although, to avoid anyone's suspicions, he maintained an ambiguous silence every time the topic came up, hoping that the others would take it as implicit proof of his experience.

They were inside the tall, green cornfield during a summer siesta, him, El Bebe, and Benito's hunting dog, Rosilla, for the following reason: Benito, who was about seventeen, was secretly dating La Cuca, who was somewhat younger, and under the pretext of spending a day in the countryside, he'd invited Nula and El Bebe to bike to the farmhouse that was half a mile from the town, arranging beforehand with La Cuca that she'd be with them *to make sure they didn't get into too much trouble* and that they got home before dark. Obviously no one had explained to Nula the way in which Benito and La Cuca had planned it, but he was aware that that's how it was, that the outing with himself and El Bebe was the last thing on Benito's mind, and that in any case he and El Bebe were able to take care of themselves, something which Benito and La Cuca were more than aware of, because, under the pretext of shooting off a few rounds a bit farther off, they'd left them alone in the cornfield for the last ten minutes. In fact, Nula had felt relieved when they'd left for a while: the conversation they'd been having all morning, full of innuendo, if somehow it seemed that Benito's parents didn't notice it, its childishness disgusted Nula, so much so that, to his experienced ear, the veiled allusions and the ostensibly unstated obscenity sounded obvious. Only to the adults, ignorant of sex, exiled in that melancholic world of domestic chores, of work, and of morals, did they pass unnoticed. Nula and his band of inveterate smokers and tellers of off-color tales, on the other hand, were like doctors of the law when it came to the matter: they knew every last thing about sex, which despite their sensitivity to its mysterious attraction apparently exempted them from practicing it, like the theologians who, utterly familiar with divinity and fascinated by the possibility of its existence, as a result of thinking about it exclusively, forget, in their remote and tenebrous sanctuary, to ever seek it out. Benito and La Cuca, meanwhile—at the time, Nula wouldn't have been capable of thinking in these terms—were sexual monsters, two strange creatures that lurched in another dimension, separate from everyday places, made of off-color jokes and populated with ridiculous, monomaniacal, and grotesque characters, where the human beings, lost in muddled dramas and tangled in language, coexisted with the beasts that not only spoke but sometimes even had the last word, a dimension where priests had girlfriends or wives, grandmothers behaved like prostitutes, and the men, in their extreme credulity, let themselves be cuckolded by their wives in a blatant, scandalous way, a dimension where one spoke plainly about things, like semen and excrement, which adults were ignorant of. It's not that Benito and La Cuca behaved this way, but it didn't take much effort for Nula to translate their obvious allusions to the language of the stories. For instance, before leaving them alone under the pretext of shooting off a few rounds at a distance where the children wouldn't be in danger, Benito had started talking about the corn with the obvious intention of causing La Cuca to prolong the misunderstanding and to degenerate into all kinds of semantic nuances, of associations, and even of gestures that apparently had nothing obscene about them but which seemed to really alter them, so much so that Benito's voice turned hoarse and labored, and La Cuca's manner, usually open and decisive, became hesitant and serious, bewildered and disconcerted. Benito

273

insisted that the corn silk was smooth and pleasant to the touch, and then, compelling her to rub it, and pretending it was a joke, grabbed her wrist, trying to force her hand to grab the corn, and La Cuca, resisting sometimes with more and sometimes with less conviction, would let him do it and then would try to pull her hand away, mixing protests with smiles, struggle with surrender, indignation with laughter. They'd made themselves red with excitement, with contained violence, and Rosilla, frenzied by what, with some reason, she must have thought was a joke, in which at times, judging by the nervousness of her bark, she must have intuited an uncontrollable seriousness, started to jump and chase around them. Nula watched them, more incredulous than disgusted, but El Bebe, sitting on the ground, motionless and serious, seemed to have fallen asleep with his eyes open. Then Benito pulled off an ear of corn and showed it to La Cuca after separating the silk and pinching it between his mouth and his nose, pursing his lips to sustain it, pretending it was a mustache, and when the ear was fully unwrapped, showing all its compact, tender, milky white grains, he tried, at all cost, to make La Cuca taste it, but she forced her mouth shut, squealing, laughing, while Benito, under the pretext of getting her to eat the corn, took the opportunity to rub his hands over her arms, her neck, her buttocks, her hips. Nula asked himself how it was possible that Benito's parents didn't realize what was happening, how the adults in general could be blind to everything that had to do with sex (though he still didn't call it that), not realizing that Benito's family not only wasn't ignorant of it, but in fact were thrilled that Benito had chosen to fall in love with the notary's daughter, and hoped that when Benito started agronomy classes in Rosario the following year, things might take a more formal turn than their adolescent holiday fling. But none of that happened: the following summer, before starting agronomy classes, Benito drowned one afternoon in the Carcarañá.

Finally they relaxed and sat down to smoke a cigarette. El Bebe remained motionless. He generally spoke very little, especially in a crowd, but he sang very well, and at parties, with the family or in town, he'd sometimes sing in public. Before the new year they'd held a tango-singing contest to celebrate the anniversary of the foundation of the town, and even though El Bebe was the only child among the fourteen contestants he'd come in second; that external contrast, between private shyness and public exhibitionism, intrigued Nula. After a while, Benito suggested to La Cuca that they do some hunting a bit farther away and told Nula and El Bebe not to move from that spot so they didn't risk catching a stray bullet by accident, and not to let Rosilla follow them, a superfluous assignment because Rosilla, still disoriented by the earlier confusion, needed time to put her thoughts in order, as they say. They'd given her that mare's name, Rosilla, because her coat alternated between white and brick-colored spots, and around her eyes, on her snout, and everywhere else that her hair thinned out, the white skin faded to bright red—she was an intelligent and frisky red head, and Benito always took her along when he went hunting. For a while, Nula could hear the loud snapping that, as they crossed the cornfield, La Cuca and Benito produced as they separated the corn plants or brushed past them. After a while the sound vanished, and two or three minutes later a shot rang out, reverberated, followed almost immediately by another—one from each barrel of the shotgun—and after echoing a few seconds in their consciousness the sound and its echo passed to their memory, where it continued a while longer, while the external silence, interrupted only by organic creaks, the whisper of corn stalks, the passing cry of a bird, closed around them once again.

La India, on the other side of the desk in the bookstore across from the courthouse, recalling the phone call from El Bebe, who'd ordered a set of law books from the town because he'd taken over

275

the notary practice after his father's death, suddenly caused the memories of that summer day to resurface, maybe seventeen years before, when they biked with La Cuca and Benito to his father's farm, to spend the day there, and during the siesta, because his parents had to go to San Genaro on some family business, the four of them had gone hunting in the fields, or at least that's the pretext Benito had come up with, because soon after they entered the cornfield, after joking and wrestling a little with La Cuca, he'd said they were going away to *shoot off a few rounds*, which immediately awoke Nula's skepticism since, curiously, they didn't take Rosilla, who, in fact, was somewhat confused to see them go, and when she tried to follow them Benito frightened her off by stomping on the ground a few times, the last time in such an exaggerated way, purely as a gag, that his sandal flew off. After they'd disappeared into the corn and the noisy rustling of the leaves and the cracking and the organic murmurs had become completely inaudible to Nula and El Bebe's ears, Rosilla, her ears nervous and erect, apparently continued to receive signals from the direction in which Benito and La Cuca had been swallowed by the corn, and finally, just as she was about to calm down and was coming back to Nula and El Bebe, the two shotgun blasts rang out, with a couple of seconds interval between the first and the second, and when she heard them Rosilla turned back in the direction of the shots, struggling and moaning, running back and forth in such a nervous way that Nula and El Bebe laughed, seeing her so worked up in such a tight space, because she didn't dare pass the line, between two rows of corn, where Benito's sandal had threateningly struck the ground several times. Eventually she calmed down again and came over to them, looking every so often, without apparent anxiety, into the vague point in space, invisible from where they were, from which, every so often, unmistakable signals reached her, more real than for the two boys lying on the ground, who in their sensory realm could only rely on their memories to verify the persistent and real existence of those evaporated sounds.

Nula is amazed by the fact that, in the middle of an energetic and friendly conversation with his mother, who's only separated from him by the width of the desk, at the same time, behind his forehead, through the silent flux, like in a dream, of memories that quickly and sharply condense events that in the cloudy material world would take hours, days, weeks, or centuries to complete, are now taking place in the bright space of his mind because of a telephone call that La India has just told him about, things that had once been real, pieces of his own experience that he'd completely forgotten. And he remembers: Rosilla had sat down between himself and El Bebe, lying on the ground, unsure what to do, waiting for Benito and La Cuca to come back. El Bebe, in fact, was always happy to be left alone with Nula, and as soon as the other two disappeared his expression lost the sort of hypnosis he'd been under recently and took on a contained exuberance that Nula, who knew him well and who actually loved him a lot, but with a certain condescension that only just now, as he remembers it, is he aware of, knew was the result of their being alone together. El Bebe's unconditional devotion to his person, which was at times somewhat suffocating and at other times amusing, could also bring out in him a tyranny that, although mitigated, caused him to permit himself a certain self-regard and even to exaggerate the qualities he considered valuable in order to intensify the admiration he received; he liked to think of himself as admirable, and in order to feel the gratification of that sensation he did whatever he could to increase this in El Bebe. It was because of this that, slightly out of curiosity and probably also to show off an admirable quality, and especially because Benito and La Cuca had left behind them and continued to disseminate over the cornfield, over the countryside, over the summer afternoon, and possibly over the whole universe, a sexual fluid whose existence the adults, Nula believed, were unaware of, and which impregnated everything and transformed them into something different from what they were ordinarily—possibly because of all of this—Nula remembered that once in a while his gang of smokers and tellers of off-color jokes, who boasted uncommon sexual experience, would grab a hen or a dog or some other animal and examine its anal and vaginal private orifices, and if it was a male they'd fondle its penis or its anus or its testicles with a stick. Grabbing a stick from the ground he pinned Rosilla and started poking her vagina, softly, in order not to harm her or scare her. At first she tried halfheartedly to escape, but Nula pushed his forearm against her back to hold her down, and half lying on the ground, continued slowly poking, gently, the rose-colored crevice that, like the other bald terminuses, because of their bright red color, had earned her that mare's name, an attribution which no doubt was at first ironic, given that horses are named by the color of their hair. Rosilla froze, her head twisted slightly up and back, possibly so as to concentrate better on the sensations and, if not to make sense of them, at least to know their cause, to explain to herself why, in an unprecedented and abrupt way, she was receiving the untimely transmission of what, ruthless yet familiar, formed part of the cyclical repertory of her instincts, whose coming and going was the weave of her pulsating presence, assemblage of intricate but precise organs from which emanated, like shadowy exhalations, confused emotions and ritual behaviors that could sometimes be confused for intelligence. Absorbed in this activity, Nula completely forgot about El Bebe until a sort of accelerated murmur, which El Bebe had been emitting for several seconds, distracted him, and when he looked up, in surprise, the stick fell to the ground (Rosilla took the opportunity to run away and, standing apart from them, between alarmed and confused, forgot their presence): El Bebe, intensely pale, had turned onto his knees and was hitting the backs of his fingers on one hand against the curled-up palm of the other, marking the rhythm with an unintelligible mutter. His eyes were narrowed and his blonde hair shook as his head bobbed in rhythm with his hands and the murmur; two drops of white saliva had formed at the edges of his mouth—he'd remembered this another time, about five years before, when Riera had jumped out of the car, downtown, to treat a boy who'd had an epileptic seizure. Nula, frightened, tried to understand what El Bebe was muttering, something which at that moment had the tone of both a command and a plea: *mifact, mifact, mifact, mifact!* and suddenly, thanks to a sort of hiccup that interrupted the litany, the only word, or two words, in fact, that it consisted of—*fuck me*—were instantly and astonishingly clear, like the moment when the endless repetition of a mantra leads, suddenly, to enlightenment—except at this moment he, Nula, was passing from a summer siesta within the green stalks of a cornfield, where patches of light filtered in, bleaching the dark earth, to a new world, one of confusion, of desire, and of guilt, and from which all certainty, in that instant, had been abolished. Without opening his eyes, as if he were alone in the field, El Bebe pulled down his pants and threw himself face down on the ground, and Nula, after hesitating a few seconds, his mouth dry, half open, pulled down his own pants and threw himself on top of him; his prick, hard, its round tip practically transparent, like a bluish red ball of glass, still half covered by his foreskin, sank into his buttocks, flattening against them, and Nula rubbed himself against El Bebe, not feeling any pleasure or knowing exactly what he was doing, while Rosilla, who must've been absorbing the maximum dose of unaccustomed experience, started jumping and running around them, barking more and more furiously, until Nula stood up and grabbed his pants, but he saw, with fear, that El Bebe's buttocks were slightly bloodstained. El Bebe, meanwhile, calm and quiet again, pulled up his pants and sat back down on the ground, looking at Nula with the same admiring and beatific smile; but now Nula was the one in a state of intense agitation: it was as though El Bebe, in offering himself, had transmitted the agent of his frenzy to him, unburdening himself of this agent just as quickly, in order to recover his normal state as soon as possible. Benito and La Cuca showed up soon afterward. They must not have been far away, because the dog's insistent barking was what had caused them to hurry back, and they must've had their own cause for shame (Nula thinks now, remembering them) because they accepted the vague and practically absurd explanations for Rosilla's barking that El Bebe, in complete control over himself, had offered them without the slightest hesitation. Only he, Nula, seemed altered, and was mortified, realizing that when El Bebe got home his parents would see the blood stains and would make him confess. He was panicked for the next two or three days, never leaving his grandfather's house, and every time someone knocked on the door to the house Nula was sure that it was El Bebe's parents, looking for answers. The idea that his grandfather would find out about what had happened was terrifying and, more so, shameful. Finally, on the third day, he had to run an errand for his aunt Laila, on the other side of the station, and when he was walking into the pharmacy he bumped into El Bebe and his mother just as they were walking out. His mother not only didn't accuse him of anything but actually bent over and kissed him and invited him over for some milk that afternoon. And El Bebe seemed happy about the encounter. The day before he'd been in Rosario, where he'd gotten fitted for his first communion.

—El Bebe, Nula says, smiling softly and shaking his head theatrically.

—He's a shark for business, apparently, La India says.

—It wouldn't surprise me, Nula says.

It was already after twelve, but La India, comfortable in her chair behind her desk and in her conversation with Nula, hadn't yet decided to close the store. Her two employees—although she isn't a rabid feminist, La India prefers, on principle, to give priority to hiring women—have already left for lunch. The extraordinarily bright April morning is visible in the street, through the window, and the light reflects, on the opposite sidewalk, off the side of the courthouse building. There's not a single cloud in the sky. As he left his house, around ten, to visit a client at the other end of the city, in Guadalupe, before coming to the bookstore, Nula stood for a moment, measuring the temperature, and finally decided to go back inside and change, leaving behind the jacket and putting on lighter pants than he'd worn the day before. When he saw the cloudless sky, a vivid memory returned of the static, massive, white clouds that he'd seen the day before on his way to Rincón to deliver Gutiérrez's wine order so that the bottles could rest a while in case he decided to serve them on Sunday; he'd run into Soldi and Gabriela just as he was turning off the pavement onto the sandy road, and had talked with them a while, but when he arrived at Gutiérrez's the woman who took care of the house told him that he'd gone for a walk in the countryside, and so he unloaded the wine, walked a while along the street, with no apparent goal, and then returned to the city. This morning, on his way to Guadalupe, in the porous and radiant ten o'clock light, he thought he could perceive the probably fleeting return of summer. It was still early when he finished with the client, so he'd decided to have a cup of coffee at the pastry shop on the lagoon, which, before one of the recent floods inundated the beach forever, when it was still crowded with people, had once been a fashionable place. He watched the water in the lagoon form ripples, still a milky beige, and in the silence of the bar, in which he's the only customer and from which even the waiter has disappeared, into the back rooms or the rear courtyard, he'd started to think about Lucía, but also about Diana, with a remote sense of anguish, like a soldier returning from a pointless

281

war. The sun, high at this point, rising, almost in front of him, from the east, warmed his face and covered the water, the distant vegetation on the opposite shore, the empty sky, with a golden shimmer. A few drops of sweat dampened his forehead and his upper lip, and his freshly shaved cheeks burned slightly. When he walked into the bookstore, La India looked at him a moment, and as he leaned over to kiss her on the cheek, asked him, in a low voice so that the employees, who were still in the office, wouldn't hear:

—What's wrong?

Nula took his time before answering. He walked back around the desk and sat down opposite her.

—My mother doesn't love me, he said, smiling.

—*He who lives most, loves most, a lie*, La India quotes, and taking, as usual, Nula's appeal for affection (believing he needs the protection less than her eldest son), like the whim of a *cynical fin de siècle dandy*, as she'd once described him, in love with her verbal invention, and repeating it often, makes the gesture of symbolically washing her hands of him and goes on to tell him about the call she got from El Bebe.

Law textbooks are stacked on the shelves, on the edges of the desk, on a table, and on the floor, in neat piles, or carefully displayed in cases or in unopened packages, or otherwise recently packaged, prepared to be sent to customers in towns or cities close to the capital. At random, Nula reads, silently, disinterestedly, the titles on the covers and the spines: *A Treatise on the Law of Promissory Notes and Bills of Exchange, Handbook of the Argentine Constitution, Notarial Practice, International Public Law, Annotated Civil Code, National Law of Administrative Procedure, Civil and Commercial Prosecutorial Code of the Province*. Shaking his head and sighing, Nula asks:

—Is Calcagno's *Roman Law Course* still sold?

—There are more current books, but it's still a reference. It's in every bibliography, La India says. Why?

—What made you want to sell such boring books? Nula says, as though he hadn't heard the question, and the moment the words are out, although he's looked away and therefore can't see the look of displeasure on La India's face, he knows that he's just added cruelty to what was already a blunder. But when he meets La India's eyes he sees only a vague, mocking irony, as though his mother hadn't heard a thing. The brutal question that, without knowing why, takes shape in his mind every so often, but which never surfaces, nor in all likelihood will ever reach his lips, now occupies the bright space of his mind, tantalizing and insistent: *What if it were us, his wife and his sons, who he was actually fed up with, and a heroic sacrifice was just a pretext for starting his successive escapes, first to politics, then to the underground, and finally to death?* But instead of formulating it, despite its peremptory insistence—he loves La India too much to allow himself anything more than the occasional minor blunder—he smiles and thinks again that, ever since he arrived at the bookstore, first with the memory of the cornfield and now with the question that sometimes rises from the blackness, tantalizing, insistently, in his conscience, his frontal bone has intercepted the width of the desk, the bright and calm space that separates him from his mother, taking, behind his forehead, the empirically measurable distance and multiplying it by infinity. Finally consenting to answer La India's question, in the most cheerful tone he can muster, he says:

—No reason. We sold it a lot at the kiosk. All I know about Roman law is the famous precept: *Mater certa, pater semper incertus,* and along with a deliberately atrocious pronunciation of the Latin phrase, Nula shakes his extended index finger in the air, threateningly and apodictically.

—The constant specter of masculinity, La India says as she checks her watch.

—Oh, don't let me keep you; I'll get up and leave right now, Nula says, obviously parodying an offended tone.

—On the contrary, La India says. This is the happiest moment of my life. After this I'm retiring to a convent to reflect upon the blessing of having you as a son. But I thought you had a meeting at twelve thirty. Don't forget that they're my clients too and I don't want you to spoil them for me.

—My mother does love me, Nula says, and, looking at his watch, announces, But there's still fifteen minutes left and it's right next door.

It's true. La India had recommended some friends of hers, lawyers, cops, judges, and since it's Friday and the courthouse closes for the weekend at noon, five of them had organized a group purchase at the law school, which is just a few meters away, on the same block as the bookstore. Nula expects to make a good sale—afterward, he plans to return home (maybe take some sun, which seems to be as hot as in November) before going back out, to *the supercenter*, where the Amigos del Vino promotional stand is set to open.

—Mami, Nula says. On Sunday, Diana and I have a cookout in Rincón. Would you be able to tolerate your grandchildren for a whole day?

—Of course I would, La India says. It'll be nice to interact with people somewhat more mature than my own children.

—I assume you're not referring to me, Nula says, and standing up and walking around the desk, he leans toward her and kisses her forehead. You're amazing, India, he says, and picks up his briefcase and turns toward the door.

—All that show just to avoid telling me what's wrong, La India says.

—I swear if I knew what it was I'd tell you, Nula says, and without turning around he waves goodbye with his free hand and walks out to the sidewalk after closing the door behind him. Although the sidewalk is still shaded by the houses, the air feels very warm, in contrast to the cool atmosphere inside the bookstore. Across the street, meanwhile, on the courthouse side, the April light shimmers, pervasive, becomes once again summery over the last two or three days. Nula remembers, again, the sky the day before, in which bright white masses of clouds, their curvy edges clean and hard, floated, static, scattered across the blue sky. An unexpected nostalgia for the day before attacks him, and the idea of constant flux, of *the becoming*, is embodied in those clouds that existed and that, bit by bit, unseen by the eye or by the mind, transforming, scattering, stopped being clouds and disappeared without anyone knowing it. Now, the day before seems like an intimate possession that, suddenly, he's been dispossessed of: because it's still impregnated with fresh traces of sensation, of experience, he senses that it's more his own than the totality of his past, knowing at the same time that, like a dead body, its deceitful presence disguises the immeasurable distance that separates the present moment from its obliterated precursors, the fossilized substance of the memories of the flesh that pulses, sees, hears, touches, feels, and breathes.

Although it's not yet twelve thirty when he enters the law school, three doors down, the five potential clients, and two more they've brought with them, are already there. They invite him into a small conference room with a large, oval table surrounded by numerous chairs, and they sit down to listen to him, as though he were giving a lecture. Nula opens his briefcase and takes out his brochures, magazines, and price lists, yet despite his movements being exact and his words measured, he continues to think about the clouds the day before, so intensely white, the shape of rocks, now disappeared, and he regrets not having written something down in his notebook before coming in, because he doesn't know how long the interview with these clients will last and whether he'll remember what, though he never formulated it exactly in his mind, he thought, at some point, to note down. The clients want to buy an assortment of a dozen bottles each, which is why they'd gotten together, in order to buy a few cases of six, of different varieties and from different wineries, and split them up. In total, it's eighty-four bottles—with the sale he made that morning in Guadalupe, he's earned enough for the day. But when he explains to the clients the unique characteristics of each wine, the technical terms that he employs and that his clients seem to consider attentively don't seem at all convincing, suitable, or appropriate. The essential thing, the taste of wine, is unnamable: the metaphors and comparisons are only allusions. The flinty aroma of certain white wines, for instance, is only a comparative, and incomplete, description, pre-dominant at the beginning, but which combines immediately, after the first sip, with the complex flavors that the wine unfolds over the palate. To him, the sensations, from a philosophical point of view, are incommunicable, and so when he explains to a client that such and such a wine is tender or robust, meaty or velvety, it's impossible to imagine how the client senses those adjectives when he tries the wine. Comparisons are more useful from an empirical point of view than those metaphors, but they don't describe the flavor of wine itself, only one of its qualities, the sudden recollection of a fleeting spark, smothered immediately by the mass of sensations poorly designated by the abstraction known as *the taste of wine*. Another obstacle follows that philosophical complication: wine is in fashion. That's fine enough for Nula, but that somewhat coarse daily novelty, not entirely disconnected from a dogged publicity campaign, easily reveals a sordid contradiction: the fashion for wine gives enthusiasts the illusion of cultivating an exquisite, rationalized individuality, while he, the common denominator among them,

286

knows all the ways they've been primed by advertising. What he really likes are the hints of flavor that surface every so often in every bottle, in every glass, and even in every sip, and then evaporate, an empirical spark that precipitates unexpected memories, of fruit, of flowers, of honey, of apricot, of grass, of spices, of wood, or of leather. Unforeseeable and fleeting, those sensorial sparks that, paradoxically, make the taste of wine more strange and unknown, ignite suddenly in the mind, promise a vivid display, but immediately after they appear, surreptitiously, are snuffed out.

He sells them eighty-four bottles, five cases of white and nine of red: among the white, a chardonnay-chenin blend, two chardonnays, a sémillon from Río Negro, and one sauvignon blanc, the same wine they drank three bottles of last night—the first paid for by himself, the second by Tomatis, and the third by Soldi—at the Amigos del Vino bar. Among the reds, he suggested a few varieties, a malbec, a merlot, a syrah, and a few blends, a mixture of cabernet sauvignon and merlot, for instance, which Nula never forgets to describe as a fundamental blend in the production of Bordeaux wine, something which, as a consumer incentive, never fails. At around two, he's arriving at his house; the kids are at nursery school and Diana is tanning, naked, out back, lying on a plastic mat in the yard. A red bathrobe, glowing in the sun, is hanging from a wicker chair. When she sees him come out, she picks up a small towel and covers her pubis and hips, hiding the triangular patch of pubic hair and the protuberance that marks the beginning of an even more intimate region; the rest of her body, from her head to just below her bellybutton, and from the tops of her thighs to her feet, remains exposed to the sun, and her skin, still darkened by the summer sun, has a light shine, and is dampened, especially on her face and around her breasts. Her arms, stretched out alongside her body, display the only visible asymmetry, product of her missing left hand.

—A Doctor Riera from Bahía Blanca called, Diana announces. His number is next to the telephone.

—A ghost from the past, Nula says. What did he want?

—He arrives tomorrow, and he wants to meet me, Diana says, laughing and sitting up, resting on her left elbow, which makes the forearm that ends in the stump elevate obliquely at her side. She looks at him.

—Tomorrow? Well you'll definitely meet him in that case, Nula says. I'll call him back later. Right now, I'm going to eat something and I'll be right back to get some sun with you.

—Oh, hurry, please! Diana says, shaking her only hand, parodying an exaggerated happiness combined with a simulated desperation. And immediately she stretches out again on the mat. Eventually, Nula comes out, naked, from the front of the house, with a white towel wrapped around his waist that covers him to his knees and a plastic mat under his arm; he carries a jug of cold water and a book: *One Hundred Homemade Pasta Recipes.* He places the jug under the chair, so that the shade will keep it cool, and covers it with the book to prevent an insect from falling inside. Then, laying his mat out next to Diana's, he removes the towel and lies down, face up. Finally, he picks up the towel and, laying it between his open thighs, pulls up a corner of the white cloth and carefully, delicately, covers his genitals. Diana, who's been watching him ever since he appeared through the kitchen door, comments, in a low voice:

—His most precious garment. His identity. The torch that guides him through the darkness. The spear that leads him through the world. The cosmic megalith. *Omphalos.*

Motionless, face up, keeping the towel still, in place, Nula smiles, his eyes closed, and a few seconds after she stops talking, motionless in a similar position, her smile identical to his, he adds:

—The diver that makes you crazy when he touches bottom.

Diana's fingers caress him softly on his left thigh.

—The battle of the sexes is growing worse, Nula says. How about a truce?

And matching, as they say, actions with words, he extends his hand and places it softly on Diana's pubis, in the center of the white rectangle formed by the towel. Diana doesn't even flinch.

—Can't happen before tonight, she says.

—But I'm getting back late tonight, Nula says, adding with a deliberate but neutral vagueness, which no doubt makes him slightly uncomfortable: There's a dinner with the people from the hyper. I don't even know when or where it'll be.

With her eyes closed, laughing silently, Diana shrugs.

—Tomorrow, then, she says.

Nula doesn't answer and removes his hand. The conversation, which he would have preferred not to happen, has made him uncomfortable. The lying upsets and disturbs him: on the one hand, Diana deserves the truth, and on the other, in a sense contradictory to the first, to what extent does she believe him? Luckily, the internal flux, made of flashes of lucidity, of autonomous images, of capricious and fragmentary memories and passing emotions, displaces his misgivings in a current that ceaselessly churns that heterogeneous, loose material, replacing it with recurrent, obsessive fantasies and sudden and insistent desires. The sun begins to warm his skin, especially on his belly, on his face, and on his thighs, and an indulgent image of his own naked and tanned body appears, so unexpected and savage that his penis, which was resting peacefully under the towel, begins to harden and swell, something which, beyond the pleasure it produces, embarrasses him slightly: despite his close intimacy with Diana, that untimely erection, just when they've decided not to make love, has something coarse and even ridiculous about it. If Diana noticed it, she'd probably laugh. Nula looks for an explanation for that sudden arousal, caused by his own body, and he realizes that he'd caught a glimpse of himself in a strange, empty room, preparing to move through a doorway into the adjacent room—he's unaware of what might be in that other room, or who might be there, but what he's sure of is that what aroused him was *a gaze*, the specter of a gaze, regarding and desiring his naked body, that, because it was absent from the image, he substituted for his own. Now, the solar fullness erases every image inside him, and the last contours of the visible world, persisting under his closed eyelids, change shape and color, becoming more and more abstract on his retina. Drowsy, forgetting his desire, which distends his alert genitals, Nula surrenders himself to the light that flows from the empty, blue sky, refracting at moments and becoming visible, like drops of rain, invisible in the darkness, are made visible—he thinks, or remembers rather—as they cross a beam of light. Groping along the grass, he seeks out Diana's hand and grasps it softly.

—So, Riera wants to meet you, he says, laughing tersely, skeptically, suggestively. I should warn you that he insists that there are two kinds of men: the kind who wants to reform prostitutes and the kind who wants to corrupt the wives of the bourgeoisie. He belongs, by his own admission, to the second category.

—Actually, both kinds overlap in the middle, Diana says after a few seconds of thought. In both cases the object is a sexually experienced housewife.

—That is not untrue, Nula agrees, cautiously, and releasing Diana's hand, lets his own fall on the grass, his arm outstretched next to his body, grazing the length of the narrow mat, and he falls silent.

Lying on the ground, motionless, naked, their eyes closed, they'd appear to be their own effigies if their hands were crossed over their bellies, peacefully spending eternity since the Roman or medieval afternoon when death fished them, together, from the agitated and contingent waters of time, the cloths that cover their private parts representing the supplement of some over-punctilious bishop who despite himself preferred to include a realist ornament in the composition so as not to rely on the conventional recourse of a fig leaf. They might also represent Adam and Eve, owing, in fact, to the white towels, forced to cover with these what they noticed immediately after they distinguished good from evil, before falling asleep, cast out into the elemental wilderness under the burning eye of the only sun, scorching them, outside the walls of paradise, contemplating the invisible substance that floods them, disturbs them, and alters them, pulling them gently through the ineluctable and mysterious waves, unknown in paradise, of succession, working against them, toward their ruin, with every heartbeat or breath or flutter, however much they try to protect themselves, sometimes, with a deceitful immobility. They are a married couple in a state of repose, the complementary protagonists that, when they joined, brought into contact the two inert halves of the world, and as such activating the force of the present, casting aside, without brutality but also mercilessly, the past that pretended, chimerically, to continue limitlessly, in a sterile, desiccated, and oxidized limbo. They are themselves a world, a reality, certain to generate, in every action, more world, more reality, they are, moreover, the very present that, as it moves, creates more present. Lying in the sun, naked, smiling, their eyes half-closed, they appear peaceful and eternal, and yet they float in the center of a whirlwind. Turbulent, inchoate, the island of the moment in which they believe they've found refuge, incessantly and at once fleetingly, is unmade as they are, and with regard to their surroundings, nothing gives way more profoundly to that corrosive alchemy than what seems permanent, stable, or in repose, rock, metal, diamond, earth, sun, moon, firmament.

Nula feels the sweat beginning to form on his forehead, on his neck and under his nose, and on his upper lip. As he lifts his head slightly and turns to look at Diana, a few drops fall from his forehead, slide horizontally across his cheekbones, under his eyes, and then across his cheeks, leaving tortuous tracks, and eventually falling from the edge of his jaw onto his chest. He knows that Diana has seen him sit up, watching him through half-open eyelids, and lying down again and squinting his own eyes, he begins to speak, certain that, from within her comfortable and alert motionlessness, Diana is listening to him.

—Before I met you, I fell in love with his wife, he says slowly. For months I was insane, but then I got tired of it and went back to Rosario. A year later, I met you and I forgot about them. The three of us loved each other a lot, and we went everywhere together, but I didn't want to hear from them again. I'd suffered too much. Eventually, I heard that they'd moved to Bahía Blanca; and then I learned that they'd separated. And last month I went to visit a new client in Rincón, Gutiérrez, who was recommended to me by Soldi and Tomatis, among others, and she was there. Apparently, Gutiérrez is her real father, but only the mother knew, and even Gutiérrez himself didn't know about it for thirty years.

Omitting, for understandable reasons, the Wednesday encounter in Paraná, Nula tells her what he remembers. Since Wednesday afternoon he's known that everything between them has moved, definitively, into the past, and because he knows that nothing will ever happen between him and Lucía again, and since what happened on Wednesday wasn't anything more than a separation ceremony, he feels less guilty omitting it—according to the singular logic with which he analyzes his sexual life, ethics are only in question when feelings that might resemble those that he considers exclusive to his relationship with Diana come into play, and that is what happened on Wednesday: for the first time, he felt somewhat guilty toward both women, toward Lucía for having pretended to still love her, and toward Diana, because from Tuesday night at

Gutiérrez's, when Lucía denied knowing him, until he went to bed with her the next day, the feelings seemed real. And now, Riera's call, announcing his arrival to the city, intensifies the suspicion that he'd had on Wednesday afternoon, that Lucía was probably thinking about her ex-husband when she slept with him. And her practically imploring declaration when they said goodbye, *You're my only friend*, loses some of its pathos and takes on a distinct meaning, exempting him, naturally, from any affective obligation, as he grows more certain that the moment he left the house she called Riera to tell him what had happened.

What he remembers: the morning when, coming out of the Siete Colores, he bumped into her and started following her; the incredible coincidence that Lucía walked up to his own house; the mysterious circuit around the block that she made, stopping and examining, with different attitudes, the houses on the four symmetrical points on each of the four streets that formed the block; how he found her for a second time one afternoon at the neighborhood pastry shop and sat down next to her, and how she invited him on a walk and without dissimulating had followed the same route as the time before, stopping at the entrance to Nula's house, at the house around the corner, which was Riera's office, on the cross street around the corner from the office, and finally at the house parallel to the office, which was her own. Nula tells Diana that he was so fascinated by Lucía that, without knowing why, he'd made the same circuit that same night, but in the opposite direction, and even rang the bell at the house on the cross street, and that a boy answered, that afterward he'd passed by Doctor Riera's office, where by that time everything was dark, had peered in, and then had turned the last corner and went inside his own house. He tells her that the next day he went to the office pretending to be sick and had met Doctor Riera for the first time, that Riera had examined him, but that he'd refused to charge him for the visit, but a while later, that same afternoon, on his way home from doing some lunch shopping for La India he'd seen Riera get out of a double-parked car, cross the sidewalk, and stop at the entrance to the apartments where he and La India lived; Nula had stopped and waited and when he saw him get back in the car and turn the corner slowly he kept walking all the way to the ice cream shop, just in time to see Riera jump out of the car, cross the sidewalk, and enter his office, and so he'd taken the opportunity to walk down the street, noticing when he passed it that Riera's car was still running, and when he reached the next corner had crossed the street and waited there; from where he was standing he could see both streets, the one with the office, where the car had now started to move slowly, and the other one, perpendicular to it, where the mysterious house sat, and where Riera stopped the car, double parked again (his typical method, apparently), crossed the sidewalk, and rang the bell; almost immediately the door opened a crack and Riera carried on an animated conversation with someone inside, invisible to Nula from where he was standing, then reached in, and finally went back to his car, almost at a run, as the slightly open door closed behind him; and Nula followed him (his own typical method, apparently)—Diana laughs somewhat more loudly when he says this—seeing that, as he'd expected, Riera finished the ritual circuit at the front door to his own house.

He would eventually learn that there was nothing strange about any of it, but before this something happened that was so incredible, so dark and singular and at the same time so humiliating and absurd to him, that in the three months that the relationship between the three of them lasted he interpreted it countless different ways, and when he finally thought he'd found the correct one he stopped seeing them, thinking that he'd be able to stop his suffering, though a couple of months later he'd seen them by chance one morning in Rosario, outside a house that, according to a friend of his, had an abominable reputation, and because knowing this had increased his suffering he'd decided never to see them again; and, eventually, he met Diana, and, as he later learned, Riera and Lucía had moved to Bahía Blanca.

And he tells her: a couple of weeks after she met him, Lucía invited him to her house for the first time, to have a tea, at six. Nula had arrived at six on the dot, his temples throbbing intensely and his hands shaking, bringing with him a small package of delicate pastries and the resignation that he'd have to drink a couple of cups of tea, which he detested. But Lucía hadn't prepared tea or anything, and, apparently distracted, seemed indifferent to his visit. When she asked him in, she looked at her watch and compared it to the clock on the wall, checking that she had the exact time. Not only did she not prepare tea, but she didn't offer him anything else; she threw the package he'd brought in the fridge without opening it or making a point to offer him any of the pastries. They sat down on a couch, and Nula, as he would every time they were alone, on dark streets especially, pressed himself close and tried to kiss her. Lucía resisted a little, but not as strongly as she would when they were in the street. He caressed her over her clothes and she let him do it, without returning the caresses. If she'd asked him to stop he would've obeyed, because he loved her a lot; he'd never loved anyone up till that moment the way he loved her, feeling, with an almost adolescent innocence, the most irreconcilable contradictions, like thinking she was both attractive and unattainable, pure and lascivious, maternal and whorish. Much later, he realized those painful contradictions had a romantic quality: according to a theory he was developing, which argued that each stage or station in life corresponds to a specific philosophical or literary movement; thus, for instance, romanticism predominates in the adolescent; you're a Hegelian when you join a political party; a Pre-Socratic in childhood; an Empiricist in your infancy; a Skeptic in your later years; a

295

Stoic at work; and so on, and so on. Falling in love with a married older woman was without a doubt the apotheosis of romanticism, and though (to follow the literary thread) it would be necessary to be Platonic if she forced the issue, it seemed impossible to Nula not to go on, a completely erroneous assumption on his part given that she was clearly letting him do whatever he wanted despite not returning his caresses with the same enthusiasm, and so despite her relative impassivity he explored deeper and deeper into her intimate territory: he unbuttoned her blouse, put his hand in her bra, between her warm, constricted breasts; he kissed her on her neck, on her ear, on her shoulder, while he took off her shirt and unbuttoned her bra, pulling it away, so that she was left naked from the waist up. It was already October, and it was hot. As he kissed and caressed Lucía's warm, damp skin with one hand he started to unbutton his shirt with the other, twisting it off, and standing up, pulled Lucía with him, pressing himself against her and taking off her skirt, which had a small clasp and a zipper down the side. Nula unhooked it and pulled the zipper down and the skirt fell around Lucía's ankles. Moving her feet slowly and clumsily, letting Nula, who was pressed hard against her, kiss her continuously, Lucía, helping with the heels of her shoes, removed the last of the skirt, but when he tried to take off her panties she rejected him forcefully and then violently when he tried again. They sat back down on the couch and Nula forced her to stretch out, and when she was lying down, face up, he got naked and threw himself on top of her but she shook him off and changed position, turning onto her side. They were lying there naked—she with only her shoes and panties on, he with nothing on—but every time Nula tried to pull down her panties she rejected him, although when he grabbed her hand and guided it to his penis so she'd rub it, Lucía grabbed it without the slightest hesitation and instead of caressing it squeezed it and released it, squeezed it and released it, and eventually just held it in her hand, motionless. They were lying there, sideways, face to face, on the couch, him naked like he'd just emerged from his mother's womb and her in her panties and high-heeled shoes, allowing Nula to caress her and squeezing his penis in her hand, when the door opened and Riera walked in.

Diana lets out a quick exclamation, opens her eyes, and sits up slightly, leaning on her elbows, causing, from the other side of her belly, at more or less the height of her hips, over her left flank, at an angle, her stump to appear. And her beautiful breasts, round and tanned, with their almost black nipples, like two identical copies of a ceramic object, highlight the principal feature on the elegant torso whose silhouette, from her wider shoulders to her narrower waist, could be represented, in an abstract form, by an inverted trapezoid.

—Wait, wait, let's clarify, she says.

Nula sits up too, and their eyes meet, Diana's lively and a bit excited, and Nula's, from what he can tell, recovering, in a vague way, the echo of the affliction of that time.

—The thing with the panties can be explained in two different and opposite ways that men, even medical students, never think of: because of her period, or, on the contrary, because she was ovulating. That's the best theory: when a woman's gone that far, there's no other reason for her to stop. There's a third explanation, but it would be too cruel: that she simply wanted her husband to find you two like that. To make him jealous, maybe.

Nula lies back and closes his eyes again, thinking, *If that was all it was it would never have been a problem at all.* He remembers: Riera closed the door and started walking around the room looking at them and shaking his head. Nula started to get dressed but Lucía didn't move; to Nula, when he'd finished dressing and was standing there unsure what to do, it seemed there was something excessive, even theatrical, in Riera's behavior. Then Riera approached him and said, as though they were old friends, *So she hooked and reeled you in too? Sometimes I ask myself if she ever does it with anyone.* Hearing these words, Lucía laughed and shook her head, as though what she'd just heard had gone too far; she stood up and started getting dressed, as though she were alone in the room, and told Nula, *Don't pay any attention to him, he'll say anything. He's rotten to the core.* And, as she finished buttoning her shirt, she started to laugh. Riera, still speaking to Nula (they each spoke about the other as if they weren't there), said, *That's the way she is; she gets you high and leaves you dry.* Nula was petrified with humiliation—at first he'd been afraid, and then, as he was dressing, ashamed, and now, combining with a hint of absurdity, humiliated. For the last fifteen days, since he saw them for the first time, beautiful and enigmatic, they'd seemed distant to him, resplendent, benevolent, and sacred, like gods who allowed him to glimpse, through their sudden appearance, a less-imperfect world, sheltered from contingency, and here they were slithering at his feet, sordid, vulgar, and perverse, adding vice, frivolity, and duplicity to the external world. *I have a deal with my wife, of course,* Riera said, calming down, referring to Lucía with certain consideration, *proposed by myself from the very beginning, because I'm a clean sportsman, and accepted by her with full awareness of the consequences, that a successful marriage requires the complete—and I mean complete—liberty of both parties.* As she listened to him, Lucía, laughing, shook her head slowly, to show her anger: *That degenerate theory suits you well.* Riera started to laugh too: *No insults, please, let's maintain a certain level of decency.* Lucía stepped toward him and interrogated him, defiant: *And what about you, haven't you just finished spewing barbarities in front of a stranger?* Apart from being referred to as a stranger, the tone of Lucía and Riera's conversation and behavior, though they seemed excessive and unexpectedly offhand and vulgar, seemed familiar, as if he'd seen the same scene many times before, realizing eventually that, with the exception of the vulgar allusions, of course, the scene reminded him of a comedy show on television, only without the music and the canned laughter, and although they seemed to have forgotten about him, Lucía and Riera acted, constantly, as though they had him in mind, the way actors practicing their roles in an empty theater never forget that their words and their actions are ultimately intended to produce a determined effect on a crowd of hypothetical, ghostly spectators. During a pause in the discussion, Nula, in a barely audible voice, tried to suggest that maybe it would be better if he left them alone, but Riera, protesting, moved toward him energetically and patted him on the shoulder: *Oh no. After what we've put you through you have to stay for dinner, isn't that right Lucy?* And Lucía replied, without irony or resentment, *It goes without saying*, and left the living room, which, without a doubt, was the only room in the house that Nula knew. Two or three times he'd followed her to the entrance and had managed to see the hallway and the interior door, whose colored glass kept him from seeing what was inside; that afternoon he'd crossed it for the first time, without going any deeper than the couch in the living room, and when Riera proposed that they move to the courtyard, where it would be cooler, Nula accepted. Riera intrigued, even fascinated, him. He followed him down a passageway, away from the living room, with two or three doorways, and then into the darkened bedroom, where the white bedspread, made of a silky material, glowed in the dim light that filtered through the cracks in the white Persian blinds over a glass door beyond that large, queen-sized bed. A sudden despair overwhelmed him when he saw the bed, accentuated by images of lust, of poorly controlled impulses, of ruin, and that anguish increased even more when, after harshly lifting the Persian blinds and leading him out to the courtyard and through a red-tiled space that separated the house from what would strictly speaking be called the courtyard, he realized that they could have gone out to the courtyard, avoiding the intimacy of the bedroom, through the dining room or the kitchen. What Nula learned from them in those months was the infantile cruelty of their perversion, their innocent reflexes, most likely unscrupulous and guiltless, that attained their ends with expertise and charm, without deceit or coercion, simply to follow their desire, so intrinsic to the most intimate fibers of their own beings that they confused themselves with it, coloring it with their strange hues but not covering its more banal qualities; and he learned that each one's intense singularity, in radical contrast to the other's, somehow allowed them, through a unique combination of elements in each one, unconsciously and blindly groping dark passages, against all reason, to be together; all of this he learned at his own expense. As they sat in the courtyard, the intimate touch of Lucía's flesh persisted, trembling, in his memory, but at the same time, that easy dinner with them in the garden, first in the warm dusk and then under a soft light hanging from a tree, revealed to him an alternate world: styles, tastes, habits, behaviors, and conversation different from anything he'd known up till that moment; he had the feeling, that night, of emerging for the first time from the magical circle of the familiar: the years in Rosario, the dormitories, the university dining hall, the department, the bars, were in a certain sense an extension of his family life. With Riera and Lucía, starting from that night, his point of view changed, and from that new perspective the whole universe seemed altered. Others, outside of himself and Chade and La India, his murdered father, his philosophy books, molded, in their own way, in a parallel tunnel, the material of the world, giving it the inconstant shape of their loss and their desire, and that unknown world that Nula had begun to glimpse attracted him as much as the living flesh of Lucía.

—You were in love with both of them, Diana says, with an echo of retrospective pity in her voice.

—No, Nula says, with the fresh light that they projected over the world.

—Isn't that basically the same thing? Diana says.

After a thoughtful silence, Nula responds with certainty:

—Yes, but only partly.

That same night he learned the reason, which was much more simple than he'd imagined, behind the four symmetrical points on the four streets of their block that had become so popular recently: Riera had a lover, Cristina, around the corner from his office, and the morning when Nula had followed Lucía from the city center and had seen her peer into the garden of his own house, Lucía, who suspected what was happening, hadn't known exactly where, halfway down one of the two parallel streets, her husband's new lover lived, having only heard a couple of vague allusions to it from her husband. She wanted to know who she was and what she was like—every one of Riera's new lovers, despite the reciprocal liberty that she enjoyed, but which she'd never make use of, could represent a new problem—and when she peered curiously into the apartment building where Nula and his mother lived it was because her calculations suggested that her husband's lover might live there. After she'd turned the corner and had glanced furtively into the office to verify that Riera was still there, she'd continued around the corner and had walked the half block to the next house, the symmetrical point relative to La India's apartment, whose features coincided with what she knew about Cristina. Stopping outside the half-open door, to show that she considered herself justified to the privilege, she'd adopted an ostentatious and defiant posture, and when this didn't yield any results she kept walking and went into her house: Nula had clearly heard the metallic sound that the key made as it turned in the lock. When he saw her the second time, in the evening, sat down at her table in the pastry shop on the corner, and followed her on her walk around the block under the darkness of the trees, he could tell, though he hadn't solved the enigma, that Lucía was making the same circuit as before and that her walk around the block coincided with the hours, at midday and in the evening, when her husband usually finished work and left the office. In fact, there was nothing mysterious about any of it, and his mistake, as occurs, meanwhile, with almost every mystery, was the result of insufficient information. But the biggest shock came when Riera told him that while he'd been sitting with Lucía at the table next to the window, he, Riera, had passed by in his car with Cristina and had seen them together, and he'd recognized him immediately when he saw him in the waiting room, and because Nula had given him his address on the medical form, Riera, after closing the office at twelve thirty, had gone to see where he lived. He told him this last detail that first night, laughing, after Lucía had gone to bed, saying that he hadn't wanted to charge him the visit because he didn't really consider him a patient: on the one hand, it would have felt like he was taking advantage of him, and on the other, he preferred not to mix the exercise of his profession with his private life. He'd been surprised to see him in the waiting room, but he'd understood immediately what was happening: whenever he had an affair with a married woman, he, too, always felt the irresistible urge to see the husband up close and, if the husband was an upright person, to befriend him even. When Cristina's husband, an electrical engineer who was doing an eight-month course in California, came back at the end of the year, he'd invite them over for dinner one night, if his relationship with Cristina was still going on, an intimate dinner, just the four of them, Cristina, Lucía, Cristina's husband, and him, Riera, and even five of them, if Nula wanted to come too. Riera accompanied that false declaration, as in other situations and with other declarations, with an open, juvenile, and slightly degenerate laugh that, as Nula saw on several occasions, seemed to open, as they say, every door for

302

him. While he listened to him talk, Nula thought of Lucía, asleep in the large white bed, or possibly listening to him too from the bedroom, through the half-open glass door that led to the garden, and after a while he realized that he was staying so long because he wanted to delay as much as possible the moment when, after accompanying him to the door, Riera would lock it behind him, go back to the bedroom, and lie down naked next to her. But when Riera suggested that it was getting late, because he had to go in early the next day, and Nula got up to leave, Lucía's sleepy and smiling face appeared in the half-open door, and in a playful voice pleaded, *Come find me tomorrow afternoon; we could get something to drink, like the other day.*

—They had that number well-rehearsed, Diana says, and kneeling on the mat, propping herself up with her only hand, she adjusts the white towel around her hips, and nimbly, almost effortlessly, she lunges upward, grabs the edge of the mat, steps backward, and ends up standing, the mat in her hand. The story is moving, she says, but I have to be back in the office by three thirty.

—And you'll meet them on Sunday in any case, Nula says. Seen from below, from the upward angle that transforms the most pathetic jester into an emperor or a mythological hero, Diana appears to become, instead of a local beauty, a young, modern wife, an intelligent, sensible mother, which she usually is, a Venus emerging from the waters, or better yet, a White Goddess.

—I'm dying of anxiety, Diana says, and blows him a kiss.

—From here you're like a queen, a goddess, Nula says. And between your legs, beneath the golden fleece, there's a half-open fault line that leads, down treacherous slopes, to the center of the earth, in perpetual flames.

—*Voyeur,* Diana says, and picking up the red bathrobe from the back of the chair, she turns toward the house. I won't wait for you tonight, then, she shouts as she walks away, without turning back toward him, as if she preferred, for some special reason, not to meet Nula's gaze when it comes to the topic of his nocturnal regressions.

—I don't think so, Nula says. He pulls off the towel that covers his genitals, removes the book that covers the jar, and takes a long drink of cold water. Then he covers the jar again, places it in the shade of the chair, and dropping the towel on the grass, stretches out face down on the mat.

After that October night, for several months, until the following fall, they were almost always together. Lucía didn't work, which meant she had lots of free time, but Riera went to the office early, and later, during his lunch hour, and in the evenings, he made house calls; Nula worked at the law school kiosk several times a week, and when he stayed home he pretended to prepare for his philosophy exams in November and December, but the thought of returning to Rosario, of leaving the city and Lucía, and Riera too, even for a single day, seemed intolerable: it would have been like stepping out of a magical world, a novel and seductive place, not exempt from sordidness and cruelty, to return to the uncertain, grayish days, with their perpetual seesaw between doubt and serenity, where he'd been treading water, resigned, since his childhood. He wanted to be Lucía's lover, but he was barely her friend, her confidant, and sometimes he even reached the status of lap dog. Even though it would've been enough for him to know her, to sit calmly and silently at her side, she allowed him certain gratifications: every so often she let him touch her, kiss her, put his hand down her brassiere, and even suck on her breasts, and two or three times she'd accepted, submissively, when he guided her hand to his open fly, squeezing his penis in that strange way, squeezing and releasing, but once when he'd put his own hand over hers, forcing her to rub until he finished, she'd jumped up, rearranging her clothes, indignant and flustered, protesting, *Oh no, not that, definitely not that!* And she'd practically run to the bathroom and the bedroom to clean up and change. But despite that, when she returned she seemed content, with an abstracted, placid smile. After being with them a few times, Nula realized that Lucía and Riera were joined by a feeling, or whatever it was, that wasn't exactly love, in the altruistic sense of the word at least, but actually something more turbulent that combined with a sort of voluptuous interdependence in which their differences generated a sarcasm more mocking than violent and their affinities a blind, impulsive, almost animal fusion. It was strange to see how the most insulting nonsense from one, verbal or otherwise, first produced indignation and then complicit laughter in the other. Nula felt momentarily excluded in those situations, but they, together or alone, always rushed to recover him. There was always the perpetual enigma: were they manipulating him, were they laughing at him, were they using him for some incomprehensible ends? Or did they really appreciate him and acted like that with everyone? Even now, lying face down on the mat, his chin resting on the back of his superimposed hands, feeling the sweat run down his face and back, even at this very moment, when they've reappeared, unexpectedly, into his life, he still doesn't know. The fact that he'd been with Lucía two days before, finally possessing what five years before he'd sought in vain, and then the coincidence that Riera had called to announce his arrival from Bahía Blanca, restarts the mechanism of the past, and though he knows that he'll never be trapped by them again, a distant, even vaguely ironic curiosity suggests that he should be alert in the days ahead. With his eyes closed, his face sweaty, pressed against the back of his hand, Nula laughs, shivering expectantly, and he realizes that his affection for them persists, but that its charge has been reversed, that it doesn't have the same painful dependency of the first period, which had lasted a while after he voluntarily decided to stop seeing them, and has now taken on a paternalistic forbearance, a sympathy without a trace of possessiveness, governed by a completely atheoretical and

305

in fact sporting inclination, to anticipate their curious reactions, for pure entertainment, without inverting any sentiment in the issue. This attitude provokes in him an excessive impatience to see them again.

Lucía was rich, but Riera, on the other hand, had come from a family of petty merchants in Bahía Blanca, and he always said that because petty merchants and the rich had more or less the same things weighing on their conscience, that it was only a difference of proportion, he and Lucía had been made for each other from the start. Lucía always complained that, because she was expected to marry rich, she hadn't been allowed to pursue secondary studies. She'd had a rancher boyfriend, but she'd left him for Riera. Her mother disapproved of the relationship (Lucía's father had died long before), but her own sentimental complications didn't allow her the occasion to worry about Lucía's future; Leonor, for her part, had been born rich, and because she'd married a rich man from whom she'd inherited a second fortune, she knew instinctively, and from personal experience, that money made intelligence superfluous. But Lucía's ignorance tormented her: when Nula and Riera discussed science and philosophy (each loathed the other's specialty), Lucía's mood would sour, and Riera, mercifully, would change the subject. The sexual disarray of Riera's life contrasted with his professional diligence. When he finished at the office he went on house calls, and he also worked with a group of doctors who treated people from the shantytowns and the countryside free of charge; they distributed medicine, and, in the worse cases, sent them to the hospital. He also saw the novitiates of a semi-clandestine brothel and though the owner paid him he gave the girls condoms and free samples that pharmaceutical salesmen had left with him. One Saturday afternoon, Nula was in Riera's car with him when suddenly he stopped, opened the door, and ran out onto the sidewalk, leaving the car running; they were downtown, and because it was Saturday, it was crowded on the street. The row of cars and buses behind Riera started to honk, but Riera didn't seem to hear a thing. Nula got out and saw that a boy who was about ten, a shoe shine who always worked on that corner, was lying on the ground, convulsing and drooling. Riera bent over him, and with two or three quick operations, did something to his jaw and laid him on his side, trying to contain his seizures. It was an epileptic fit. The boy calmed down gradually—the scene lasted two or three minutes—and Riera told Nula to open the rear door of the car and then to pick up the shine box, while he himself picked up the boy, laid him down on his side on the back seat, set the shine box on the floor of the car, closed the door, and sat down behind the steering wheel. He told Nula to kneel on the front seat and watch the boy in case the seizures started again. The boy was pale but calm, and seemed lost and drowsy. Riera took him to the hospital, to the neurological office, and didn't move until he was sure he had a bed and a specialist to examine him. Nula had gone to his office to meet him for an afternoon swim at the beach in Rincón (Lucía had gone to Paraná to see her mother), but at two thirty they were still at the hospital, so when they left, shortly after three, they ate a slice of pizza standing up at a pizzeria across from the hospital, and Riera, although he didn't usually work on Saturday, decided not to go to the beach after all, and leaving him at the entrance to La India's, went back home.

In late November, Nula had a fight with La India because he'd decided not to take his philosophy exams in December and push them back to March, under the pretext that he still wasn't prepared. *You're one of those people who thinks that the mayonnaise gets made whether you beat the eggs or not!* La India had exploded; she'd noticed that something strange had been going on with him since September, though she didn't mind that he was staying in the city, working at the kiosk and living at home. Ever since their father had left, and especially after he was killed, her sons' emotional life worried her, and she preferred to always have them on hand, but it was difficult (with Chade, who was more reserved, almost impossible) to talk about things in a clear and direct way. The offhand and somewhat aggressive talks she had with Nula contributed more to hiding the real problems than to revealing them clearly. Nula listened with a serious expression to La India's remonstrations, but every free moment he had he spent with his new friends. Sometimes he was alone with Lucía at their house, or they went out walking, and other times he met up with Riera for a beer and they'd talk a while, but what he preferred was for the three of them to be together, because he got the feeling that Lucía and Riera really appreciated him and did everything they could to make him feel welcome. But with them there was always something false that came through despite the fact that everything they did seemed so natural, so much so that Nula ended up thinking that they must have been unaware of it. Riera would sometimes take him to Cristina's—he remembers a week in December when her son was in Córdoba, at his grandparents' house—and the thing that seemed unconscious with Lucía became obvious, even brutal, when they were with her. Riera's political theories were as expedient as they come: the problem with society wasn't the poor but rather the rich families that controlled the banks, the military, the seats of political power, the media, the factories, the press, and so on. Because they were very few, the simplest solution was to kill them all, but because this was impossible, they had to start by corrupting their women, and he'd taken on the task of corrupting the wives of the bourgeoisie in order to precipitate social change. And he always followed that brief discourse with that terse, somewhat degenerate laugh that no one, male or female—and he knew it—was capable of resisting. Cristina wasn't particularly rich: if her family did have money, it was certainly less than Calcagno's fortune, of which Riera never touched a dime, referring to it often with contempt and even disgust. Riera subjugated her, and she, Cristina, accepted everything he gave her. Sometimes, in Nula's presence, he even ordered her around, and one night even suggested she should sleep with him, something she accepted immediately, but Nula, although he was very excited, didn't dare do it and went home. He heard them laughing as he went out to the street, and then, after taking a few steps along the sidewalk, he stopped and stood for a couple of minutes, thinking about going back, but he changed his mind and went home, past Lucía's house, which was dark and silent, and since it was almost midnight he didn't want to ring the bell, so he just went to sleep.

The summer passed in this way; March, and the exams, were approaching. Nula studied, and because the law school shut down from early December to early March, the kiosk closed too. The bookstore, meanwhile, closed in January, for the judicial holiday, and reopened in February, half days only. Nula worked there twice a week, Thursdays and Fridays, which allowed La India to spend long weekends in the country or at the shore. Riera and Lucía didn't leave the city all summer, and all that time Nula was trapped in the aura that they secreted, trying to prove to himself that he was capable of controlling his desire, his suffering, and even his lust. Their company became a kind of addiction: wherever they were was the center of the world, solid and brilliant; everything else was soft, shapeless, and gray. He knew he wasn't getting any farther with Lucía, but while they continued to make him feel like he existed as something other than the theater of their wretched war—a feeling he often had—he'd be able to tolerate their machinations. One night in early March, having already decided to go to Rosario for his exams, he decided never to see them again. The heat was dreadful, so they ate in the courtyard, but suddenly, in the middle of their conversation, a storm drove them inside. After the lightning and thunder of a dense and turbulent storm had passed, a rain settled in that would surely last till the morning. Lucía proposed that they watch a movie she'd rented, a detective story that had made a big splash the previous winter, but which she hadn't been able to see in the theater. They moved to the bedroom, with fruit and cold water, and sat down together at the foot of the bed to watch the movie. After a while, Lucía said she preferred to lie in bed to be more comfortable, and five minutes later, without saying a word, Riera followed her. Nula felt his heart beating harder and harder in his chest. His throat dried, and he opened his mouth to breathe, trying to be silent, because it felt like he was drowning. At first he thought these were the symptoms of desire, but immediately he realized they were of pain, and that, in fact, he wouldn't have been able to tell them apart. The unnamable, the inconceivable, was happening. Because they'd turned on a bedside lamp so as to not watch the movie in the dark, the room had a warm glow, which from time to time brightened even more when the film passed from a dark image to a clear one, and which meant that everything happening was perfectly visible. But Nula didn't want to turn around. Suddenly he heard Lucía's voice behind him saying, *Poor thing, we left him alone*, and then, directly to him, *Are you alright there, on the floor?* with a distant, absent voice, as if she were falling asleep. But Nula was sure that she wasn't falling asleep—just the opposite; their barely audible voices, their movements, their sounds, signaled not only that they weren't sleeping, but that in fact they were wide awake, though in a somewhat different state of consciousness, which may have even pushed them radically farther from consciousness than a dream, believing they liberated in a whirlwind of sensation that defined them most intimately, when in fact they had been possessed and were now controlled by what was most external to them. Up till that moment, Nula had thought that the strange laughter that connected them precluded intercourse, that they left that extenuating labor for others—an illusion that, later, when he thought it over, seemed at once hilarious and pathetic. For several minutes, he was frozen, rigid, leaning against the edge of the bed, trying to ignore their whispers, their laughter, their moaning, the squeaking and creaking of the bed, the rustle of the sheets, but when Lucía finally started to emit a guttural noise, increasing in intensity, he crawled out on all fours, like a cat, trying not to make a sound, all the way to the hallway, where he stood up and walked out, practically running, through the darkened house that, over the last few months, he'd come to know by heart. Except for the morning when he'd seen them from a taxi, in Rosario, he never saw either of them again, until about a month back, in March, five years after that night, when he saw Lucía come out of the swimming pool in a green swimsuit, and when Gutiérrez, looking at him, had said, *It's not what you think. She's my daughter.* After the March exams, Nula stayed in Rosario under the pretext that classes were starting soon and he didn't want to get behind that year, and when he came to visit La India on the weekends he almost never left the apartment, and if he did he never took the walk around the block; he always walked straight to the city center. Later, from Cristina, who he bumped into that winter, with her husband, he learned that Lucía and Riera had moved to Bahía Blanca. That October he met Diana, and he forgot about them completely; with Diana everything seemed easy and transparent, which was why, when she got pregnant and she told him she was willing to get an abortion he responded that it would be better if they got married. With his Greek philosophy professor he'd studied Problem XXX.1, attributed to Aristotle, or to Theophrastus, where the affinity between wine, sex, poetry, and philosophy—common ground of the melancholics—was discussed, and because he had to find work and just then an introductory seminar in enology was being offered at the Hotel Iguazú, and which created the possibility of finding a job if he did well, he enrolled with a loan from La India, and, soon after, with another brief course in Mendoza, he was offered a job with Amigos del Vino, which meant that the next year, when Yussef was born, he had enough to provide for him, and by the time Inés was born he was already one of the top salesmen for Amigos del Vino, at least the only one who Américo allowed to bend the rules. And now he's lying on the mat, face down, tanning in the sun, feeling the sweat drip down the corners of his face pressed against the back of his hands superimposed on the edge of the mat.

Drying the sweat from his face with his forearm, Nula turns over; above him, in the blue sky turning white in the intense light, the sun, declining from the zenith, blazing, a metal yellow fusion that splinters and overflows from the circular nucleus, is impossible to look at directly. When he closes his eyelids, he brings with him several golden blotches, vibrating and shifting on his retina, and which take a long time to diffuse into the reddish darkness that protects his pupils. Groping at the lawn, he picks up the towel and covers his genitals again. With his eyes narrowed, his forehead slightly wrinkled, and his mouth half-open, exposing his clenched teeth, his face has a look of suffering, but no thought, neither unhappy nor joyful, reaches a state of consciousness inside him, and his expression is rather the result of lying in the sun, exploiting its energy and at the same time suffering the flame that, indifferent and almost disdainfully, scorches him, but which with the slightest act of carelessness would consume him. After a while, he takes a drink of water and pouring a small amount in his hand splashes it on his face and then he puts the almost empty jug of water under the shade of the chair again and turns back over. But less than a minute after turning into that position Diana reappears, clean, dressed in a flowered skirt and a white linen jacket the starched lapels of which conceal her prominent chest, crossing just below the very low, angled side pockets that allow her to bury her stump

312

in the left side and hang her purse from her forearm. The upper straps of her relatively high-heeled white sandals are tied above her ankle bone. She carries Nula's cell phone and a scrap of paper. Nula turns over and sits up slightly on his elbows.

—Are you sure you're going to work? he says.

Without needing him to continue, Diana takes the suggestive question as a positive assessment relative to her appearance, and she smiles, condescending, enigmatic.

—On judgment day all will be revealed, she says. Here's your cell phone and your friend's number in Bahía Blanca. And, seeing his somewhat helpless nakedness, his face darkened by sweat and by the heat that has reddened sections of his skin, plus the horizontal wrinkles formed on his belly by the position of his half-upright body, plus his penis and testicles, submerged in a layer of soft, amorphous skin below his curly pubic hair, plus his sweat-dampened thighs and his bony knees, which appear older than the rest of his body, plus his curled toes and the wrinkled and dirty soles of his feet, Diana says, *You look like you're all set to receive them.*

Diana leaves the paper on the chair, and though there isn't a hint of breeze she puts the cell phone on top of it to keep it from flying off. Nula watches all of her movements with deliberate, excessive attention. Without looking at him, she knows what he's doing, and when she straightens up she hides her smile. *She's happy,* Nula thinks. *Maybe because of the secrets I've just told her, or maybe the idea of meeting them on Sunday makes her think she might learn something new about me even though they're not important any more.* Diana, without saying a word or dropping her mysterious air, waves goodbye silently, her palm turned toward him, with her fingers. Though he doesn't lie back down, Nula, with a distracted movement, covers his genitals again and watches her walk away: her flowered skirt, undulating at her knees, her straight back, now, because of the cut of the linen jacket, forming a white rectangle from her shoulders to her hips that hides the true geometry of her body, the inverted trapezoid of her torso, her semispherical, pointed breasts, the dark triangle of her pubis, the curvy, pronounced bulge of her circular hips, which safely transported to the world the two little animals who right now must be taking a nap at the day care, as opposed to her, who, because her umbilical cord had been wrapped around her wrist, is now forced to hide her stump in the angled pocket of her jacket and to hang her leather purse from her forearm. An unexpected emotion seizes him, a mixture of affection and guilt, of distress and happiness for his luck that lasts a few seconds and then passes, after which he lies back down face up, closes his eyes, and tries to erase the last traces of that unbearable emotion, which has extracted him suddenly from his neutral state, neither painful nor pleasurable, in which the minutes, the hours, the days, the weeks, the months, and the years slide by. Eventually, he calms down, and the sweat that touches his lips every so often tastes something like tears. Sitting on the mat, he picks up the cell phone and the white paper and dials Riera's number. The phone rings once and Riera answers.

—I was about to leave for the office, he says in a soft, affable, and vaguely paternalistic voice. I didn't think you were going to call.

—Did she already tell you about our meeting? Nula says. Despite the separation, she's still under your influence.

—First of all, we're not separated, we're estranged, Riera says, without losing an ounce of affability despite the severity of Nula's tone. Secondly, I've been planning this trip, to see the baby, for a long time. It's Holy Week, remember? And finally, it's such a pleasure to hear from you after so long, and how enchanting your wife is! Why'd you disappear without saying a word, you son of a bitch?

—I didn't want to bother you. You two seemed so busy, he says, repressing a smile.

314

—Now I have to ask your permission to fuck my wife? Riera says obscenely. Despite the time that's passed, Nula recognizes the overtones.

—There are more important things that you don't . . . Nula starts to say, but Riera, cheerfully, deliberately compounding the vulgarity of his previous question, interrupts him:

—Horseshit! he says, raising his voice slightly. I've told you a thousand times: what there is is what is there and what it does, no more no less.

—And I've told *you* a thousand times: vulgar empiricism, or worse yet, bourgeois pragmatism, Nula says, laughing. You're in decline, Oscar.

What there is is what is there, no more no less: that aphorism contained the entirety of Riera's materialist monism (though he'd never called it that), and Nula had heard him say it over and over back then, as a way to start or finish any discussion, never losing his grave voice or his cheerfulness. A kind of euphoria seems to overcome him when he expresses that conviction, as if everything, reduced to the primitive, unsophisticated tendency of primary material to diversify through countless combinations revealed its essential transparency, its immediate and distant clarity, its mechanical predictability, facilitating not only his way of being on the physical plane, but also, and especially, on the moral one. (Riera's worldview, at least as or possibly more crude than the world to which he applies it, is, to Nula, his most enviable trait.)

—You can criticize me in person. I'll be in the city tomorrow at noon, Riera says.

—At noon? Nula says, incredulous.

—I take off from Bahía Blanca at eight thirty, connect in Aeroparque at eleven, and at twelve, more or less, I land in Sauce Viejo, Riera says.

—Should I pick you up? Nula says.

—Lucía will be waiting for me, Riera says. And we'll see each other Sunday, in any case—your wife is coming I hope—and I stay the rest of the week. I have to run to the office. Ciao.

When the line goes dead, Nula hangs up the cell phone and holds it cupped in his hand, which shakes distractedly, confused by the conversation he's just had and whose echoes, empirical traces that resonate, more and more uncertain, until they crystallize, or fossilize, like flowers of experience desiccated between the yellowed pages of a book, move to their place in the dark archive of his memory. Nula leaves the phone on the chair and, throwing the towel carelessly on the grass, he stands up, naked, and takes a few indecisive steps across the lawn. The courtyard is a rectangle of green grass, closed at the back and along the sides by an unplastered brick wall tall enough to prevent the neighbors from seeing him walk around naked; a curved, white slab path dives the rectangle of grass in two; on the path an overturned tricycle bakes in the sun; and on the lawn a small plastic truck full of dried avocado leaves seems to wait for someone to push it away; a few trees grow along the wall, a bitterwood, a very tall avocado tree, and a rose laurel. Suddenly, a butterfly appears a meter away, as if, filtering through an invisible fissure in the air, it had fluttered from nothingness into being, from the impossible other world that Riera consigns to inexistence without the slightest hesitation, to the living interior of the material, taking shape, dense and rough; it flutters a while in the daylight, and then, disintegrating, returns, darkly, to the indifference and muddiness of the diurnal.

After shaving for the second time that day, Nula's mind, clouded by the sun, awakens under a warm shower, where he remains a long time, and before stepping out he finishes with a thick burst of cold water; his muscles tense up, and as he dries himself, he feels energetic, compact, hard, and he rubs his body vigorously, opening the bathroom door and causing the steam from the warm shower, which fogs the mirror, to dissipate. It's somewhat cooler outside the bathroom, so he walks to the bedroom, naked, to dress, constantly rubbing his body with the towel to dry the wetness, which he can no longer distinguish as water or sweat. In the bedroom, which, in darkness, is actually cold, he senses, with pleasure, that his skin is drying, and after rubbing deodorant on his armpits he starts to get dressed with the kind of special attention that has nothing to do with the inauguration of the promotion for Amigos del Vino but rather with the expectation of another kind that the night has in store for him. He puts on a lightweight tan suit over a cream-colored short-sleeve polo shirt, without a tie, and a pair of shiny brown loafers, without socks. The local criteria for elegance, more or less valid for the previous forty years, and suited to a middle class man whose work does not preclude him from certain touches of bohemia, which includes the selective commerce of wine and other gastronomical products, are followed scrupulously by Nula, but his age, twenty-nine, the last symbolic barrier from entering the adult world forever, allows him certain touches of studied negligence, exhibited to the world in general, but especially for certain people, at night, and in secret. When he's ready he picks up his keys, his pen, his wallet and credit cards, a few coins from the night stand, his cell phone, his notebook, and a clean handkerchief that he puts in the right rear pocket of his pants, and turning toward his desk he switches the computer on, looking for the lines by Omar Kayyám that, last night, after he and Diana got back from the Amigos del Vino bar, where they were having drinks with Gabriela Barco, Tomatis, Soldi, and Violeta, and, around midnight, after taking home the girl who'd stayed late to watch the kids, he'd finished polishing and typing out on the computer, expurgated of all allusions contrary to the aseptic postulates of publicity technique, of marketing strategy, and of the porous and drowsy understanding

317

of the consumers. If the ideas on this topic, which he's been turning over in his head for a long time, could be expressed in a more or less organized way, they would develop as follows: *Inebriation, the primary function of wine consumption, cannot be mentioned, though by definition it's the very reason for its existence; and inebriation begins with the first glass, which means that only a hypocrite could pretend that drinking in moderation is possible. The feeling produced by the first sip of wine and the ultimate drunken black-out are only separated by degrees. After the first glass, the other, an other—the otherness—that we're seeking begins to bloom from within the only place where it could rationally be found, that is to say, within ourselves. Wine transforms both the drinker and the world around him. The sensorial shift provokes a momentary forgetting of the abyss, allowing, almost immediately, joy, wit, and energy to take its place; it doesn't matter that later, with the second or third bottle, distress, anguish, confusion, and fury return, taking possession of the body and the mind. Inebriation is an easy gift: the ability to finally be oneself. Sobriety expels us from our true inner life, and inebriation restores it to us. That is the only purpose of wine, and because of this alcohol is sacred in every civilization but ours, where, like everything else, it's been transformed into merchandise. It must have something to do with Christianity, because in* The Thousand and One Nights *the wine sellers are always Christian. Rather than attempt to excise inebriation from the consumption of wine, it's necessary to admit that in fact inebriation without wine also exists, and that seeking it through wine constitutes a search for the self, which sobriety, in general, refuses. It stands to reason that in order not to find one's self it's necessary to practice a ritualized sobriety. Natural inebriation, without the aid of toxins like wine or other drugs is also looked down upon. Insanity, for instance, can be considered a kind of inebriation caused by a combination of internal and external agents. Mysticism is another: that's why the mystics, drunk on divinity, are shunned by every religion. But there's a passing, non-toxic inebriation that can suddenly assault the individual,*

318

allowing an internal transformation and, for a few moments, an inward sight along with a different vision of the world that is estranged, in transition, where the banal is exalted, the familiar is uncanny, and the unknown, familiar. That autonomous inebriation, which can cause exaltation or panic, puts one into contact with the otherness sought through wine, and is therefore as suspect as the other, which wine produces. The earnest search for that otherness from the self, which is within the self, and within the world, can be considered an exercise in practical metaphysics. And the contact with that otherness, exultant or painful, like a passing mystical experience, shouldn't be worried over. Nula takes the notebook from his pocket, opens it on the desk, and, with a black pen removed from a jar, after drawing a line, a squiggle, and then another line in order to separate the new note from the previous one, thinks for a few seconds and then writes: *A dialectical materialism conceived from multiple and contradictory viewpoints, in a single individual or in several: the otherness of the self, like the front and back of a thin disc, which, when spun, reverses front and back, each occupying the place of the other. One transforming, continuously, into the other.* But as he writes he's assaulted by a doubt: what if his fear of having been betrayed by Lucía is what's inspired his revenge on the ridiculous conspiracy that adjudicates Riera and Lucía. He leaves the pen in the jar, closes the notebook, puts it in the inside pocket of his coat, and, after picking up the briefcase, passing through the bedroom to take one last look at himself in the mirror, he turns off the light and, crossing the living room and the cool, shaded front hall, opens the door and goes out onto the bright sidewalk.

Over the past two days the city has returned to a summer that, judging by the increasing heat, would naturally be called intense and, for the same reason, temporary. The rain earlier that week, on top of the humidity it brought with it, had given renewed life to the vegetation: first the water had cleansed the foliage, and then, penetrating the earth over two consecutive and almost full days and nights, had helped the sap to feed the branches, rising and extending to each leafy tip, to every tiny filament at the farthest ends from the trunk, and as a result of this secret, periodic trajectory between the earth and the water, the light and the air, appeared, in passing, traces of reddish or tender green buds, little flowers opened temporarily, and branches loaded, once again, with new, firm, and very green leaves. Even the people on the street have let themselves be conquered by this extension of the summer, and the deserted streets reveal that the sense to not be seen on the street until at least after six, when the sun begins to fall, is now intrinsic to the city's inhabitants, always alert, though the summer may have passed, to the menace of the heat. Everyone who's braved the outdoors, at least in the streets far from the city center, now walks on the western sidewalk, in the shade, and if they're forced to cross they do so at the very last moment, risking as little time in the sun as possible. As he pulls out, the air conditioning starts to hum, and Nula advances slowly down the empty street, staying close to the curb, unsure yet which route he'll choose to the hypermarket: because the space that separates him from it could roughly coincide with the surface of a right triangle, the two most direct options from his house are to travel the *catheti*, which is to say, drive straight to the boulevard, turn east, and drive the full length of the boulevard to the bridge and then continue along the straight highway that in a certain sense extends the boulevard all the way to *the supercenter* and beyond, to La Guardia and the Paraná fork, or he could choose the hypotenuse, which is to say the port road, and because it's still before five he decides to drive through the center, and so, somewhat randomly, following the impulse of the moment, he turns at this or that street, always to the north or to the east, driving into the downtown that, in fact, for a sunny April day, around four thirty, is practically deserted. Because the fall business schedules are already in effect, most businesses are still open, though for the most part they're empty, and very few people get off of the buses that come from the outskirts, advancing almost at a crawl, one behind the other, down particular streets. Nula knows that it's not only the heat that drives the people from the downtown, but also *the supercenter*, which, though deserted during the first part of the week, is transformed, over the weekend, into the principal attraction in the region.

When he turns onto the avenue he accelerates slightly, passes a couple of trucks—the second one, painted red, has the words VISIT HELVECIA, FOR THE GOLDEN DORADO printed in large, black letters on the trailer—and moves ahead, alone, toward the bridge. Coming out of the bridge onto the highway, he looks, through the gap left by the suspension bridge after it fell during one of the last major floods, at the large circle of water known as the lagoon, which he was contemplating that morning from the empty bar in Guadalupe, and though, for the moment, the full length of the surface, seen from a distance, appears to be made of a luminous, fractured substance, the quality of the light has changed since this morning. Closer, on the opposite shore from the waterfront, at the Piedras Blancas beach, which had been deserted the past few weeks, he sees several bathers splashing in the water and others, stretched out on the sand, tanning in the sun. The short, dark green station wagon, bought second-hand a couple of years ago with the money he earned from selling wine, leaves behind the road bridge and, accelerating, starts down the four-lane asphalt road that everyone simply calls *the highway*, and which narrows over the next three or four kilometers until it splits to the right toward Paraná, and to the east, along the coastal road. But the hypermarket is right there, barely a kilometer from the bridge, on the right hand side of the road.

Though the parking lot isn't yet full, he has to drive around a couple of times before parking because there isn't a single spot left

321

in the first three or four rows closest to the main entrance. There are lots of cars from around the region that have been parked there all day, while their owners run errands downtown, leaving the shopping at *the supercenter*, the movies, and other activities for later in the afternoon, and even that night. The specialists who built *the supercenter*—the autonomous society to which they belonged must have been headquartered in the United States, in Europe, or in Switzerland, for instance, or in some other fiscal paradise like Monte Carlo, Luxemburg, or the Canary Islands—were not concerned in the least with the swamp on which they constructed it; after all, Venice and Saint Petersburg had been built on swamps, and they hadn't sunk yet. The primary function of *the supercenter* was to create a strategic point where customers from many points around the region could converge; although a couple of bus lines from the city extended their routes across the river for the first time in the history of local public transportation, the city's inhabitants would be grossly mistaken if they thought that *the supercenter* was intended exclusively for their use. The strategists hoped to attract (and they were quite successful at it) clients from upward of sixty or seventy kilometers away, and even beyond, along the coastal road, the route that runs north along the west bank of the Paraná and its tributaries, but also, across the Colastiné bridge and the underwater tunnel, several kilometers after the fork, people from Entre Ríos province, on the eastern shore, not only from Paraná, the capital, but also from important cities to the south and east of the capital. From the other side of the city, to the north, to the south, and especially to the west, the towns and cities of the plain also send their processions of the faithful every weekend. Every social class sends its delegations; everyone that has something to spend, however little that may be, spends it at *the supercenter*, where even the most intimate desires are anticipated, given that the hypermarket is intended to replace, by incorporation, every kind of business,

322

large or small. Every new product that appears on the market has a place there, and unlike specialized businesses, in *the supercenter* every novelty is like a new song added to a performance. When, for instance, endives appear in the produce section, the customers rejoice and offer their commentary; and when a product that's usually in stock is missing, the winds of dismay, if not panic, begin to blow, as they say, among the customers. For those who have nothing to spend, which is practically the majority, the hypermarket also has a feast prepared: every so often, tired of seeing the circus from outside, they take it by force, attempting, diligently, to demolish it, and, ultimately, it's overrun.

Before getting out of the car, Nula takes the copy of the verses by Omar Kayyám from his briefcase and, folding the white pages carefully down the middle, he deposits them in the side pocket of his jacket. As he crosses the parking lot, from the sixth row parallel to the entrance, the sun seems stronger than it did during his siesta, possibly because of the sensation of increased heat from the warm asphalt, over which his obedient shadow, the sharply drawn silhouette that follows him, diminished by the position of the sun in the cloudless sky, is projected. And when he enters the coolness inside the building, the change in climate, which includes, in addition to the air conditioning, a continuous loop of saccharine movie soundtracks in the background—"Love Is A Many Splendored Thing," just now—contributes, Nula remembers every time he walks in, to the sensation of passing from the air to the water, like when, as a teenager, diving into the river from the floating dock at the regatta club, he'd penetrate the subaquatic medium, completely different from the land above. But immediately, to the left of the entrance, a small crowd, somewhere between passive and unruly, calls his attention: a disorganized line, gathering and dispersing in accordance with the contained agitation of its constituents, mostly men, but also a few women, teenagers, and children, from various social classes, judging by their clothes, causes Nula to wonder what new, magical product can produce that reconciliation of classes, genders, and generations, equalized by the common denominator of appetite. Apparently, certain sporadic irregularities in their behavior, motivated by the impatience and even the anxiety of some of its constituents, produces a momentary disturbance that disrupts the line, eventually reconstituted by the vigorous protests emerging from the crowd. Nula approaches a dark-skinned older man who watches the scene with cold, vaguely disdainful calm.

—What are they selling? Nula says.

—Tickets to the Sunday match, the man says, without even turning his head to look at the face of the person who's asked him the question, concentrating instead on his observation of the crowd's behavior, possibly with the intention of making use of his observations to find an advantageous place in line, or simply with the philosophical neutrality of someone corroborating with this scene a specific preconception of the human race. Nula hesitates a moment, observing for himself the people who swarm around the entrance to the small room, and then he takes a few steps away, toward the empty passageway, and taking his cell phone from his pocket, dials a number and waits a few seconds for an answer.

—Good afternoon, he says. This is Mr. Anoch, from Amigos del Vino. Is Ms. Virginia there, please?

—One moment, says a feminine voice. And after a few seconds: She's in a meeting. Can you wait ten minutes in the cafeteria, please?

—Of course, Nula says.

The voice on the other end says *thank you* and hangs up. The cafeteria is almost empty just now; the customers seem to prefer, being as they are brighter and more suitable for light fare, the two bars in the hypermarket, one at each end of the building, the farthest one near the phone bank, and the other just before the entrance to the food section, in a wide passageway, along with a car dealership and, across the way, a few meters before the bar-cafeteria, a travel agency and a sporting goods store. Without intending to, or even realizing it, Nula sits down at the same table, in the same seat, and in the same position as Wednesday, on his way back from Paraná. The moment he sits down, a detail that he'd overlooked disorients him for a minute, and while amusing, insistently, though intermittently of course, it torments him: the guttural pigeon-like cooing, increasing in frequency and in amplitude as the paroxysm approached, that at once savage and tender cooing issuing, hoarsely, from Lucía's chest the night when he decided, crawling on four legs, almost in tears, from their bedroom, to leave their lives forever, the cooing that, as he listened to it for the last time, from the living room, seemed to have transformed into a growl, hadn't appeared the day before yesterday in Paraná, in fact no sound whatsoever had come from Lucía's chest. She might have clung to his body somewhat more tightly at the moment when, shuddering, he finished, but the unequivocal signal of pleasure from another, more remote from her own body than the distant stars, the impotent and painful fury of desire reaching its upper limit of incandescence as well as its momentary obliteration, the sonorous evidence rising from the dark jungle of her organs, had remained silent during her calculated and blatant pantomime. *And I felt guilty! She acts, thinks, and breathes for him. He commands her from a distance, like a remote-controlled robot. They're beyond united; they're a single entity in two separate bodies.* He's assaulted by a tenuous humiliation, and, almost immediately, by a battered, acquiescent relief. Remembering that he's in a cafeteria, he stands up and, walking toward the passageway, separated from the room by a moveable metal railing a meter high, parallel along the full length of the shelves, refrigerated or otherwise, displaying food and drinks, picks out a carbonated mineral water, and after paying for it and having the cashier open it, he puts several cubes of ice and a slice of lemon, which he picks up with metal tongs from a receptacle, into a tall glass and, arriving at the end of the line, starts to cross the silent room, past the empty tables, toward his table. Halfway to the table, he stops, sprays some mineral water into the glass, shakes it, and takes a sip. And, while he's drinking, the following idea, like a surge of emotion, strikes him: *Everything is real, probably, but if we sometimes see things as unreal it's because of their transience. Only in dreams are things absolute, when in reality we see things as relative and transitory. And so, while dreaming, we believe more in the reality of the dream than in what we believe while awake in the reality of the world.*

When Virginia enters the cafeteria, Nula checks the time on his watch: it's ten to five. She moves through the tables, dressed in yellow linen, so slender, firm, beautiful, and decisive, that, while she appears to incarnate the feminine ideal *par excellence*, her energy has a kind of virility that Nula intuits to be somewhat uncontrollable, and beyond his own powers. Nula stands up and waits for her.

—What punctuality, Virginia says.

—For you, I'd wait for hours, Nula says.

—Please, no clichés, Virginia says.

—Should we have a drink? Nula says.

—There's no time; it's almost five, Virginia says.

—Did you remember that we had a date if everything went well? Nula says.

—Of course, Virginia says. And if it goes to hell, too. How about we meet at Déjà Vu, the little bar on the boulevard across from the Alianza Francesa, at nine fifteen? I get off at eight, and that'll give me time to change.

—Sounds perfect, Nula says, and he makes a small, parodic bow that produces in Virginia sudden, happy, surprised laughter. Don't change too much, he says, because you're perfect the way you are.

Virginia shakes her head, defeated, and waits for him to come around the table before starting to walk. When they go out to the passageway, the music is interrupted and a masculine voice inter-jects the sonorous flow audible even in the most distant corner of the hypermarket: *Two announcements, one for children and another for everyone over eighteen: In the toy section, there's a raffle for a soccer ball, in honor of the Sunday Clásico; no purchase necessary, the raffle tickets are available at every register in the hyper. For the adults, starting at five o'clock and continuing all week, in the beverage section, there's a free tasting from the prestigious Amigos del Vino, introducing a new line of red and white wines for the selective palate, at moderate prices designed for the discerning clientele of the Warden hypermarket.* The voice is cut off and the volume of the music increases slowly, reoccupying, alone, the ambient space.

—What do you think? Virginia says.

—Exactly what we hoped for, Nula says.

When they are close to the intersection where the stand has been set up, Nula sees Américo and Chela, approaching in the opposite direction that he and Virginia are, and when they're almost there, Nula raises his arm, exposing his wrist watch, and shakes his head with exaggerated amazement.

—Perfect timing! he says when they arrive.

And Américo, falsely solemn and serious, announces: Punctuality is the politeness of kings.

The four of them smile at each other.

—This is Ms. Virginia, who runs the beverage section for Warden. Américo, my esteemed foreman, distinguished proconsul of the northeast region for the best wines in Argentina, and Chela, his exquisite wife, Nula says.

—Ms. Virginia, charmed, Américo says, shaking her hand while he points to Nula with the other hand: Trust me when I tell you never to buy a used car from this youngster.

The four of them laugh and approach the stand. Two girls, dressed alike—a white, short-sleeved blouse and a light green pleated skirt—are standing on either side of the stand, which is a narrow, collapsible counter at the ends of which two vertical metal bars sustain a sectioned wooden board painted a green similar to the skirts and on which a vine has been painted on one end and the word Amigos del Vino Tasting on the other. Two open bottles of white wine sit in a small ice bucket, and, on the counter, two of red, along with several rows of plastic cups and a stack of colorful brochures. Behind the stand, the shelves are full of bottles of red and white wine, differentiated only by the color of the label. Chela approaches the girls and gives each of them a kiss on the cheek.

—Steady, girls, this only lasts a week, she says.

—Alright, Américo, Nula says. A few words to start us off.

—Always remember that Amigos del Vino isn't a sect, but a revealed religion, Américo says.

—Exactly, Nula says. I present to you the selected fragments of its godless mystic: the divine Omar.

Reaching into the side pocket of his jacket, he pulls out the carefully folded white pages and hands them over.

—With this, no one can stop us, Américo says, and he puts them in the side pocket of his own jacket. Then, turning to Virginia, he says, Have you ever tried our product, ma'am?

—Of course. Behind the scenes, last week. It's high quality; otherwise, it wouldn't be here.

From the end of the aisle perpendicular to them, Moro, the real estate agent, makes his sudden appearance.

—Morito! Américo says. They've known each other since high school, and he held one of the first positions in the reliable client list that he gave Nula when he debuted as a salesman.

—Américo, Moro says. And, turning to the others, he says, ironically, I heard them announce the event over the loudspeakers and decided to come by. Good thing I did, with the chief maximus here in person.

One of the girls approaches him:

—Would you like a taste, sir?

Unsure, Moro quizzes first Américo and then Nula, the experts who guide his wine consumption, with his eyes:

—It's a high-quality product, Américo insists with a serious expression, further accentuated when he explains the premise of the marketing campaign they're putting on: We want to put an end to the scandal that in a democratic society the table wines within reach of every budget are always terrible quality.

—And you, Nula? Moro says.

—Don't think I'm going to commit *harakiri* contradicting my boss, Nula says, pleased to hear the others' laugher, especially Virginia's, which sounded vaguely surprised and somewhat stronger than the everyone else. But he adds, in a confidential tone, gesturing to the girls at the same time: Try the white and then tell us.

—Why not? Moro says.

The girl takes out a bottle of white from the ice bucket, pours a small amount of wine in one of the plastic cups, and extends it to Moro.

—Would anyone else like to try? the girl says.

—I'm saving myself for later, Virginia says, an apparently innocent sentence that Nula interprets as directed to him and overflowing with suggestion. And she adds: I have to get back to my office. Friday's are always crazy. Make yourselves at home.

Moro, seeing her walk away, beautiful, impeccable, and attractive, her firm body draped in yellow cloth, on high heels that click when she takes her first steps down the drink aisle before disappearing, stands frozen with the plastic cup in his hand halfway full of wine as yellow as Virginia's clothes.

—The longer you hold it, the hotter it gets, Américo says as his eyes, glowing maliciously, search fruitlessly for Nula's, standing motionless with a calculated expression of indifference.

Moro raises the plastic cup, trying to see the color of the wine in the light, but the plastic isn't transparent enough for him to see clearly what's inside, and so he resigns himself to lowering his hand and examining the wine through the cup's circular opening. Then, slowly, he brings it to his lips, but before allowing the plastic edge to touch them, he pauses mid-movement and shifts his nose slightly toward its contents. Under the eager and curious looks of Chela, of the girl who's just served him (the other one, curious to know what's happening in the rest of the hyper, isn't even paying attention), of Américo and Nula, Moro takes the first sip and, rather than swallowing it immediately, holds it behind his teeth, attempting to lift it to his palate, murmuring slightly, narrowing his eyes, until finally he swallows it, shaking his head solemnly in approval, still concentrating, overdoing it somewhat, in Nula's opinion, as he thinks that Moro, were he alone with the wine, wouldn't have felt the need to demonstrate so excessively an experience that, ultimately, even for him, Nula, and for Américo, who know the wine by heart, having tried it many times before deciding to sell it, is now and will continue, till the end of time, to be unique, incommunicable, and remote. Forgetting the wine, Nula thinks, *Moro was the first to see Gutiérrez when he returned to the city without telling any of his friends.* He'd picked him up at the Sauce Viejo airport, had taken him to the house in Rincón that Doctor Russo had built with every luxury with the fraudulent credit from the bank that because of so much shady business between the doctor and his friends ended up *banca rotta*, and when he, Moro, the man who at this moment is taking the second sip of white wine, which he detains intentionally in order to qualify as exactly as possible the fugitive evidence of the experience, the man who on behalf of the real estate agency in Buenos Aires collaborated on the sale of the house, allowing Nula to see Lucía, after five years, coming out of the swimming pool in

330

that fluorescent green swimsuit, and had suggested to Gutiérrez, with the recommendation of the agency in Buenos Aires, to have some fish at a fancy restaurant in Guadalupe he, Gutiérrez, had preferred to go to the San Lorenzo grill house, which had last been fashionable in the late fifties, probably, and which Nula knew because, when he was finishing high school, he and some friends would often go there to learn the ways of drunkenness. Moro had shown him the features of the house one by one and Gutiérrez had passed through them practically at a run, thinking not on the state of the amenities, corroded prematurely by neglect and the humidity, or on the price they were offering, which he didn't even discuss and which he could've lowered significantly because very few people were interested in the house and almost no one had the means to buy it, but rather on ghosts that, for decades probably, he had been projecting into it. *The houses in this city*, Moro had told Nula one day when he'd come on a sales call, *that my family has bought and sold and rented for the last three generations are the result of a compromise between the whims of their owners and the whims of their architects, constrained, fortunately, to a certain level of realism by zoning laws and the laws of economics*, and so Nula figured that from a man who could speak in such an exact and disillusioned way about what he was compelled to sell, the rather gentle, sympathetic assessment that he made of Gutiérrez the day he first met him, suggesting that he lived in a different dimension than everyone else, actually seemed plausible.

—It's very good, Moro says, after taking the second sip of wine, his eyes narrowed.

—Would you like to try the red? the girl says.

—No. That's fine, Moro says.

—Let's sweeten the deal, Américo says to the girl. Give him a bottle of red to take home, and a receipt for the cashier. And, turning to Moro: With this receipt they'll let you through. Cool the bottle down a bit before drinking it; it'll go really well with some tagliatelle.

While Nula and Chela listen to Américo's recommendations, their eyes meet with quiet sparks, enjoying the imperceptibly theatrical zeal with which Américo displays his promotional talents. Moro takes the bottle and the receipt and is about to say goodbye when a woman of a certain age suddenly walks up to Nula and starts talking to him:

—Aren't you India Calabrese's baby? she says in an overly loud and emphatic way.

Everyone freezes, surprised, and Nula blinks a few times, hesitating, before he responds:

—No. I was definitely that baby once, but now I'm not sure what to tell you.

Although Moro, Américo, and Chela laugh when they hear his response, the woman remains serious, and finally introduces herself.

—I'm Affife, do you remember? I was friends with your father and your mother before I moved to Córdoba.

—Affife, of course! Nula says, and kisses her cheek.

—I'm on my way to a movie, and it's about to start. Give your mother a kiss from me, she says, then turns the corner, almost at a run, and disappears down the next aisle toward the registers.

—She bounced me on her knees when I was a kid, Nula says, to explain himself.

But Moro and Américo aren't paying attention to him any more, and Chela is talking to the girls at the stand. After Moro leaves, and because several people are arriving to try the wine—the masculine voice interrupting the music has announced the presence of the stand over the loudspeakers two more times—Américo suggests to Nula and Chela that they have a drink at one of the two bars, but

Chela says she wants to browse around the hyper and makes a date with them for six thirty back at the stand. They go to the bar near the phone bank, because it's the most well-lit, and quietest one, although the crowd is increasing, and if there are still some free tables, by six thirty when they leave to meet up with Chela, there are already people waiting at the entrance for a table to open up. While they drink a mineral water, Américo, halfway seriously, tells Nula to be careful, that mixing business with pleasure, especially for a married man, can be dangerous. Nula pretends to be oblivious to the reasons for his advice, but Américo, who has a taste for psychological observations as well as detailed and complex elaborations, practicing these the same way others might fish or do amateur theater on Sundays, interrupts him:

—I was watching you with her: it's obvious that you've got something going. If not, you would've said something when she left, and you didn't move a muscle; you didn't even say goodbye or turn around. Ignoring her so much can only be explained because you thought it prudent not to call attention to yourself. Let's see: Have you already made a date? For when?

—Américo. She's a mother of children. You've got me all wrong, Nula says, conscious that his words have been chosen specifically for their false sound, implying to Américo, in this way, that he recognizes the truth of his observation but that he can't admit it openly, which satisfies Américo, whose supposition and interrogation are not made for ethical, but rather sporting reasons. *I'm not buying that*, Américo says, waving, in the air, an index finger covered with hair on the back all the way to the phalanx, and, immediately, without transition, he starts talking business: if they sell a hundred and twenty bottles through the hypermarket, give or take, it'll cover the costs of the marketing campaign, with some profit left over. Nula listens to him with pleasure: for some time, business, at moments, produces a pleasure similar to what he's experiencing

333

now, a pleasure that comes from a sense of security, of release, of surrender to the world. That pleasure assaults him, tinged with happiness, and the first time he felt it, suddenly and unexpectedly, he spent a while analyzing it in retrospect, until he realized that allowing himself to live like that put him in contact with the world, incorporated him into it, recovering, for a few seconds, the unity that thought, reason, and philosophy, had, from the beginning, understood to be lost. The same way Diogenes the Cynic refuted Zeno's paradoxes as he walked, he could sometimes refute the contradiction between being and becoming just like that, *by being*. But he knows it can't last: if one day he managed to forget philosophy and surrender himself, blindly and completely, to the supposed spontaneity of life, sooner or later, the torment, the division, forcing his return, would find him. And this somewhat literary and in fact extremely naive idea unfolds into a detailed vision of his own future life as a wine salesman who, having completely abandoned his reflections, his notes, his readings, *now hopelessly addicted to the opium of being*, as per the expression that he discovers in the midst of the images that define his new condition, would be reduced to what you might call an existence confined forever to the external: a family man, traveling salesman, with a graphic designer wife; in a few years, Américo retires and he, who'd taken on a partnership with Américo a while back, becomes the new manager of the branch; Diana, meanwhile, because of her agency work, will be forced to give up painting, but she'll be a successful designer, often hired by agencies in Buenos Aires, and when the kids are older, he and Diana will start to travel frequently to Buenos Aires, to Rosario, and even abroad; he'll have to be away more and more often, and for longer periods, not only to Buenos Aires, and Mendoza especially, but also to Paraguay, to Corrientes, to El Chaco; he'll frequent the international wine fairs in Europe, in New Zealand; the kids will finish school, they'll get married, they'll have kids of their own; he and Diana will be left alone in the house; La India and Diana's parents will have died by that point; they'll retire and the days will seem endless; they'll wander aimlessly in their slippers around the empty house until, finally, they'll turn on the television and eventually fall asleep with it on, until their servant turns it off and takes them to bed; there haven't been books in the house for years, except for a small collection of books on wine, cookbooks, graphic design manuals, and some books on painting, which Diana will use every so often for ideas to use in her jobs; Diana will never again describe her theories about *the real world as abstract form*, and he, Nula, will have forgotten even the existence of the riddle that Gabriela asked him last night at the Amigos del Vino bar, and to which he immediately replied, *Timaeus 27: What is that which always is and has no becoming, and what is that which is always becoming and never is?* Everything will be over, but without their really knowing why it'll seem unfinished to them; from the outside, their lives will give the impression of comfortable achievement, but they themselves will be harassed, continuously, secretly, by a muted and constant sense of disquiet; others will think that in their old age they display an enviable serenity, but they'll actually live in a state of monotone bewilderment, with a sense of drowning in a rough magma; later, though they'll still be together, they'll start to forget each other's name, and then, though they spend all day sitting on the same couch, even the other's very existence; they'll no longer recognize the faces of their children, or their grandchildren, when they lean in to give them a quick kiss on the cheek; and finally, one afternoon, one night, one morning probably, in summer, in winter, what's the difference, everything will come to an end.

—You're not listening to me, Américo's voice says. Is everything alright?

—No, Nula says, with a quiet smile, I haven't come to terms with you doubting my intentions with Ms. Virginia, that's all.

—I'm just not buying it, period, Américo says, and swatting the air with the back of his hairy hand, he decides to continue: a typical, high quality wine fractionated here in the province and not in the production region would be a good business right now, because the taste for wine has always existed in this country, but because of all the noxious sludge that's been bottled here the customer of limited means, especially after all the crises, has stopped drinking wine and prefers a good cold beer, especially in the hot months. The good wines are too expensive, and the cheap ones are undrinkable. What's missing, therefore, is that one, Américo says, gesturing energetically but vaguely at something somewhere in the hypermarket, beyond the registers, and despite the vagueness of the gesture, Nula imagines the intersection in the beverage section where the publicity stand has been set up alongside the neat rows of red and white wine bottles, distinguished clearly from a distance because the label of the red wines is red and the white wines a pale green. The feeling of happiness has vanished, and commerce no longer offers the return of a world without reflection, and so he listens to Américo's ideas skeptically: first of all, after his experience with Aconcagua—*the pinnacle of table wines*, according to a radio campaign at the time—Chela won't let him try to build his own fractionator and, in his opinion (which is to say, his as in Nula's), the arrangement that Américo has with Amigos del Vino is less risky and more profitable because he can also count on the support of the owner, who is in fact a friend and who's incorporated him to the firm under especially advantageous conditions; and on the other hand, expensive wines have a better profit margin.

—Why do you want to build a fractionator of average wine, Nula says, if fine wines have a better margin and the risk falls totally on the central house? For us, everything is profit, it's a gift.

—What you lack is a sense of the social aspects of business, Américo says with a beatific smile that he accompanies with a slow movement of his head both sideways and slightly upward, his eyes narrowed, meant to connote the sublime, and adding: With our whips we'll drive the merchants from the temple.

As though on cue, the background music, which had been Rififí, is interrupted, and the masculine voice of the booster announces: *For Holy Week, the Warden hypermarkets are hosting a raffle of fresh-water and saltwater fish, both fresh and frozen varieties, Norwegian salt cod, tuna, or Gran Paraná pejerrey, for instance, essential for the banquets at the end of Lent,* and the music resumes.

As they leave the bar, they see that the crowd has now invaded *the supercenter.* Through the windows of the bar, which face the parking lot, Nula, while he talked to Américo, had been watching the cars pull in and drive around and around looking for an open parking space. The sounds of footsteps, of voices, of laughter, can only be distinguished when they issue from a nearby source, because as the source moves away the different sounds merge into a single hum that, in contrast to the ambient loop and the voice over the loudspeaker that interrupts it every so often, sounds like a dull, monotonous, and continuous hum, which, intermittently, is punctuated by a set of chords and a recitative. Moving slowly through the crowd, Nula can discern fragments of voices and laughter that almost immediately fade and disappear into the background. They cross the toy section, the electrical appliances, the kitchen supplies, they take a loop around the cheeses, around the prepared foods, and past the frozen produce, and after glancing quickly at the labels and the prices on the shelves of wine that comprise the hypermarket's typical stock, they turn toward the stand. Although it's ten of seven, Chela isn't there, but when they approach the stand, one of the girls tells them that she was already waiting for them but that she'd left again, saying that she'd be right back. Some five or six people are waiting for their turn to taste the wine, and another three or four already have a plastic cup in their hand,

337

apparently studying its contents, or simply waiting to be served a second time. Américo elbows Nula discreetly but enthusiastically so he'll look at all the bottles that are missing from the shelves, whites as well as reds, more than twenty altogether. At five after seven, Chela appears, pushing a cart with some things that she's picked out: two or three cleaning products, a small box of frozen salt cod, a small box of homemade ravioli, makeup, a small garden spade, and a necktie with red and blue angled stripes for Américo. She picks it up and shows it to him, and then she folds it in half and holds it up to his bearded chin, letting it fall against his chest, over the one he's already wearing, to see how it looks. Then she pulls away the tie, kisses him on the part of his face, near the cheekbone, where there is no beard, and puts the tie back into the cart. Nula watches them, at once sympathetic and sorrowful; he thinks about La India, alone for years, and about his father, lying on the cold floor of a pizzeria—the crumpled and bloody corpse that actually may not have been killed by the gunshots because the man who occupied it was already dead to himself, since the time of delirium and frenzy, long before the superfluous bullets reached him.

To pass the time, Nula accompanies Chela and Américo, who are heading back to Paraná, to their car. They get in line at a register, and when they walk out to the parking lot the warm and somewhat humid air sticks to their cheeks. Although it's already seven thirty, it's still not completely dark. In the west, above the city, an enormous, bright red stain extends, smooth and uniform, over the sky, and below, through the shadows on the ground, the lights of the waterfront are visible. Américo suggests, possibly with an implicit warning, that he should leave too, but Nula says that he prefers to stay a while longer, until after eight, in case the girls at the stand need anything. His eyes follow Américo's car as it drives away, and then he lifts his head toward the tense, brilliant stars in the dark blue sky. Ceaselessly, cars enter and exit the parking lot, they form lines for gas at the service station, they drive around looking for an open space, and their occupants come and go with their carts, empty or full of merchandise, all distinct and very real in the evening, yet at the same time improbable and somehow vague. The extensive facade of *the supercenter*, with its many entrances, the one to the hypermarket, to the mall, to the multiplex, illuminates the dark air with its neon signs, its geometric, outward projections of light, its lamplights indicating the edges of the cement that separates the sidewalk from the parking lot. Nula goes back in through the multiplex, studies the show times, and sees that there are lines forming for the eight o'clock show. Then he passes through the cafeteria, which is now full, and observes the crowd from the entrance: the line that fills the passageway between the main room and the dishes and beverages; the customers who, leaving the registers, carry their loaded trays, moving slowly, uncertain and somewhat discouraged, looking for a table. Farther off, the small room where they were selling tickets to the Sunday match is closed, and a small sign taped to the wooden door announces: TICKETS FOR THE *CLÁSICO* SOLD OUT. A man and a woman practically running from the parking lot freeze, stupefied, when they see the sign. Nula walks into the hypermarket, and, moving slowly through the crowded aisles, without stopping once to look at any of the many products on display, eventually arrives at the stand and stops a certain distance away. The prospective tasters of the new line of table wines swarm around the counter. As she's serving a customer, the girl who offered Moro the wine, and who's seen him approach, gives him a friendly gesture, and so Nula walks up to her.

—Everything alright? he says.

—Perfect. There's barely enough to go around, the girl says.

—Do you need a hand? Nula says.

—No, no. Don't worry about us. Ms. Virginia is sending someone at nine to help us pack everything up. You can leave if you like, she says, handing a cup of red wine to a man who was watching every one of her movements carefully.

Nula looks at his watch: it's five after eight.

—Alright, Nula says. I'll leave before the return of Affife.

The girl doesn't get the joke, but she laughs politely and starts to fill another cup, this time of white wine. Nula turns around and starts walking toward the exit. The infinite loop of musical soundtracks heard in every elevator of every luxury hotel, in every supermarket, in every mall, in the variety shows on planes and in airports, the infinite wave of saccharine music that has been assaulting the West, and probably the East as well, for decades, like a soft requiem for the slow extinction of a species dying from a plague of conformism punctuated here and there by a marketing campaign, the thin molasses propelled by a plethora of violins, at the very moment when Nula crosses the exit, is playing "The Godfather," and as if he'd been infected, without knowing it, by the virus of that same plague, as he steps into his car, Nula starts, softly, humming the melody. Because he still has time, he decides to get in line for gas at the service station, which takes awhile, and then he drives on, not really knowing what to do. After crossing the road bridge, rather than continuing along the boulevard, he turns up the waterfront along the edge of the lagoon, all the way to Guadalupe. At a bend, he sees the water glowing through the trees; it makes him want to get out and he starts to slow down but immediately changes his mind and drives on. At the Guadalupe roundabout he turns west and then back onto the same road, to the south. Thirty blocks later he reaches the boulevard, and, two blocks west, the bar Déjà Vu, but because he can't park on the boulevard he turns at the corner, to the north, and parks halfway down the block. He walks slowly under the trees, in the warm night air. At nine fifteen on the dot he walks into the bar; Virginia is already there, not at a table but rather behind the counter, talking on the phone.

The bar is full, and although it's been open for over a year and Nula has passed it many times in his car, looking at it curiously, it's his first time inside. It's a simple and pleasant bar, with French posters on the ochre walls and wooden tables and chairs. It's full of young people—*a hip place*, Nula thinks with a hint of arrogance that he immediately regrets, and sidestepping the tables, which are all full, he walks toward the counter. Virginia sees him arrive, and as she talks on the phone she gestures for him to wait. As she talks she looks through the window at some vague spot on the dark boulevard, and Nula is able to examine her ample, firm body, her wide back and her well-proportioned, slender arms, their tanned, smooth skin revealing, discreetly, below the short sleeves of her marble-colored shirt, hard muscles. After a couple of minutes, Virginia hangs up.

—Muriel, my daughter; on Fridays she and her five friends all sleep over at someone's house, Virginia says. Like old ladies getting together without their husbands.

—Like some of them, enjoying the liberties of widowhood, Nula says.

—What are you drinking? Virginia says, using *tú* unexpectedly. It's on the house.

Nula, with a half smile, slowly shakes his head, unsure. Despite being a wine seller, he has a strong preference for more colorful, eccentric drinks, like Kir Royales, Bloody Marys, screwdrivers, Negronis, San Martín Secos, or Lemon Champs. Finally he decides:

—A Negroni, he says.

Virginia pours the liquors in a cylindrical glass, over three or four ice cubes, mixes them with a long-handled spoon, and, folding a paper napkin in half, puts the glass on top and slides it to the outside edge of the counter. Before touching it, Nula observes, admiringly, the deep red of the liquid mixture that Virginia has just prepared.

341

—Well? she says.

—Aren't we going to toast? Nula says.

Virginia pours a small amount of seltzer into a glass and raises
it. Nula raises his own, and the glasses, when they touch, produce
a faint, momentary tinging. They take a drink, and Nula, with a
gesture of approval, pursing his lips, concentrating on the flavor of
the drink, looks up slowly.

—Excellent, he says. I didn't know that you worked here, too.

—I don't work here. I'm the owner. Well, one of the owners.
There's three of us, Virginia says. Him—she points to the waiter,
serving a table—his wife, who should be here soon, and me. Do you
mind if we wait for her five minutes before we leave?

—Of course, Nula says. I knew from the first time I saw you that
you were a business man.

—No, Virginia says. The first time you saw me was a few years
ago, at the enology course at the Hotel Iguazú. That's the secret
that I wanted to tell you: that we already knew each other.

—Seriously? he says, laughing. You're joking. How could I not
have noticed you?

—I was a little fatter then. And in some situations it's better to
go unnoticed, Virginia says. I wanted to approach you, I was very
attracted to you. But you seemed so serious back then. And besides,
a pregnant girl came to see you two or three times. When I saw you
the other day I recognized you immediately. You look better.

—I'm sure you do too. I can't imagine you looking better than
you do tonight.

Virginia laughs lightly, but immediately her expression turns
serious.

—Thanks, but it's not necessary for you to keep repeating that
nonsense, she says. Here comes my associate.

Nula, who is taking a sip of his Negroni, turns toward the door,
through which he sees a girl in a tight, short-sleeved black dress

with a tight band around the knees; a low, rectangular neckline begins at her collarbones and falls to the upper edge of her breasts, leaving her neck exposed. She stops at a table occupied by a couple, says a few words, and then, leaning over, gives each of them a conventional kiss on the cheek. Then she walks to the counter and arrives just at the moment when Nula deposits the glass with the rest of his Negroni on the white paper napkin.

—Flaca, Virginia says. This is the friend I told you about. Nula, La Flaca.

La Flaca approaches Nula and kisses him on the cheek. Then she apologizes for making them wait. Her husband arrives from the other side of the room and now it's his turn to receive the quick kiss from La Flaca on his left cheek. Virginia picks up her purse from somewhere behind the counter, invisible to Nula, walks to the end of the counter, where the register is, turns around, and comes back in the opposite direction, toward them, along the outside edge of the counter. White pants made of a silky cloth hug her legs, her backside, her hips, her flat belly, her groin. Her white shoes click, evenly and firmly, against the reddish tiles. After a general exchange of perfunctory kisses, Virginia and Nula walk out to the street. They turn at the corner, walking under the shadows of the trees, toward the dark green station wagon parked along the curb a few meters ahead. Before pulling out, in the darkness of the car, with the dashboard lights projecting upward at an angle, their faces, looking in the same direction because of the position of their bodies in the seats, as though each of them was unaware of the presence of the other, reflecting the weak light, covered with highlights and shadows, indecisive and expectant, exaggerate their strangeness. A heavy silence surprises them, unexpected considering the casual relationship they've settled into since the beginning, submerging them among rapid, contradictory thoughts for a few seconds, as if the fragile cortex of urbanity whose surface retained the overflow of an indifferent, anarchic substance above turbulent, profound depths had split and both of them, exhibiting their openness up till that moment, assaulted by a sudden flood, were trying desperately to contain it. Nula, his voice coming out slightly hoarse, having to cough a couple of times before he can speak naturally, suggests the restaurant at the Hotel Palace, one of the most popular in the city, where they're sure to run into at least one person they know, according to the rule whereby he carries out his most suspicious behavior where everyone can see it, precisely with the intention of dispelling those suspicions. Virginia accepts with a quick laugh that, Nula thinks, suggests she intuits his rationale. The mood has changed: their casual, quick humor, their worldly cynicism, their erotic double entendres, have lost their *use value*, and, without meaning to, they've moved inside something, a zone or a dimension that they are less than halfway in control of, and where, however much they pretend to move through it openly, they know that trembling, shudders, moaning, and heaviness are waiting for them. The restaurant is very full, and when the waiter offers them a discreet table in the back, Nula says he prefers a more central one, next to the window that faces the street, so that they'll be seen easily from anywhere in the room, and from the street as well, a preference that once again provokes Virginia's laughter, about which, in this new phase of their relationship, where they're forced, for the moment, to intuit the meaning of each others' words and reactions, to Nula, not the slightest shadow of a doubt, as they say, remains.

—Do you drink wine? Nula says.

—Why not? Virginia says. For me, first a glass of white and then a red.

—Very good, he says. The cellar is good here; we're partial suppliers.

And, as they wait for the wine to arrive, they start to talk. When she was twenty-nine, Virginia, who studied French at the Alianza, went to France, to Bordeaux, to perfect the language, thinking she'd come back to the city to teach, but when her grant finished the following year she started to take an interest in wine, and as her French improved, her desire to teach it waned. She enrolled in enology courses and eventually found work with a supplier. Everything was going well: she'd been in Europe for four years and she was unsure if she would stay forever, but when she got pregnant it seemed, though it was never clear why, that she had to return. She waited for her daughter to be born so she'd be French. The girl's father, who had another family, offered to recognize her, but Virginia refused; she respected the father, admired him even, but she didn't love him. Recognizing Muriel would have created enormous complications for him, Virginia was convinced that he was relieved when she said no. For seven years he sent her money every month, until suddenly, one day, the money orders stopped. Eventually she got a letter from a friend in Bordeaux, saying that the man had died in a car accident. At the time, Virginia was giving private French classes, and sometimes the Alianza asked her to fill in, but wine, as a profession, attracted her: in Bordeaux, she'd seen the business side up close, of course, and also a lot of scheming and fraud, but wine itself, the successive transformations of the fruit into a drink and then into madness, sacred or otherwise, fascinated her. She'd promoted a few lesser-known Mendoza wineries around the littoral region, and had taken other courses (like the one where she'd seen Nula for the first time), but she wasn't that interested in traveling, so when they built *the supercenter*, she applied to manage the beverage section. And him? Nula hesitates a few seconds before responding. Him? Nothing special: he started out in medical school and after a while got bored with it and transferred to philosophy.

Then, because he was about to be a father, he had to get serious about work, and, well, the chance to work in wine presented itself unexpectedly. It's not that bad, but since he has two kids now—a boy and a girl, Yussef and Inés, four and two, respectively—it would be impossible to stop working and commit himself to philosophy. (Nula's interest in philosophy is amusing, and somewhat surprising, to Virginia.) In any case, Nula says, philosophy isn't strictly speaking a profession; one is a philosopher in any situation, and any object in the world can be of interest to a true philosopher. Furthermore: any object in the world is the cipher for the whole world; if one discovers its essence, the whole world is revealed. And, considered properly, wine could be, after all, an optimal object of study. And, with a theatrical gesture, Nula raises a glass of white wine and makes a silent and delicate toast before taking a sip. When he places the glass back onto the tablecloth, he looks Virginia in the eyes and asks her gently:

—Aren't you worried about having deprived your daughter of a father?

—Yes, very, Virginia says without hesitating, but she doesn't elaborate on her response.

Nula doesn't insist, though he thinks again about his mother, his brother, his murdered father. Still, he doesn't really want to discuss the topic, first of all because it's too intimate and painful to describe immediately to someone who's practically a stranger, but especially because he prefers to avoid disclosures, not out of caution or discretion, but rather because he doesn't want them to become too human; he'd rather avoid opening the fissure through which shame and compassion might pass, the first being confused for the second in a swamp of relativity, removing them from that limbo of exteriority where their desire, sheltered from shame and reluctance, moving with ease, irrational, makes pleasure from ghostly stereotypes. Thus the meal passes with the kind of polite and expectant formality where each of them—at least this is how Nula imagines it—tries to discern, analyzing, in transit, the other's intentions. They try the red wine and say some things about it, attempting to describe with everyday images the incommunicable depths of the experience, and when they coincide in some detail they reveal an excessive, childish enthusiasm that in Nula is not simulated in the least, though its excessiveness may come from the anticipated pleasure of what, though it hasn't been named once all night—maybe they've both decided it without they themselves deliberating it, each of them possibly unaware of their own decision—inexorably, approaches. Every time that Nula thinks of the possibility, a violent emotion overwhelms him, and he has to concentrate so intensely to keep it from manifesting outwardly that, from time to time, he loses the thread of the conversation and can only respond with vague monosyllables and slow, indistinct nods, projecting into the immediate future the intense disorder, impenetrable to the words that Virginia, concentrating on the thoughts that those words attempt to translate, speaks in the present. Though she protests energetically, Nula pays the bill, and when they finish their last sip of wine, he gets up, says he'll be right back, and starts walking toward the bathrooms. Because it's Friday night, the restaurant is packed, and Nula sidesteps the tables with an unhurried, distracted agility. Two large tables of older women who get together, without their husbands, on Fridays, exude a singular energy, an overblown joy, possibly because they've freed themselves, for a few hours or forever, from the protection, tender or despotic, it makes no difference, of the men who, for decades, imagined that they possessed them. And a few meters beyond them, in a discreet corner in the back of the room, where the waiter, because of his experience, though he was ignorant to

Nula's private custom—hiding in plain sight—offered to seat them when he came in with Virginia, sits Gutiérrez in the company of a woman of a certain age, older than him—or at least that's the impression that Nula gets as he approaches.

Gutiérrez has seen him approach, and because he's also seen Nula notice him, he waits for him smiling, half-standing. When he sees him, Nula thinks that if there were a restaurant that Gutiérrez, having returned to the city after more than thirty years away, would definitely pick, it would have to be the Hotel Palace, which already existed, very similar to how it is now, before his mysterious departure. Gutiérrez might be unaware that, like the tumultuous history of the country and the city, the restaurant, so similar to how he left it, suffered many setbacks, changes of fortune, decline, death and rebirth, successive closures and triumphant but ephemeral reopenings, periods when it was even a ruins and a house of ill repute, until a few years ago an international consortium of hotels bought and restored it, improved by the prestige that age inexplicably endows, to the same look it had the day it first opened in the mid forties. *I'd bet my life that he couldn't have paid for it back then, but the real reason he's here tonight is that he'd wanted to be here during those years, doing the things that he imagined that the ones who were here kept doing, as though he'd never left, as though nothing had happened in all that time, and the Hotel Palace, with its most recent and umpteenth inauguration, must shore up that illusion, given its attachment, according to everyone who knows him better than I do, to that same world that was his until the day he left,* Nula thinks, constantly smiling, as he approaches the table, holding out his hand to Gutiérrez, who waits with his own extended.

—How are you? Gutiérrez says. Mr. Anoch, wine seller. Mrs. Leonor Calcagno.

Nula is about to hold out his hand to her, but something in her posture, neither suspicious nor aggressive, but rather absent behind a vague smile, either her typical grimace or the involuntary side effect of repeated plastic surgery, tells him that she will not change position, and so he chooses instead a subtle, stiff, but friendly bow.

—Good to met you, he says, and she responds with an imperceptible movement of her head.

—I saw you when I came in, but you didn't see me. Your wife, I take it, Gutiérrez says, nodding more or less in the direction of Nula's table.

Thinking that Virginia is my wife is as far from the truth as taking Lucía for his daughter, Nula thinks with unjustified cruelty, but instead he responds in the most neutral tone he can muster: Not at all. She's a colleague from the supercenter; a typical business dinner.

—Of course, Gutiérrez says. Now that you mention it, it's obvious a mile away. I hadn't looked closely.

And he looks, quickly and just as vaguely, at the approximate place in the dining room where Virginia must be sitting at the table, though both he and Nula know, of course, that it's impossible for him to see her from where he's standing.

—The other day I tried the viognier with Gabriela and Soldi. Thanks for the recommendation, it's excellent, Gutiérrez says.

—So I heard. I ran into them when they were coming back from there, happy as anything, after eating my catfish, Nula says, and Gutiérrez receives this allusion with a cackle.

—*La forza del destino*, he says. And in a kindly threatening tone, he says, Be sure to bring your swimsuit on Sunday. I read that the weather is supposed to be excellent. I already called the others; you were the only ones left.

—I'm sure it'll be great, Nula says, but, for several seconds, he finds it impossible to turn his thoughts or his eyes from Leonor Calcagno: from between those legs, probably, though he can't see them under the table, as thin and feeble as her blackened arms, at

349

one point, Lucía Riera had emerged, irritated and bloody, wailing in shock and terror, from the placid lethargy in which she'd been vegetating for nine months, possibly sowed by the very man he's just spoken to; suddenly, time has started to run backward, and the first cause of his encounter with that attractive, firm body, swaying, dressed in red, across that spring afternoon, attracting him like a magnet, or, better yet, like a promise, is now in front of him, the clandestine hours when in cheap hotels or in some apartment far from the city center, with fury and tenderness, they copulated—if, after all, it's true that Gutiérrez, and not the author of the still-usable *Roman Law Course*, is the real father, although the refusal, by all the parties in question, to verify it categorically, something which would be so easy to do, tends to suggest the opposite. Maybe it seems dishonorable to Gutiérrez to believe DNA more than Leonor; in any case, if that demented pact between the mother, the daughter, and the supposed father is inexplicable, it's no more so than the apparent devotion that Gutiérrez demonstrates for the wreckage he's taken out to dinner at the Palace restaurant tonight: clearly she has the cerebrum of a bird, and not just its cerebrum, actually. If she was beautiful once, she no longer conserves even the faintest shadow of that beauty; she can't weigh more than forty kilos; her dark skin, devastated by constant exposure to the sun, or worse yet, to artificial tanning lamps, along with the creams, the diet regimes, the face lifts and skin grafts, the hair transplants and dye jobs, the silicone breast implants and lip fillers, supposedly to make them more sensual, have eroded whatever beauty she ever may have had; her arms, which extend like two dry twigs from the short sleeves of her dark blouse (perhaps following the precept that dark colors are thinning), loaded with bracelets, just like her gaunt fingers with rings, are wrinkled, and a thick layer of makeup disguises the wrinkles on her face, but no face lift could hide the skin on her neck that, as blackened as the rest, collapses into irrecoverable folds, which the two or three necklaces that lay on her flat and bony chest cannot manage to conceal. And now, to top it off, she opens her purse and, removing a makeup case, opens it, looks at herself in the interior mirror, and starts to retouch parts of her face with a small brush. Her skin is so dark, her body so withered, that her eyes, which are large and brilliant and yet inexpressive, look like two artificial lights occupying the place where her eyes should be, shining through their respective orifices in a dark, crumpled, and lifeless cardboard mask. When he turns his head away, Nula's eyes meet Gutiérrez's; his eyes are serene, and glow with a lucid and benevolent irony: *I know what you're thinking. But to understand what this is you'd have to live through the entire life of someone else; my experience is untranslatable, so it's useless for you to waste your time wondering why I ran back to this rotten city after she and I met in Europe and she told me I was the father of her daughter. What do I care if it's true or not? No matter what, the external always takes your place, the world, with its capricious, impenetrable laws, will always take you wherever it wants. You can't imagine how beautiful she was, and so different from your associate tonight, and even though she couldn't follow through to the end, she had more than enough courage for the enormous risk of giving herself to me, a nobody, for several weeks. Wouldn't it seem terrible to you if I left her now that she's alone, exhausted from her battle with age, after she'd given me, at the exact moment when I most needed it, what none of the gigolos who have exploited her would ever have? It doesn't matter to me that she's gone to bed with a thousand men; frankly I don't think she gave a single one of them the gift the she gave me and that she herself is probably unaware that she possessed, or in any case that, from the effect that she continues to this day to have on my life, was only meant for me.* In fact, Nula can't tell with any certainty if these are the words hidden in the look that Gutiérrez has just given him, or if it's he himself who attributes them to him, connecting the fragmentary histories in circulation and projecting onto Gutiérrez what, without knowing it till that moment, he's thought of him since he first met him. Several curious and even absurd things, if taken separately, acquire a certain sense, not entirely clear of course, but totally coherent: for instance, his insistent declaration that he became a screenwriter and took on a pseudonym in order to disappear better, or on Tuesday, at the fish and game club, when he took out his false teeth, causing him as much surprise and even discomfort as to the man tending the bar, but which nevertheless seemed strangely reasonable to Escalante, so much so that he rewarded him with two live catfish, which, as an immediate consequence, restored the bartender's respect. Many things escape him, and while there's nothing actually disconcerting about Gutiérrez, just the opposite in fact, some aspects of his personality seem, in the end, not exactly absurd, but rather enigmatic.

—Well, it's great to see you both, he says.

—Until Sunday, then, Gutiérrez says cheerfully, infected by Nula's intensified friendliness.

—Yeah, of course. At what time? Nula says.

—I get up at six, Gutiérrez says. But if you want to sleep in a little, or go to mass . . .

—Right, right, Nula says. Let's say around eleven?

—That's what I was thinking, Gutiérrez says.

And, with a silent wave, Nula continues toward the bathrooms. In the approximately forty-five seconds that the conversation lasted, Nula thinks, he's become more lovable, possibly, but definitely more mysterious. And, on his way back from pissing, washing his hands, checking himself out in the mirror to confirm that everything along the exterior region of his person is in order, he passes by the table again, and the quick greeting that Gutiérrez gives him, consisting of waving the fingers on his slightly elevated hand, an indifferent and momentary although friendly gesture, similar to what Nula gave La India that morning, intensifies both his familiarity and his enigma. Leonor Calcagno ignores him, not out of disdain or suspicion, but because she finds herself, as always, trapped in the muddy material of her own person, where in all likelihood she's been splashing frantically since her first moment of consciousness.

Though he hasn't been delayed long, Nula hurries back, but between the occupied tables, the busy waiters passing him, the clients coming in or going out, he doesn't advance very quickly. When he is close to the table, he sees Virginia, calmly gazing out at the street through the window, her clean, thick hair, her round, tanned face, her wide shoulders, and her at once smooth and muscular arms. For the first time, he sees her without her noticing, and the virility of her body and the serenity of her expression forms an exciting contrast that attracts and repels him simultaneously. But when he reaches her side and sees that she already has her purse and her white jacket in her hand, ready to leave, that contradictory impression is erased, and he follows her decisively into the street. As they walk toward the car, Nula realizes that, at least in her high heels, she's few centimeters taller than him: *It'll be a difficult body to control,* he thinks, and when, thinking this, he laughs momentarily, Virginia looks at him with an inquisitive expression.

—Nothing, Nula lies. I was thinking of someone I ran into at the restaurant.

Virginia doesn't respond, but shakes her head thoughtfully. They get in the car and, before putting the key in the ignition, Nula leans in to kiss her on the mouth; she lets him do it, but without allowing him to embrace her yet, and when he extends his hand to touch her, her hand traps it and their fingers interlace; Nula, who pushes forward softly, feels the resistance of her palm, and the two opposing forces find a stable equilibrium as they practice the ancient custom of testing with their mouths, first of all, like newborns and animals, the flavor, the value, the viability of the external, its beneficial or noxious, gratifying or repulsive qualities. When they separate and their hands release, through his sudden arousal, Nula, who still holds his car keys in his free hand, concealing his trembling, tries two or three times to put them in the ignition, until finally he's able to; the dashboard lights come on and he looks quickly at Virginia, but she is motionless, her head leaning against the edge of the seat, her eyes narrowed. Nula turns the car on, pulls slowly away from the curb, and advances down the dark, deserted street toward the bright intersection. It's almost midnight. Remembering the sensation of the fleshy, humid, and warm borders that he's just tasted, Nula thinks that, although everything is alike, nothing is ever repeated, and that since the beginning of time, when the great delirium began its expansion, each one of the buds with which it's revived, reincarnating and withering immediately, every event is unique, flaming, unknown, and ephemeral: the individual does not incarnate the species, and the part is not a part of the whole, but only a part, and the whole is in turn always a part; there is no whole; the goldfinch that sings at dawn sings for itself; what it sings was unknown before that morning, and its previous song, which even it doesn't remember singing, and which seems so much like the one before, if one listened carefully, would clearly be different.

Nula reaches out his hand, seeking Virginia's, and he finds it, warm and relaxed, on her thigh; their fingers intertwine again, but without resistance.

—What should we do? he says.

—Whatever you want, if you can imagine that I don't do this every Friday, Virginia says.

—It wouldn't matter to me, Nula says.

—But I don't, she says, and after a pause: I'm paying for the hotel.

Nula, incredulous, shakes his head: And is that typical? he says, with a laugh that sounds like a protest.

—I'm not going to explain it, Virginia says, without laughing.

—Alright, alright, Nula says. I accept.

They go to a motel room on the outskirts of the city, to the north. An employee meets them in the shadows of the entrance. Nula rolls down the window and the man, without leaning out too much, out of discretion for sure, offers them a special room, which he calls the *Palais de Glace*.

—Why not? Virginia says before Nula has time to consult her. And, giving him a nudge on the arm, holds out a few bills.

—The last garage on the left, the man says, and Nula drives away slowly, in first gear, down a brick gravel path flanked by hedges and surrounded by a series of garages, of which two or three are occupied. Dim lights barely illuminate the garden, and when the car enters the garage, a faintly luminous strip designates the entrance, which they cross without incident thanks to the car's headlights.

A door in the middle of the wall leads to an almost completely dark passageway in which the man from the entrance is waiting for them. Without turning around—discretion is a house rule—he leads them to a door, opens it, and before disappearing, he murmurs: The light switch is to the left of the entrance.

As soon as they enter, Nula switches it on and closes the door to the passageway. The contrast with the passageway, the garage, the garden, and the turbulent night in the outskirts dazzles and at the same time amuses and fascinates them. A chandelier hangs from the ceiling, and its illuminated lamps are reflected in an array of mirrors surrounding a large bed, without a headboard, covered in a red bedspread. The back wall, the two side walls, and the ceiling from which the chandelier hangs are covered with mirrors. Standing in the middle of the room, at the foot of the bed, each one of their movements is repeated ad infinitum in the mirrors, sharp and clearly visible in the glaring, multiplied lights. They embrace and kiss, but without the other seeming to notice it, both are less attracted to the carnal experience than to the infinite image of themselves experiencing it, returned to them, simultaneously, by the mirrors. Nula wants to go take a shower, but it's difficult for him to abandon that embrace, reproduced as far as the eye can see, acquiring a dreamlike quality in which the multiple images of himself carry out the gestures that he imagines, without the sensations that he experiences, ultimately confusing the empirical plane with the countless images that mimic him until he loses his own sense of reality. Eventually, he lets go and walks into the bathroom. He undresses, and when he steps into the shower to wash himself off and cool down, he's so excited that his penis makes it difficult for him to wash his groin, his thighs, his testicles. Finally, he reemerges, drying himself off as he walks into the room. Virginia is lying on the bed, naked, her forearm resting on her forehead and her eyes narrowed, one leg bent and the other extended across the bed, the black triangle of her pubis half-hidden by a fist resting softly on the pillow of hair. Nula lets the towel fall to the ground and, standing at the foot of the bed, rests his left hand against his own groin to make his penis stand out more, and then, with his fingers, pulls back the foreskin to reveal the reddish head, inflated by the impatient blood, and then, looking sideways, sees his own image multiplied in the side mirrors, then in the one in front of him, and finally in the one that returns his image, inverted, from the roof. But when he looks back toward the image reflected by the side mirrors his eyes meet Virginia's and he realizes that she isn't asleep and that in fact, with her eyes narrowed, she's gazing, lost in thought, at her own naked body in the mirror. Suddenly, she realizes that she's being watched, and looking at Nula through the mirror, feeling discovered, she starts to laugh, and Nula, removing his hand from his groin, laughs along. For several seconds, countless naked bodies, that of a young woman lying in bed, and that of a man standing at the foot of the same bed, laugh with a curious joy, but the laughter rings out in a single dimension, without it being clear where it comes from, whether from the rough bodies made of blood, of impulses, of thoughts, and of time, or from the ghostly pantomime that, sheltered from contingency, mimics them, seething, in the mirrors. Virginia opens her eyes and moves her arms, which end up alongside her body. Her legs, stretched out across the bed, open slightly, and along the inside edge of the black triangle of her pubis, barely visible, the reddish promise is revealed, the legendary entrance beyond which, inaccessible and remote, in an unknowable space, like the most distant and invisible galaxies, the sensations of the other take shape.

SATURDAY

MARGINS

Before the central market was torn down, the alley behind it was full of cheap restaurants and boarding houses. In one of these, La Giralda, on August 6th, 1945, precisionism was born.

There was no broadside, no Battle of Hernani, no exquisite corpse. Mario Brando, its creator, had his sights elsewhere: precisionism should take its place not among the avant-garde, in opposition to the times, but rather as its most faithful representation. According to Brando, newspapers, radio stations, universities, and large-circulation magazines should be the natural media for the expression and expansion of the movement. Scientific magazines not only weren't excluded but in fact were, in a certain sense, the immediate precursors of the precisionist aesthetic. A proto-precisionism could be found precisely in the latest scientific treatises and the reviews of these in popular magazines.

At the time, for the writers of the city, it was a sign of good taste to be seen, every so often, at one of the precisionists' Thursday dinners. Only the post-modernista old guard refused to yield, but it's important to note that, from Belisario Roldán onward, they'd labeled every new literary movement as wayward, prosaic, and incomprehensible. Anyone still left over in nineteen sixty was still making the same joke about modern art, namely that everything represented by abstract painting was a fried egg.

The rest of the opposition, which is to say the neoclassicists and the regionalists, was much more elastic, if not opportunistic. The regionalists, who met on Fridays at the San Lorenzo grill house, would individually attend the dinners every so often, and would invite this or that precisionist to their cookouts. But they didn't suffer from any illusions: they knew that Nexos, the official organ of Mario Brando's movement, would never welcome a regionalist text. The neoclassicists, whose magazine, Espiga, had been published triannualy since 1943, had some official exchanges with the precisionists, inasmuch as Brando and his clique thought that certain neoclassical subjects, like Christian mysticism, for instance, could yield to the precisionist aesthetic. And the neoclassicists, meanwhile, appreciated the precisionist inclination for traditional forms. In private, the regionalists referred to the neoclassicists as sanctimonious Bible thumpers and to the precisionists as outdated futurists and fascists; the neoclassicists said that the regionalists, with every one of their criollo cookouts, were slowly devouring the subjects of their literature, and that the precisionists, with their absurd scientism, were the medical school pages; and the precisionists, who weren't satisfied with the occasional slander and in fact launched fully clandestine smear campaigns, referred to several members of Espiga's editorial committee as Curia spies, to their writing as an intentional amalgamation of mysticism and faggotry, and said that the interest of the regionalist group's leader for the countryside could be explained by the fact that he was actually a horse.

Brando was born in 1920. In 1900, his father, an Italian immigrant, arrived in Buenos Aires with the certainty that every one of his compatriots huddled alongside him in the boat, along with everyone who'd come over in the last thirty or forty years, crowded in other boats, and still crowding in Buenos Aires slums until they got the chance to finally own a farm or a business, that every one of those compatriots, who came from everywhere in Italy, still shared the same weakness, pasta, and that he would be the one to supply them with it. After three or four years of adventures, he finally landed in the city and started to manufacture, in small, artisanal quantities, fresh pastas that he distributed to a fixed clientele in wicker boxes, carefully wrapped in immaculate napkins cut from bags of grain. Two years later, the customers would be coming to buy their pasta at the Brando family delicatessen, in the center of the city, and if by 1918 their dry spaghetti, wrapped in cellophane or in twenty-kilo bags, was sold in numerous shops in the north of the province, by 1925, Pastas Brando was one of the top businesses in the province, and Atilio Brando was the president of the Círculo Italiano. (In 1928, one black ball thrown in the vote would keep him out of the Club del Orden.)

To the annoyance of many local patricians, Atilio Brando's Spanish was flawless. Five or six years after having come to the country, all that was left of his Italian accent was a slight aspiration. His family was full of lieutenants to Cavour, to Pellico, and to Garibaldi. In the sixties, Taine had eaten with one of his relatives in Rome. And when the manufacture of pastas had achieved a regular pace, when the complex, futuristic harmony of the factory was producing an uninterrupted chain of identical packages of fragile, yellow pastas ready to be circulated by a perfectly oiled and efficient distribution network, the elder Brando handed over the factory to a loyal manager with a share in the profits and started spending long periods in Italy or writing novels and memoirs in his house in Guadalupe.

It was said that, without a doubt, the Brandos had come to this world to demolish stereotypes. The delicate Romans who conversed with Taine in French and supported unification ended up forgotten and scattered, while the visionary who, to reconstruct his patrimony, had only a couple of secret recipes for tagliatelle and rigatoni, could boast a virtuously nonchalant attitude with regard to his children's education and to the destiny of Pastas Brando after the death of its founder. Memoirs and realist novels were the polestars of his life. In contrast to every gringo imagined by the Argentine theater, Atilio Brando wasn't a slave trader, work wasn't his religion, and he didn't demand a law or a medical degree from his son as the first step toward an advantageous marriage with a patrician young lady.

In contrast, to Mario Brando, social status had true value and wasn't the tenuous and somewhat degenerate simulacrum that the old pasta maker described in his realist novels. To him, urbanity was an extreme form of historicism, and materialists, if they were consistent, should venerate snobs. But Mario Brando wasn't a snob, inasmuch as, every time he used the word, he knew what he was referring to. His poetic vocation was authentic, and his historicism was in fact manifested in his romantic life and in the tenets of precisionism, of which he was the primary author. The relationship to his father was original for reasons diametrically opposed to those that literature has accustomed us to think of as typical of generational conflict. Of the two Brandos, the father was the romantic and the son the pragmatist; the father was generous and the son miserly; the father, indifferent to social conventions, and the son, utterly dependent on public opinion. The father walked around shabbily dressed, lost in daydreams, while the son never left the house without a vest or a gold cigarette case. Like a millionaire father who tries to hide from his board members the vagrancies of his heir that might endanger the business, Mario hid his father's flirtations with realism from landowners and his disciples, considering them a mockery of precisionism's scientific exactitude. Luckily, Atilio Brando wrote in the language of Dante, as he proudly declared, and apart from a few articles in La Región from the thirties, his books (Against Hermetism, for instance), published in Italy, did not circulate beyond a few members of Unione e Benevolenza. The old man was bothered by worldliness because it distracted him from literature; for the son, literature was the pinnacle of worldliness, in the noble sense of the word, and he told himself that it was the only noble thing he could boast of.

For several reasons: first, because precisionist mechanics were essentially worldly, which is to say historicist (historicizing might be the most appropriate word). The idea of translating a traditional poetic vocabulary into rigorously contemporary scientific and technical language demonstrated a blind faith in the knowledge of the age and in an exact correspondence between its terminology and reality. The heart in "El corazón, viejo, tan mentado," in "El alma que canta"—Brando would often say at the dinners—isn't a forced rhyme, it's a muscle. And he would stare at his interlocutor, his eyes wide, with the hint of a slightly defiant smile, taking in the effect that his words had produced.

Second, Brando and his underlings were convinced that the mass media, like newspapers, radio, and later television, along with traditional cultural institutions, should play a dominant role in the dissemination of precisionist tenets. It wasn't simply exhibitionism: Brando was convinced that precisionism's social function was to purge the language of the masses, modernizing it and making it correspond with scientific terminology. It's very simple, Brando would insist, it's about speaking with precision. That simplifies things very much. Look at the etymology of the word "precision," from the Latin "praecisus," cut off, abbreviated. Every word that the precisionist poet uses should correspond to a verifiable thing. In this way, all misunderstandings in the social exchange of concepts and emotions disappear. The precisionist movement hoped to occupy the totality of the social field, acting on each of its articulations in order to transform it completely. Was this optimism or extremism? the neoclassicists asked themselves, somewhat lost, pretending, with their perplexed tone, that despite every good intention and everything they knew about them, they couldn't find any conceptual coherence in the movement. And yet, when those echoes of bewilderment reached his ears, Brando said that the answer had already been given in the first sentence of the first manifesto, published on the first page of the first issue of the first volume of Nexos (December, 1945): To preserve the economy of ideas, in the field of verbal commerce we are protectionists.

By 1945, Brando was already finishing law school. He'd done it rigorously and swiftly, on his own initiative, inasmuch as the elder Brando was not subject, as mentioned above, to the fetish of the diploma. Furthermore: by 1940, he'd already turned the factory over to his manager, an honest, hardworking criollo with more luck and more ethics than those described by Gutiérrez (Eduardo), among others; he'd transformed his capital into real estate and property (land, houses, farms) and lived peacefully from the rent, contemplating the implicit worldview in I Malavoglia. Pasta, he supposedly confessed once to Washington Noriega during casual conversation on a corner downtown, sometime around 1937, a dalliance of youth. He'd already married off his three daughters and had determined that his youngest son was not one to be disarmed by life. At twenty-one, he was already

366

dating the daughter of a general. At twenty-six, four months after the appearance of the first issue of Nexos, and with the second soon to be published, a story in the society section of La Región announced the wedding of Señorita Lydia Ponce Navarro to Dr. Mario Brando. The elder Brando shook his head deep down (to put it one way), mystified. Mario's social success impressed him less than the painstaking and efficacious way in which he passed from one stage to the next, and the almost mathematical exactitude that ruled over the realization of his projects. In short, at twenty-six, Mario Brando was one of the most cultured and elegant men in the city, he worked at an important law firm, he received a portion of his father's estate, he'd married the daughter of a general, had turned down an assistant professorship in Civil Law, and he was the undisputed head of the precisionist movement, whose magazine, Nexos, had been warmly received in the Sunday supplement of La Nación.

An article with a photo in the next day's edition of La Región had described the first precisionist dinner. Behind the apparent objectivity, the post-modernista resentment was clearly visible. Brando learned his lesson. After that day, he wrote the newspaper and radio stories for them himself. What would strictly speaking be called the group's creative labor was soon supplemented with conferences, newspaper articles, and radio interviews. The appearance of the magazine was of fundamental strategic importance: in the articles, the seminars, the interviews, and the conferences, they had to make terminological and theoretical concessions, which generated numerous misunderstandings; but the pages of Nexos, meanwhile, maintained, from start to finish, a consistent exactitude. It's precisionist manifestos, texts, and engravings formed a coherent and persuasive compendium. The first issue, for the city and for the time, was luxurious, so much so that the neoclassicists, who'd been producing the modest

Espiga at great personal cost for almost three years, started to spread venomous rumors about the source of their funding. Brando's legendary cheapness immediately ruled out the possibility that the issue was paid for out of his own pocket. There was, in fact, no mystery: the new owner of Pastas Brando, who'd known Marito all his life, the lawyers at his firm, who through Brando had contacts in the industrial and military sectors, and the bookstore-press that Brando convinced of the possibility of an exclusive series of single-author editions from precisionist poets as soon as the movement was funded, were more than enough to finance the first four issues of Nexos, which comprised the first volume.

The Thursday menu was invariable: alphabet soup (that was Brando's idea), Spanish-style stew, cheese and dessert, and red or white house wine. Cuello, the most famous regionalist, after attending one of these dinners, said to a friend, Instead of trying to reform literature, they should start by reforming their wine list. Brando had made a deal with Obregón, the owner: after fourteen guests, the price of the menu was reduced. The first group of precisionists consisted of seven people, to which four or five girlfriends were added, and because there were always a few other guests who varied from week to week, the number that Brando and the owner had agreed upon was always easily met. It was said that, with fourteen people, Brando not only got a price reduction, but he himself ate for free. In any case, whenever the dinner finished, he always took charge of gathering the contribution of each guest, and was always the one to settle at the counter with the owner. One night, the number of guests reached twenty-one, not counting a table of regionalists and neoclassicists who, apparently by chance, as though they didn't know that the precisionists got together at that restaurant every Thursday, had decided to eat there that night. When he walked in and saw them sitting at a table near the one that the owner usually prepared for them, Brando told one of his lieutenants, with great discretion, to avoid provoking them at all cost. But the others were celebrating a municipal prize, and when they started drinking champagne with dessert, two or three of the precisionists started to fraternize with them at the next table.

Someone who never missed a dinner was First Lieutenant Ponce, which is to say, Brando's brother-in-law and Lydia's younger brother. Though he'd studied at the military college in Buenos Aires, his father had obtained a post for him in one of the regiments in the city. He was shy and tanned and all of those intellectuals made him somewhat uncomfortable. He admired his brother-in-law very much, and wouldn't say a word during the whole meal. But because he would arrive before anyone, and would drink three or four Hesperidinas at the bar before the meal, sometimes, afterward, he would start to recite Joaquín Castellanos's "El temulento," which, along with "Si hay un hueco en tu vida, llénalo de amor" was the only poetry he knew. Brando's underlings, sensing that the founder of precisionism grew impatient with the first lieutenant's poetic inclinations, started to say, behind Brando's back, when describing the episodes, that the post-modernista fifth column was trying to undermine the movement from within.

For several years, precisionism dominated the literary world in the city, with a strong advantage over the other schools. It was the only original literary movement to have appeared there, inasmuch as the neoclassicists weren't in fact anything more than a branch of a movement that had circulated throughout the country, and the regionalists weren't a group strictly speaking because the only thing they had in common was their taste for cookouts and their systematic employment of barbarisms. Among the regionalists, only Cuello was known outside the province. His books were regularly reviewed in La Prensa and La Nación, and yet the invariable praise they received repeatedly affirmed that the books constituted an invaluable testimony of his native region and that their author was a profound student of the ways of the countryside. Precisionism, meanwhile, had been recognized from the beginning as something more than a simple literary movement, as a true Weltanschauung. More than as a poet, despite the many merits in that regard that even his detractors recognized, Brando was seen as a philosopher, as a man of science, and even as a reformer. Despite the jealousy that his increasing fame provoked, more than a few regionalists, and more than a few neoclassicists in particular, admitted privately that, had he abandoned his avant-garde pretensions, he might have transformed himself into a more than respectable representative of their respective schools. Higinio Gómez and Jorge Washington Noriega, who kept themselves on the margin of the literary world, referred to him, sarcastically, as "Il Duce stil novo of scientistic debris," and refused to be impressed by the fact that Buenos Aires was looking favorably on the work of a local agitator. Brando, meanwhile, took that acceptance as objective proof, and the rival groups validated his position. A sonnet of Brando's, "Chemistry of the passions," appeared in mid-1946 in the supplement to La Nación, and it should be said that, if the existence of God had been announced in that Sunday rotogravure, the regionalists and the neoclassicists, as of that moment, would have done without the miracles or the ontological proof.

As often happens with avant-garde movements, the leaders sacrifice themselves to the arduous creative labor, leaving the administrative work to their seconds in order not to overwhelm them with responsibility. Tardi, Brando's lieutenant, was in charge, during the first volume, with the trips to the press, with typing up the maestro's poems, along with the correspondence with their advisors and with the radio stations and the papers. He was slightly older than Brando, and because he'd started out publishing in Espiga, the neoclassicists called him a traitor, and because he was Brando's first disciple and his name was Pedro, they often said, in reference to his somewhat feeble intelligence, Upon that Rock he will edify his church. It's well-known that a conflict between Brando and Tardi caused the first rupture.

The groundswell that opened between the members of the group came to light with the fourth precisionist manifesto, which appeared in the fourth and last issue of the first volume of Nexos. Its title—A precisionist sonnet is like no other sonnet—gave legal force to an aesthetic position that Brando adopted in order to critique a triptych by Tardi whose publication had been postponed since the second issue. Needless to say, everything published in the magazine was discussed at the editorial committee's periodic meetings, and Brando's decisions were always final. The publication of the triptych had been delayed a third time, and for the same reason: residue of pre-precisionist lexicon. The unspoken distress among the ranks of the movement was revealed less in the passion of their discussions than in their disillusioned conversations as they were leaving, when Brando wasn't around. If he can't win, he calls it a draw, Tardi muttered in the ear of the person who followed him out. Even without Brando's psychological refinement, the discontent would have been obvious. For the purpose of a radical break, the fourth manifesto spelled out their doctrine and outlined, one by one, the deviations. Poetry, it concluded, will be precisionist or not. Precisionism is conscious of the unease that its crusade generates. But its most lucid representatives know how to recognize its enemies, whether inside or outside the movement.

To make it any clearer it would have had to be written in water. Now he'll know what it's like to spend entire days at the

371

printer, Tardi said malevolently as he left the last meeting, which resolved upon the dissolution of the movement. In order to finish the preparations for the fourth issue of Nexos, Brando had to accept the collaboration of two kids who were still imitating Espronceda and the Río Seco romances and who hadn't even finished high school. Tardi's triptych appeared in the fall issue of Espiga, after a cleansing, demanded by the neoclassicists, of all traces of precisionist vocabulary.

One less piece of bullshit, said General Ponce Navarro, who didn't approve of the dinners that his eldest daughter had been attending even before she was married, or of the literary scandals that his son-in-law was caught up in. My dear General, Brando would retort, cheerful and patient, although somewhat scalded, if the troops understand their orders it's thanks to the work of poets, who purify the language. And because he had nerves of steel and a temperament that refracted all bitterness, he didn't allow himself to be distracted by the defection of his collaborators, and had already begun to prepare a limited hardcover edition of his poems. Doubt had no place in the repertoire of his states of being. Like any good realist, the elder Brando attributed that character trait to his wife's family, and it produced a sort of ironical aversion in him. On the other hand, his literary sensibility was closer to the regionalists than to the precisionists. Not only was he friends with Cuello, but he also went native, as they say. Cuello, who was a meticulous student of the flora and fauna in the province, aroused his admiration. He'd saved enough to buy a motorboat, and on the weekends he'd often explore the islands in it. Sometimes, the elder Brando would accompany him. They slept along the coast, in a small tent, and ate whatever they caught. On Sunday nights they'd come home dirty, tired, and unshaven, and before they said goodbye they would drink one last beer at the counter of some bar. Out of mutual discretion, the topic of precisionism was never brought up.

One Sunday in April, 1947, Brando was shaking his head in disbelief over the ineptitude of the most recent issue of Espiga when he received a visit from the general and his bother-in-law, the first lieutenant. Lydia and her mother were at mass, and the general wanted to take the opportunity to speak to Brando. In short, it concerned the following: there was a possibility of obtaining a post for Brando as cultural attaché in Rome, but because Lydia had always been very close to her mother he hadn't wanted to speak of the matter in front of the women, given that Brando wouldn't have been the one making the decision. The general, for his part, recommended that he accept. A new era had begun in the country, and new blood was needed in every field. The general added that, when he brought up Brando's name at the ministry, the acceptance was immediate and practically enthusiastic. And that, no doubt, owing to what you call bullshit, Brando responded thoughtfully, smiling condescendingly. Although he'd decided on the spot to accept, he asked for forty-eight hours to think it over, arguing that this sort of decision shouldn't be taken lightly, something which increased the general's respect, but also his anxiety, given that he'd already given his word at the ministry that his son-in-law would accept.

The news caused considerable commotion in the literary media. Gamarra, the head editor of Espiga, repeated the same joke everywhere he went, namely that Brando, who took himself for avant-garde, was arriving twenty years late to the march on Rome. But La Región published a very long piece that Brando practically dictated to the journalist, in which it said that the nomination recognized less the value of a man than of an aesthetic and philosophical doctrine. In the three or four weeks

373

leading up to his departure, Brando made himself visible often, on San Martín and at parties, as though he wanted the density of his person, highly polished and neatly combed, to be engraved on everyone's memory during his absence. His elegance was sober, not that of a dandy, as may have been expected from his avant-garde tendency, but rather that of a tasteful bourgeoisie, who isn't trying to call attention to himself with extravagances, but who always dresses in the manner that his station both obliges and permits him to be seen in the street, adding two or three personal touches to show that a bourgeois fits naturally into his social class while at the same time being a well-differentiated individual. Some golden accessory, whether they were cufflinks or a tie clip or a ring that stood out when juxtaposed with his wedding band, always gave him an additional glow. Cuello said sarcastically that he always looked like he was on his way to or from a wedding.

With Brando's departure, the rest of the precisionists scattered: Tardi and two others, Carreras and Benvenuto, fell in with the neoclassicists. Benvenuto started to specialize in German romanticism and eastern philosophy. Tardi and Carreras ended up on the editorial committee for Espiga, which was last published in 1950. Among the other four, two abandoned literature completely, and of the two who were left, one moved to Buenos Aires and the other one committed suicide sometime later (it was rumored that he was a pedophile). There was less activity in the literary world, and politics seemed to be the main topic of conversation. Members of the opposition spoke in low voices, like conspirators, and those who had joined the government or the official party pontificated openly, demonstrating their enthusiasm. Gamarra, who refused to join the party, arguing that he was apolitical, lost his post at the university, and thanks to his relationships at the Alianza Francesa, went to live in France.

374

The regionalists were also divided. One, who had been an anarchist, ended up joining the communist party after Cuello joined the official party. Among the neoclassicists, two or three radical Catholics joined the government, but the rest, who'd joined the opposition, claimed that El Gran Conductor had a brain tumor—in the sella turcica of the sphenoid bone, to be precise—and didn't have long to live. Somehow, everyone kept publishing chapbooks and hardcover editions and individual poems in literary supplements. But the era of the precisionist dinners and the Friday cookouts at the San Lorenzo grill house had come to an end.

Every so often there was news of Brando. Someone had seen him in Trastevere, driving around in an Alfa Romeo. Someone else thought they'd heard, though they couldn't quite remember from whom, that he was summering in Sicily. The elder Brando, who was now too old to accompany Cuello around the islands, but who had a cookout with him every so often, and who'd taken to calling his son Il Dottore, said that Lydia had just had a baby girl and that the post at the embassy left them plenty of time to travel. In 1950, Lydia had another daughter, but, according to the first lieutenant (who was a captain by then), who'd run into Gamarra once on a bus to Buenos Aires, they were getting tired of being away from their family, and Lydia didn't want their grandparents to die without knowing their granddaughters.

Most Tuesdays at eleven in the morning, Tardi would pass by the Highway Administration, where Benvenuto worked, to meet him for a cup of coffee at the corner bar. Once, Benvenuto was waiting for him with a copy of the previous Sunday's La Prensa (which had been banned by the government). There was an article by Brando in the rotogravure. He's worth his weight in gold! Benvenuto had said, brandishing the rolled-up newspaper. While Benvenuto finished organizing some forms, Tardi read it, shaking his head and issuing surprised, scandalized laughter every so often. It was an essay on Dante, written practically at the foot of the Florence Cathedral. According to Brando, contemporary literary language was like Latin in the era of Dante: it was dead. De vulgari eloquentia, and if it couldn't stand up as a valid program, it had, nevertheless, the value of a universal token inasmuch as it demonstrated with clarity that every great poet should forge his own language. Dante couldn't express himself with precision in Latin; he needed a new language. Given this, he didn't go against his time at all, because he'd adopted the language of his time. Without shrill, false rebellions he'd managed to express a complete philosophical system. That had cost him more than one hardship. For instance, his disciples, his friends, his group Dolce Stil Novo, were no doubt unable to stand it that Dante, elevating himself above doctrinal squabbles, and above the limited reach of every little courtesan poet, would have dared to take on, in his great philosophical poem, all knowledge, both human and divine. Yes, but Dante was forced into exile, and he lives off the fat of the dictatorship, Tardi exclaimed, throwing the paper on the table and lowering his voice slightly when offering that aside.

The elder Brando died in late 1950. In the final years he may have glimpsed the reason for his repudiation of his ancestors, the ones who had Taine for dinner and led him through a labyrinth of palazzi: it was a kind of melancholy. He ended up taking with him to his grave the interior chuckle with which, not without some compassion, he regarded the known universe. The following autumn, Brando and his family arrived from Italy. According to Cuello, who knew one of his brothers-in-law, an agronomist who managed some family farms near Malabrigo, Brando, while still in Rome, had demanded that all actions concerning the inheritance be frozen until his arrival, and so no one touched a paper, but when Il Dottore arrived (always according to Cuello, who was sarcastic yet incapable of slander), the first thing he did was burn the manuscripts of his father's realist novels. Everything else, which he was not indifferent to after all, came second.

He never left again. According to him, family complications kept him home, but coincidentally, a few months later, soon after an aborted coup, the general retired, and the embassy was never spoken of again. Brando did not seem too upset. The polish of his gold accessories was now supplemented by the splendor of his time in Europe, giving him, that winter, a particular luster. That veneer remained forever, and even for those who knew him later, the new generations of poets who didn't care much either for precisionism or its inventor, it worked. Brando was one of those people who exemplified better than most, from a sort of personal density, the old idea that all men are unique. He was recognizable from a distance; his arrival was always remarked; his presence was never ignored. And, once he had been seen, it was immediately understood why six or seven poets, some even older than him, had given themselves to his aesthetic doctrines, and for several years had put themselves almost exclusively at his service. The poets who publicized his tenets or typed up his poems must have found, in his compact soul, a possible model for counteracting the uncertainty of their own beings and the interminable afternoons. It had nothing to do either with ethics or with literary talent, nor with any particular capacity for seduction, because, in that regard, Brando was in no way industrious or demanding. In fact the opposite could be said: he was someone who rarely, if ever, demonstrated his affection, and his relations with people consisted rather of an icy and seemingly distracted courtesy. The contradictory nature of his principles was immediately obvious, given that it would never have occurred to him to conceal his irreconcilable inclination for scientistic poetry and social position within the heart of the philistine bourgeoisie. If he read his disciples' poems it was, invariably, in order to tear them to pieces in the name of the precisionist aesthetic; if he published them in the magazine it was, unequivocally, because they clearly demonstrated that the hand of the chef de file had given them their final touch. To the company of poets he preferred that of rich and illiterate frivolous attorneys from the Club del Orden, that of Rotarian doctors, and that of neat, brutal, and shaven-headed horsemen of the Círculo Militar. If he went for coffee with some local writer who survived on a meager pension from some public office, he, who had considerable assets and who upon returning from Europe had left his old law firm in order to start his own, always managed to make himself invisible when the check came. It was difficult to imagine him in those tasks or positions that are the burden or delight of most other humans: defecating, fornicating, cutting his toenails, relating in some way or another to contingency. Every so often, an extremely faint scatological echo, which one had to be very alert to perceive, vibrated in his conversation. Whenever he made an observation that he considered keen, and which often were, he would sit for several seconds, as I've said before, staring at his interlocutor, waiting for his reaction. But, otherwise, it was impossible to meet his gaze. He was always looking at something over your shoulder, if he was taller than you, and at the knot of your necktie, if he was shorter. To be more precise, it should be said that what he actually had were listeners and not interlocutors. When he stopped speaking and the conversation passed to the other party, to what might be called the external field, his eyes, which were large and brilliant while he talked, narrowing, clouded over or shut down. And, all the same, three or four months after his arrival, in June or July of 1951, the precisionist machine began to function once again.

An article in La Región, in mid July, outlined the theoretical precepts of the second volume. Its theme was the decadence of the west, manifested in the irrationality of thought and the increasing relevance of the masses in historical events. If he goes on like this, he'll end up publishing for Reader's Digest, someone had told Benvenuto, who, however, received the sarcasm with constraint. In some ways, Brando's article coincided with two of his favorite theories, namely that a first, enlightened romanticism had been distorted after the fact by one that was irrational and vulgar, and, meanwhile, that the decadence of the west, which was an incontrovertible fact, confirmed the supremacy of eastern thought. Furthermore, Benvenuto perceived, in Brando's article, certain veiled critiques of the government. For several days, Benvenuto asked himself whether or not he should call Brando to suggest a meeting at a symbolic and neutral location, the restaurant behind the market, for instance, but in the end coincidence took care of that, when, one afternoon, coming out of his office, he ran into Brando as he was walking through the door. The two men embraced on the sidewalk, under the lukewarm July sun, and walked together two or three blocks, talking about the past, about their friends, about Leonardo da Vinci, and about Chinese jurists. After remarking on the suicide of R, Benvenuto learned that Brando had been aware of his problems, and that on two or three occasions R had come to see him, deeply depressed, and that Brando had tried to calm him down. (Less sympathetic versions asserted that Brando, after hearing R's more or less veiled confessions, had demanded that he remove himself from the movement.) According to Benvenuto, in his final days, R lived on uppers and barely slept. He'd spend whole nights walking through the city and in the morning would go straight to work, without going to bed. Brando asked Benvenuto about Tardi, and suggested that they get together for a cookout at the house in Guadalupe, where he'd moved after he got back from Rome (and where, meanwhile, he continued to live until his death). Noticing Benvenuto's hesitation, Brando asked for the numbers of Tardi and other former members and said that he would call them himself, which would discharge Benvenuto from a difficult task, making things much easier, because if Brando himself was in charge of making contact with the other precisionists a reconciliation would be much more likely. And so, two Sundays later, at around eleven, the precisionists from 1945 that were left in the city, along with their families, began to arrive for the cookout at the villa in Guadalupe.

A surprise was waiting for them: Captain Ponce himself was preparing the cookout. He'd arrived the day before from Córdoba, where his regiment was stationed, due to one of those unexpected troop movements, since his headquarters were in the south. The continuous punishment of the Patagonian wind had removed his frail look and had given him the consistency of leather. He greeted them cheerfully, with a glass in his hand, but worried about the progress of the coals. He himself had brought the demijohns of Caroya wine that were one the table, and he filled their glasses with generosity and insistence, under Brando's slightly reproving gaze.

Also present was a stranger to the historical precisionists, a Doctor Calcagno. He was a serious, almost sad, and well-educated man, and although he was several years older than Brando, he seemed intimidated by him and acquiesced to everything he said, even to things he didn't seem to agree with. He taught Roman Law at the university and enjoyed a considerable reputation in his specialty, and two or three years after Brando left his old firm in order to start his own they became partners and were never separated again. Calcagno was like Brando's silent and obedient shadow. He accepted everything, and even Tardi, who had been almost literally Brando's servant during the first period of the precisionist movement, was scandalized by so much submission, possibly feeling irritated that as of that day Brando would prefer Calcagno's servitude to his own. The firm made a lot of money, but while Brando kept a few cases for himself, which he managed personally, at the margin of the firm, Calcagno was the one who took on all of the work, something which would have been more or less understandable if the reason had been to leave Brando free time for his literary activities, but Calcagno also took on all of the practical work for the movement, editing, distribution, public events, proofreading, correspondence. Even years later, when he married a much younger woman, Calcagno still maintained that religious obedience to Mario Brando. What's curious is that Calcagno wasn't even a writer, and, moreover, that he was an honest man, but even when Brando, who'd become a provincial minister after the revolution, had to resign his post due to obscure accusations of corruption that were never completely clarified, and which, despite his opportunism, prevented him from ever aspiring to a public post again, Calcagno, whose honesty was unquestionable, continued to support him till his death.

With that cookout, precisionism's second institutional era, after the announcement in La Región and Brando's article, was inaugurated. Brando, upon his return from Europe, must have badly needed the restoration of the group, because otherwise he wouldn't have invited his disciples and their families and everything else to the house in Guadalupe. It was a gesture of reconciliation that would not be repeated. Once he was assured of the collaboration of the three or four poets from the old guard, he went back to meeting them at peripheral and depressing bars and restaurants. His social life, meanwhile, took place at his house and in the houses of his rich and ignorant friends, at the Jockey Club, or in political circles, although, as the regime lost popularity, and though he'd had a diplomatic post in Rome, he started to move imperceptibly toward the side of those who, three or four years later, after a couple of aborted coups, would end up over-throwing it. The only person who shared both worlds with him was his faithful shadow, Doctor Calcagno.

Even Brando's most intransigent enemies admired his political opportunism. Over five or six years he'd managed to be named cultural attaché in Rome by one government, to spend several years in Europe with his family, on a diplomatic salary, without any sort of declaration or public stance, and even without seem-ing to carry out any political activity, and then, just after the provincial inspector formed the first cabinet after the coup, he was asked to take the post of Secretary of Public Works. Had it not been for that obscure embezzlement incident, which was never clarified, and which had no other consequence for him than his retirement from politics, it was almost certain that a national trajectory awaited him.

What interested him was poetry and science, and astronomy in particular. At the house in Guadalupe, in a kind of tower at the back of the garden, which served as his office, he'd built an observatory where he'd shut himself up every night. Apart from Calcagno, who often went to visit him, very few people had enjoyed the privilege of an invitation. But from some poet or journalist from Buenos Aires, which is to say, anyone who could spread, beyond the city, his image as poet and scholar of art and science, a visit was particularly appreciated. After the coup, when he was Secretary of Public Works, in the photo that accompanied an interview with him, he was seen bent over, look-ing at the sky through the telescope. What's surprising is that the story, which occupied a whole page, came out in La Prensa, after its legitimate owners recovered the paper, and despite the fact that he'd published his "Meditation at the Foot of the Flor-ence Cathedral" while the newspaper, seized by the government, had been transformed into an official organ. Someone once said that Brando didn't own an umbrella because when it rained he was able to walk through the drops without getting wet. What one had to admit, according to this same person, and to several others, including some of his enemies, was his fidelity to poetry, though it was rumored that when he wasn't writing precisionist texts he wrote more traditional poems that very few people, if anyone, had seen, and through which he hoped to save his reputation if precisionism ever fell out of fashion.

This may have been an error on his part, because precisionism was an authentic local product, the most original literary movement in a city that, since romanticism and even since Góngora, had always welcomed every artistic novelty, adapting it to the regional climate and incarnating it in a local artist. We produced romantic poets in quantities greater than it would have been prudent to desire, and a story from the same movement, "The Novel of a Pale Young Man," even appeared almost simultaneously with the first wave of realist and later naturalist novels, from which the group of regionalist writers captained by Cuello and Righi emerged. Symbolism and French poetry circulated thanks to modernismo, and, as I mentioned above, its last representatives, in the sixties, could still recite Belisario Roldán's discourses by heart. In the forties, at the local level, the first surrealists began to appear, along with mystics and orthodox neoclassicists, who gathered around the magazine Espiga. We also had writers who practiced social realism, expressionism, what you might call a virile North American style, the objective novel, and even the writing, the practical life, and the physical appearance of the Beat generation. Every one of these movements had begun somewhere else, had traveled the world, and had ended up winning some acceptance in the city. Only precisionism had been born here, whatever the political or moral convictions of its inventor may have been, if he had any, and, likewise, whatever credit its creator may have given to his creation. Mario Brando, precisionism, and the city were as inseparable in the minds of the literary critics from Buenos Aires or Asunción or Montevideo as the three elements of the trinity probably were to Christian theologians. Anyone with a personal conception of literature wasn't intimidated by Brando's success in the forties and fifties (later, in the third period, he was already somewhat forgotten), and many local personalities who understood the deserved rejection of their own mediocrity before the eternal injustice of Buenos Aires toward the interior identified with the recognition that Brando and his poetic school enjoyed, and felt proud to have it as the fame of the city. They were local products like river fish, like Coronda strawberries, like the suspension bridge, and, later, like the underwater tunnel. At last, an author from the city wasn't writing about the landscape or the flora and fauna characteristic to the region, but rather about universal relations that, according to precisionist theory, should exist between poetics and scientific language. As dubious as the aesthetic may have been, there was no doubt that it found attentive and objective interest in its time.

Brando's life was the complete opposite of what one might expect from a poet, in any case according to the current stereotypes used to imagine the life of the poet. Brando didn't drink, and he smoked very little—apparently the doctor had prohibited him to carry. His family life was conventional and quiet, and was limited to his wife and two daughters. After the death of the elder Brando he'd stopped seeing his sisters. He almost provoked a lawsuit when the inheritance was distributed, but the conflict was resolved quietly before reaching the courts. His sisters never forgave him for having burned their father's literary papers when he got back from Europe, or for taking the house in Guadalupe, which their father had built in the late twenties for the whole family, without ever discussing the issue with them. Two of the sisters had moved to Rosario and the third now lived in Italy. Like her brother, she wrote, but in Italian, like her father: realist novels with a certain social and even erotic vulgarity, and in which bread was called bread and wine was called wine, without disguising provincial hypocrisy behind ridiculous scientistic neologisms, as she wrote to me once in a letter from Rome, shortly after Brando's death.

In the last years of his life, long before he got sick, in fact (a tumor in his colon finished him off in a couple of months), Brando lived a very reclusive life. He was more occupied with his law firm and with his social and familial connections than with precisionism or with poetry in general. All the same, his articles and poems still appeared every so often in La Región, in La Capital, or in some other Buenos Aires newspaper. But the precisionist movement itself already belonged to the past. In 1960, La Nación published an article celebrating the twenty-fifth anniversary of the first dinner at La Giralda, authored by Brando himself, along with a photo that he provided.

·

When he finishes reading, Tomatis turns over the last white page, printed from a computer, and puts it on top of the others, with the printed side facing down. Then, picking up the stack of pages, he taps their bottom edge against the manila folder on his knees several times so that the sheets all line up neatly. On the first page, halfway down the page, the title, PRECISIONISM, appears in capital letters, and below it, in italics, *by A witness of the time*, and after a space what strictly speaking would be called the text begins. While he carries out all of these movements, Tomatis holds, between the index and middle fingers of his right hand, and resting as well in the space between his index finger and thumb, the red pen with which he's been making annotations in the margins every so often. Finally he closes the manila folder, slides it into one of the compartments of the open briefcase in the adjoining seat, the one on the aisle side, and lets it fall, along with the pen, not before pushing down on the button that retracts the tip into the metal cylinder that protects it. Then he puts his elbows on the arm rests that surround his seat, and turning his head and falling still, he stares at the landscape that rolls by on the other side of the window without seeing any of it.

Gabi's fear that Tomatis would guess the true identity of *a witness of the time* was justified; before he read the text, even before he'd gotten a copy, the moment Gabi mentioned his existence, Tomatis had already solved the supposed mystery of its authorship, deciding at that moment that he would never reveal his certainty to Gabriela. In any case, it's always the text that speaks, never the writer, at least when it comes to literature, and especially literary fiction, in particular the kind that pretends not to be and instead presents itself as a straightforward report. Every word, as simple and direct as it may be, is already a fiction. What else could we expect, therefore, from the gloss of a supposed *witness of the time*, written several years after the events it narrates, the majority of which he never attended, like the evangelists who never knew the source of *the good news*, whose existence, meanwhile, is based on such little evidence? And, shifting in his seat, satisfied, Tomatis smiles and then looks around him to verify that no one in the bus has seen him laughing to himself.

It would be practically impossible for that to happen. The upper level of the two-story *executive comfort* class bus is almost empty. On Saturday afternoons, on the scheduled five forty (from Rosario), and though it is the night before the start of Holy Week, the buses between Rosario and the city that roll down the highway in either directions, green, red, white, or metallic according to

386

their company, are never very full; on Friday and Saturday mornings, on the other hand—and those who travel frequently know this—it's wise to buy a ticket well in advance. For decades, and for a thousand different reasons, Tomatis, who is rumored to never have taken a local bus, has traveled frequently on those interurban buses, ever since the heroic period, when traveling the hundred and seventy kilometers—if it was a local and not the express—could take four hours and sometimes more because the bus stopped at each of the towns along the two-lane route, and if there was traffic after San Lorenzo, in Rosario's industrial suburbs, it could take another fifteen or twenty minutes each way. Since the inauguration of the highway, in the seventies, the trip was reduced to two and a half hours, which sometimes forced the drivers to go almost at a walking pace down the empty highway for the last thirty or forty kilometers so as to not arrive ahead of schedule.

On the upper deck, barely half a dozen seats besides his own are occupied, and only two at the very back, behind him. There're two female students in the first row, just behind the panoramic window, above the diver's seat; a much older woman with a child who, Tomatis gathered when he saw them board, are no doubt a grandmother and a grandson whom she picked up in Rosario so he could spend the Holy Week holiday with his grandparents; two rows in front, a boy with a suitcase whom Tomatis had seen before at the terminal bar, drinking a coffee like himself, at a table close to his, and who caught his attention because he was reading an old translation of *A Sentimental Education*; just in front of the boy, a middle-aged couple, forty or forty-five at the most, whom he saw on the platform, giving the porter a large wheeled suitcase covered with stickers from hotels, from other countries, and from airlines, two of which hung from a string attached to the handle, suggesting that they were returning from a recent trip. Finally, in the back row, two boys, probably students as well, making an early trip to the Sunday *Clásico*, or at least that's what Tomatis gathered when, after he'd already sat down, he saw them come up the spiral staircase from the lower level, from the fragments of enthusiastic and somewhat loud conversation that he heard as they passed by his seat and sat down in the last row, on the other side of the aisle. From their position relative to himself, they would be the only ones, meanwhile, who could have caught him laughing to himself.

The air conditioning alone isn't enough to explain the pleasant coolness inside the bus; of course it's the cause of the sensation, but there's something more general than a simple sensory detail, the *impression* of coolness is the result of the fact that all of the passengers sitting on the sunny side of the bus, with the exception of Tomatis, who's folded it back in order to see the exterior, have kept closed the curtains that shield them from the sun, as they found them when they boarded, probably left that way by the cleaning staff. It hasn't been necessary, meanwhile, to close the curtains on the other side of the aisle, because the shade from the bus itself protects the passengers from the rays of the sun. And so, between the shaded side and the sunny side, with the curtains closed, with the exception of Tomatis's, in addition to the air conditioning, a cool penumbra has formed in the bus, pierced at various points by streaks of light that filter through the edges of the curtains, which sometimes don't completely cover the glass, a penumbra that Tomatis, carrying in his memory, though no longer in his body, the recollection of the heat outside, experiences with a sense of relish. The open curtain attenuates this slightly, but the combination of the heat that the sun, still high in the sky, radiates through the window, and the interior coolness that sticks to his skin, causes him, after half an hour on the road, despite the eighty-five degrees with which, in early April, the late summer is extended, to suddenly feel a physical sense of spring that, by association, returns him over several seconds of unexpected and violent happiness to the person

388

he used to be years before, in what he's taken to calling his youth, which he's unsure whether to consider a past stage of his life, an invention in the ceaseless chain of interior images, or an illusion, or, better yet, a legend.

The physical source of the happiness comes, no doubt, from a set of random elements: the temperature of his body and the outside temperature, light and shadow, the traveler's calm and temporary passivity, the repetition of a situation, sitting on a bus between Rosario and the city, that he's been in many times since his adolescence, but in the present instance, reading the history of precisionism has recalled memories of other times, starting in the mid-fifties especially, at the end of his adolescence, drawing them from dark depths and making them fully conscious. One repeated memory from that time, apparently singular yet in reality composed of fragments of many similar memories, returns often: his canoe trips with Barco, from the regatta club, across the river. They'd leave very early in the morning, when it was just getting light, and, taking turns on the paddles, would plunge into the labyrinth of channels and islands that they knew well, though not well enough not to get lost every so often at some turn in which the width of the channel, the direction of the current, the vegetation, or the shape of the islands that they came upon were so identical to all the others they'd already passed that they temporarily had the impression of having remained at a fixed point, without advancing a millimeter, across the omnipresent and disproportionate river. More than once they found themselves in some unknown channel; they would stop paddling and let the canoe drift, correcting its course only every so often with a thrust of the paddle, knowing that at any moment they'd find themselves at some familiar point along that vast and empty extension of islands and water. They'd paddle from the dawn, as they watched the sky brighten ahead of them, in the east, well into the morning, sometimes protecting themselves from the sun along a shady bank, resting a while, sprawled out inside the canoe, taking sips of water or eating pieces of fruit in order to trick their stomachs until the afternoon, when it was time for lunch, under a tree inside some island, fleeing from the cruel, blinding white light of the sun at the zenith, radiating its incandescent sparks over the entire visible space, as though there were no longer a sky or an earth, water or vegetation, material gathered into distinct things of different colors and consistencies, but rather a single fluid glimmer replacing the multiform and multicolor diversity of the existent. That moment, Tomatis thinks now with the words of an adult about an experience that was then unnamable, when the diversity of appearances into which the world decomposed was reabsorbed by the flux that, every so often, allowed him to drift for an incalculable lapse into its proprietary space only to be erased almost immediately. That multiple memory, made of many repeated memories, differs from one that's more intense and unique, the distant but sharp recollection of a November morning when, for a long time, as the canoe drifted through channels in the river that were at once familiar, because they seemed like so many others, and unfamiliar, because it was the first time they'd crossed them, the light flowed in such a way that the whole surface of the water, the air, and the sky transformed into a white, homogeneous, radiant incandescence, while the reddish earth of the islands and the bluish green vegetation seemed suddenly covered in a kind of brilliant lacquer, and the flowers along the riverbanks, both aquatic and terrestrial, both white and bright colored, shone, glazed with a ubiquitous, active light that, paradoxically, even made the spaces in shadow glow. This brand-new world had risen from a deep well of nothingness and now floated in a channel of light, wrapped in its undulating, velvety tunic. Tomatis, lying against the edge of the slowly drifting canoe, observed it, overwhelmed with an intense, inextinguishable happiness. Both the islands and the water were equally still, the liquid surface seemingly veneered in a luminous substance, and the canoe, without the traction of the paddles, slid through it silently, without resistance. The present became a magical illusion in which everything that took effort or caused disillusion or pain—uncontrollable impulses, corrosive memories, the passage of time, the external world, indifferent and even hostile to desire—had been neutralized. In that generalized stillness, the canoe's drift differed from its typical movement, not only because of the silence, but also from the ease with which this luminous, undulant, and vibrating substance, endowing things with an extraterrestrial halo, allowed itself to be crossed, slowly and calmly, acquiescent and benevolent. Every so often, a bird, flying, suddenly and colorfully, from the interior of some island, crossed the motionless landscape, gliding, compact and quick, over the water, almost without flapping, and disappearing into the vegetation of a nearby island, and yet the movement required to complete that trajectory seemed fictitious and strange, and though the eye absorbed the totality of its flight in a single gaze, in the seconds that immediately followed its disappearance from the senses, when it transformed, imperceptibly, into memory, the uninterrupted flight was transformed into a series of disconnected and ecstatic fragments, frozen in various, discontinuous stages of the flight. Tomatis looked at Barco sitting on the other end of the boat, his eyes narrowed, the paddles gathered up in his hands, and thought that he'd fallen asleep, but later, when they started to talk again, Barco told him that he'd been trying to listen for something that might explain the intriguing silence that had fallen over that section of the river, listening for every imperceptible whisper on the water or on the islands that the current usually prevented him from hearing. Barco's response, though it didn't help him understand what had happened, calmed him down, because the unusual silence that Barco had sensed meant that the singular impression that the flux of morning light had caused in him had an objective source and wasn't merely a hallucination. Cool and glimmering, brought within reach of his senses by that fluid radiance, the visible, by its simple appearance, had transmitted a contagious euphoria that kept him, for several minutes, in a light and peaceful state of exaltation.

Tomatis, content, turns around in his seat, though first taking a quick and discreet look at the row behind him, to his right, on the other side of the aisle, where the two boys who'd been chatting since the bus left the terminal have grown quiet, wanting to verify that the cause of their silence isn't that they're watching him, as if, studying him closely, they could have gathered from some tiny detail in his behavior the intense emotion that has just struck him and that, more than anything in the world, he'd like to keep from exposing to outside indiscretion. But from what he can tell with a quick look, the two boys have simply grown tired of speaking and are now resting, reading a sporting magazine that one leafs through slowly so that the other, the one on the window side, leaning toward him, can also see the headlines and look at the photographs. Satisfied, Tomatis forgets about them almost immediately and leans back against the seat. The six o'clock sun in the cloudless sky is still high and yellow, yet the shadows from the trees, from the houses, from the warehouses, from the mills, extend to the east, projecting over the grasses that the past week's rains, which lasted till Tuesday night, and even into Wednesday morning, have revived. After leaving the Rosario terminal, the bus crossed the city's western neighborhoods until it reached the loop road, and after taking this along the long belt of shantytowns that surrounds the city, it reached the highway and turned north toward the city. It was only then that Tomatis picked up the text about precisionism again—though he knew the ones around Rosario by heart, the poor sections of any city, seen from the bus or from the train, attracted him, and he liked to observe every one of their features in careful

392

detail, the facades, the businesses, the cross streets, often unpaved if they were deep into the outskirts, that disappeared, perpendicular, into the horizon. In the poor neighborhoods of Rosario, in the narrow front gardens, in which there's barely space for a large bush, there's often a hibiscus, and every time Tomatis sees one of those plants, he remembers that Frazer says that among many of the ancient tribes of the planet it's the species whose wood best conserves the primordial fire of the universe, after which the universe was reborn, because it's the best wood for lighting a fire simply by rubbing it with a stick. According to others, among some tribes the hibiscus symbolizes the universe itself, possibly, Tomatis once thought, because of its continuous and ephemeral blooming: its red flowers (there are other colors, but the red hibiscus is the most common) take shape and bloom over a few hours, but not much longer, and as they whither and fall others take their place, which means the plant grows in a process of continuous change, just like the universe, where worlds, stars, and galaxies are ignited and then extinguished, are born and die, in a constant flicker whose exact duration and interval could only be calculated from some improbable exterior.

The shantytowns, an endless collar of poverty that surrounds the city, just like a slip knot around the neck of a condemned man, Tomatis thinks, have a sense of calm, if not warmth, this Saturday afternoon, despite the paralyzing indigence among the precarious shacks that, miraculously, hold each other up; Tomatis senses this from having passed them many times before over the years. Since his first trips to Rosario, the belt of poverty around the city had been growing, until now it surrounds it completely. It's been the stop for everyone who, coming from the depths of affliction, from the northern provinces, from Paraguay, from Bolivia, and even from Peru, thought they'd find some relief or some hope in the littoral cities. For the majority, still blinking from astonishment and incredulity after discovering the overwhelmingly stupefying proof that they were raw flesh senselessly thrown to the world, forced to survive with only the placenta that nourished them for nine months, poverty was already progress, the inferno of work a gift, their shack a refuge, and the city to which many come to work, seen from a distance, the promised land. For others, poverty perpetuated the scandal, and to them the ones who weren't splashing frantically, the ones who through inheritance, luck, perseverance, merit, larceny, or the exploitation of their neighbor, lived in the legendary aura of a world without privation, were like an alien species to them, serpents, black widows, scorpions, with whom it was impossible to identify and who had to be crushed without hesitation so as to avoid the deadly sting, the bite of the atavistic enemy defending its territory. Others were resigned to rummaging in what the city discarded, among the trash heaps, searching for the gold mine of cloth, of paper, or glass, of metal, that would provide them with a day or two of food. There were those who, from an adolescent body, theirs or another's, sometimes even the one they loved most, where they could have sated their thirst, drawing relief, as from an inexhaustible source of calm, built a chaos of venality, contempt, and perversion, and, from this lifeless decoy, made a business. Some killed or got themselves killed for no reason, inspiring fear not only in their enemies, but especially in their mothers, in their grandparents, in their siblings. And yet, the ones who had come from other places—rural zones lost in the north, impoverished Indian reservations populated with the last representatives of the starving tribes that, had they gone to school, would have learned that there hadn't been any more Indians in the region for many years—thought, rightly, that they had progressed, from nothing to something, a job, a tiny schoolhouse among the ranches, under a blue and white rag flapping in the air, a clinic, a cafeteria, a chapel or an evangelist temple, but also dances, the political events where the candidates distributed food, clothing, and blankets to buy their votes, or a vacant lot with a white arch at each end where ragged and sweaty kids chased a ball for hours, shouting and gesturing, until they were swallowed by the night. In fact, the bus had earlier passed a group of younger and older kids who were playing a pickup game, and a group of onlookers watched, spread around the edge of the field. To one side, in an open-air courtyard closed at the front by a low mud wall and an unplastered brick arch—the sign above the arch read *La Quema Social and Recreational Club*—preparations were being made for a dance that night. Some sections of the long belt of poverty are worse than others; in the worst ones, the shanties, caves of stick, straw, cardboard, cabinetry, and rusted tin predominate, but in other parts the construction is tidied up with clean adobe, unplastered brick, doors, and windows. Out front of some of those houses there's even an old car, a motorcycle, or a bicycle with a delivery basket behind the seat. A wide strip of grass, split in two by a ditch, separates the ribbon of buildings from the asphalt of the loop road. Around the ditch, the grass is littered with twisted paper, plastic bags, empty cans, broken or mud-stained bottles, and empty cigarette packs; every so often, stands of enormous eucalyptus, of tall acacias, of leafless carob trees with brown vines hanging from their branches, or of bitterwoods recall that at one time that congested strip was countryside, farms, estates, and empty plain. The porous, uniform six o'clock light covers the earth, the buildings, the grass, and the trees in a reddish, pulverized gold patina, its fine dust still floating in the air. The afternoon is so calm that, on one dirt street perpendicular to the avenue, Tomatis saw a cloud of dust, motionless, like an evanescent monument, lifted by some vehicle that had already disappeared, holding together in the warm and windless air without dispersing or falling to the ground. After the turnoff to the road to Córdoba, at the entrance to the highway, two or three kilometers from the loop road, they passed the dump, surrounding them on both sides with its compact strata of steaming garbage, and men, women, and children bent over the mountain of discards expelled by the city, digging through it, searching for their day's wages. And then the first houses, many of them extremely old, wavering between the country and the city, surrounded by trees, with a horse grazing in the rear pasture, a farm, a rusty, unused windmill, brick smoke floating over the truncated pyramid where they have been stacked. As soon as they left the city, Tomatis started to read the pages that remained, looking up every so often and glancing out the window, and now, after putting away the text, which he'd annotated in the margins, after being struck by a sudden and intense happiness, he has leaned back against the seat and watches the landscape roll past through the window, the only one not covered by a curtain, the others closed to protect the interior of the bus from the setting sun, which is still strong, falling, imperceptibly slowly, toward the western horizon. They left the Rosario terminal thirty-five minutes ago, which means that within an hour and forty-five minutes, at eight on the dot if everything goes well, they'll be pulling in to the terminal in the city.

For the past year, since Alicia started pharmaceutical school in Rosario—the implacable, overwhelmingly determined pressure from her grandmother, which Haydée, her mother, had never been able to resist, had ultimately won out—Tomatis has gone to visit her every so often, on Saturday mornings, with a routine that never changes: at ten o'clock she's waiting for him at the terminal, from which they take a taxi downtown, where they walk along the prom-enades and the arcades; when Alicia sees something she likes, she goes inside to try it on, and if she decides to buy it, Tomatis, who stays on the sidewalk, goes inside to pay for it. At eleven thirty they drink a quick coffee on Calle Córdoba, and then continue their walk. At twelve thirty they browse through a few bookstores,

Tomatis buys a present for his sister, and at around one thirty or one forty-five they have lunch at some fashionable place popular with young people, where they serve unique sandwiches and salads that you build yourself from an assortment of ingredients laid out on a table. Tomatis orders a beer and Alicia asks for soda. For a while now, Tomatis has been resigned to the idea that Alicia will inherit her maternal grandmother's pharmacy. He would have liked for her to study philosophy, music, fine art, diplomacy, anthropology, physics, any of those romantic careers that certain parents, moved by the chubby little angels they've watched in the cradle since the day they were born, project into their future, one in which all contradiction, adversity, and contingency, at least from a distance, have been eliminated. The day that Alicia told him and his sister over lunch that she was going to Rosario to get a pharmaceutical degree, Tomatis choked on the spoonful of soup that he was eating at that moment, and the discussion that followed was loud and prolonged, especially because the idea seemed excellent to his sister as well, something which in fact meant nothing because she and Alicia were always on the same side anyway—which is to say, against him—when they argued. Tomatis was bitter for a while, but he eventually calmed down, telling himself that, in the end, it was what was best for Alicia, a life planned out in advance, free of any surprises, either beneficial or harmful. All the same, he still catches himself now and then, trying to detect some indication of rebellion in her, however small.

Over the previous week, after having told Alicia on Monday about his visit and having bought the seven forty ticket for Saturday that same afternoon, he has been living, in his own words, *the tedious life of a provincial bourgeois pensioner*, although, as he declared on Thursday night at the Amigos del Vino bar, over a few bottles of sauvignon blanc with Violeta, Nula and his wife, Gabi, and Soldi, *luckily interrupted every so often by a wake, a by palatable story, or by intoxication.* Apart from Nula and Diana, his wife, everyone knew those lines, and though it was much newer than the one about the buses not being full enough, which they'd discussed that night, it got the usual positive reception, provoking laughter not only in its recipients, but also in the one who uttered them. Only Nula and Diana were unaware that the supposed modesty of describing himself as a *provincial bourgeois pensioner* was actually a sly way of comparing himself to Flaubert, and when now, in the bus, Tomatis smiles again, it's out of empathy with the other three, who always understand the veiled allusion and not the literal sense of the lines. After saying goodbye to the others and leaving the bar, rather than taking him home or inviting him over for a drink, Violeta suggested that they take a drive along the waterfront—she liked to lock herself in her car, put on music, and drive around the city and the surrounding towns all night if she didn't have work the next morning. That inclination in Violeta pleases Tomatis. She put on Beethoven's "Grand Fugue" that night, remarking, after the first few notes, that, *It doesn't sound like anything else,* making her way through the empty streets toward the waterfront, along the avenue, where some trucks were parked but where nothing moved and there was not a single sign of life. Their intermittent affair over the past few years is faithful but without passion, a tiresome excess that they certainly don't miss. And though they fornicate without complexes or taboos, within the limits allowed by their occupations and their physical condition, it's the friendship, the intellectual and affective part of their relationship, that keeps them together. The two are coming off romantic and familial lives (Violeta has two children) from which neither joy nor periodic catastrophes were lacking, and those two extremes have caused them to prefer, each in their own way, a less ambitious and more reflective and calm sensuality for their later years. Despite the fact that Tomatis is ten years older, Violeta doesn't repress her critical faculties, something which delights

Tomatis. According to him, his relationship with Violeta helped refute what all his oldest friends think of him, namely that due to his unrestrained egocentrism he passes through life altogether too pleased with himself, insensitive to the faults that the word justifiably attributes to him. Violeta, aware of this, always makes the same cheerful, self-satisfied observation to the third person, *It's extremely practical because we have everything in common—we're both in love with Carlos Tomatis.* They'd crossed the darkened city, driving up the avenue and turning onto the waterfront, isolated from the external world in the car resonating with the notes of the "Grand Fugue." The black surface of the lagoon, whose invisible presence could be intuited beyond the trees along the waterfront, became perceptible from time to time when a ripple in the distance, fragile and fugitive, betrayed it. Violeta stopped and parked for a couple of minutes, with the engine still running, and Tomatis took the opportunity to get out of the car and stand on the sidewalk, under the trees, in the warm shadow. Although some twenty meters of wooded terrain separate him from the bank that leads down to the water, Tomatis was able to recognize, after a few seconds, the strong odor of the river, of the silt washing up on shore, a mixture of rotten plants and dead fish, nourishing the paradoxical world that blooms again and again, feeding off its own decomposition, without anyone knowing why, though some can describe how and with that they're satisfied, from the swampy detritus. The notes of the fugue carry into the night through the open door of the car, dispersing in concentric waves until they disappear, swallowed by the silence of the incalculable blackness. Soon, Tomatis got back into the car and closed the door and Violeta steered the car slowly away from the curb, gaining velocity as she moved along the empty waterfront. Finally they arrived in Guadalupe, circled the equestrian statue above the roundabout, and turned to the west, away from the river. They drove the transversal avenues that connect, from east to west, the poor neighborhoods north of the city, poorer to the west, where, beyond the melancholy shores of the Salado, the last decrepit ranches are scattered, and where the last parcels of the city are confused with the barren plains. Driving through one of these forbidden neighborhoods, which are impossible to enter, night or day, without some specific reason, they saw, along the cross streets, under the trees along the sidewalks, hidden and confused shadows that moved, that shuddered, that froze in the thresholds of houses, behind a half-open door, or among the trees. Farther along, a girl in shorts and a bra, no more than fifteen or sixteen years old, smoking a cigarette in a doorway, illuminated by the hallway light, revealed a backlit silhouette that, even to the most excessive desire, would signal more danger than pleasure. And Violeta accelerated when, as they crossed one intersection, they saw a group of human shapes running toward the car, down the middle of the street, shouting and waving their arms, most likely alerted by the sound of the engine, to make them account-able for the invasion of their territory. Tomatis sat up in his seat, looking through the rear window at the intersection they'd just crossed, just in time to see the group pour into it and stop, shouting in the middle of the street, while two or three continued to run, without the slightest chance of catching them, toward the car that moved away, and that, two blocks later, turned again to the east, toward the city center. Violeta dropped him off at the door to his house and went home to her own. And the next morning, at around ten, Gutiérrez called to tell him not to forget his swimsuit, because as long as the weather permitted it the swimming pool, after the select company and the barbecue, would constitute the principal attraction.

The highway crosses empty fields now, and in some parcels, where the corn and sunflower have already been harvested, the truncated stalks remain, brown, ragged, and scorched, like a field of ruins. But the grass is green along the shoulder and on the strip of ground that separates the two sides of the highway. Against the pale, cloudless sky, there's considerable agitation among the birds, coming and going, landing on the ground, on the posts, on the barbed wire, on the trees, then taking off again and landing again, as though, intuiting that the light is fading, they are accelerating the rhythm with which they live out the last hours of the day, trying to get ahead of the night. Inside the bus, the angle of the rays that filter through the edges of the curtains is less severe, declining to the horizontal, without reaching it of course, and while sometime earlier they projected onto the floor, in the middle of the aisle, now they touch the seats on the other side. Tomatis checks his watch: it's six sixteen. After forty minutes on the road, the dusty afternoon light is now concentrated in the rays that, all at the same angle, indifferent to the movement or the displacements of the vehicle, and despite the vibrations that the force of the engine and the inconsistencies of the road transmit to the bodywork, impassively cross the penumbra of the bus, only changing position because they're changed by the distant, flaming disc from which they come. A momentary estrangement comes over him, the sense of being in two planes of space and time at once, the first in a typical bus driving down the highway between Rosario and the city on a Saturday afternoon, and the second in an embalmed stretch of time in which motion is stillness and all known, familiar space is a universe in miniature, enclosed in a crystal ball, cast about, without its inhabitants noticing, within an igneous whirlwind swirling in a infinite blackness. It's an estrangement without panic, a possible image of what, wrapping us in its cocoon of flammable gasses and fusing metals, accompanying us from our imperceptible birth to our imperceptible death, is our true home. He's pulled from that daydream by an external contingency, a slightly more conspicuous bump tells him that they're passing over the Carcarañá, in La

Ribera, and he turns toward the window in order to see it better, narrow, turbulent, and swift between the pale banks populated by shrubs and weeds, and higher up, in the surrounding area, by weekend houses built in the shade of the trees. The river is revealed and then disappears, a flash of moving water that, because it flows at the bottom of a bank, enters into shadow long before the flat, exposed earth dominated by the overwhelming afternoon light. Tomatis leans back against his seat again, and for about a minute he doesn't think of anything, his hands crossed at his belly, his eyes open but not looking directly at any object, his expression calm and empty. Now he's aware that he's getting hungry: the salad he had that afternoon, despite the indisputable variety of ingredients laid out on a table, meant to give the clients complete freedom to serve themselves as much of whatever they choose, in fact reveals an deft sophism, because it's obvious that in order to prepare a salad with some rationality not all of the elements on display are mutually compatible, and only a few make sense to combine, one always chooses between lettuce and chicory, between cured or fresh pork, between hard and soft cheeses, between sardines or tuna in oil, and though he no longer remembers all the ingredients that he chose, he can tell by his sensation of hunger—actually agreeable for the moment—that the salad, though they ate pretty late, wasn't enough to keep him till dinner, at around eight thirty, assuming that the bus arrives at the terminal at eight, and adding the time it takes to get to the taxi stand and then to his house. He could eat something at the grill house or at the outdoor bar across from the terminal, but because he got up early this morning he wants to get to bed soon, then read a while, to be fresh and rested tomorrow morning for the cookout at Gutiérrez's. He remembers that one of the two chorizos that Nula gave him the other day when he picked him up downtown is still in the fridge; he'd eaten part of the first—exquisite—with his sister that same night, and the rest of it yesterday, but the second was intact. Tomatis hopes that his sister hasn't invited over her friends for lunch or to drink vermouth today, serving them the salami in slices, on a cutting board, with pickles and olives, as she usually does. But he doesn't worry: despite her constant criticizing, his sister always keeps the best food for him, at least when Alicia isn't around, and so, especially because she knows that he'll arrive tired and hungry from Rosario, he's almost sure that, after the praise they showered on the salami that they ate on Wednesday night, his sister will have all or part of the second waiting for him when he gets back.

But would the city still be there? When we are not empirically present in a place, does it still exist, at least in the same way? Though he's well aware that the thought is absurd, that a professional philosopher could easily refute his naive doubt, Tomatis can't help but ask himself the question every so often, though it's more an irrational, almost animal confusion than a philosophical inquiry. Just like thinking too much about breathing can make it difficult to breathe, becoming conscious of living in both space and time at once can make even the most simple things complex and strange, and thus, from the time he left the city early that morning until he returns to it that night, its existence, which is completely dependent on his memory, becomes extremely problematic. Though he's actually a fervent defender of the existence of *the external*, Tomatis can never discard the ideas, the impressions, and even the sensations that support the contrary thesis. Only habit, and distraction, furthermore, interfere with the observation or the conclusion that the place that we left some time earlier, decades or seconds ago, is no longer the same when we return, though all the elements may seem identical to how we left them. The passage of time, though imperceptible, whether of a few seconds or a few minutes, leaves clear traces in the apparent immutability of things; one only has to be conscious that those traces exist in order to perceive them. For the duration of our absence, the places outside of our empirical horizon continue to churn, a continuous, shifting network woven of various threads by a loom that incessantly produces, both archaic and new, the same interconnections: the world continues to spin, along with the solar system and the entire universe, and when we return to the kitchen from the dining room, or to the dining room from the kitchen, in the time it takes to find a clean knife in the utensil drawer, everything has changed, and sometimes we even have the vague or clear sensation of that change. If the same thing happens when we're motionless, and we feel time pass through us, modifying space from within, how can we not feel, after leaving a place for a few hours or a day or a decade, that when we return, that momentary feeling of estrangement which follows our brief ceremony of recognition, is waiting for us? Just now, in the bus, he once again intuits the silent murmur of that change, and one might say that, with every displacement of our attention, the familiar is submerged into the unknown, and when we reencounter it, it's no longer completely the same as it was.

Tomatis, tangled up in the vagueness of his thoughts, jumps when he sees one of the two boys from the back standing in the aisle next to his seat, smiling. *That's last night's La Región, isn't it? Could we borrow it a while?* Tomatis, reacting quickly after the surprise, notices the copy of *La Región* that he bought that morning because the Buenos Aires papers hadn't arrived yet; as he was taking the manila folder from the briefcase to finish reading the history of precisionism, he'd taken out the paper as well, and because the vibrations of the bus had caused it to fall to the ground twice, he'd put it under the briefcase to keep it still, intending to leave it on the bus when he reached the city. Tomatis hurries to pull it from under the briefcase and extends it, politely, thinking that if what they want is to deepen their knowledge about the Sunday match, they'll be happily surprised to find that the sports page contains two large color photos of the local teams, in addition to a detailed history of every *Clásico* over the last fifty years, with the results, team rosters, and highlights of the matches, which Tomatis of course didn't read, but which from having worked at *La Región* for years, as a section editor and intermittently as an editorialist, he knows the paper has an unfailing tradition of publishing two or three days before the game. The outcome is important: the winner keeps a spot in the first division, while the loser is forced to move down, *Or something like that*, Tomatis thinks, having not been to the stadium for a soccer match once in his life. *You can keep it, I've already read it*, Tomatis says. *Thanks*, the boy says, and returns to his seat, but as soon as he opens the paper he stands back up and walks back to Tomatis's seat. *Are you sure you aren't collecting it? Did you see the color photos of the teams?* he says. *Don't worry*, Tomatis says, *I have another copy at home*. And the boy returns to his seat, walking backward, bent forward, reverent, in disbelief over the gift he's just received. *He's probably a medical or architectural student*, Tomatis thinks. *Or maybe electrical engineering, degrees that our university doesn't offer, at least not to the highest level. Maybe, if it's the first of these, he gets his medical degree, he'll take on a specialization, gastrointestinal surgery, for instance. And if some day, because of my inclination for white wine and gin on the rocks, my chronic gastritis becomes an ulcer or a cancer and they take me to the operating room and I see him walk in, smiling, and he pats me on the shoulder to reassure me about the operation just before they give me the anesthesia, I'll remember that he collects color photos of the local soccer teams, and just as I close my eyes I'll know that I've put my life in the hands of a dangerous man.* Tomatis laughs to himself, trying to maintain an impassive, absent expression, though he knows that the two of them, concentrating on the sports page, have already forgotten that he even exists.

His right hand rests on the open briefcase, his fingers playing along the vertical, soft leather dividers that separate the four compartments, which, in fact, contains very few things: the manila folder containing the treatise on precisionism, which he finished reading a while ago, adding a few annotations in the margins, another folder, this one of light green card stock, containing an old article from *La Región*, with an even older photo picturing several well-known collaborators on the first volume of precisionism, during a dinner at La Giralda, along with a few other papers, in particular a letter that Pichón had sent him from Paris the month before, and to which, for lack of time, he'd only responded to the day before yesterday. In another compartment of the briefcase is the gift for his sister, a fantasy bracelet that Alicia picked out, wrapped in metallic paper, which he bought that morning on Calle Córdoba, and finally, in the fourth compartment, an *alfajor* given to him by the driver as he was getting on the bus, compliments of the house and included with the price of the trip, and next to the *alfajor*, a book about Hujalvu, the butterfly painter, which he'd been thumbing through on the way there, and whose French introduction *"Vie et mort des papillons,"* he'd begun to read (the book is a gift from Pichón, which he'd sent him from France for his birthday). Finally his fingers, and not Tomatis himself, decide to grasp the green folder, half-opening it, shuffling through the papers that it contains, and picking out Pichón's letter and opening it in the light, unfolding it, to reread it:

Carlitos. How's the March heat treating you? We're still in the middle of winter here. You must be surprised to be getting a letter from me after our phone call on Sunday, but that night, after dinner, I came up with a poem that, from a distance, has to do with our conversation. So I'm sending it to you. It's a vague parody of La Fontaine.

Maître corbeau là-haut perché
rien de bon n'annonçait,
ni d'ailleurs, rien de mauvais.
Il se tenait là-haut, neutre et muet.
Aucun présage ne l'habitait.
Aussi extérieur que l'arbre, le soleil, la forêt
Et aussi privé de sens que de secret:
forme noire sans raison répétée
tache d'encre dans le vide imprimée.
Maître corbeau là-haut perché.

What do you think? Don't tell me anything right away. The question begs reflection. What, on the other hand, I want you to send me soon is a detailed explanation, on paper, of your thesis on Oedipus. Certainly in this century Oedipus has become a stereotype, a two-dimensional caricature like Batman or Patoruzú, but one of his characteristics, his blindness, still fascinates me. Hugs to everyone. Pichón. P.S., What do you think of Hujalvu? A western specialist says that he'd specialized in a single species of butterflies (Inachis io), *but one of his students wrote, in the mid-eighteenth century, that he always painted* ONE SINGLE *butterfly.*

Tomatis finishes rereading the letter, but he continues to hold it, motionless, even with his face, just below his eyes, without re-folding it. For the last month the problem has intrigued him. The same butterfly? Aesthetically, the choice is reasonable, and, one might even say, necessary, but how would it be possible to keep a single butterfly intact over an eighty-year life without it eventually disintegrating, unless, after a certain point, he was painting from memory, not from the material, pulverized after a few decades, but rather the shape imprinted on him forever, which, having observed it to the point of possession, he was able to turn in every possible direction. Tomatis shakes his head thoughtfully, with an almost imperceptible slowness, and without much conviction refolds the letter, handwritten in green ink, and drops it into one of the compartments of the briefcase.

Moving directly north along the highway in which, over a hundred and sixty-seven kilometers, there's not a single curve, at ninety kilometers per hour—the legal speed limit for interurban passenger transport throughout the country—Tomatis has the west to his left, the east to his right, and the south to his back. After leaving Rosario, along the loop road surrounded by shantytowns, in the right lane of the highway, as far as San Lorenzo more or less, the traffic was very dense, but afterward it began to thin out. All the same, at the moment when he drops the folded letter into the briefcase, an engine roars to his left, and the most likely empty tractor trailer that passes at a high speed hides the sun for several seconds, and the increasingly horizontal rays of light are erased, intercepted by the double trailer of the truck, and almost immediately, when the truck has finished passing them, they reappear. Every so often, cars also pass them at full speed, advancing along the fast lane, and disappear quickly to the north. In the opposite direction, cars, trucks, and buses follow each other mechanically, but at moments long stretches of the highway are empty. The buses, green, red, and orange, announcing the names of their companies in large letters everywhere along the highway, drive toward Rosario and Buenos Aires, and some, the specials probably, toward Mar del Plata and even Bariloche, from the city or from Paraná or Resistencia or Asunción del Paraguay. Once, at a stop between Rosario and Buenos Aires, in San Pedro, Tomatis saw a double-decker that was going to Machu Picchu. Tomatis remembers thinking, *A bus to Machu Picchu? And why not Tibet?* And he smiles again, and turns around discreetly again, afraid that the two at the back will catch him laughing to himself, but apparently they've been subjugated by the sports page from *La Región* that he's just given them.

Half opening the light green folder, separating its edges, he carefully pulls out, from between the few papers alongside it, the yellowed clipping from *La Región*, which is at least five years old, with the photo that, if the date that the article attributes to it is correct, is around half a century old at the moment in which he's now studying it carefully. There are eleven men, all of them in suit and tie, except for one, who wears a dark bowtie. Though it's difficult to tell much about the location, because the photo was taken from a practically empty corner of the room, Tomatis doesn't need to read the caption printed below the photo to recognize La Giralda, gone for years now, since they tore down the central market. The article is titled "The Precisionist Group," and a lead-in explains, *On the eve of another anniversary of the creation of precisionism, this article recalls the history of the movement and the personality of its leader, Mario Brando.* The caption printed below the photograph mentions the place where it was taken, but not the date, and identifies the people present. Seven are sitting, and four are standing behind them; in the background, turned away from the camera, standing in front of a black rectangle below a hanging lamp, there's a waiter, facing what could be the entrance to the kitchen, obscured by the photograph's narrow depth of field. It's a classic after-dinner photo; the four who have stood up must have been sitting with their backs to the photographer, who must have made them move so that everyone would be facing the same way. Their chairs are not in the frame, except for one, a piece of which is visible in the far right corner of the picture, because they pulled them away from the table, and so the large, messy table is clearly visible. On top of the white tablecloth there are two siphons of seltzer, two oil bottles, half-full glasses, plates containing the remains of food, probably dessert (and probably cheese and sweets, after the alphabet soup and the obligatory Spanish-style stew), with utensils crossed on top or thrown carelessly on the tablecloth. There are ashtrays, but there aren't any bottles of wine, and Tomatis remembers, as he does every time he looks at the photo and examines it up close, that someone, describing Brando's control over his disciples, told him that if he wasn't drinking then the others couldn't drink either, and so many of them drank in secret. This same person told him that only when his brother-in-law, General Ponce, when he was still a first lieutenant, or a captain, attended the dinners, could the guests drink whatever they wanted, because the general would order large quantities of the best wines, something Brando disapproved of, though he never dared to contradict him, because the more Ponce drank, and though he never became violent, the more uncontrollable he became. Only the next day, in private, would Brando question him, thinking that family business should be conducted behind closed doors, but whenever he, Ponce, bumped into some member of the group on the street, and the first lieutenant, laughing, told him what had happened and how terrorized Brando kept his troops, it caused this person a dark pleasure to learn about his family affairs.

Though he is sitting in the far left of the photo, at the end of the table, turned decidedly toward the camera, which implies a marginal position, studying the photo closely, imagining the scene during dinner, with the four who are now standing behind the ones who are sitting, it's immediately obvious that Brando, as he must have done at every dinner, is seated at the head of the table. The absence of women makes it possible to suppose that it was a work dinner, some decisive moment in the history of the group, before Brando's departure for Rome. Despite the poor lighting of the image, his hands, pressed together, reveal his tense fingers and the knuckles jutting from his right hand, as well as the sleeve of his stiffly starched white shirt, clasped by a cufflink that in all certainty is made of gold. Everyone is very elegant, with a pointed handkerchief coming out of the breast pocket of their jackets, their shirts and even in some cases their light-colored vests, and even in silk ties, all of which betrays an equal interest in their public image and in the renovation of poetic language though the grafting of scientific vocabulary. Even the four who are standing, and who are the youngest, display the same taste; their medium-length beards (nine of the eleven have one) make them seem older, though most of them were at that time between twenty and thirty, and among the ones standing, three of them are barely twenty, and one of them, the third one from the left, not even nineteen. For Tomatis, this is the author of the extract resting in the manila folder in the briefcase. The close beard, the quiff, the silk tie, a bit more colorful and less conservative than the rest, and which, tightly knotted to the collar of his white shirt, emerges from the crossed lapels of his dark suit, would allow him to not stand out too much from the others, but something at once absent and preoccupied in his expression distinguishes him from them. Brando's expression differs from the others' too: his vague smile, the tension in his hands and the rigidity of his body, along with the almost imperceptible air of skepticism and cunning on his face, not to mention the fact that while everyone else around him rests their hands or elbows or forearms on the table, he's pulled his chair out and crossed his legs, distancing himself almost half a meter from the edge, not even touching the circular, white tablecloth falling in triangular folds. The distance that he creates between himself and his disciples, at the same table where they've broken bread together, confirms, Tomatis thinks, the rumors of his duplicity, of his shuttling between those he considered his equals, the ignorant and pragmatic bourgeoisie who could even be brutal if they felt their interests were threatened, but who were useless for his literary career, and the others, his disciples, gathered from the most diverse environments, petty employees of public offices, high school teachers, journalists, with no patrimony but their readings, their facility for expressing

411

themselves on paper, and their literary tastes (only one, years after this photo was taken, after his return from Rome, Doctor Calcagno, belonged to both worlds, and Brando made him not only into a partner, trusting him with all the work at the law firm, but also, as a literary lieutenant, the only one he trusted among the members of his own class, into a true slave). The absent and somewhat nervous look of the boy trying to go unnoticed among the others has nothing in common with Brando's, unless it's the knowledge that the pleasant end to a literary feast that the photograph pretends to immortalize—and which in a certain sense it achieves, as substantiated by the article in *La Región* and the fact that he, Tomatis, is thinking about it half a century later—is merely the deceitful surface of a mirror behind which a maelstrom of contradictions boils. Tomatis knows, from friends of Washington, that his homosexuality, which at the time the photo was taken even he was probably ignorant of, but which Brando suspected, the subtle pressure, and the low blows from the leader, without producing an open conflict, forced him to leave the movement a few months later. Around that same time the defamation campaign concerning the pedophilia of one of the members, which was never proven but which drove him to suicide, began to circulate, and several of Brando's enemies insist that he was the one who started the rumor. As regards the melancholic young man in the photograph, things were not as easy for Brando. An only child, he'd gone to live in Buenos Aires after the death of his parents, and when he returned he'd lost his shyness and fear and had gained confidence and mordancy. He wrote literary and musical articles for the papers and he sang in the provincial choir. When the symphony orchestra was created, he was named director; he also directed the national radio station—because he was intelligent and honest, whatever government came to power, he was always kept at his post, but in '75 he was let go, and after March of 1976 he decided to return to Buenos Aires so as to disappear in the vast swarm and spend some time out of sight. By the time he returned to the city, four or five years later, Brando had died. He once ran into Tomatis on San Martín and told him that he'd left out of fear that Brando would denounce him. Immediately, Tomatis sensed that he was right: he'd seen that threat in Brando's eyes one night, when he'd made the mistake of thinking that he might intercede with General Ponce for some information about Elisa and Gato, who'd been kidnapped, and, mortified, had gone to his house to ask for it. In that look, in a momentary but hateful and violent spark, he'd seen everything that Brando was capable of: a viscous, dark stain, or tear rather, had allowed him, Tomatis, to glimpse, under the uniform of an elegant bourgeoisie absorbed in the disinterested contemplation of the stars, committed body and soul to the cause of his aesthetic ideal, the shadow of the beast, blinking impatiently, waiting for its chance to leap onto its prey and tear it to pieces. So it made sense for the author of *Precisionism, by a witness of the time* to disappear from the city and withdraw discretely into Buenos Aires. For years he'd carried on a secret war with Brando, a war so subtly codified that only its antagonists knew of its existence. There had been no open rupture, and when they met in public they greeted each other coldly but courteously; at meetings, after greeting each other with confident smiles, they didn't speak again. And yet the boy thought he could sense, while he was still attending the group's meetings, veiled warnings from Brando. When *Nexos* began to appear, it systematically rejected his submissions, always under diverse pretexts—length, immaturity, transgression of precisionist doctrine. A trait that Brando had that the boy noticed immediately and that Tomatis confirmed seeing too when he confided to him: he never took direct action himself; he had the unquestionable talent for influencing others to do and say what he wanted as though they'd thought of it themselves. Tomatis and *the witness of the time* agreed: to denounce them, Brando wouldn't have gone directly to General Ponce to accuse them of subversion, but instead, during a family lunch some Sunday, probably after the eleven o'clock mass, with their wives, their children, and their grandchildren, he would have made so many allusions that his brother-in-law, fearing a sanction for dereliction, would have run straight to General Negri after the lunch to point out the evident threat of such and such an individual. When *the witness of the time* realized Brando's allusive methodology, he decided to employ the same tactic. Brando never discussed sex, for example; it was taboo for him, with the members of the group, with his intimate friends, or with his family. And yet, coincidentally of course, when the boy attended the meetings, the conversation would always take a turn such that two or three of the people at the table would end up mocking the *Espiga* neoclassicists, insisting on their effeminacy. Brando remained silent and circumspect, almost irritated, while the others exchanged rumors between guffaws, and *the witness* told Tomatis that he'd asked himself more than once if Brando himself was conscious of those maneuvers to influence others, which from the outside, to a shrewd observer, were immediately obvious, or if a carnivorous instinct drove him, without fail, to commit the injury. Tomatis answered without hesitation that in his opinion he was conscious of it, and *the witness* told him that he'd wondered about it at first, but later, after he'd left the group, he decided to put it to the test: in a local paper, less noteworthy but also less conventional than *La Región, the witness* had published an article about Louis Bouilhet, a friend of Flaubert, who a century earlier had the idea of publishing a long poem, "The Fossils," based on recent archaeological and paleographical discoveries. With that precursor, *the witness* pretended to verify the existence of pre-precisionist ideas, but in fact it was an indirect way of demonstrating that Brando hadn't invented a thing. Brando never responded to the piece, but a few weeks later he published an article in *La Región*'s literary

414

supplement about the moral duties of poets in which he alluded, coincidentally of course, to Canto XV of *Inferno*, in particular to verses 102–108, without quoting them. It wasn't difficult for *the witness* to search for them in the text, where it describes the inner ring of the seventh circle, in which those who commit violence against nature, which is to say, for Dante, the sodomites, suffer in a desert of flaming sand: *In somma sappi che tutti fur cherci / e litterati grandi e di gran fama, / d'un peccato medesmo al mondo lerci.* In the same article he cites Juvenal as an example of a poet who denounces and attempts to correct the moral failures of his time, but of his sixteen satires he only refers to the second, without specifying its content. It was clear enough: in the midst of his banalities for the general public, certain passages of the article had a hidden recipient. But *the witness of the time* had his own resources, and when he invited precisionists to a radio program he hosted, *Music and Lyric,* it was always the most unruly or the least intelligent of them, creating a less-than-brilliant image of the movement. Of course he wouldn't have made the mistake of not inviting Brando, just the opposite, but he knew that, under whatever pretext, he would always decline the invitation. Later, *the witness* learned that Brando encouraged his disciples not to go on the show, but without too much conviction, first of all because everything that created publicity for the movement was useful to him, but especially because he didn't want to *give ground* to the other groups, the neo-romantics from *Espiga,* the *criollistas,* the hardened avant-gardes, and because, without exception, publicity on the radio, in the papers, in magazines, and later on television was something that not one of his disciples or the members of other movements were capable of refusing, the search for unbridled fame and the traffic of influences being always the principal aims of literary and artistic practices. Another obvious allusion to Brando on the part of *the witness* came in a puppet show that he wrote and which was often staged at schools, at birthday parties, and at one of the first independent theaters of the city. In the play there was a lawyer who was always followed around by two other characters, slightly stupid types who constantly let themselves be tricked and robbed by the lawyer. The trio was a hit with the public, adults as much as children, and everyone would applaud whenever they came on stage, laughing and stomping the ground. The children would always try to keep the lawyer from tricking the two idiots, and would shout warnings at them, and when a policeman, who discovered his schemes, fell upon the lawyer with a whip, it brought the house down. In the fifties, those characters were incredibly popular in the city and in many towns around the province, and everyone who was five or six at the time still remembers them. In reality, the play alluded, in a veiled way, but transparent to anyone who knew the story, and especially Brando, to a rumor that had been circulating for a while about Brando's first years as a lawyer, when he worked for himself, long before he formed a partnership with Calcagno, namely that Brando had gotten power of attorney over two elderly senile men, and that he'd convinced them to leave everything to him. The rumor (if it were true) was especially repugnant if one considered that, while the old men may have had some money, Brando was already a thousand times richer. And *the witness* believes that, years later, in '75, Brando took his vengeance on him by having him fired from the radio, and, the following year, having him threatened anonymously to force him to leave the city.

Slowly, almost without Tomatis realizing it, all of these stories become soft and fragmentary, unraveling, and finally, like a trail of smoke losing its cohesion, thinning, they disappear. He remembers his brother, who had the same name as him, but because he died when he was seven days old, a year later, when he, Tomatis, was born, they gave him the same name, but inverted: his brother had been called Alberto Carlos, and he was Carlos Alberto, but the Alberto only appears on official documents, he never uses it. Despite everything, it's pleasant, now, to see him play, run, ride a horse. He seems so happy! The problem is that they both have the same name, their parents should have prevented this. Maybe they should give the name to his brother now, because, with the passage of time, through one of those ironies of chance, he, Tomatis, now an adult, has become the older brother. He's overcome by an immense sense of shame, an intolerable sympathy, and he feels like he's drowning, and so, shaking his head, confused and sweaty, he opens his eyes. When he sees the sun, he realizes that he's been asleep and he checks the time: it's ten of seven. For the first time in over fifty years, he's had a mircodream, as he calls those sharp and momentary images that, without too much development, visit him in dreams, and in those two or three instants of dreaming he saw his older brother, whom he never knew, but for whom, all the same, he still suffers a painful compassion now that he's awake. Tomatis realizes that, though it didn't look like him, the boy in the dream must have been himself, as he'd been—or as he would have liked to have been, he can't remember any more—when he was eight or nine. Seven days old! You might say that, almost literally, more than anyone else, he was born to die, Tomatis thinks, a bit more calm now that the overwhelming confusion he'd felt a few moments before, thankfully, has abated.

With the changing position of the sun, the horizontal rays of light that crossed the interior of the bus have disappeared, leaving a pale and porous shadow in which, here and there, because of the vibrations of the bus and the momentary bumps in the road—patches, potholes, or transversal lines of hardened tar that mark the layers of the asphalt—short luminous bursts appear. Outside, in contrast, the sky is veneered a singular, golden copper to the horizon, and more intensely to the east over the flat and barren land. Rain has been forecast for the weekend, even violent storms in certain regions of the plain, and Tomatis leans forward to better observe the sky through the window, but he doesn't see a single cloud. The sky is now paling to the east, and the disc of the sun, still relatively high, a yellowish green, will redden suddenly, growing, as its fall toward the horizon line accelerates. For the last fifteen days, it's rained every weekend, and then the weather clears little by little until the moment the sun reappears and the heat returns. The week that's now ending began with rain on Monday and Tuesday—there was also a brief storm on Sunday morning—and though it dawned cloudy with a light drizzle on Wednesday, by that afternoon the heat was already oppressive, and by the next day the cloud cover had transformed into enormous white clouds that appeared motionless against the luminous, blue sky, clearly visible thanks to the cleansing of the air by the rains; the summer was returning. And yesterday and today there hasn't been a sign of clouds, and the air has been suffocating. Tomatis thinks that if it manages to rain tonight, the cookout that Gutiérrez has gone to such lengths to organize, gathering his old and his new friends, will be spent under the pavilion, watching the rain fall, or at the large kitchen table, to which Tomatis has already been invited before, the previous winter. He imagines the guests eating and drinking under the pavilion, talking and laughing, but contained within its limits by the rain. Every so often, someone will be forced to cross them, to go to the bathroom or to look for something inside the house—cigarettes, a camera, papers, makeup—stored in their rain jackets or their purses piled up on the sofa in the living room, and they'll cross the wet lawn at a run before circling the white slabs around the swimming pool and turning onto the stone path that leads to the entrance to the house. It will have been raining all morning, and while the thick and loud storms may transform into a silent, fine rain by the middle of the afternoon, the water will not stop falling, just like this past week, until Monday or

418

Tuesday, and maybe, with that rain, the autumn will finally arrive. The party will end early on account of the weather, and at around three or four the guests will start to leave, especially if the rain cools the air suddenly; used to the summer heat, the guests will have come in clothes that are too lightweight and will be cold, and the teeth of the most sensitive among them may even start to chatter. Like so many other things in his life, apparently, Gutiérrez's party will probably not turn out the way he expected. Clearly his politeness isn't faked, and his sense of generosity seems genuine, but there seems to be something darker at work behind them, not against others, but rather against himself. In any case, he doesn't seem to expect anything from the world or, better yet, Tomatis thinks, he doesn't seem to desire any of the things that the majority of people desire. His calm and affectionate but slightly distant personality, isn't it indifference, detachment, unqualified absence? And yet, while the big things don't seem to interest him, the smallest ones, if not the most insignificant ones, attract and seduce him, like a one- or two-year-old baby whose mother points insistently at a mountain so that it'll notice it, and meanwhile it's fascinated by an ant scurrying over the instep of its shoe. Once, Gutiérrez dragged him to the San Lorenzo grill house, a hole in the wall that was last fashionable in the fifties or sixties, but which has been in decline more or less since 1968. According to Rosemberg, since he came back, whenever he takes anyone out he always invites them to the best restaurants in the city, but when he goes out alone he only goes to San Lorenzo—Tomatis wonders if having dragged him to that temple of precooked sweetbreads, of leftover steak, and of dubious empanadas was in fact a gesture of confidence, a sign of deference, almost an homage to his person, a thought that without ever having been made explicit more or less signified, *You, Tomatis, who know how much things are worth, will be able to recognize the hidden treasure here.* And Gutiérrez, who frequently orders Italian and French wine, along with champagne, through an importer in Buenos Aires, and serves it generously to his friends, drank wine with ice and seltzer at the grill house while eating precooked intestines and greasy, proletarian empanadas. Watching him eat, Tomatis tried to unravel the situation, the enigma of the man who kept the best wines in his cellar and took his friends out to the best restaurants in the city or, he was sure, in Rome or Geneva, but when he went out alone he went exclusively to the San Lorenzo grill house. It's a frequent topic of deliberation for Tomatis, and the day they went out together, as he watched him put ice and seltzer in his wine, intrigued, adopting a knowing air, but trying to provoke some sort of clarifying response, he told him with a smile that tried to be conspiratorial, *For the sake of consistency, you'll need to do that with your Château Margaux*, and upon hearing this, cracking up and shaking his head, Gutiérrez answered, *That sounds more like your style! It's not at all like that for me*, which did nothing to resolve Tomatis's perplexity. He often told himself that he, Gutiérrez, was frozen in his own past, which sometimes seemed evident, and once he even said to Soldi, *He confused his youth with where it took place*, but the explanation was altogether too simplistic, Gutiérrez was too lucid not to be conscious of that error. No, it had to be something else. And, every so often, Tomatis was stuck wondering, *Is it this or that thing, isn't it actually, or maybe* . . . But none of the explanations were consistent with Gutiérrez; there was always some detail, some trait, some hypothesis, that didn't coincide with him. The fact that he was so similar and yet so different from his friends from the city, both new and old, could not result entirely from his long absence; there was something intrinsic to him that had to explain it. And his friendliness, at once affectionate and distant, wasn't produced by hesitation or duplicity. What was most mysterious was the infantile pleasure that the most banal things gave him: a word that he'd forgotten after all that time and which someone had spoken as he passed them in the street, or the way some children behaved when they were leaving school, or the tree buds in September, or the suggestive look he exchanged with a girl searching for a rich client from her table in some downtown bar, produced a sort of mild hilarity in him that seemed at once exultant and sympathetic, and which intrigued anyone in his company. They seemed to provoke a kind of recognition in him, and the things that had been like loose threads of unperceived experience within the incorporeal plane of his recollections, after so many years away, suddenly, in the tactile evidence of the present, were actualized. Tomatis shifts in his seat, bothered by a slight agitation, feeling that, once again, his understanding has come up against a limit. It doesn't seem sufficient to explain him through simple nostalgia and a reencounter with the things of the past. And then, suddenly, after a few seconds in which his mind, unable to think, is submerged into a kind of painful void, he receives, through an association of ideas, the revelation: he hasn't come looking for anything; he's come back to the point of departure, but it's not a return, and much less a regression. He hasn't come to recover a lost world, but to see it differently. From the series of incalculable transformations, large and small, that he suffered since the day he left, another man has emerged, modified in imperceptible ways, especially to himself, by each change. And the man who now goes into ecstasies over the banalities of the world knows, having paid for it with his life, that every banality is shored up by a brace that flowers on the surface and stretches down into an unfinished, black depth. He seems to have reached the ultimate simplicity, but only after a long tour of the inferno. He, Tomatis, has never heard him raise his voice, and every time he thinks of Gutiérrez, he pictures him smiling vaguely, the slight smile more present in his eyes than on his lips. Even when he starts in on his enumerative diatribe against rich countries, though the terms he employs can sometimes seem too cruel, the gentle irony with which he speaks expresses more disillusion than rage, and, if you pay attention, sometimes, there's a noticeable trace of indulgence. The world that he celebrates now, with an almost constant and subtle exaltation, is not at all the one of his youth, but rather one that he came to discover over the course of his successive transformations, and the person he's become is now seeing it all for the first time. He didn't actually return to his point of departure, but rather to a new place where everything is different. And though he may have lost his innocence, his capacity for acceptance has grown, inclining toward simple things without idealization or disdain. He must've thought that if he managed to recognize and appreciate simplicity, he could reconcile himself to the world. The distant, even absent quality that is sometimes evident in him is probably a result of that exercise in reconciliation, the consciousness and effort of it long ago dissolved into the benevolent sincerity with which he regards the world; he even finds a way to qualify Mario Brando. And Tomatis elaborates a formula that seems to give him enormous satisfaction, the multiplicity of meanings it contains only apparent to him: *He left his house and had to cross the whole universe to get to the corner, and now he knows the effort required to reach the corner, and the significance of the immediate.*

The sun has now begun to redden; its circumference is sharper, and the flaming disc seems to have cooled and smoothed, losing its look of boiling metal and gaining a sort of gentleness. But the afternoon that is repeated on the plain has something solemn and disquieting about it, and an unmistakable impression comes suddenly and destroys every illusion, that the place where we thought we were living is another, larger, and this destructive realization removes every known sense of the verb *to live*. Our experience, which we thought so intimate, becomes foreign, and life reveals its remote and tiny quality, a momentary spark in an immense, igneous storm. The smooth surface of the red disc now emits magnetic vibrations in which cold and torrid shades alternate. In the absolutely cloudless sky, the disc, which appears to have been drawn with a compass, grows as it falls toward the horizon, and on the plain a reddish glow haloes the grass, the foliage of the trees, the fences—cows and horses, abstracted, graze unhurriedly, as though they don't realize that the night is rising from the east, from the side of the river. In a small pond the water has turned red, and a few motionless herons have their backs to him, as though that change of color upset them and they prefer to ignore it. Along a dirt road perpendicular to the highway, a rider, mounted on a dark horse, moves toward the red disc at a slow trot, and Tomatis senses that when he reaches the horizon he will intercept the reddening form and the rider will enter into it, submerging himself into the magnetic, quivering substance contained within the perfect circumference, the fluid mass of metal in fusion that will swallow him forever unless the horse and rider, triumphant, emerge on the other side of the road, leaving a ragged hole in the center of the disc, sabotaging the fraud or revealing the illusion. But if suddenly the sun were to stop, touching the horizon tangentially, the trot of the horse, in the distortion of space and time that the detention would cause, would be frozen, without advancing, in the same point in space for all eternity, halfway along the road between the highway and the red disc, incredibly immediate and enormous. Maybe the horse and the rider are phantasmal, incorporeal figures separated from the expired and corrupted flesh that for the past few hours has been lying vacated in a field, on their way, blurrily and hastily, to the kingdom of the dead, which as everyone knows is clustered at the far edge of the west, *to the left of the world,* Tomatis thinks, raising his left hand and touching the window glass, cold because of the air conditioning. *The publisher will have arrived by now, and he'll have started negotiating with the authorities, trying to convince them of the utility of the Fourth Estate for explaining government policy to the public, and the need for a free press in a kingdom of the dead privileged with new institutions that affirm democratic values and consolidate individual liberty and economic progress, informing them, in addition, that for a kingdom of the dead in constant demographic shift, a rigorous communication strategy is essential; he is willing to put his experience in communications at their service, of course, in addition to his contacts with the vital forces of society and his relationships among marketing and public opinion experts.* Tomatis shakes his head with a smile that is both indulgent and mocking, and, looking away for a few seconds from the red disc falling toward the horizon, he observes the ochre shadow inside the bus. The passengers in the front seats are almost invisible, and the ones closest to Tomatis are only black silhouettes encircled by a reddish halo; whenever a head moves, its dark profile is outlined in the shadow by that luminous line that emphasizes it with meticulous exactitude. But the heads that stick out above the seat backs are motionless, as if their owners had abandoned them in their seats before beginning their trip to *the edge of the west, the left end of the world,* following the dark rider trotting slowly toward the red disc that is now almost touching the horizon, and toward the publisher of *La Región,* who at that very moment is offering his *communications strategies* to the authorities of the kingdom of the dead. Behind him, on the other side of the aisle, the two boys, possibly medical students, sprawled out on their seats, have fallen silent, with their eyes wide open, possibly due to a sudden stupor or an absorbing memory, and their pupils, exposed to the sun by the excessive stillness of their eyes, glow dark red, phosphorescent, as if distant bonfires, brought to the present by the intensity of their recollection, burn as intensely in their memory as the tiny flames reflected in their pupils. *But the kingdom of the dead,* Tomatis tells himself, *isn't at the edge of the west, on the left end of the world, but rather within everyone, inside us, it's a burden carried on the shoulders of everyone that, unnecessarily and*

424

miserably, is born and dies. Those of us traveling in this bus carry that burden, that cross. And at this very moment, everyone who squirms, from morning to night, awake or asleep, in the nest of humanity, in the ball of mud in which they struggle, overwhelmed, bears it. The living and the dead share the same indivisible kingdom.

He's overcome by a kind of ephemeral rage, of indignation possibly, against the whole universe, against the red disc that now begins to dip into the horizon, condensing the shadow inside the bus. But almost immediately he calms down. He doesn't think about anything. Now, as the horizon swallows the red disc more and more quickly, the night, rising from the east, submerges the plain. At around eight thirty he'll be at home, and in order to rest from the long day, the early morning trip, the walk with Alicia along the downtown streets, the return trip, and wake up refreshed and ready for the Sunday at Gutiérrez's—as long as it isn't raining in the morning—he'll get into bed with a book at around ten and will try to get to sleep early. With any luck, his sister will have cut up some slices of the second cylinder of delicious mummified meat, the local chorizo that Nula gave him the other day. He's safely guaranteed the luxury of death, Tomatis thinks, ironically, all he has to do is keep on living. In the waning, reddish splendor, erased by the growing shadow of the bus, he checks the contents of the briefcase to make sure he has everything and then closes it after pulling out the *alfajor* and dropping it into his coat pocket, in order to give it, along with some coins, as he usually does, to one of the kids begging at the entrance to the terminal, near the taxi stand.

Where the circle was there's now a red stain spread across the horizon, and the entire plain is black except, here and there, in the puddles, in the marshes, in the lakes, there's an equally red surface that, with a bit of imagination, could seem to be the sun, which has disappeared, tinting the water from below, from the antipodes. But in fact it's the unpredictable trajectory of the light that, from the horizon, lingers on whatever surface will reflect it, resisting the invasion of the night. As the minutes pass, the red stain contracts, like a wound that closes little by little, leaving only the final bloody fissures, until finally the even blackness covers the entire space, and the diverse shapes that the world assumes are erased completely, deconstructed by the smooth, abstract, uninterrupted blackness. Artificial lights restore them at moments, in vivid, fragmentary, and fleeting bursts of reality into which, almost immediately after lighting up, improbably, they dissolve. The vehicles coming in the opposite direction are just as phantasmal, and their headlights sweep across the shadow of the bus as they pass, allowing him to see, for a few seconds, the motionless or swaying heads that extend beyond the upper edge of the seats, the grandmother's, Tomatis remembers, though the grandson's is invisible just now, the middle-aged couple who, judging by the labels hanging from their suitcases that he saw on the platform before they were loaded, seem to be returning from a long trip. At the last toll, before the exit for the airport, the bus was forced to slow down and stop, reintroducing, for several moments, the rough present that, when the bus starts to move again, accelerating, is left irrevocably behind, circulating endlessly in a past ever more archaic and distant until it finally drifts into the night of time. Soon, in the distance, the lights of the city will be visible. Abandoning the highway, the bus drives into the suburbs of Santo Tomé. From his seat on the upper deck, Tomatis looks down on the poor houses of the outskirts, as if the night, the melancholy streetlights, and the poverty especially, miniaturized them. But when they reach the center of Santo Tomé—several houses, occupied or empty, display the ubiquitous sign ANOTHER MORO PROPERTY FOR SALE—he notices its liveliness: the bars, which are still empty, have set up tables on the sidewalks, and many stores, groceries, bakeries, ice cream shops, and even offices still have their doors open and their shop windows illuminated. The fever of the hot night is visible on people's clothes and faces, but some kids, recently showered and changed for the Saturday night, talk and laugh on the corners, or walk in groups along the main street. *Though they seem to still be ignorant of it, and though some of them may pretend not to know it, every one of them already bears that crushing, agonizing burden. For now they move, healthy and careless, through the quiet of the evening, confusing their desires and their dreams with the unexamined reasons for their existence. They think they exist for themselves, but all they are is bait, tempting the thing that makes them exist. They think they're displaying themselves, but what they don't know is that they're being displayed by the archaic design that brings them to the world, gives them an attractive shape, and then, without cruelty or compassion, casts them into the abyss.* The bus leaves Santo Tomé and turns onto the road bridge over the two branches of the Salado, glowing briefly under the lights of the bridge before it disappears. The city is on the other side. Tomatis sees its lights, unfolding in long rows of brilliant points, and imagines himself coming off the bridge, entering the avenues, arriving at the terminal. The anticipated exhaustion of the return suddenly overcomes him, and his home becomes a place at once strange and familiar, immediate and remote, where the living carry the dead on their shoulders, only liberated of the burden by their own death, and so on until the end of time, which is not at all infinite, but rather condemned to end with the final exhalation of the last human breath.

SUNDAY

THE
HUMMINGBIRD

***THE FIRST TWO WITHOUT PULLING OUT!* GUTIÉRREZ THINKS**
at the moment he wakes up, even though more than thirty years
have passed since that summer morning, so similar to the one in
which he's just opened his eyes, when he slept with Leonor naked
at his side for the first and last time, because every other time
they saw each other it was always in the afternoon, the appropriate
time of day of adultery. But there's no virile pride or arrogance in
the thought, only incredulous happiness, retrospective excitement,
gratitude. Ever since that distant, scorching Sunday, somewhat
unreal because of the excessive heat, the multiplicity of sensations
up till then unknown to him, the lack of sleep, the exhaustion, until
that peaceful April morning, almost as hot as the first, Gutiérrez
has been convinced that his life began that night and ended a few
weeks later, when he took the bus to Buenos Aires and disappeared
from the city. He thinks he owes this to Leonor, and is prepared to
pay that infinite debt forever: *You get seventy years for a few hours, a*

few minutes, of life, and then there's nothing to do with the rest; it's just killing time.

After spending a while in the bathroom, shaving, defecating, taking a warm, meticulous shower, brushing his teeth, combing his hair, dressing—underwear, a white undershirt, dark blue pants, sandals—and getting the thermos and the *mate* in the kitchen and eating a few buttered buns that Amalia picked up at the bakery, Gutiérrez is walking from the kitchen to the courtyard, and moving away from the pavilion, and beyond the swimming pool, stepping off the white slab path that leads from the house to the pool—believing he would move in to that house after retiring from his many activities, Doctor Russo thought big—he steps onto the stretch of lawn that, still wet from the dew, dampens his feet through the opening of the sandals, producing, in the warm morning, a delicious sensation. At a distance, Faustino leans attentively over a hibiscus, possibly searching for dry branches or flowers, withered during the night, to prune.

Gutiérrez empties the gourd in two or three energetic pulls through the straw and falls still. The entire lawn around him is covered in multicolored drops into which the morning light decomposes. That immense, unique, often colorless substance that is incessantly scattered over even the most remote corner of the visible world rests at his feet now in a shimmer of yellow, green, orange, red, blue, and indigo drops that, if he moves his head slightly as he looks at them, seem animated, change color, grow more luminous, emitting iridescent sparks. The humidity of the night, condensing in the morning cold, was deposited into colorless drops over the green leaves of grass, and now the sun has risen to a certain height, a precise location in the sky, and its rays, striking the drops at a certain angle and at no other, refract into a manifold iridescence, as if a rainbow had exploded and its splinters continued to shine around him, tiny and multiplied, on the wet ground. This intimate, domestic enchantment gives way to a momentary and fragmented sensation, an abstract certainty about the common essence that circulates among every part of the whole, connecting them to each other and to everything else, and the at once astonished and estranged impression of always being somewhere larger than where our systems of habit mistakenly accustom us to believing we are. Gutiérrez takes two or three steps and stops at a spot where the grass is somewhat higher, and when, after having stepped on the leaves, separating them, his feet are once again motionless, they close over his sandals once again, causing them to disappear into a kind of cave of green grass in which, every time he moves, sparkling iridescently, a reflective surface of multicolored drops shimmers.

Yesterday morning at around nine, Amalia had come in to tell him that there was a man looking for him. It was Escalante. He was passing by to let him know that he wouldn't be coming to the cookout after all.

—I figured you were here for the flashlight, Gutiérrez said, laughing.

—The flashlight?

—The one that Chacho loaned us when we went looking for you at the club.

And he went into the kitchen and returned to the courtyard with it.

—Thanks, Escalante said, and for a moment neither one knew what to say.

—I knew you wouldn't come to the cookout, Gutiérrez says finally. But I never thought you were so sensitive that you'd come tell me the day before.

They started walking slowly around the courtyard, stopping every so often for no apparent reason, shooting the breeze, with

433

ironic indolence but also with long intervals of silence that were no longer uncomfortable. They didn't talk about their mutual past, but rather seemed to include it, tacitly, in the present. It was obvious that, unlike so many others, including Gutiérrez, Escalante was impervious to nostalgia. A few months before, Rosemberg, somewhat maliciously, had said, *It's hard for Sergio to admit his altruism and it horrifies him that others might speculate about his thoughts and feelings. And on top of that he has a personal ethic that no force in the world could deviate even a millimeter.*

It was strange to see them walking around the courtyard, especially Escalante, carrying an enormous flashlight that early in the bright morning. Gutiérrez pointed it out: *You're like Diogenes the Cynic,* he said, *always looking for someone.* Escalante laughed and was about to bring his hand shyly to his lips to hide his ravaged teeth, but he stopped himself, possibly remembering what had happened the previous Tuesday at the fish and game club, when Gutiérrez took out his false teeth to show him that he had nothing to be ashamed of. It may have been that gesture, and not their past friendship, that had inspired the gift of the two fresh rather than frozen fish; the same gesture that confused Nula so much seemed to have an unmistakable significance for Escalante.

Gutiérrez walked him to the asphalt road, and they stood a while longer without crossing. People looked at them curiously, but they didn't notice. Every so often, Escalante would greet, not altogether demonstratively, an acquaintance passing in a car or a bus, or on foot or on horseback. They seemed used to his distracted laconism, in fact they seemed to consider it admirable.

The first to arrive, just after eleven and even before "the family," real or imaginary, are Clara and Marcos Rosemberg. They've brought two enormous *alfajores,* made, according to Marcos, that same morning. Amalia picks them up from the pavilion table and takes them to the kitchen, where they'll stay fresher. Clara and Marcos go into the house and soon return in their bathing suits and sit down in the sun, in the lounge chairs (Faustino unfolded three others around the pool, and the bright colors of the canvas reverberate in the sun), and a few minutes later Gutiérrez comes out of the house, dressed only in shorts and clogs, and sits down to talk with them alongside the large, rectangular pool in which the water, apparently motionless because no breeze is blowing, but in reality an unstable, constantly churning mass, sparkles. Not surprisingly, the first topic of conversation is the visit that Sergio Escalante paid him yesterday. Marcos considers it surprising, but Clara only smiles vaguely, or, better yet, only expands the vague and rather absent smile that, for years, whenever she's in public, she wears constantly. Her sixty-three years, though they've deeply marked the lines on her face and have partially grayed her blonde hair, haven't managed to thicken her youthful silhouette, her thin but well-shaped limbs, her flat stomach, her delicate, subtle breasts. César Rey, Marcos's best friend, while he was her lover (the only one Clara had in her life), called her *Flaca*, which is to say, Skinny. The two of them lived together in Buenos Aires for several months, but one day, El Chiche Rey drunkenly fell, or threw himself, under a train, and she came back to the city and to Marcos. They had a second son, and now devote themselves, with punctilious affection, to their grandchildren. Marcos vibrates with politics, and Clara, who before she was thirty intensely but contradictorily loved two men simultaneously, passes through life distant but friendly, smiling and calm, without anyone, anyone at all, not even Marcos, who trusts her completely, managing to know what she's really thinking. Her conversation is at once pleasant and evanescent, so much so that it can sometimes seem disjointed and even mysterious. Often what she says sounds like an intimate thought spoken aloud, as though it had escaped her. And her sense of humor is subtle but cryptic; most of the time only her own smile, and not her interlocutor's, widens. As he talks to Marcos, Gutiérrez observes her discreetly every so often: after two or three minutes, she detaches from the conversation. And suddenly, without losing her vague smile or her calm movements, she stands up slowly and, taking a few steps during which she rearranges her adolescent breasts within the top of the two-piece bathing suit of rough fabric, stops at the edge of the pool, and after a short hesitation, dives in loudly. Marcos and Gutiérrez stop speaking and watch her: emerging from the bottom, after a few seconds of blindness, she opens her eyes and shakes her head a few times; the water, altered by the dive, trembles around her, and as though she's trying to calm it, Clara falls still. Only her head and part of her shoulders rise above the water; the rest of her body remains submerged. To keep herself afloat in the deep section of the pool, without moving, Clara slowly waves her arms and legs, or better yet, what only at moments appears to have the shape of arms and legs, because the submerged portion of her body seems to have transformed into a series of shapeless, unstable blotches which the majority of the time don't even resemble human forms, shaking as what they appear to be: exaggeratedly pale, disconnected, fragmentary shapes.

The arrival of Tomatis and Violeta finds the three of them in the water. It's around noon, and Faustino has already lit the fire; with his back to everyone, he busies himself with it. Tomatis shakes a bag from the hypermarket (the W emblazoned on it is red), and shouts, with tremendous satisfaction, even before saying hello, *This is for after lunch!* but instead of revealing the contents of the bag, wraps it around the object it contains, apparently a rectangular box.

—Does it go in the fridge? Gutiérrez says, coming out of the water, intrigued.

—Not at all, Tomatis says. But somewhere cool and humid, yes. How's it going? What a beautiful morning, no?

436

Violeta arrives behind him, waving silently. Clara and Marcos come out of the pool and, following Gutiérrez, walk across the grass, against which the midday sun falls steeply, to meet them. They exchange greetings and observations but they don't touch because Violeta and Tomatis maintain a comfortable distance from the three dripping water. Suddenly they hear the engine of a car, apparently moving slowly, and when they look in that direction they see Soldi's car (Soldi's father's car, actually) parking next to Violeta's, in front of the gate. At that same moment, a man on horseback passes behind the parked cars at a slow trot and disappears behind the trees—enormous rosewoods—that border the sandy dirt road. The group pauses, waiting for the newest guests to get out of the car, cross the gate, and enter the courtyard, but, apparently remembering his duties as owner of the house, Gutiérrez advances and starts walking obsequiously toward the entrance. The arrival has produced some curiosity in Faustino as well, and he turns around and, with his back to the flames, advances a few steps, staring at the white bars of the gate. Finally, Soldi and a stranger get out of the front seat, and Gabriela Barco from the back, each one slamming their respective door. *That's José Carlos, Gabriela's friend,* Tomatis whispers to the Rosembergs, who nod their heads affirmatively, thanking him in this way for the information. At a distance, Gutiérrez and the three visitors carry on a conversation that is inaudible to those watching from the courtyard, by the swimming pool, a few steps from the grill. But everyone imagines that it's a set of conventional displays of affection, the mundane sounds to which some sacrifice is required at any party, before beginning a conversation worthy of the name. Gutiérrez hurries to open the gate and leans over to receive a quick kiss on the cheek from Gabriela before she introduces her friend, while Soldi, taking advantage of the presentation ceremony, walks around them and hurries toward the others, their motionless, unrecognizable shadows gathered at

437

their feet because of the perpendicular position of the sun, smiling, watching him.

There's not a single cloud visible in the deep blue sky, in which, surrounding the sun, impossible to look at directly, golden sparks hover. Tomatis, who imagined in the bus yesterday that it would be raining all day today, nevertheless doesn't allow himself to believe what he heard earlier on the weather report, while they were driving to Rincón, namely that by the end of the afternoon, and that night at least, the whole region would be covered with storms. Gabriela and José Carlos listen to him with an interest that isn't overly apparent. For some time, Tomatis has noticed, with considerable relief, that in José Carlos's company the adoration that Gabriela has felt for him since she was a baby is somewhat attenuated. That affective displacement allows him to relax, temporarily relinquishing his role as the infallible, sapient role model. But, curiously, when Gabriela replaces him with José Carlos, he, José Carlos, seems to grant him limitless credibility. It's now almost one, and all the guests, with the exception of Leonor, have arrived, and the three of them are the only ones in the shade, not swimming, under the trees at the back, from which they can hear the attenuated sounds of the diving and splashing and the shouts and laughter of the swimmers. Tomatis is unaware of Gabi's reason for not going in, or José Carlos's (solidarity with Gabi), though his is perfectly straightforward: he doesn't feel like getting wet, and besides, the cool shade under the trees is more pleasant than the water in the swimming pool. Also, from where they are, the smell of the cooking reaches them from time to time.

As though he were considering Tomatis's meteorological observation, José Carlos appears thoughtful. His neatly combed black hair and his black beard betray his Sicilian origins, but he's thin and tall, the mixture of blood from some genealogical branch saving him from the stereotype. He must be around forty, more or less, and his slow, almost modest gestures, his slightly faint voice, along with thinness, contrast with his taste for a generous table and for unsparing but courteous conversation. Last night, he was the one who prepared the chicken that Ángela left in the fridge, *alla cacciatore*, which is to say, sliced up in a pot with tomatoes and other vegetables and some white wine. Gabriela, entranced, watched him cook, forgetting the very existence of "Carlitos," her mentor. After eating, they'd started watching a movie on television, but they got bored before it finished and went to sleep. They're happy with the news, and though José Carlos already has two adolescent sons from his first marriage, the thought of being a father for a third time causes him a lot of pleasure, especially because he feels good with Gabriela and is sure that their relationship will last a long time, maybe for the rest of his life.

—Weather predictions depend too much on chance, he says, just to say something, trying to shore up with a more or less scientific observation the hope that it won't rain during the cookout or the week ahead.

—It's true. That's why I prefer to organize events based on a more dignified system, Tomatis says. For example, this past month it's been raining every Sunday. On other occasions, I've observed rainfall only on even days, and so on the odd days I never went out with an umbrella.

Gabriela and José Carlos laugh, and Tomatis, satisfied, allows himself a sip of white wine.

—Weather phenomena are a useful model for the universe, Gabriela says.

—The part and the whole equally unpredictable, José Carlos says.

They sit thoughtfully. The chaos of the Genesis, the primordial explosion, the ungodly rains and cyclones, and, more reasonable but no less mysterious, the Santa Rosa storm that, contradictorily, arrives punctually every August 30th, boil and churn wordlessly in their imaginations, speechless from the excessiveness of what they are forced to evoke. Though they are all standing calmly under the trees, holding a glass of cold wine, they feel trapped by the whirlwind of space that makes and unmakes events, part of which, out of habit, with an overabundance of confidence, they call their lives.

Suddenly, the sounds coming from the swimming pool are no longer heard, as though everyone had frozen and gone silent at the same moment. Instead, from some vague point, but very close by, from one of the ramshackle houses spread randomly across the fields, or possibly in one of the nearby homes, they hear the unexpected, sweet sound of a *chamamé* playing on a local radio station, like a fragment of order that they'd forgotten to include, erasing the chaos of the world with the intimate sound of the accordion.

—So that's the great corruptor of the wives of the bourgeoisie, starting with his own? It actually looks like he could use some corrupting himself, Diana whispers to Nula when she sees Riera come out of the house in shorts and stop at the edge of the pool

—You little slut, Nula says, laughing. Neither you nor the bourgeoisie have anything left to corrupt.

They're lying on the lounge chairs, drying off after their first swim. They arrived about a half an hour ago, after having dropped off the kids at La India's for the day, bringing with them six bottles of wine (two of Nula's favorite, the sauvignon blanc), something which, apparently at least, produced extreme pleasure in Gutiérrez. Nula suggested that he let them rest a couple of weeks before drinking them. Gutiérrez invited them inside to change, but they already had their swimsuits on, so they got undressed by the swimming pool and put their clothes in the large, straw bag that had contained the bottles. Diana's tiny yellow bikini, in a certain sense

440

demonstrating the aptness of medieval realism, openly displayed her godlike body, the absence of her left hand seeming to evoke the history of a dark, mythological episode. And just as they finished undressing and began walking quickly along the lawn from the white slabs around the entrance, Lucía and Riera appeared (Leonor would arrive later, on her own). Standing on the edge of the swimming pool, they greeted the people in the water—the Rosembergs, Soldi, Violeta, and Gutiérrez—walked passed the grill and exchanged a few words with Faustino, waved politely to Gabriela, José Carlos, and Tomatis, who were talking in the shade, under the pavilion, and hurried toward Diana and Nula, who were waiting for them, hesitantly, near the pool. Nula wondered how the encounter would turn out, but they reached them so quickly that he didn't have time to think up a plan. Riera kissed Diana loudly on the cheek, as did Lucía, and then they hugged Nula with the spontaneity of old friends seeing each other again after a long time. Gutiérrez, who was coming out of the swimming pool at that moment, seemed surprised to see Lucía and Riera treating Nula so intimately, and Nula, noticing his expression, told himself that it would probably cost him some effort to make sense of the scene that had taken place the previous Tuesday, when they'd found Lucía at the house after returning, under the rain, from the fish and game club with the two catfish and Lucía and pretended not to know him. *Luckily*, Nula thought, *Gutiérrez isn't someone who worries too much about the lives of others.* After that effusive introduction, Lucía and Riera followed Gutiérrez into the house, and, without saying a word, Diana and Nula dove into the blue water. While Diana swam, Nula started talking to Soldi, whose curly, black beard clumped together into pointed thickets that dripped water. After swimming a while, Diana got out of the pool to dry off on a lounge chair, and Nula followed her a couple of minutes later. They fell silent under the sun, lying in the lounge chairs, until they saw Riera come out of the house, dressed only in shorts, and because he was barefoot, and the white slabs were roasting by that time, he chose to walk along the lawn. He's now standing at the edge of the pool, smiling.

—I think it's you he's smiling at, Nula whispers, but without concealing his comment very much, and Riera realized that they were talking about him and, with a hesitant smile, approaches slowly and stops in front of them, with his back to the pool.

—What kinds of nasty things are you saying? he says.

—None, actually, Nula says. Diana was asking me if we're really in the company of the great corruptor of the wives of the bourgeoisie.

—At your service, madam, Riera says, staring at Diana. They exchange a quick, almost imperceptible smile that Nula nevertheless understands as a sign of recognition, as though they were two members of a secret society who, when they meet in public, have to perform certain ritualized gestures that only they know in order to identify each other. Or as if, after a long search, two creatures destined to find each other had met unexpectedly, recognizing each other in the act without the slightest hesitation. Though Nula believes he knows Diana deep down, a slight and momentary twinge of jealousy at once surprises and mortifies him.

—Well, he says. It's not really as bad as all that.

—I could already tell on the phone that it would be worth meeting you, Riera says.

—But, you see, Diana is incorruptible, Nula says.

—It's my primary charm, in fact, Diana says. Or am I wrong?

Nula, with considerable relief, realizes that the imperceptible smile that Diana just exchanged with Riera does imply a kind of recognition, but also a sense of defiance.

—*Incorruptible bourgeois*, Riera mutters with affected thoughtfulness. A contradiction in terms.

Nula and Diana laugh, and Riera follows with a brief cackle. Amalia comes out of the house with a platter of plates of olives, cheese, mortadella, and salami. She distributes them around the table under the pavilion, which has already been set for lunch, and turns back toward the house. Tomatis, José Carlos, and Gabriela approach the table and, in a highly educated manner, withdraw pieces of food with their fingers and bring them to their mouths. Soldi, completely wet, shaking himself off energetically to remove some of the water, comes out of the pool and stands a moment at the edge, unsure. Finally, seeing that the yellow lounge chair in which he sat on Thursday is empty, he hurries to it. From the other side of the pool, sitting in adjoining lounge chairs, Nula and his wife laugh with Doctor Riera. Soldi would like to approach, but he prefers to watch the scene from a distance, especially because Gabi has gestured warmly from the pavilion, where she talks with José Carlos and Tomatis, and, if he gets up now, he ought to walk over to them.

—An oxymoron. Like saying *cold fire*, Nula says after he manages to contain himself.

—An oxy-what? Riera says, alarmed.

—Nothing a man of science would understand, Nula says, with feigned condescension.

They laugh again. It's the easy, expressive, and vaguely complicitous laughter that, as usual, the immediate affection for Riera, product of his physical presence and his spontaneous and tempestuous friendliness, creates in everyday interactions, and not only with women. Amalia comes out of the house again with a bottle of wine and an ice bucket, and behind her, carrying identical objects, Lucía and Gutiérrez appear. This arrival produces a subtle but unmistakable euphoria among the guests: the appetizers were merely a preface of the start of the feast that the procession of the three wine-bearers signals in earnest. For now, the guests, scattered around the pool, inside it, or under the pavilion, will serve themselves a glass of wine and pick at something from the plates at their own pace, until the announcement that the cookout is ready will gather them around the table, which has already been set. With a vague gesture, and in a very loud voice, Gutiérrez encourages his guests to serve themselves from the table, and though no one seems to pay any attention to him, as soon as he disappears into the house, José Carlos, Gabriela, and Tomatis each serve themselves a glass of wine and eat avidly from the plates, this time using toothpicks arranged in glass jars to pick at the cubes of cheese or mortadella, the salami slices or the oval-shaped green and black olives. Though he isn't much of a drinker, Soldi looks curiously at the table from his yellow lounge chair, but doesn't make a move to stand. The Rosembergs and Violeta are talking in the water, at the shallow end of the pool, and Nula is too busy with Diana and Riera, and somewhat too anxious in fact, to think about eating just now, and his anxiety heightens when he sees Lucía, rather than following Gutiérrez and Amalia back into the house, walking toward them and stopping next to Riera.

—It's so great to see you, she says with a happiness that is paradoxical, given that it's the first time in her life that she sees Diana, and that, five days before, in front of Gutiérrez, she'd pretended not to know who Nula was.

Nula is confused, and even somewhat worried. Lucía's dependence on Riera could motivate her, with the hope of recovering him, to exceed her husband's allusions and ostensibly humorous insinuations, especially with regard to their encounter Wednesday afternoon in Paraná. But after her excessive comment, Lucía falls silent and her expression turns serious and slightly disoriented, and Nula's alarm takes on a hint of shame and compassion. It seems to him that Lucía is more lost in the world than she was the morning he first saw her, dressed in red, when he started following her, eventually penetrating her aura, and Riera's, for months and months. He sees them from the outside now, and though they don't

444

seem much different, he interprets their words and actions in a way that seems more reasonable to him, though he's unsure if it's more accurate. Diana, meanwhile, smiles, urbane and expectant. *I'm going to help Amalia with the salads*, Lucía says finally, and with the gentle suddenness typical to her, she steps around Riera and heads to the kitchen.

—Should we go for a swim? Riera says.

—Why not? Diana says, getting up, and, without saying a word, Nula does the same. They move slowly and lazily toward the deep end of the pool and then, loudly, first Riera and then Diana and finally Nula, they dive in. For several seconds they move under the transparent water that transforms their solid bodies into fragmentary, unstable, inhuman blurs, but when their heads and shoulders emerge, though their faces are wrinkled, their hair disheveled and stuck to their head, and their eyes squeezed shut to keep the water from entering them, they recover a vaguely human appearance, as if the disintegration threatening from below lost efficacy on the surface, even though traces of its corrosive action, capable of deconstructing both the material and the illusion of reality, will linger for several seconds. And the three of them laugh, carefree, happy to be in the water where, paddling skillfully, they stay afloat and come together, in the middle of the pool.

Soldi, from the yellow lounge chair, watches José Carlos, Gabriela, and Tomatis, who, after picking at a few things on the plates distributed over the table, each serve themselves a glass of white wine and, walking slowly, leave the pavilion and head once again toward the back of the courtyard. Soldi follows them with his eyes until they stop under the trees and, turning around and observing from their position the house, the courtyard, the pavilion, and the pool all together, they begin to talk. They must be very far back, in the shade; he, on the other hand, lying lazily in the yellow lounge chair, feels the sun, which has dried him completely in a few minutes, causing the skin on his stomach to itch, and making him drowsy.

The operation seems complicated, but for Diana it's easy: she does it several times a day with a variety of similar artifacts each designed for a different function, and though some in the group consider it polite to pretend they don't see her, whether or not they do doesn't matter to Diana or Nula; it consists, simply, of strapping a leather wristband to her left arm, over which a metal hoop, probably of stainless steel, is attached, and which extends into the shape of a fork. Once this maneuver is carried out, Diana, just as casually, picks up the glass into which Nula, with affectionate deference, has just poured a considerable quantity of white wine, and takes a long drink. Across from her, on the other side of the table, Soldi wonders whether it wouldn't have been better to sit down to eat with the prosthetic already in place, but eventually he decides that to Diana it must seem more natural to put it on in front of everyone.

Before sitting down at the table, the bathers, after drying themselves off with a few minutes of exposure to the sun, have gotten dressed again, the men in a shirt or an undershirt and the women in their light dresses, easy to take on and off, and which they now wear over their one- or two-piece swimsuits. Though Faustino announced the cookout several minutes ago, and all of the guests including Amalia are sitting at the table, the two empty seats, one next to the other, delay the service for a few moments. A taxi has just stopped in front of the white gate without turning off its engine, and Gutiérrez has hurried outside to meet Leonor Calcagno. Walking slowly, they cross the gate and, with a satisfied look, turn toward the table. Just as he was that Friday night at the Hotel Palace restaurant, Nula is once again astonished at the fragility that radiates from Leonor's body, from her arms and legs, scrawny and blackened by the sun and by tanning lamps, from her face, ravaged, along with her chest and buttocks, in all likelihood, by surgeries as useless as they have been recurrent, from her reddish dyed hair, from her upper lip, swollen from an injection of silicone; her skeletal fingers, almost as black, are covered with rings, her wrists with bracelets, and several fantasy necklaces attempt to conceal the recalcitrant wrinkles on her neck. And yet, despite the impression of fragility, Leonor moves with a litheness that suggests an indifference to her surroundings, and when they reach the pavilion, her free hand (in her other hand she carries a white purse that matches her white dress and her white, high-heeled sandals, made of chunky jute, and knotted around her ankles) lifts to her head to straighten her hair, and she offers a distant smile when Gutiérrez, raising his voice, presents her to his guests:

—For those who don't know her, Mrs. Leonor Calcagno! and he makes a quick and vaguely circular gesture with which he attempts to encompass the large, rectangular table. The others offer a variety of conventional responses that no one hears because, in being spoken all at once, they annihilate each other. Amalia, who is sitting at the end of the table closest to the house, starts to get up, but Gutiérrez, shaking his head, tells her with a friendly look that it's not necessary. The two empty chairs are just to the left of Amalia, and Gutiérrez invites Leonor to sit next to her, while he occupies the other empty chair. Marcos and Clara Rosemberg are sitting across from them; Marcos leans over the table, standing up slightly from his chair, and, grabbing Leonor's free hand, gives it a quick squeeze. Next to Clara is Soldi, who's sitting next to Gabriela, who's next to José Carlos, who's next to Violeta. The opposite end of the table, at the back of the pavilion, is occupied by Tomatis, who's to the left of Lucía, who's next to Riera, who's next to Diana, who's next to Nula, who's next to Gutiérrez, who's next to Leonor. The only one standing is Faustino, next to the grill, tending the meat and the offal that are browning over the fire, and on a tiled side table that extends from the grill, which is separated from the coals and the reserve fire by a short wall, he has a plate already prepared, a dish of salad that Amalia brought him, and a half-full glass of white wine. Suddenly, with a long fork in one hand and a substantial knife in the other, he turns, his face flushed and his graying beard matted with sweat, and, in a solemn and professional tone, whose irony is not lost on any of the guests, he asks:

—Ready, don Willi? Shall we proceed?

Half standing up, with parodic gravity, offering a gesture of consent, Gutiérrez responds:

—You may proceed, don Faustino.

Electrified by the mini-farce they have just attended, the audience breaks into applause. (Diana clinks her metal fork against the edge of her plate and Leonor Calcagno merely hints at a few silent claps with her bony hands that resemble little blackbirds' feet.) Browning on top of the generously proportioned, and for now, entirely covered grilling surface, are strings of chorizo and blood sausage, equally crisp spirals and tubes of chitterlings and tripe, golden clusters of whole sweetbreads, split kidneys protected by their own grease, and three long and wide strips of ribs, which have already been cooked on low heat on the bone side, display it now while the meat receives its share of the fire in order to reach the proper level of doneness. Given that their passage over the fire is a simple formality, the blood sausage is the first thing served, followed by the chorizos, and Faustino cuts a number of each on a dish, with the number of guests in mind—fifteen including himself—and then passes the dish to them, starting with Violeta, the one closest to the grill, while those sitting nearby take the opportunity to serve themselves as well. One inconsistent detail in the bountiful table calls Soldi's attention: the asceticism of the salads. Being in love with celery, grated carrots, radishes, and beets, he's intrigued that at the table of Gutiérrez, with such an imposing cookout, there're only two kinds of salads that, while certainly of an abundant quantity, are unquestionably monotonous: mixed greens and chicory with a dash of chopped garlic. And suddenly he realizes that it reveals a conservative purism on Gutiérrez's part, a bookish purism to which even the two classic salads might seem like a concession, because he considers the colorful plethora of complex salads an urban corruption that betrays the original asceticism of the cookout. *He seeks an imaginary perfection in everything, not realizing that the myths he yearned for over those thirty years had changed, eroded by contingency, while he was away,* Soldi tells himself.

The first minutes of the lunch, with the exception of a few approving comments meant to bolster the satisfaction of the cook, transpire in silence. Gutiérrez, chewing a bite of food, stands up suddenly and walks to the small room attached to the pavilion, where the gardening supplies along with every species of tool and maintenance product are kept. From where he's sitting, Nula sees through the open door that it also contains a small, supplementary fridge meant to prevent unnecessary trips to the house, from which Gutiérrez removes a few bottles, with which he returns to the table; they're three bottles of cabernet sauvignon that he himself sold Gutiérrez, and that he put to cool, already uncorked, in the fridge. Gutiérrez distributes them around the table and sits back down between Nula and Leonor.

—Red! Just what I'd been missing! Violeta declaims, adopting a masculine and undeniably vulgar tone, making three or four people laugh or smile, Clara Rosemberg among them, unless her smile has been caused by some intimate stimulus, memory, or association. Violeta matches her words with actions and immediately throws back the rest of the white wine that was in her glass and, grabbing a bottle of red, serves herself generously. Then she puts down the bottle, picks up the glass, and tastes the wine.

—It's cold, beautiful, she says.

Simultaneously, Nula, whose glass is empty, serves himself a glass of red from the second bottle, without serving the people around him first because they still have white wine in theirs. Nula takes a drink and puts the glass back on the table. *He knows how to handle wine,* he thinks. *It must be over thirty today, and this red should be consumed at fifteen or sixteen, so it needs to be kept longer in the fridge, given that the bottles will be on the table a while, which means that they need to be colder than they otherwise should be because the temperature of the wine will increase as it comes into contact with the outside air. And that's what he did.* As though guessing his thoughts, Gutiérrez, gesturing to the glass with a movement of his head, asks him:

—How is it?

—Exactly how it should be, and it'll improve over the next few minutes, Nula says.

—Your professional opinion is very reassuring, Gutiérrez says with a calculated modesty that Nula takes as a gesture of deference. And then, after a moment of silence, leaning closer, confidentially: And how's the metaphysics coming along?

—Always both more and less arduous than the sale of wine, Nula says after thinking it over a second.

Nodding, Gutiérrez issues one of those loud and open peals of laughter, uncommon from him, that tends to produce curiosity and even, out of sympathy, laughter among those who hear it. Everyone sitting around the table looks at him with expectant surprise, hoping for an explanation, but when Gutiérrez, with a negative gesture of his hand signals that he won't offer one, they return to their conversations. Nula, who didn't think that his mundane comment would cause such a visible impact, smiles, satisfied, though slightly disoriented by the man sitting to his right, Willi Gutiérrez, who seems to him, as he sees him more frequently, deserving of friendship of course, but increasingly incomprehensible and strange. His laughter just now, disproportionate to the comment, seems to reveal a certain familiarity not only with metaphysics, but also with the consciousness of what's necessarily abandoned in order to survive in life. *What must have been the parabola traced by his life from the town north of Tostado to Rome and Geneva to make him who he is today, and who really is the person who he appears to be? What strange people he and his oldest friends and Lucía's mother are!* Next to him, Diana is talking to Riera, and no one is paying attention to him now, but when he sees Soldi scrutinizing him openly from across the table, Nula realizes that he must guess what he's thinking about. Their eyes meet and Soldi nods very slowly, and it seems to Nula that his dark eyes display a conniving smile.

With the wine and the food, the conversation is electrified. After the blood sausage and the chorizo, Faustino serves the offal and switches, in turn, from white wine to red, under Amalia's reproving gaze from the other end of the table, which Nula glimpses quickly. The conversations move, in loud voices, from one end of the table to the other, or are whispered among neighbors, and are punctuated frequently with exclamations and laughter. Everyone seems content, if not happy, with the possible exception of Leonor, who, preoccupied with her appearance, repeatedly takes a mirror from the white purse hanging from the back of her chair and touches up her makeup, fixing the places she thinks need it. No one seems to notice her, but Nula is sure that many of them watch her disapprovingly. When the meat is ready, Faustino asks each of the guests the ritual question: *Well done or juicy?* And when Tomatis enthusiastically replies *Juicy*, Soldi's voice rings out, droning sententiously as though in an echolalic fit, *Juicy immanence, the universe incarnate*, which causes Gabriela, Violeta, and Tomatis to laugh, along with Gutiérrez, at the other end of the table, who looks at him, surprised.

Although Diana seems to be intensely concentrated on the conversation with Riera, her right hand places the knife on the edge of the plate and, sliding it under the table, she grabs Nula's left thigh, and he in turn reaches down and grabs her hand. Their fingers remain interlaced for several seconds, and the few quick squeezes they give each other seem to signal the ratification of a secret complicity that persists despite their mundane obligations. Then Diana's hand releases his, reappears on the table, and picks up the knife; not once has she picked up her head to look at him, nor has she interrupted for a single instant her conversation with Riera. Lucía, meanwhile, is talking to Tomatis about the majestic look of the river when seen from the hills above Paraná, while Violeta is in an exchange with José Carlos about the architecture in Rosario. It may be the food, the proximity of the fire, the intensity of the conversation, and in particular the hour of the siesta, and while the shade of the pavilion protects them, their sweaty faces have lost a good portion of the freshness that they displayed that morning, and though the wine must also have contributed to their exhaustion, the alcohol's artificial energy paradoxically redoubles, in all of them, their enthusiasm. Nula observes its effects among the guests: their faces glow from the sweat, and their eyes from the wine that burns in their intense and alert gazes. Amalia brings out three more bottles of red wine from the room attached to the pavilion and distributes them around the table, and, from the kitchen, she brings a dish of salad. For most of the time, she's been talking to the Rosembergs and watching her husband, who, because of the wine, is speaking more and in a slightly higher register than usual, something which seems to cause Gutiérrez a great deal of satisfaction; it may not only be the wine, but also the familiar atmosphere oozing from the gathering that provokes Faustino's expansiveness. Even Leonor, who hardly speaks, not even to Gutiérrez, seems to feel at ease at the table. Gabriela, who's discussing the provincial avant-garde with Soldi, as they've been doing for months, in a low voice, smiles enigmatically, which causes Soldi to give her an inquisitive look, but Gabriela shakes her head, signaling that she won't say anything: because Soldi doesn't know that she's pregnant, it would be difficult to explain to him that what made her smile was the thought that the other guests must have thought that she wasn't swimming because she had her period, when in reality the complete opposite was the case.

Suddenly, interrupting her conversation with José Carlos, Violeta takes a Polaroid camera from the bag lying at her feet and, standing behind the table, turns toward Faustino and asks him to pose next to the grill, which Faustino agrees to with intense pleasure. After preparing her shot, Violeta takes the photograph, and the camera, with its characteristic sounds, produces through a horizontal slot across its base the print which Violeta removes and extends to Tomatis, who shakes it gently as it dries, glancing every so often at the faded image until eventually he stands up and puts it in his pocket so that the darkness that reigns there will accelerate its development. Gutiérrez, at the other end of the table, stands up just as Violeta is preparing to take a photo of the whole table. Crossing the lawn with a quick step and then continuing along the white slab path, while the Polaroid starts to develop the second photograph, Gutiérrez disappears into the house. A moment later, the second print appears in the slot and Violeta, withdrawing it, extends it to Tomatis, who starts shaking it while with his free hand he withdraws the first one from his pocket, examines it, and, smiling with satisfaction, shows it to Faustino, who looks at it briefly and then hands it to Violeta. The color image passes from hand to hand, and each guest, more or less attentively, gazes at it, studies it, interrogates it perhaps, marveling, after having lived it a minute before through the confusion of their limited senses within the intricate network of the event, at the sight of an infinitesimally thin cross-section of time on that glossy paper square. When Tomatis finally takes it from his pocket and passes it around the table, the second photograph produces and even greater effect than the first: every one of the guests recognizes themselves in it while simultaneously rejecting themselves, resenting the image that differs so harshly from the one that, a minute earlier, idealized by a kind of credulity, they'd had inside. Everyone is looking at the camera except Gutiérrez, who, with his back to it, in the background, behind Amalia's erect head, is on his way to the kitchen.

Violeta takes several more photos from various positions, as if she were hoping to reconstruct the multidimensional totality of the courtyard through those one-dimensional fragments. Because Gutiérrez is taking a long time to come back, Tomatis asks for the camera in order to surprise him the moment he reappears outside, but when, after a couple of minutes, he finally does, Gutiérrez is holding a video camera and is already filming the table of guests, and when Tomatis presses the shutter release, the two men capture each other reciprocally, which produces a possibly excessive outburst at the table, more a result of the wine than the actual comedy of the scene. While Tomatis withdraws the print, shakes it momentarily, and then puts it in his pocket, Gutiérrez approaches the table, still filming, and walks down the length of it, focusing on each person, and then, passing behind Tomatis's empty chair, films the other side as he walks back to the other end. *He'll keep us embalmed in his video tapes, in the office he calls the machine room, the same way he kept embalmed for over thirty years the memory of his youth and everything his youth represented*, Soldi thinks, and, though he's unsure why, a faint but unbearable and devastating sense of pity for Gutiérrez, for himself, for the whole universe, seizes him.

When he reaches the head of the table, Gutiérrez passes behind Amalia and starts backing up, still filming, to capture the gathering at the table again, moving away, panning out, until finally, when he's several meters from the pavilion, in the middle of the courtyard, he stops, lowers the camera, which had hidden his face, and

454

because the demands of the filming had caused him to be slightly hunched over, he straightens up, displaying a satisfied smile. From the pavilion, Tomatis, taking advantage of Gutiérrez's distraction and his isolation in the middle of the courtyard, at the right distance for the camera to capture his whole body, lifts the camera to his face, closing his left eye and resting his right against the eyepiece, but when he presses the release there's no reaction from the machine, empty because the ten prints on the roll have been used up. Attempting to disguise the catastrophe, feeling slightly ridiculous, Tomatis lowers the camera, not realizing that Nula, from the table, has seen what happened and is grinning mockingly, and then returns to the other end of the table, puts the camera back in Violeta's bag as he passes, and lets himself fall into his chair.

No one serves themselves any more meat, though there's still a full strip left on the grill, along with some chorizos and blood sausage. Considering the cookout finished, Faustino stacks everything on the edge of the grill so that it doesn't overcook while staying warm in case someone changes their mind and decides to take another piece. But a short while later, seeing that no one seems to want another round, he removes the leftovers from the grill and arranges them on a dish. Amalia stands up and starts to clear the table, and, seeing her, Violeta and Clara Rosemberg do the same, and the three women walk in a line toward the kitchen and disappear into the house. Diana removes the prosthetic fork, keeping the leather wristband in place, and sets it on the table, and Nula, without hesitating, picks it up along with an empty salad dish and its corresponding wood utensils, walks across the courtyard, and disappears into the house. As he walks away, Gabriela, discreetly watching his movements, thinks, *He must love her very much, unless he reserves that deference exclusively for the public.* But, though she doesn't know why, she hates herself for the cruelty of the thought; she took a dislike to him because of an absurd dream in which

455

Nula served her a live fish as a mean joke, when the poor guy isn't at all responsible for her dream. Gabriela forgets that her antipathy preceded the dream, and that when they were talking between the cars, when they were on their way back from lunch at Gutiérrez's and he was on his way there to drop off some cases of wine, she was already bothered by his over-confident womanizer attitude. But Gabriela immediately forgets Nula and remembers that Thursday afternoon, the blue sky after the rain the led up to it, and the giant, bright white masses of scattered clouds that seemed motionless but which by the afternoon, when she was walking to the Amigos del Vino bar, had already disappeared.

Nula comes out of the house before the women, bringing Diana's fork, now washed and dried, and walks to the large, straw bag, where they'd carried the wine and where he's kept his neatly folded pants (he put his shirt back on before sitting down at the table), and from which he now takes a long cardboard box containing two or three metal prostheses with various functions, and puts the fork in it. The bag also contains a sketch pad and a box of colored pencils that Diana always carries with her whenever she travels or goes out the countryside for an afternoon or attends an unusual event, and which could be considered her tools, visual rather than textual, for taking notes. Just then, of the three women in the house, Violeta is the first to come out: she carries a rag to clean the table and a stack of dessert plates, and almost immediately, following her closely, Clara appears with another stack of plates, and when Violeta finishes cleaning the table and starts distributing the plates, Clara does the same with hers, placing on each of them a small desert fork that clinks faintly against the white china. Tomatis signals to Violeta, who leans in to hear what he whispers to her, and when Tomatis finishes speaking, Violeta nods in a way that makes her look like an obedient young girl, and goes back inside. Before she walks in, she steps aside for Amalia, who's carrying the two *alfajores.* Marcos, in a serious tone, says, *They're from this morning,* pointing when Amalia places them, one next to the other, in the middle of the table. They're wrapped in white paper that for now Amalia does not unwrap. And, directing himself to the table at large, with the same seriousness of his first qualification, Marcos adds, *They couldn't be any fresher.* Amalia returns to the house, but when she's about to go inside she has to step aside, exactly like Violeta had to do several moments before in order to let her pass, thinks Tomatis, who watches them from the end of the table, and who was watching the door with some anxiety, asking himself if Violeta had found what he'd sent her in the house to look for, smiling with relief when he sees her come out of the house with the supermarket bag emblazoned with the red W that corresponds to the meat section and which contains the mysterious object that Violeta hands over discreetly when she reaches Tomatis, who places it carefully on the corner of the table, between himself and Lucía. Finally, Amalia comes out of the house with a special knife and a cake spatula that, as she moves across the courtyard toward the pavilion along the white slabs and then the grass, catches the sun.

Clara and Violeta sit down in their respective seats, and when Amalia reaches the table Gutiérrez asks her for the knife and the spatula and, getting to his feet with an elaborate bow, extends them to Clara Rosemberg; without hesitating a second, Clara receives them and, after Soldi pushes the *alfajores* to her from the center of the table, she picks them up delicately, places them side-by-side, and unwraps them extremely slowly, revealing two bright white circles fifty centimeters in diameter and six or seven thick. The entire surface is covered in a fragile shell of frosted sugar, and when the knife begins to cautiously slice more or less equivalent segments from the circle, neither the three layers of dough separated by a dulce de leche filling nor the solidified white bath that covers the cracks, indisputable proof, as though anyone would doubt the word

457

of Marcos Rosemberg, of their freshness. Clara places the segments of the circle on the white plates as they are passed to her, and these then move between hands until they reach the seat of their intended recipients. After serving the last slice—there are still four or five pieces of the second *alfajor* left—Clara sits down and, after checking to make sure that she hasn't forgotten anyone, starts to eat her own.

—It's time, Tomatis says after they've finished eating the dessert and an indecisive silence has settled on the table. Opening the plastic bag, he takes out a large box of Romeo y Julieta cigars, his favorite brand, and tearing off the sticker that holds it closed, he lifts the lid and extends the box to José Carlos, who exults at the neat rows of thick cigars before picking one and passing the box to Soldi, who examines them quickly, curiously, before giving the box to Clara Rosemberg. Clara and Marcos study the contents and take out a second cigar. The box passes around the table to Gutiérrez, who seems ecstatic over the situation, and after looking admiringly at the rows of cigars, passes the open box to Nula without serving himself. Nula, studying the box, feigns a look of skepticism, which creates a degree of anticipation at the table, until finally, still scrutinizing the cigars suspiciously, he says loudly, *Che, Tomatis, they swindled you—this box is full of Romeos!* General laughter receives the joke and the box continuous its course, without stopping, to Tomatis, who offers it to Faustino, who rejects it emphatically, shouting, *I don't smoke!* Tomatis takes a cigar for himself, closes the box, puts it back in the plastic hypermarket bag to protect it from the heat, and leaves it on the table.

José Carlos smokes a cigar alone, but Tomatis and Violeta, Clara and Marcos Rosemberg smoke it in pairs: they pass it back and forth every so often, pulling slowly and loudly, and then return it. Clara narrows her eyes, apparently concentrating, before every pull, and discharges mouthfuls of thick, gray smoke into the warm afternoon air, while Marcos regularly checks the fire at the end. All of them, with the exception of Tomatis, are occasional smokers, what you might call *enthusiasts,* but, under the circumstances, their pleasure is apparently authentic. They are, in fact, happy under that pavilion, outside that house, with that company and that singular host who disappeared from the city one day without telling anyone and reappeared, for good it seems, some thirty years later, with the same economy of explanations as when he left. A gentle mutual acceptance, a surrender to the moment, allows them an unexpected sense of well-being, removing them from the internal murmur, the solitary rumination, that fills the hours of the day, allowing them to find in the external, like a momentary source of relief, an interesting and pleasurable life, if only for a few moments, in the exceptionally hot April Sunday that gives them the illusion of living in an endless vacation. The wine, in particular, has contributed to that sensation, and now the cigars provide the moment with a meditative perfection. Their words are slower, more carefully thought out than usual, and private conversations have disappeared in favor of a collective attention to which anyone who speaks directs themselves. Everyone hopes for something interesting from the others, not a revelation so much as a story, a well-turned series of events that lead to an unexpected conclusion, to a surprising and unforeseen situation, filling the colorlessness of time with a bright glow as they're recorded by the imagination, settling like a layer of sediment in a glass of wine in their at once receptive and deceitful memories. And suddenly, Violeta begins: after taking a pull from the cigar, she hands it back to Tomatis, and while she exhales the smoke she says that during the dictatorship, during the terror, when fear, disgust, randomness, cruelty, and pain occupied everything, in the middle of the contempt and the killing, things happened that were simultaneously agonizing and comical, so absurd sometimes that they ended up being hilarious. Because at that time the military

459

was hunting out so-called subversive books, people were forced to scatter their libraries, burning or burying suspicious books in the backs of their courtyards. One night she was having dinner at the house of a studious but incredibly naive colleague, and when she commented on a set of books covered in brightly colored striped paper he'd explained to her that they were among the books considered subversive at the time and that he'd covered them like that so if the police came they wouldn't be able to read what was written on their spines. *Good idea, wasn't it?* Tomatis adds to reinforce the effect of Violeta's story, intending to make it more humorous to its recipients. Several people laugh, and Faustino, impatient to tell his own story but somewhat inhibited by the size of his audience and the anxious gaze of Amalia who, from the other end of the table, seems to fear an incongruous comment from her husband, refers to some neighbors in La Toma, public servants who one afternoon were taking some fresh air at their window when they saw a caravan of Ford Falcons, from whose open windows extended the barrels of machine guns, coming down the street, which prompted the woman to say to her husband that they must be looking for someone and that they must be making a raid, and since they weren't guilty of anything they remained sitting calmly in the window. But it was their house that they were coming to. Twelve men got out, all armed, and entered the house, but they didn't touch anything, they simply wanted to terrorize them, and by the next week the couple was already in Barcelona. After the dictatorship they returned, and they still laugh when they remember what the woman said, and tell it to their friends, *They must be making a raid,* and, according to Faustino, *it turned out that they were coming to theirs.*

Amalia relaxes, and Faustino, still excited by the success of his story, collapses into his chair, satisfied. And then Marcos Rosemberg interjects from the other end of the table, using the cigar as a kind of pointer with which he underscores his words. He once had to go to some military official—a sort of legal advisor to General Negri who had the rank of colonel, celebrated for his bad faith and his dangerousness and his evil nature in particular—to get some information about a disappearance. The colonel asked him in and ordered him to sit down on the other side of the desk, and without speaking to him again he continued doodling on a paper for several minutes, deliberately forcing him to wait as a way to assert his authority. He finally looked up and gave him a studied look somewhere between inquisitive and severe, and so he, Marcos, started to inform him that he was there as an attorney, trying to get some information on the whereabouts of someone who'd disappeared three days ago, but the colonel, pounding the table, shouted that no one had disappeared in the country, only subversives who'd fled abroad to escape justice and that to pretend otherwise amounted to an insult to the armed forces and to the government. The problem was that, with the violence of the punch that he'd given to the desk, his wig had shifted slightly on his head, and his supposed assertion of authority was contradicted by the incongruence of the poorly pasted wig against his scalp. Drunk on his own words, the colonel continued to pontificate and threaten, but Marcos wasn't listening any more, and was instead making a tremendous effort not to start laughing, fearing, simultaneously, that if the colonel's state of excitement didn't subside his wig would fall off his head, and as the situation continued, it became increasingly obvious to Marcos that if the colonel realized it, *he was a dead man, he'd never walk out to the street again.* And so, in the middle of the colonel's speech he stood up, making to leave, muttering that they'd never see eye-to-eye, but with two energetic strides the colonel walked around the desk and stopped thirty centimeters from his face, giving him the most threatening look available in his repertory. But with his sudden movements the wig had shifted even more and was now almost hanging over his left ear. Split between laughter and fear,

Marcos decided to exaggerate his fear, thinking that if he didn't manage to contain himself and started to laugh the colonel would think it was out of nervousness. Suddenly the colonel gave him his most underhanded insult, addressing him as *tú*, and shouted, *You'll walk out that door or it'll cost you dearly!* and Marcos turned toward the door just as the first wave of laughter started to shake him, just like a retching before vomiting, and the colonel, seeing him from behind, must have thought that he was shaking so much out of terror, and ratcheting up his insults as Marcos was crossing the doorway, he muttered, *Bolshevik shitbag!* But Marcos continued laughing, so much so that the soldier who was on guard, without knowing the reason, started laughing too, infected by it. And when he got in his car and started driving along the waterfront toward his house and remembered that the colonel had called him a *Bolshevik* even though he hadn't been a communist for years, because he'd become a socialist, he told himself that, for a security agent, he seemed very poorly informed, and this detail redoubled his laughter, though he didn't know, ultimately, if his laughter was humorous or nervous.

Now it was José Carlos's turn. He'd also lived through an experience that was at once hilarious and agonizing. Like many other members of the university, students, staff, professors, he'd received several threats over the telephone, and at first he hadn't taken them seriously, until someone told him that some army commandos were looking for him, and that he would be kidnapped, and he was forced to leave the city and go to Buenos Aires, where it would be easier than in Rosario for him to go unnoticed. A friend loaned him an apartment in an isolated neighborhood, and to avoid being recognized he decided to change his appearance: he shaved his beard, dyed his hair blonde, and changed his hairstyle. He also dressed differently, less formally, more in keeping with the current fashion, but in a subdued way so as to not call too much attention to himself. When José Carlos says that he dyed his hair blonde, there's laughter among the listeners, and Gabriela grabs his arm, smiling tenderly, and rests her head on his shoulder. It's clear that she's heard the story many times before, but his past troubles, though she enjoys hearing about them, knowing the ending already, also move her because of the real danger he faced during those dark times. Almost immediately she releases José Carlos's arm and sits back up in her seat. And José Carlos continues: during a February siesta, when the heat was unbearable, because he was drowning in his friend's apartment, he decided to sit a while under the trees of a nearby plaza, where it would be cooler. Though he never went out, while he was in Rosario, without a suit and tie, he put on a sleeveless shirt, what people call a *muscle shirt*, board shorts, and sandals, and picked up a leather satchel and went out into the street. He thought that the long, curly blonde hair, his summer tan, and his lack of a beard would make him impossible to recognize, but as he was walking into the plaza, which was practically deserted at that hour, he saw a man sitting on a bench near the corner, watching him openly, but hesitant, unsure if he knew him or not. When he was approaching the bench, José Carlos recognized him immediately: it was a staff member of the department in Rosario, who hadn't seemed very trustworthy to him, and who must have been passing through Buenos Aires. He tried to act nonchalant as he passed him, but feeling the other man scrutinizing him, trying to decide if it was or wasn't the assistant professor of economics whom he saw every day at school. Rather than sitting on a bench as he'd imagined he would, José Carlos continued across the plaza at a diagonal, but before disappearing down an adjacent street he turned around visibly and saw that the man had stood up alongside the bench and continued to watch him, intrigued.

He felt finished. For a while he went outside as little as possible, and, of course, he never went back to that plaza again. A few months later, thanks to the intervention of the Italian embassy, which had given him and many other descendants of Italians dual citizenship, he was able to travel and he moved to Milan. One day, a colleague from Rosario came to visit him and he told him the story. But the colleague, laughing, told José Carlos that he already knew it, because the staff member at the department had told everyone that one day, completely by accident, during a vacation in Buenos Aires, he'd found out that José Carlos was a homosexual.

José Carlos's classic and immaculate professorial appearance, almost severe in contrast to the picture the listeners have of the bleached blonde and shaggy man in sandals, carrying a handbag, his legs and shoulders exposed, is probably what provokes the widespread laughter, causing Riera to strike the edge of the table with the palm of his hand, Nula and Marcos Rosemberg to double over in their respective seats, Gutiérrez to remark on the story to Leonor Calcagno, and for the rest of them to revel in the story long after it is finished. Only Tomatis, who'd heard it before, smiles thoughtfully. Suddenly, in a spark of clairvoyance, he realizes why they are together, gathered around the table, relaxed and happy, because, he thinks, no one among them believes that the world belongs to them. They all know that they are apart from the human swarm deluded into thinking that it knows where it's going, and that separation does not paralyze them, just the opposite, it actually seems to satisfy them. Every one of them, not to mention the owner of the house, who guards an impenetrable mystery behind his forehead, insists on being something other than what's expected of them: the wine seller, for instance, who aspires to be a philosopher, or Soldi, the son of privilege who, rather than taking over the family business, prefers to take an interest in literature, or Marcos and Clara Rosemberg, who have been glued together for over thirty years despite the fact that she left him for their best friend and only returned after he threw himself under a train, and he, who'd let her go without a

464

fight, received her with open arms when she decided to return to him. Or the girl with the stump whose remarkable beauty had been marred before she was even born by that conspicuous deformity to keep her perfection and radiance from overshadowing the goddess after whom she was named. Or the strange woman sitting next to Gutiérrez, whom he came back to the city for and who was no doubt a goddess to many in the past, and who, from an obsession with her supernal past, mutilates herself more every day in the vain hope of recovering it. And myself, who has been given the head of the table at this feast of the displaced as though coincidentally. Tomatis, within the slow smoke of the cigar, lets himself get tangled up in his thoughts, and suddenly an affection tinged with admiration for the people sitting at the table overcomes him: they're right to be the way they are, apart from the crowd, flying solitarily in the empty sky, their destination uncertain, their delirium as their only compass, with no determined path to track along. And while it's true that the ones who will one day wake the drowsy masses have walked among them for long stretches, it's no less true that the ones who live at its margin, sometimes without even knowing it, are the most justified to judge it; they're fodder for their own delirium, it's true, but they're also the color of the world.

Their arrivals were scattered, on their own or in small groups or pairs until the lunch gathered them under the pavilion, and now that the long meal has finished they scatter again across the courtyard or into the house. Gutiérrez and Leonor, along with the Rosembergs, have gone inside; Diana is sitting in a white lawn chair, sketching, under an umbrella that Gutiérrez himself set up so she could work in the shade; Riera and Nula are talking, still at the table, which has been cleared and cleaned completely by Clara, Violeta, and Amalia. After putting out the flames and cleaning the grill and taking the leftovers from the cookout to the large fridge, Faustino has disappeared; he's actually sleeping a siesta in the shade, under a tree, an activity similar to what Tomatis is doing, lying on the lawn, under a tree, his head resting on Violeta's thighs, her back resting, in turn, against the truck of a tree. José Carlos, Gabriela, and Soldi are talking on the bench at the back, and Lucía is playing in the swimming pool's blue water, moving almost without making a sound. For now, she's the only one not seeking the shade, but Diana hadn't intended to either, and if Gutiérrez hadn't set up the umbrella she would have continued sketching with her pencils, lost in her work, the afternoon heat forgotten. After setting up the umbrella, Gutiérrez glanced at the pad of paper on which Diana was sketching: there were fourteen blotches of color in an oval arrangement, plus one, the fifteenth, in which the color orange predominated, somewhat separated from the rest; the blotches, despite their abstraction, could vaguely suggest human shapes. Diana, realizing that Gutiérrez was looking at the sketch, explained, without looking up, *It's your guests sitting around the table. The different colors represent each person's main qualities.* Gutiérrez shook his head, asking, at the same time, *And that orange blotch is the fire?* Diana, still sketching, explained, *No, that's the owner of the house.* Gutiérrez asked again, intrigued, *And why the orange?* And this time, Diana, looking him directly in the eyes, said, *Among certain religions in India, it's the color of surrender.*

The rest of the planet is dying of hunger and all they know how to do is buy things; and they pretend that the whole rest of the world is like them; it doesn't cross their minds that it's possible to live differently from their way of life, which they insist they've chosen freely but which is clearly just a state in which they've been shipwrecked. And they've exported this disaster to the rest of the world, and everywhere they go everything has been left in ruins. And everyone who travels there from the most remote corners of the world, dazzled by the counterfeit shimmer they can make out from a distance, arrive finally at what they believed was an inexhaustible well of happiness but quickly discover its mistrust, its rejection, its exclusion. *But I'm repeating myself,* Gutiérrez says with an apologetic smile, unsure how he has once again, for the umpteenth time, punished his friends—Clara, Marcos, and Leonor—with his favorite diatribe, always spoken without hatred or violence or anger, but rather with a sense of irony, or reproach perhaps, as though he would have preferred that the place which, in reality, didn't offer him such a bad reception, had been more similar to the idealized fantasy that had been constructed for him long before he entered its noisy and colorful aura.

The four of them are sitting in the darkness of the living room, cooled by the floor fan that hums in a corner, sending them, along its semicircular trajectory, periodic bursts of gentle air. On the low table between their chairs, on a metal platter, there's a pitcher of cold water in which, when they serve themselves, ice cubes clink, along with the four tall glasses that they drank from, and in which there're still some traces of water. The four of them have a common past that at this distance has become legendary, as if, now unchangeable, it had happened in a different dimension from the one they now occupy, made of space and time, of hesitation and uncertainty. And yet they appear to be seated calmly in their chairs, as if they were lodged in a segment of the eternal. That common past distinguishes them from the others, who wander around the courtyard, seeking a place in the shade, in order to let the wine settle maybe, and to recover from the exhaustion of the lunch and the demands of their digestion; or this is how Gutiérrez imagines it from the cool, dark living room, in any case. His friends, meanwhile, and the lover he had for a few now remote weeks, have in fact listened to him, though they've already heard him discuss the same topic many times before, with interest and patience, but also

467

with a degree of skepticism: Marcos, for instance, who is a senator and has traveled widely and is in frequent contact with European parliaments, while he's not unaware of the brutal contradictions of so-called *late capitalism*, thinks that many of the social gains made by rich countries wouldn't be detrimental for the poorer ones. Leonor finds it inexplicable for Willi to find so many faults with a continent that can boast places as picturesque and pleasant as Saint Tropez, Nice, Liguria, and Marbella, with so many magnificent hotels and such impeccable service—anyone who's seen the dawn in Cadaqués, even though its beaches are small and overcrowded, doesn't have the right to complain about the European continent. Leonor thinks that Willi is too complicated, and that may have been one of the main reasons why she didn't leave with him that time, so long ago now. Clara Rosemberg's skepticism, meanwhile, has a different source than the others': she gets the feeling that Gutiérrez himself, because of his tone, doesn't really believe in the seriousness of his accusations, or that he considers them of secondary importance, in any case, and that he'd like his listeners to do the same, following rather his irony and his rhetorical distancing. Clara asks herself if his cruel critique of Europeans isn't actually a subtle gesture of reverence toward his local friends. And, with her vague and enigmatic smile, she gives Gutiérrez a look of acquiescence, whose cause or significance Gutiérrez, somewhat perplexed, is not able to guess at.

Yes, Nula thinks, *but I saw them in Rosario, on the sidewalk outside that awful house, with some strange and dubious people, the morning when I passed in a taxi.* And, simultaneously, though he didn't for a second doubt that he'd seen them, he still couldn't believe it. At times, he was sure that it was them, Lucía silent and sleepy and Riera, as usual, cheerful and animated. Because it was winter, they were dressed warmly, Riera in a black overcoat and Lucía in a fur.

The people they were talking to, in a circle, two women and a very young-looking man, were different from them in a way that Nula couldn't quite define. Later, at other times, it was as if he'd only imagined them, or had seen them in a dream, or had been told about it by someone, or had read about it somewhere. But every time he passed the house, in a taxi or on the bus, and even on foot, during the day, when it seemed empty and closed, he would see them again, sharply, in the icy morning, speaking in a circle with their strange friends, and he would try to block out, without managing to, the intolerable images of what might have happened just before, inside, according to what the friend who'd pointed out the house had told him. And now Riera is saying something about how hard the separation with Lucía was for him, and that for months they've been trying to get back together. *Yes, but I saw you with her in Rosario, on the sidewalk outside that awful house,* Nula thinks again, more as a hurt protest than as an accusation. And he's about to tell him, to make him remember, *to make him know that he knows,* but no matter how much he tries to give shape to and pronounce the words that would put his doubt to rest (Riera is incapable of lying), he isn't able to, though his expression must betray his effort somewhat because Riera interrupts his conjugal disclosures and looks at him quizzically, and when Nula doesn't catch on, he asks him directly:

—What's wrong?

—Nothing, Nula says, I was thinking that you and Lucía are a perfect match, and I'm absolutely sure you'll end up together.

—Seriously? Riera says, his smile full of suggestion, clearly signaling that in the words Nula has just spoken there are numerous, darkly hidden allusions that to him are more amusing than offensive or worrying. And suddenly he stands up and shouts to Diana, who sits several meters behind them, sketching under the umbrella:

—Should we take a swim?

Nula laughs, defeated. He realizes that Riera has wanted to demonstrate to him, through his attitude, not only that his allusions aren't a threat to him, but that he can do things that are even more disturbing, something which translated into words would look something like, *Anyone who would suggest to me that the relationship I have with my wife is perverse should know that I would be more than happy to have one even more so with theirs.*

—Sit there for two more minutes without moving from those positions and I'll accept, Diana says without looking up, because she's finishing the sketch of them from behind, sitting in their chairs under the pavilion, near the empty table. They freeze for a minute more or less and finally Diana shouts, *Done!*

She closes the pad and the pencil box and, standing up, heads toward the pavilion.

—Immortalized, she says when she passes them on her way to drop the pad and the pencils in the straw bag. Nula and Riera stand up and start to unbutton their shirts, removing them almost simultaneously, as though they'd been competing to see who could take theirs off first. Riera leaves his on the back of his chair, but Nula folds his carefully and puts it in the bag, where Diana is dropping the leather band that she's just removed from her wrist. *Go ahead, I'll be right there*, Diana says, and Nula understands that, though she already has her bathing suit on, she doesn't want to undress in front of them. The two men walk toward the pool, and only when she sees them standing with their backs to her, at the edge, looking at the water, does Diana remove her dress and her sneakers and put them in the bag. When she reaches the pool, Riera is already in the water, but Nula has waited for her at the edge. When she sees her arrive, Lucía, who is standing in the shallow end, opens her arms to receive them, shouting, *Come in, come in!* Diana and Nula dive in to the deep end, and Diana, swimming under water, moves toward Lucía, but by the time she surfaces Lucía's enthusiasm seems to have vanished. They stand there motionless, without knowing what to say, in the four o'clock sun that projects unstable sparks on the water disturbed by the movement of the bodies that have just dived into it and which continue to move and twist inside it. Lying on his back, Nula observes the completely empty blue sky, almost the same color as the water, possibly a bit lighter due to the intense light of the sun, which, though it's not visible to him in the portion of sky framed by the courtyard, the trees, and the house, flows ceaselessly in the April afternoon, as hot as any January or February. The serene stillness of the blue sky contrasts with the sparkling undulations of the water, and Nula concentrates on that contrast, telling himself that it only exists within the human incapacity to perceive with only our sight the prevalence of that same agitation in what, because of that same optical illusion, its earlier observers named the firmament.

Sitting up, he sees Riera swimming, with vigorous strokes, toward the women, and, submerging, he does the same, but under water. When he reaches her, he wraps his arms around Diana's waist and lifts her, as he emerges, his head pressed against her firm, naked back. Diana protests, laughing, shaking her arms and legs, and Nula drops her loudly into the cool water. When his attention returns to his friends, he realizes that Riera and Lucía are kissing and caressing each other openly, intensely, without false modesty, and, at least apparently, with the world around them forgotten.

—A beautiful reconciliation scene, he whispers to Diana, taking the opportunity to nibble softly on her ear. In fact, the caresses to which Riera and Lucía have abandoned themselves have given him a sudden erection, and, trying to calm down, he wonders if that hadn't been their primary motive. Under the swimming trunks, his penis engorges slightly, but remains a soft thickness that sticks, agreeably, to the skin on the inside of his thigh. If they were alone he'd convince Diana to make love. He'd put it in her right there, in the water; it would be easy to lift her up and make her cross her legs around his back, pull his shorts halfway down his thighs, and, pushing aside the tiny bottoms that Diana has on, when his penis was hard enough, penetrate her. It wouldn't be the first time they'd done it in the water: they'd done it once in the river, two or three times in the bathtub, even with the discomfort, and one night in a hotel pool in Córdoba. He'd lower her bikini top and suck her tits, harder than Lucía's despite her two maternities, and better shaped than Virginia's, whose taste and consistency he still has in his mouth, or rather, which are still so present in his memory than they seem to persist in his senses. Though Diana is next to him and their bodies are almost touching, the scene that he imagines has erased her presence, and while the physical attraction that it evokes is more distant than her real body, it has a mythic perfection, sheltered from all contingency, that magnetizes him, heats him up, and blinds him. He's become so excited that he submerges himself again in order to see if the cool water will remove that turbulent fantasy, but when he's under water he can't resist the temptation to fondle Diana's buttocks, but then he sees that Lucía and Riera's hands, under the water, are grabbing each other's crotches. Curiously, rather than excite him like the apparently passionate caresses to which they'd abandoned themselves did a moment ago, this detail calms him down immediately, as if the sexuality that seemed, as he grew excited, to exist only for himself, concentrating in his body all the desire of the universe, was now revealing its pedestrian vulgarity in showing that it was shared by others. He will have to live through more experiences in order to understand that it's the desire of the other and not our own that creates pleasure, and though he doesn't yet know this, he still hasn't reached full adulthood.

—We have to separate tonight; I—persona non grata at my mother-in-law's—am staying at a hotel, Riera says, as though in apology, but

472

they remain intertwined, their arms around each other's waists and their free hands submerged.

—Legally you continue to be husband and wife, Nula says. You have every right.

—Of course, Diana says. And even if you weren't.

Gutiérrez, in a white undershirt, shorts, and sandals, appears suddenly at the edge of the pool.

—The younger generations seem to understand each other well, he says affably. You're not plotting against you elders, I hope.

But there's a hint of doubt in his words. Nula thinks that the familiarity among the bathers, who only met this morning, *doesn't quite make sense to him.* Actually, Nula doesn't know if Gutiérrez's confusion is real, or if he, who has at his disposal every element of the situation, is projecting ideas onto him. Lucía stares at the surface of the water with a conventional smile, but Riera and Diana exchange pleasant looks with the owner of the house, who, seen from below, is amplified by the perspective, and he offers the four of them a welcoming expression that contains more than a pool-side afternoon cookout in the country. Nula believes—hopes—that Gutiérrez is able to understand everything, and though it was Lucía and not himself who on Tuesday night said that they didn't know each other, he feels guilty about what happened. With him, the lie seems more absurd and superfluous than immoral.

—Lucía, Gutiérrez says softly. I'm taking your mother to Paraná.

—Don't worry, Lucía says, finally looking up at him. I have to leave too, to take the baby to a birthday party.

—I'll call a cab later. We'll talk tonight? Riera says.

Lucía kisses him on the cheek and, without saying a word, separates from him, walking heavily through the water to the metal ladder. As soon as she steps on it, she turns to Nula and Diana: I'll come say goodbye on my way out.

—It's okay, Diana says.

Gutiérrez, it seems to Nula, observes the scene with curiosity. Or, maybe, with an irony that is at once amused and benevolent.

Now Tomatis is the one sitting up with is back against the trunk, and Violeta the one who is lying on the ground, drowsy, her head on the lap of Tomatis, who amuses himself listening to the sounds around him, the ones coming from the pool, of course, but also from other swimming pools in neighboring houses. Every so often a car passes, invisible to him, the muted sound of its engine audible, along with, from the asphalt road, the distant vibrations of passing trucks. Televisions and radios are turned on nearby. The *Clásico* starts at seven, but other games are being played in Buenos Aires or in Rosario and more than one fan must have taken his television or portable radio out to the courtyard, contributing to the cloud of noise pollution that has devastated every Sunday in the republic from time immemorial, Tomatis thinks sarcastically. Luckily, the announcers' voices come from too far away to disturb the calm drowsiness of the courtyard, and besides, they're so typical of Sundays that, as strident as they may be, many people don't even hear them anymore. All day, he's been paying attention to the birds, who are relishing the good weather: around noon, he'd heard the pigeons, cooing in the shade, the constant chirp of sparrows all morning, and, after lunch, at the hottest time of day, the flocks of guira cuckoos gathering noisily in the trees, enjoying the unexpected summer. Two or thee times he's seen a pair of nesting birds passing, looking among the grass for something to eat. Every so often the cry of a kiskadee rings out, or a kingbird passes, or a cardinal, crossing from tree to tree, from courtyard to courtyard, from the sandy streets to the countryside perhaps, beyond the asphalt road and the town and the river and the islands, across the river.

From where he's sitting he can see, beyond the clearing for the courtyard, the house, the pool, the pavilion. Gutiérrez and

474

the Rosembergs, who'd disappeared inside a while before, appear through the side door of the house. Gutiérrez walks to the edge of the pool and speaks to the people in the water. Marcos, who is only wearing swimming trunks, sits down in one of the lounge chairs and leans back. But what catches Tomatis's attention is Clara Rosemberg; from that distance, he can watch her easily. Clara, with hesitant slowness, starts to cross the courtyard. Despite the heat, she walks with her arms crossed over her chest, as if she were cold. Her vague, thoughtful smile, which is actually a kind of mask, remains on her face. With long, slow strides, her youthful silhouette crosses the courtyard in one direction, then in another, distant from the afternoon, from the rough and bright present, from the whole universe possibly. Tomatis, who always found her interesting, thinks that's she's carried, since she was a child, an abstracted sadness. Now a sudden movement of her head reveals that she's discovered some flowerbeds planted in the shade under a few trees, and then, without uncrossing her arms or accelerating her walk, she approaches and examines them carefully. Every so often, she leans down, and, stretching out a hand, touches a flower carefully, so as not to damage it, then withdraws her hand, stands back up, and crosses her arms again, still observing the multicolored flowerbeds. She does this three or four more times, walking among the flowerbeds: she leans over, touches a flower or caresses it, studies it a while, and then straightens back up and crosses her arms. Tomatis thinks he can see, from that distance, the thoughts that bubble behind her enigmatic forehead. It's as though he were seeing her naked, at her most secretly intimate, and ashamed at his indiscretion he narrows his eyelids, so as to not continue watching her without her realizing it. But his curiosity is stronger than his reservations and he opens his eyes again. In any case, Clara is too far away for what he's doing to be considered indiscrete, and besides, to him the scene is unexpectedly enchanting, as though

475

he were seeing her in a theater. Clara's gaze passes calmly over the flowers, and Tomatis remembers a haiku by the nun Seifu: *an aged butterfly / letting its soul play / with a chrysanthemum.*

Gabi, Soldi, and José Carlos, sensing some movement around the pool, stand up and walk to the front part of the house. They've seen Violeta and Tomatis, who for a while now have been taking a siesta, resting in the shade of the trees not far from the bench where the three of them have been sitting, do the same. They've been discussing a little of everything, politics, economics, literature, in particular the local avant-garde, which has occupied Soldi and Gabriela's time for months, but also the personality of the owner of the house, his not at all ordinary life, his mysterious past, his tact, and his slight eccentricity had filled a good part of the conversation. All three agree that there's something elusive about him, and that in some of his apparently inconsequential actions there's nevertheless something deliberate, an effort to show things in a different light. His elusiveness, Soldi has said, is definitely a result of that tacit exercise. It's like he's trying to say something, but without words, and that's what feels disturbing. The three of them also wonder about the unique relationship that Gutiérrez has with Leonor and Lucía Calcagno, but out of discretion none of them comment on it. The arrival of Leonor, whom none of them had ever seen, surprised them, but what was immediately obvious wasn't mentioned by any of them: she and Gutiérrez couldn't have been more different, and it seemed impossible that they could ever understand each other or even maintain a conversation, and yet he left everything he had in Europe to move into that house, near her, and had accepted the idea that Lucía was really his daughter without demanding any serious proof of it. Of course, when they were alone, Gabriela and José Carlos would talk about it, and she and Soldi would bring it up as soon as they saw each other again, but doing so in Gutiérrez's own house seemed, to all three of them, though they never discussed it, sordid and disloyal.

When they reach the area between the pavilion and the pool, they realize that almost everyone is there: Nula, Diana, and Marcos are sitting in adjoining lounge chairs; Diana, Soldi observes without saying anything, is sitting in the yellow one; Faustino arrives from the front of the house, carelessly shaking his clothes, because he's been lying on the ground, in the shade of the trees out front, taking a siesta; Clara, Violeta, and Tomatis are talking in the sun, standing on the white slab path that leads from the house to the pool and the pavilion; Riera swims noisily through the rectangle of blue water; and Amalia takes in, politely but without too much interest, from the doorway to the room attached to the pavilion, the tableau vivant that they seem to represent: *Sunday in the country: Afternoon.* When he arrives, Faustino deviates slightly from his path and walks up next to her. Amalia, seeing him, notices that he still has some branches and blades of grass sticking to his shirt and pants, and she brushes them off, passing an expert hand over her husband's back and buttocks. Riera starts to climb slowly up the metal ladder in the shallow end and steps out of the pool, shaking water, concentrating, absent from his surroundings, like an animal passing from one element to another, adapting to the change, not realizing that everyone present is looking at and perhaps admiring him, the forty-year-old man without a single gray hair or a single wrinkle, tall, without a belly, his damp hair sticking to the tanned skin of his arms and legs and chest. Surfacing from his animal self-absorption, he notices the others' gazes and brandishes, without an ounce of affectation, the wide and slightly degenerate smile that, as paradoxically as it may seem, awakens the immediate sympathy of both men and women, so much so that, because of his inexhaustible energy, his frank and open amorality, several women he tossed aside still talk about him with a tolerant smile, and a few husbands whose wives he seduced, or, in his own words, *corrupted*, are still his friends today. Hesitant, unsure what to do, he finally decides to sit down in one of the unoccupied lounge chairs on the other side of the pool, immediately across from the ones occupied by Diana, Nula, and Marcos. Almost at that exact moment, dressed to leave, carrying a bag in her hand, Lucía comes out of the house followed by her mother and Gutiérrez. Seeing her walk out, the three guests who occupy the adjoining lounge chairs stand up simultaneously, but Riera continues sitting; because Lucía has given him a conspiratorial gesture, Nula gathers that he's preferred to remain sitting so as to not have to run into his mother-in-law. Lucía begins her circuit of goodbye kisses with Diana, marking her fondness with a few caresses and pats on her naked back, then Marcos, and finally Nula, an extremely fleeting brush against his cheek, as if her lips had rebounded when they touched it. Looking around, Lucía decides to move on to the door of the utility shed, and gives Amalia a kiss and Faustino a handshake; she crosses under the empty pavilion and approaches the two groups of three: José Carlos, Soldi, and Gabriela, and on the other side of the pool, standing on the white slab path, Clara, Violeta, and Tomatis, whom she avoided a moment ago when she turned toward Diana. Once the round of kisses is finished, Lucía walks toward Leonor and Gutiérrez, who wait for her near the door. Gutiérrez pats her affectionately on the shoulder and, waiting for Leonor to give a general farewell to the group, consisting of an imperceptible smile and a slight movement of her head, accompanies them to the white gate, but after taking two steps he stops suddenly, causing the two women with him to do the same, and pointing toward the middle of the front courtyard at a flowering bush, lowering his voice, but not so much that they can't hear him, and then moving his extended index finger and placing it vertically against his lips to urge them to be silent, he says:

—Look. The hummingbird.

Everyone stops speaking and turns their heads toward the yellow-flowered bush; even Riera, who had been sitting with his back to that section of the courtyard, twists around and looks: flapping continuously, the bird's tiny body hovers in the air in front of a yellow flower while its beak is inserted into it. Its vertiginous flapping creates a doubly surprising effect, in contrast with the utter stillness of the courtyard, the trees, the lawn, the blue water in the pool, now that no body or breeze disturbs it, and in particular of the human figures, frozen in various positions, their gaze directed at the yellow bush and the tiny body frantically shaking its wings to neutralize the force of gravity. The people, alive as of a few seconds and now transformed into petrified effigies of themselves, the garden, and the house with all its rooms, and what is beyond its limits, streets, paths, towns, rivers, cities, the world, which issue no sound, no movement, are like an elaborate backdrop, worthy of the legendary magic of the hummingbird, which appears suddenly, with the regularity of the constellations, in their gardens and disappears again just as quickly, like a mirage or a vision. The totality of the world seems to be concentrated, for several minutes, in one of its parts, winged and bright, and yet, despite its fame, all of the energy that it draws with its beak from the yellow flower is consumed at the very moment it's obtained because of the exhausting flapping with which it fights against the terrestrial pull. The curious stillness of the bipeds who have conquered verticality nevertheless contains an element of cruelty, as they delight, from their comfortable position on the ground with their vigorous feet and legs, in the beauty of the spectacle. As indifferent to the pain of others, Tomatis thinks, as the Roman masses, which included the emperor, before the portentous blood of the gladiators and the martyrs. But the desperate effort of its wings and the eagerness with which its beak enters and exits the yellow flower give that beauty a tragic element that overcomes its decorative futility.

As though its movements were discontinuous, their trajectory escaping the human eye, the bird moves from flower to flower without needing to obey the laws of space to do so, or as though it had been allowed to travel by means of sudden temporal cuts as compensation for the entropy produced by its constant flapping, until, suddenly, it shoots up into the sky and disappears among the trees. The statues into which its admirers had been transformed take on life again, once again endowed with movement, with the gift of speech, of laughter, of surprise. They seem to congratulate each other for the fleeting apparition—already an image of dubious reality in their memories—that they've just seen. Gutiérrez tells his guests:

—He appeared earlier than usual today.

—Because a storm is coming, Tomatis says.

Faustino concurs with an affirmative gesture of his head, after which the visitors from the city, through the silent confirmation of a representative of the rural zone, allow themselves to take Tomatis's sententious assertion seriously, knowing that his taste for parody, for comic effect, for witty retorts, which have become a kind of second nature for him, are by now so intrinsic that sometimes not even he himself seems to have access to the less predictable corners of his infinite internal jungle.

At around six, though it was still sunny, and, at least from the courtyard, not a single cloud was visible in the blue sky, the sound of distant thunder could be heard, and because Amalia and Faustino had to leave, Gutiérrez offered to take them, but he insisted that his guests wait for him to return. Shortly before, Soldi had taken José Carlos and Gabriela to the city, because José Carlos was returning to Rosario that night and Gabriela had decided to go with him. Now, when the sound of Gutiérrez's car can no longer be heard, his guests have gathered around (or inside) the swimming pool, waiting for the storm. And yet, apart from the thunder, which gives no indication of approaching, there's no other sign of it: the afternoon is sunny and peaceful, and there's no breeze at all. None among the people remaining in the courtyard seem at all worried about the development of the weather. The three couples plus Riera have scattered as a result of their conversations and their movements in the following way: Tomatis and Clara Rosemberg sit on the lawn, talking, in the shade projected at that hour by the house over a section of the courtyard; Riera and Violeta are playing in the water, and Diana is showing Marcos her sketch pad. Only Nula is alone, at a distance: he's resting in the shade, in the same chair that, after lunch, Gutiérrez set up for Diana under an umbrella. Though he can see the courtyard, the pavilion, the pool, and can see or hear the others splashing in the water, it's as though, as he thinks about Gutiérrez, he's become absent: *You'd have to include the relationship he has with his employees, even more mysterious because they actually didn't meet that long ago, and yet there seems to be a certain familiarity, if not complicity, between them. It's as though practical matters were also of secondary relevance in that relationship, and he applies the same elusive standards with them as he does for everything else.*

He pulls his cell phone from the straw bag on the ground, under the pavilion, rummaging briefly among the clothes, the pencil case, some things of Diana's, and then, looking hesitantly around, walks to the white gate, dialing La India's number as he crosses the courtyard and stopping in front of the gate when she answers.

—It's your favorite son, Nula says when he hears his mother's voice.

—I don't have a favorite son, La India says. But I do have some adorable grandchildren. All four are here, because your brother and sister-in-law went to watch the *Clásico* at seven and then they're coming for dinner.

481

—So it would be okay if we came by for them a little later than planned? Nula says, aware that the question is actually a rhetorical one for which the response he expects isn't long in coming:

—It would take much longer than a single Sunday for me to educate them properly.

—Despite what a disaster I turned out to be?

—You didn't turn out that badly, La India says. And, after a short pause: And to what do we owe the delay?

—Because it's going to storm, our host, who is a very friendly man, took the gardener and the cook home so they don't get rained on, and he asked us to wait for him so we can have a drink before we go, Nula says. And Diana is showing her sketches to a senator. The house is magnificent; it has an amazing courtyard and pool. He'd make a good match for you, *mamá*.

—If I wanted a boyfriend I'd find one for myself, La India says, laughing intensely.

—Admit that you like the idea, Nula says. So, we could come by later than we thought?

—Get here whenever you want, La India says. The less contact my grandchildren have with their perverse father, the better off they'll be.

—You're a rock, India. I'm sending you a big kiss.

—And I'm dodging it, La India says. Goodbye.

She hangs up. Nula stops moving, thinking, next to the white gate posts, tapping the now disconnected cell phone softly against the palm of his right hand. Finally he decides, opens the gate, and goes out into the street. The cars, shaded by the large trees, seem somewhat more dusty than when they arrived from the city late that morning. Nula travels the few meters that separate him from the corner, and, stopping at the intersection, he looks two blocks down, at the asphalt road, on which, toward the city, numerous cars are driving, most of them returning from a weekend or a Sunday in the country, but there are also a few trucks, loaded with fans waving the flags of the clubs that will shortly battle over the *Clásico*. Nula disregards the cars and his gaze shifts toward the embankment where, three days before, during the Thursday siesta, he talked a while between cars with Soldi and Gabriela Barco. The weather had been good that day: for the first time in several days the sky was very blue, and there were immense, incredibly white, and apparently motionless clouds scattered among sections of open sky, but by Friday morning they had already disappeared. Nula takes a few steps along the sandy ground in the direction of the road, scanning the sky to the southeast; if there's a storm, it's sure to come from that direction: and he can just make out, beyond some tall trees, on the river side, the tips of dark clouds from which seem to come, precipitous and fleeting, numerous lightning bolts, along with the thunder that they engender, more sharp, prolonged, and audible than the weak spark of the distant flashes. *If the wind picks up, it'll be on top of us before long*, Nula thinks, and as he thinks this he watches the movement of the trees behind which the clouds are gathering. He turns around slowly and, after traveling the meters of street that separate him from it, pushes the gate open and enters the courtyard, closing it behind him. He can now see that Tomatis, Clara, Marcos, and Diana have gathered in the middle of the courtyard, standing, enthusiastically discussing the sketchbook. As he walks up to them, Marcos is saying:

—The problem today is, who legitimizes the legitimizers?

—I agree, Nula says when he reaches them, though his gaze still scrutinizes the trees in the courtyard to see if they display the same movement as those on the distant mountain. There's nothing for now: not one leaf moves on the highest, sunny branches, and so Nula leans over to see the sketch that the others are looking at.

It's the pencil sketch of him and Riera, sitting under the pavilion, perfectly recognizable despite their faces being invisible because Diana has drawn them from the back without their knowledge, except in the final minutes, when they invited her to go swimming and she asked them to pose a while longer so that she could finish.

—Wonderful, he says, and kisses Diana on the cheek. But what actually attracts his attention just now is the racket coming from the pool, and so, moving away from the group—he and Diana will talk about the sketches tonight when they look at them—he walks up to the edge of the water: Riera and Violeta are playing with a multicolored ball, standing on opposite sides of the shallow end, throwing it back in forth and trying to keep the other one from catching it. It's immediately obvious that Riera is dominating the game, and that rather than giving Violeta an advantage he's happy to beat her ostentatiously, which makes her laugh and protest simultaneously, as if that minor vexation caused her a degree of pleasure.

—Sadist victimizer! Nula yells to Riera, who still hasn't seen him.

—And if she likes it? Riera says, and because he turns around to say this, Violeta takes the opportunity to throw the ball at his head with an impotent fury that causes the multicolored sphere to drop halfway along its trajectory, in the middle of the pool.

—I forfeit, she says, and with heavy steps, intended to overcome the resistance of the water, she moves toward the metal ladder and starts to climb up. Riera makes a sudden lunge and, before Violeta has finished climbing, steps up onto the edge of the pool, splashing Nula's naked legs. The multicolored ball continues floating on the water, rocking violently, but always at the same point on the surface of the water. Riera sits on the edge of the pool, shaking his head to dry the water from his thick, soaking wet, chestnut hair.

—So she declared you persona non grata, Nula says.

—Yes, and since you've seen the house you'll know that it's not like there isn't plenty of room, Riera says.

Nula decides not to register the allusion, opting instead for mocking laughter. And then: You'll see that everything will work out.

—It practically is already worked out, Riera says with unusual severity.

Violeta approaches them along the edge of the pool.

—I've had my share of aquatic pleasures for the day, she says, insinuating that Riera's behavior has spoiled them, but apparently happy that this has happened. She continues toward the group talking between the pool and the house. Riera sees the cell phone in Nula's hand.

—Were you about to call someone? I can disappear, if you want, he says.

—It doesn't matter; I don't have a private life anymore, Nula says. Ignoring the effect that his sibylline words have caused, he studies, curious, without anxiety, the trees at the back: there seems to be a faint undulation among the highest branches. *It's coming, the storm*, he says, even more ostentatiously disinterested in the mocking, complicit smile that Riera is giving him. It's difficult to tell how much Riera knows about his visit to Paraná, and though he knows that Riera would tell him immediately and that if he doesn't do so now it's because it's not the right time, he has no desire to reenter their aura, like five years before, when, as he was coming out of the bar, he bumped into the girl in red and started to follow her. The magnetic aura that surrounded them, more luminous and vivid than his own life, confronted with the bitter roughness of possession, during the Wednesday siesta, has dissipated. Nula thinks that, if he wanted to, he could be the one to arrange events according to his fantasies, although he owes them too much to want to do that. But a thunderclap, much closer than the previous ones, pulls him from his thoughts. The thunder causes Riera to look up as well and scan the peaceful blue sky, in which not the slightest sign of a storm is visible. Nula puts the cell phone in the straw bag, under the pavilion, and then takes the umbrella out of the base, folds it, can leans it up against the wall, under the pavilion, near the grill. Then he returns to the edge of the pool, from which Riera watches him, intrigued, and starts folding up the lawn chairs. Riera stands up and does the same with the ones around him and then follows Nula submissively as he leans the ones he's already folded against the wall of the pavilion, next to the umbrella, to protect them from the rain. When they've put away the last of them they walk out of the pavilion and toward the others, who continue talking, apparently unaware of them, in the middle of the courtyard. When the second thunderclap rumbles, Diana closes the sketch pad and puts it carefully in the straw bag. Now everyone is scanning the sky, and though they don't see anything in it that indicates a storm, they all see the momentary flash of a lightning bolt and notice that the tall trees on the sidewalk are starting to shake, just as the white bars of the gate open for Gutiérrez, who, after closing it, moves toward them at a run, but in slow motion, pointing up and back, as if he was being chased. His guests watch him, amused but also somewhat surprised because they wouldn't have expected, from him, the kind of parodic behavior that diminishes his mystery and reduces him to the banality of every other mortal. Only Nula and Tomatis intuit, though still vaguely, that this is also a reconstitution, the playing out of something lost that he's not actually trying to recover but that he stages, purely as an intimate game, in the theater of his disenchanted imagination. When he reaches the middle of the courtyard, a heavy thunderclap makes the house, the pavilion, the trees, and the earth vibrate, disturbing the blue water in the pool, and suddenly the light turns livid and the air darkens.

—Right here, right here! Tomatis shouts, pounding his chest, standing at the edge of the pool, looking toward the darkened sky, and

486

speaking to the endless series of long lightning strikes and the deafening, continuous thunder that, for a while now, has been shaking everything, creating a tremor in the rainy shadow of the evening. And then: If you exist, swine, hit me right here! I'm defying you! I'm talking to you, coward!

—Don't pay any attention to him, he's quoting Flaubert again, Violeta says to the group, which is surprised by Tomatis's suddenly theatrical behavior, jumping from the table at the edge of the pavilion and berating the turbulent sky.

At that moment, Tomatis stops yelling and returns to the table, calmly, with a satisfied smile.

—You see? he says. He doesn't exist. And picking up his glass of whiskey, he shakes it a moment, clinking the ice against the glass, and takes a long drink.

—Either he doesn't exist or he's gone deaf, Marcos offers sententiously.

A dense, loud rain has been falling continuously for a while now, multiplying its intensity with every volley of thunder and lightning. The southeast wind brought with it a thick curtain of black clouds that completely obscured the sky along the entire visible horizon, and though by now the wind had calmed down considerably, or perhaps for that same reason, the storm had settled in, dumping endless, thick streams of water, pierced constantly with electricity and noise, over the evening. Gutiérrez suggested that they move indoors, but his guests preferred the pavilion, which protected them from the rain while at the same time allowing them to enjoy the delicious coolness of the air after the sweltering afternoon. Assisted by Nula and Violeta, Gutiérrez prepared the table and served them the cold leftovers from the cookout, bread and butter, and a few bottles of red wine. So that she wouldn't have to put the prosthesis on her arm again, Nula prepared chorizo and steak sandwiches for Diana, or put pieces onto a dish from which they both ate. Eventually, Gutiérrez announced that Amalia had made a cake that she hadn't dared serve after the *alfajores*, and which she'd left for that night. Violeta brought it out—Nula took care of the plates and the dessert utensils—and Gutiérrez appeared last with a large ice bucket that, when he brought them out, fit two bottles of French champagne very well. They made their trips to and from the house at a run, forced to cover the food, and the cake in particular, with white napkins, but they themselves arrived soaked, though this didn't seem to bother them much, just the opposite: judging by their happy laughter when they arrived, the euphoria with which they distributed the food and the bottles, they seemed to be enjoying themselves, thanks to the effects of the wine, which had been partially spent over the hot afternoon. After the first glass of champagne, when Gutiérrez moved to serve him a second, Tomatis put his hand between the mouth of the bottle and the top of the glass and asked:

—Do we have anything stronger, by chance?

And so when he finished pouring the second round of champagne, Gutiérrez ran into the house, returning eventually with a bottle of whiskey, a dish of ice cubes, and several glasses. And now, just as Tomatis finishes his sip of whiskey, after clinking the ice against the glass, hearing Marcos's comment, Diana, gesturing vaguely with her head to the sky, the night, the storm, adds thoughtfully:

—If he's gone deaf he definitely wouldn't have heard him over this racket.

—Even within the most deathly silence he cannot hear, Marcos says with an apodictic and deliberately theatrical seriousness, and after taking a sip of champagne, savoring it ostentatiously, raising his voice to Gutiérrez with worldly confidence, says, Willi, darling, this *champagne français*—and he exaggerates the French pronunciation of the two words—is a disaster!

They exchange an ironic, knowing look. Of the ones that Gutiér-rez knew back then, to whom he'd granted such prestige, Marcos is most similar, even physically, to how he was when he knew him: the same blonde hair, thinner and more faded now, and the same blonde beard, now more white than golden, which, at a gentle slant, encircles his mouth.

—I save it for special occasions, Gutiérrez says, and Nula, who is watching him, smiling, vaguely fascinated, thinks that this must be true, but that what Gutiérrez considers a *special occasion* probably doesn't have anything to do with what most people consider as such. Marcos smiles, less pleased with the courtesy than with some mysterious double meaning that he seems to have glimpsed among the conventional words. Ubiquitous, omnipresent, the storm echoes over the courtyard, over the fields, over the night, and the eight people who sit or stand at the table under the illuminated pavilion seem to be staging a realist play, to the point that their words issue with celerity and precision from their lips, as if they hadn't needed formulation inside themselves beforehand, being as they were rep-licas of a previously written text that they'd already memorized.

Seeing them exchange that practically imperceptible ironic look, Nula remembers that on Tuesday, at the fish and game club, when they brought up Marcos and his political activities, Gutiérrez and Escalante had also exchanged an affectionate but mocking look, as if those activities were just another character trait rather than a true political vocation. To Nula, Marcos is more than a good client, he's a lawyer who meets him in his office, whose library, alongside the legal volumes, visibly displays books by Hegel, by Gramsci, by Stendhal, by Tolstoy, and by Sarmiento. Nula does not know that Marcos's father, a communist German Jew, came to the country in the late fifties, and that, to survive, he'd built a secondhand bookstore in the city, Martín Fierro Books, after the national poem whose sestinas, which served him as a guidebook

489

for ethical behavior, he could recite from memory in a Spanish that became increasingly fluent over the years. For most of his youth, Marcos was a communist, but over time he grew distant from the party, breaking with it definitively during the dictatorship. He was among the men who thought they could change the world until they realized that the world changed on its own, and dizzyingly, but in the opposite direction toward which they'd worked, and even in unexpected and strange directions, at which point, neither innocently nor cynically, they started working for what was worth saving, even if that attitude sometimes made them seem antiquated or even conservative—at least compared to those that, while they unscrupulously cut the biggest slice of cheese for themselves, insisted on self-identifying as modern.

—It's stopping, Riera says suddenly, and taking two or three sudden strides he stops at the edge of the pavilion and scans the black and rainy sky. Yes, yes; it's stopping. It's time to get going.

—A momentary letup, Gutiérrez says.

—No, no, listen, Riera says, and cupping his hand around his right ear, he concentrates his attention. Everyone listens to the sound of the rain as though it were incredibly important, when in fact what's happening is that at the end of their long stay the conversation has been exhausted and, as often happens, while the alcohol has at first contributed to their gregariousness, it now pushes them once again within themselves. But the rain allows them a last jolt of sociability.

—Let's see, Clara says, and, with her delicate steps, she walks past Riera and stops in the middle of the white slab path, her arms crossed over her chest and her eyes closed. She stands motionless in that position for several seconds, and then, completely soaked, she returns to the refuge under the pavilion, saying, It'll be a while before it stops completely.

—Are you sure? Tomatis says, and still holding on to his whiskey glass, but covering it with his hand so that too much water doesn't get inside, he does the same circuit as Clara, stepping out of the pavilion and stopping on the white slabs more or less in the same spot where she had. And, at that moment, a sudden fading of the sound and the water is immediately perceptible. The unexpected change at first disorients Tomatis, but a satisfied smile illuminates his face, and raising it to the rainy sky, he announces prophetically, or rather mystically, like a circus magician announcing a revelation to his audience: It's still sprinkling, but when I remove the hand that protects the contents of this glass, the rain will stop completely.

He carries out a set of pseudo-esoteric movements, balanced with his eyes closed, turning slowly on the white slabs, his face, entranced, lifted to the rainy blackness, and after turning around two or three times, he stops, facing the pavilion, completely still for several seconds, and with an ostentatiously theatrical gesture, he removes the hand that covers the glass and gestures to the others to come out to the courtyard. Applause, shouts, and whistles respond to the invitation, and everyone hurries outside, most of them with a glass in their hand.

—Whoever comes out last, turn out the light, let's look at the night, Tomatis suggests, and matching words with actions, he steps off the white slabs and begins to walk slowly across the wet lawn, toward the back of the courtyard. Someone behind him—he is unaware that it's Clara—turns off the light and Tomatis moves into the darkness, perforated every so often by near or distant flashes of green lightning that, like the traveler his shadow, are followed a few seconds later by the faithful thunderclaps, the inoffensive slaves of the cruel light that forces them into displays of aggression and melodramatic sound. Tomatis hears the crowd of feet splashing behind him across the wet lawn, hurrying to catch him, and finally his friends, arriving breathless and enthusiastic, gathering around him in the darkness.

—What's the latest? Marcos's voice says.

—Still sprinkling, Tomatis says, and there are a few short bursts of laughter. They move slowly, as a group, and suddenly a sequence of lightning strikes illuminates them intermittently, creating an effect that is dubious from an aesthetic point of view but which is appropriate for the situation.

—See that? Did you see that? Diana's voice says.

—What? What is it? several voices, with exaggerated alarm, inquire.

—I saw it. Above the trees. A lost soul, Riera says. And I spent so much time looking for one during dissections. Look closely, up there. You can just see it through the darkness.

—Oh yeah, there is it, floating above the tree with its arms extended, it's completely white, confirms the chorus with drowsy reverence. And it's true: an evanescent white form, with its short arms extended, similar to the representations from the nineteenth century, when they were no longer believed in, of the souls in purgatory, floats in slow descending circles, against the trees at the back, closer, in its shape, to a microbial creature than to something from the celestial spheres. After a moment of silence, Nula's voice is heard in the darkness:

—It's Hamlet's father.

—No, no, Diana says. It's Athena, rerouted by the southeastern on her way to Troy to pacify the rage of the Greeks.

—It's not, says the voice of Gutiérrez. It's Mario Brando, sent by Dante to confirm his recognition of precisionism as the only legitimate heir of the *dulce stil novo*.

—You're all wrong, Marcos says. It's Doctor Russo, coming to occupy, *definitively and gratuitously*, the house he sold to Willi.

And at that moment, as though it had heard him, the somersaults of the evanescent, whitish shape grow increasingly unstable and it rushes to the earth. Everyone runs to it, but Nula is the one who traps it, announcing what everyone already knew:

—It's a plastic bag from the hyper. It has the Werden W.

—*Warden*, Tomatis correct him. What color?

—Blue, from the seafood section, Nula says.

—Blue, Tomatis repeats after a doubtful silence. Adjacent to black.

MONDAY

DOWNRIVER

WITH THE RAIN CAME THE FALL, AND WITH THE FALL,
the time of the wine.

TRANSLATOR'S AFTERWORD

Juan José Saer died in Paris on June 11, 2005. During his final days, in the hospital, he worked on the book you hold, *La Grande,* published posthumously in October of the same year. The manuscript was prepared for publication by his longtime Argentine editor, Alberto Díaz. In his afterword, Díaz notes that the last line of the book we have is in fact the first line of an unwritten final chapter:

> In his notebook [for the final chapter], Saer wrote the title and the first line. We know that he thought of it as a brief *coda* (no more than twenty pages long), and that he'd decided to end the novel with the phrase ANOTHER MORO PROPERTY FOR SALE. The reader might infer a possible ending from this phrase (perhaps Gutiérrez has decided to sell the house), but there are no indications or notes that provide any certainty to what the ending would have been.

In short, the precise manner in which Saer would have concluded his vast and intricate *corpus* will forever remain in the territory of speculation. This, to me, seems apt. Arguably, the distinguishing formal quality of Saer's later work, in particular after *Nadie nada nunca (Nobody Nothing Never)* (1980), is its incompleteness, its "openness" in the sense that Umberto Eco would have it.

If *La Grande* is an "unfinished" novel, it's not so in the sense that we mean in reference to posthumous novels by Scott Fitzgerald or Kafka or Bolaño. Likewise, the *La Grande* that we have is not strictly speaking a "draft" if only because Saer was a meticulous draughtsman, and the prose that made it into type was most often very close to the final version. (His papers, which now rest in the archives at Princeton, are somewhat disappointing in this regard.) *La Grande* is unfinished in the sense that *incompleteness* is its central motif as well as the manner in which it is narrated—Saer's fashionable philosophical term, in the mouth of Nula, the book's protagonist, *devenir*, means "to become." The hesitation, false starts, inconsistencies, and awkward mid-sentence tense shifts that mark the prose style should not be taken for roughness or errors that would have been "corrected" upon further revision. These qualities, typical of Saer's style, follow from the two central concerns of his novels: the substance of memory and the problem of narration. The question of *being and becoming* was implicit in all his writing, it was his metaphysics.

It wouldn't be unreasonably far-fetched to suggest that Saer actually offers us not one but two *coda* to *La Grande*, and that, as a last wink, these don't appear at the end of the book, conclusively, but rather are insinuated somewhere in the middle, just as, on the level of the sentence, he tends to fold the crucial idea of a paragraph within an otherwise apparently superfluous parenthetical subordinate clause. The book that Nula is writing, his *Notes toward an ontology of becoming* is one of these *coda* (or maybe *cipher* is the better word); this title perfectly describes the book in which it appears, as well as Saer's writing generally. The subject of Nula's work-in-progress, like Saer's, is the manner in which the human mind comprehends and reproduces reality. Saer, like Proust or Sebald or Woolf before him, practiced what might be called a phenomenology of the mundane.

Another recapitulation, in miniature, is the story of the fictional painter Hujalvu, who, according to a letter from Pichón to Tomatis, spent his life painting not one species of butterfly, but rather *one single butterfly*. "The same butterfly?" Tomatis wonders, rereading the letter:

Aesthetically, the choice is reasonable, and, one might even say, necessary, but how would it be possible to keep a single butterfly intact over an eighty-year life without it eventually disintegrating, unless, after a certain point, he was painting from memory, not from the material, pulverized after a few decades, but rather the shape imprinted on him forever, which, having observed it to the point of possession, he was able to turn in every possible direction.

The butterfly here can stand in, metonymically, for the infinitesimal provincial world, *la zona*, that Saer wrote and rewrote continuously throughout his life. This anecdote, a barely mentioned postscript in an otherwise inconsequential letter, practically a throwaway moment in the novel, comes as close to a manifesto as anything Saer ever wrote.

For Saer, style itself, prosody, was a form of combat against the counterfeit brutalization of "realism." Saer made prose in a baroque, draping style, from multiple viewpoints simultaneously, shifting registers dramatically from one clause to the next, circling syntactically, then back again, and maybe once more, then a dip, and a final turn. Reading Saer is like dancing inside the mind of someone who sees everything through the looking glass, always the skeptic. (No wonder, then, that Diogenes, the madman philosopher, often appears in Saer's writing as a stand-in for the author figure.) If sometimes dizzying, for the reader this dance is intensely pleasurable, a supple antidote to our contemporary moment of pixilation and radical constraint, but for the translator this manner presents considerable challenges, and I would not have been able to make English from Saer's prose without the invaluable help of many informants, among whom Eamonn McDonagh, Sergio Chejfec, and Rafael Arce deserve special thanks. Any trips and falls in the translation are entirely the fault of my own ineptitude.

—Steve Dolph, 2014

Juan José Saer (1937–2005), born in Santa Fé, Argentina, was the leading Argentinian writer of the post-Borges generation. In 1968, he moved to Paris and taught literature at the University of Rennes. The author of numerous novels and short-story collections (including *The Sixty-Five Years of Washington, Scars, The One Before,* and *The Clouds*—all in print or forthcoming from Open Letter), Saer was awarded Spain's prestigious Nadal Prize in 1987 for *The Event.*

Steve Dolph is the founding editor of *Calque,* a journal of literature in translation. His translation of Saer's *Scars* was a finalist for the 2012 Best Translated Book Award. He lives in Philadelphia where he spends his summers rooting for the Phillies.

Open Letter—the University of Rochester's nonprofit, literary translation press—is one of only a handful of publishing houses dedicated to increasing access to world literature for English readers. Publishing ten titles in translation each year, Open Letter searches for works that are extraordinary and influential, works that we hope will become the classics of tomorrow.

Making world literature available in English is crucial to opening our cultural borders, and its availability plays a vital role in maintaining a healthy and vibrant book culture. Open Letter strives to cultivate an audience for these works by helping readers discover imaginative, stunning works of fiction and poetry, and by creating a constellation of international writing that is engaging, stimulating, and enduring.

Current and forthcoming titles from Open Letter include works from Bulgaria, France, Greece, Iceland, Latvia, Poland, South Africa, and many other countries.

www.openletterbooks.org